Anonymous

Northern Notes and Queries

The Scottish antiquary - Vol. 3

Anonymous

Northern Notes and Queries
The Scottish antiquary - Vol. 3

ISBN/EAN: 9783337239138

Printed in Europe, USA, Canada, Australia, Japan

Cover: Foto ©Andreas Hilbeck / pixelio.de

More available books at **www.hansebooks.com**

Northern
Notes and Queries

or

The Scottish Antiquary

Edited by the Rev. A. W. CORNELIUS HALLEN

M.A., F.S.A. Scot., ALLOA

ESTABLISHED 1886

Vol. III., with Indexes

Issued in Quarterly Parts, 1s. each
Annual Subscription, 4s.

EDINBURGH: DAVID DOUGLAS

MDCCCLXXXIX

LIST OF ILLUSTRATIONS

Northern Notes and Queries

OR

The Scottish Antiquary

CONTENTS.

NOTE.—*The Editor does not hold himself responsible for the opinions or statements of Contributors.*

114. LORD WILLIAM GORDON.—In Wood's *Douglas's Peerage*, vol. i. p. 656, it is stated that Lord William Gordon (who was born 15th August 1744, as second son of the 3d Duke of Gordon) resigned his commission in the 37th Foot in 1769. This circumstance is thus referred to in the *Scots Magazine* (xxxii. p. 515): 'LONDON, *August* 23, 1770.— Thursday last set out for Dover on his Journey for Rome, Lord W——m G——n, once esteemed by the British court as the most accomplished young nobleman of the age. He is gone with a full determination never to return. He has cut his hair close to his head and carries a knapsack on his back, and intends walking to Rome on foot, with no other companion but a very large dog. He was ever

remarked for his generosity, and has divided his horses, dogs, etc., among his acquaintances, several to his particular friend the young Earl of T——lle. He has never appeared in public since the much talked of connection between him and a certain Lady, by whose friends he was never pardoned, and from their behaviour he has adopted the above extraordinary resolution.' Lord William did, however, return to England, and married, 13th February 1781, the Hon. Frances Ingram, daughter and co-heiress of the 9th Viscount Irvine. Regarding this marriage the *Scots Magazine* remarks (xliii. p. 110): ' The marriage took place at Lady Irvine's seat in England ; the bride was a ward of the Chancellor, who opposed the marriage.' Perhaps some of your readers can throw light on these occurrences.   Σ.

115. ARCHER FAMILY IN THE NORTH OF ENGLAND (Note 53).—The following notices of the name may be useful to G. H. R. :—

1. The Mayor of Newcastle-on-Tyne delivers, in Sept. 1302, some arms, including ' 21 crossbows from Roger Archer at 2s. each' (*Cal. Doc. Relating to Scotland*, vol. i. p. 391).

2. Patrick le Archer, ' tenant du Roi du Counte de Are,' does homage in 1296 (*Ibid.*, p. 202).

3. John Archer of Oxenholme, Westmorland, was first husband of Elizabeth, daughter of Sir William Pennington of Muncaster.

4. The widow of John Archer of Oxenholme was 2d wife (about 1740) of Thomas Strickland of Sizergh.

5. Mary, daughter of James Archer of Preston, was 2d wife of William Patten, Alderman of Preston (*b.* 1604, *d.* 1660). Her grand-daughter was mother of the 11th Earl of Derby.

6. In a list of from 50 to 60 Archer marriages the above three are all that refer to Archers of the North.   Σ.

116. MUMMERS CENSURED.—' Clackmannan, 6 January 1713. The which day Session mett & after prayer the Minr informed the Session that Francis Donaldson son to Francis Donaldson weaver in green & Wm Stirling son to Isobell Hadden in toun were going about disguised on new years Eve, causd cite them, they were this day called. Compeard Francis Donaldson and confessd that he had on him womens cloaths night foresaid & that his face was blacked : Compeard Wm Stirling confessd his going about disguised with his face blacked & straw ropes on his legs the foresaid night, but that he went only into one house. They both acknowledged their sin, & promised by Gods grace never to fall into the like again. The Session thought fit to dismiss them, having held forth to them the sinfulness & abominableness of their deed with certification.'—*Kirk Session Records.*

117. SPANISH ARMADA (Note 97).—D. A. will find information regarding 'Spanish Wrecks off Aberdeenshire' in *Scottish Notes and Queries* for January last.   J. E. LEIGHTON.

I well remember that when I lived as a boy at Peterhead, more than fifty years ago, there was a common tradition that one of the ships of the Spanish Armada, the 'St. Michael,' had been wrecked on the rocky coast there.

In support of this tradition a piece of timber, about two and a half feet high by one and a half broad, on which was carved a representation of the offering up of Isaac, an angel in the upper corner intercepting the stroke of Abraham's knife, remained built into the gable of an old house on the North Shore, the most ancient part of the town.

A number of brass cannon, said to have belonged to the same ship, remained for a long period in the town, and were used for defensive purposes at the rising of 1715, after which they were removed to London.

W. B.

118. NAME OF THE ISLE OF MAY.—The following letters, which appeared in the *East of Fife Record*, have been sent us for insertion as likely to prove of interest :—

FAREHAM, HANTS, *7th Jan.* 1888.

DEAR SIR,—In a Gazetteer of Scotland (1842) the derivation of the name of this island is supposed to be taken from the Celtic word *Magh*, signifying a plain ; and in support of this view it is stated that the surface of the island is, on the whole, flat, which is certainly far from being the case. It would therefore seem necessary that some other source or root of the name should, if required, be sought for. This subject has occasionally attracted my attention, but it was only the other day that I arrived at what I consider to be a satisfactory solution of the question.

It may be as well to premise that, according to Edmunds's *Names of Places*, such names of islands as end in *ey*, *ay* always mark them as unquestionably Norse. I consequently came to regard the *ay* in May as indicating its being an island ; but the meaning of the *M* I could not understand.

I think, however, my difficulty has been removed, in this way. In a map attached to Dasent's rendering of an old Icelandic Saga, called in English *Burnt Njal*, the ancient Norse names of several of the Scottish islands are given, from which I shall select for remark two only, viz. Hoy, in Orkney, and the May.

Hoy, in the map, is spelt Hàey, which, according to Edmunds, means the high or lofty island, by which appearance, as is well known, it is remarkably distinguished among its neighbours.

The May is named Màey ; but another authority must be referred to for the interpretation of this word. From what has been above said, the meaning of the first syllable only is required, and this is afforded by Dr. Jamieson's *Scottish Dictionary*, which gives the derivation of *maw*, a seagull, as coming from a Danish word of the same sound and meaning. And this old name Màey, signifying Gull Island, seems to be a very appropriate appellation as respects the seafowl-frequented May—none perhaps more simple or evident.

It will be noticed that in the modern pronunciation both of Hoy and May they have been reduced to words of one syllable, whereas the old names give them two.

This may seem to many to be a very trifling subject about which to write ; but from what has been above said it will be observed that an erroneous derivation has been assigned to the name of May, and an attempted correction of this may not be without some interest, at least to the good folk of the East Neuk.—Yours obediently,　JOHN MARTIN.

FAREHAM, HANTS, *3rd March* 1888.

DEAR SIR,—Since my late communication about the name of the Isle of May I have succeeded in obtaining a confirmation of my views respecting it.

Having requested a friend in London to consult an Icelandic Dictionary on the subject, he writes me that he has done so, and that under the word *Ey*—island—it is stated that in compound names of place it was often used with those of birds and beasts; and Má-ey strangely enough) is there given as an instance of this combination. (Again under *Már*—seafowl—the Scottish 'Maw' and English 'Mew'— 'Má' is given as one of the forms which this word also took in compounds. So it would appear 'the May' has been named—and that in very remote times—from being an island frequented by sea-gulls, as it continues to be.

I may instance as examples of many of these old Norse names being retained among us, that the word 'Már' above quoted forms part of the name given in the East of Fife to the common diver—the marrot, and that 'goat'—a narrow inlet into which the sea enters—is, according to Dr. Jamieson, derived from the Icelandic word 'goota,' of the same signification.—Yours obediently,   JOHN MARTIN.

119. PAUL ROMIEU (p. 170).—Having had occasion lately to look over some volumes of the records of the Incorporation of Hammermen of Edinburgh, of which body clock and watchmakers formed a part, I find that Paul Romieu was admitted a freeman of the Incorporation on 2d June 1677, and 'presented ane essay, viz. the movement of ane watch which was found to be ane weill wrought essay able to serve his Mäties liedges,' and was admitted in the art of 'Cloackmaker.' 'This essay was made in his own chamber.' Again, on 19th August 1682, Paul Romieu, son and apprentice to the above Paul Romieu, was admitted a freeman in the 'clockmaker art,' his essay being also a watch movement. On 17th May 1711 David Murkerson, apprentice to 'the late Paul Romieu,' seeks a discharge of his indenture, although not expired until 2d December, 'as both Paul Romieu and his wife are dead.' This was probably the younger Romieu, as no further notice appears of either, with the single exception of the discharge of another apprentice, named John Coustiel, on 6th November 1714.   D.

120. COLONEL NEWCOME—Note 111—(from the *Scotsman*).—SIR, I have received an answer from Mrs. Ritchie, and shall be glad if you will allow me to give the substance of her remarks upon the memorial brass which she has placed in our church.

Mrs. Ritchie informs me that there is no foundation for the statement made in the paragraph which first appeared in your columns, to the effect that the deathbed scene in *The Newcomes* was suggested by the circumstances of Major Carmichael Smyth's death.

Nor does she think that her grandfather was at Charterhouse. His father was a doctor, and lived in or near Edinburgh.

She adds, 'The "Adsum," and the rest of the quotation from *The Newcomes*, was put upon the brass because I knew that Major Carmichael Smyth had suggested the character of Colonel Newcome to my father, and so it seemed appropriate and natural.'—I am, etc.

                                                    J. M. LESTER.

AYR, *February* 24, 1888.

121. CARMICHAEL [GIBSON?] PEDIGREE (Notes 67 and 71).—In his note on the Gibson Carmichael pedigree G. B. stated that a

daughter of Sir John Gibson married 'Major Thomas Dalziel.' Somewhat doubtful about the correctness of the Christian name, I sought for information at the War Office and elsewhere, and am able now to state that this daughter, Anne Mary, married not *Thomas* but *Robert Dalziel*, of whom Col. Gibson in a letter (Brit. Mus. Add. MSS. 28887 fol. 345) dated Portsmouth 29th October 1701, addressed to J. Ellis, says, in asking for the appointment of 'Towne Major' for his 'Sone in Law, Capt. Robt. Dalzell' that 'he carried arms in Holland several years before the Revolution, was made ensign at the Revolution, and was Cap. in my late Reg. all the four years it stood—he is both a good man and a good officer, and no man better attached to his Maj. and which it would be a great ease and help to me in my old age to have such an officer under me upon whom I could entirely rely,' John Gibson had been appointed Colonel of a Regiment of Foot to be forthwith raised, and Captain of a Company in the same, 16th February 169⁴⁄₅; this Regiment, afterwards known as the 28th Foot (now 1st Battalion Gloucester Regiment), was reduced in 1698 after the peace of Ryswick, and reformed in 1702, having, like several Regiments about this period, served for a time as Marines. When reformed most of the officers of the old Regiment were reappointed, holding the same rank as formerly. Therefore in the succession of Colonels at the end of the Annual Army Lists Sir John Gibson appears as Colonel of the 28th Regiment from 16th February 1694 to 5th February 1704, when he was succeeded by Sampson de Lalo.

The first notice I have obtained from the War Office of Robert Dalzell is his commission, 1st June 1690, to be Ensign to Captain Carr in Sir David Colliear's Regiment, which in 1689 had been sent to the Netherlands under the Earl of Marlborough, and was afterwards disbanded. He was appointed Captain and Lieutenant to Colonel Gibson 16th February 169⁴⁄₅; Town Major of Portsmouth 6th December 1701. Notwithstanding his promotion to higher rank, he retained this appointment until after Gibson's death in 1717. He rose to be General of Foot 26th March 1745 ; was, 9th July 1730, Colonel of a Regiment, afterwards the 33d Foot ; was transferred to the Colonelcy of another Regiment, afterwards the 38th Foot, and was superseded 13th March 1750. This is the last notice of him at the War Office.

In the Register of Baptisms at Portsmouth there are the following entries :—1697, August, Annie Francis, daughter of Captain Robert Dazall and Anne Mary his wife. 1698, March, Gibson, son of the same. 1700, August, Thomas, son of Captain Robert Dalzell and Anna Maria his wife. 1706, September, William. Again, 1714, March, William, son of the Honourable Robert Dalzell and Mrs. Mary his wife. This last entry shows that Captain Dalzell was most probably son of an Earl of Carnwath.

Having so far written the above, a friend sent me, from the *Dictionary of National Biography*, vol. xiii. 1888, the biography of 'Dalzell, Robert (1662-1758), General.' It is much to be regretted that it contains errors and omissions, some of which I note. The name of his wife is not given, but it is stated that 'Sir John Gibson, Knight, . . . married Dalzell's sister'—an error which has arisen from Dalzell in his will calling Susannah Gibson his sister instead of sister-in-law. His earlier services are stated on 'possibilities' and not on certainties.

The career of a Robert Dalzell has been followed up, but it is probable that more than one of the same name was serving in the army at this period. The account given in the article does not coincide with the facts I have stated. The dates of the earliest mention of him in the War Office Records, and of his first appointment as Town Major, are also wrongly given, etc.

The biography states that 'he made eighteen campaigns under the greatest commanders in Europe.' He eventually became Chairman of the Sun Fire Office, and his son Gibson a Director, who died in Jamaica 1755, and was buried in St. Martin's-in-the-Fields, London. His father died 14th October 1758 in his 96th year, and was also buried there. At the time of his death his only surviving descendants were the two children of his son Gibson, Robert of Tidcome Manor House, Berkshire, and Frances, married to the Honourable George Duff, son of the first Earl of Fife.

To return to Sir John Gibson. The earliest notice I have obtained from the Commission Books is dated 28th February 168$\frac{8}{9}$: 'Sir Robert Peyton Knt. appointed Colonel and Captain of a Regiment of Foot.' 'John Gibson Lt. Col. and Captain of the sd Regiment.'

Having been unable to discover who was the mother of his children, where they were baptized, any particulars about his sons, or where Sir John was buried, I shall be grateful for information on these points, and for any account of his services previous to 1688. I note that on his seal there are no Arms impaled with his own. The will of Susanna Gibson, proved in London 10th March 1758, mentions a nephew and his family : 'I Susanna Gibson of the Parish of St. Martin's in the Fields Middlesex Spinster . . . give all the rest of my estate to Hannah Gibson wife of my nephew John Gibson of James St. Covent Garden Upholsterer . . . upon trust to apply the Interest and Dividends to the sole and separate use of her children.' Signed, 26th November 1755, 'John Gibson, sole Executor.'

F. N. R.

122. GENEALOGY.—'It is strange that while the study of genealogy used to be thought the sign of an obsolete, effete, and worn-out nation, at the present time in America the study of genealogy is drawing a larger expenditure of money, investigation, and literary power than in any other country in the world.'—DR. STUBBS, Bishop of Chester.

123. AN ACCOUNT OF THE FAMILY OF YOUNGER, ALLOA.—The name Younger occurs in 16th century wills and parochial registers, both in England and Scotland ; it is, however, by no means common. It is clear that in England it was the form of spelling assumed by the members of the Flemish family of Joncker, who came to London, and were members of the Dutch Church, Austin Friars, in 1580 ; the name occurs several times in the Baptismal Registers of that church, and also in other London Church Registers a few years later as Yncker, Younckeer, Yeounger, and Younger. The arms of the de Joncker family are 'Franché au 1, d'azur à une étoile d'or; au 2, de gu. à 2 roses d'arg. rangées en band.' The earliest known instance of the name occurring in Scottish documents is David Younger, 'nuncius et vice comes' of the County of Kircudbright in 1509 (*Reg. Priv. Coun.*). Next in date comes Henry Younger, who, with Gilbert Coston and Herbert Broun, is described as one of the 'inhabiters of Lord Erskine's land in the Ferryton' in the

parish of Clackmannan, 20th March, 1524 (*Bruce Charters*). In 1569 William Younger was a Prebendary of Trinity College, Edinburgh (*Reg. Priv. Coun.*); in 157⅔ William Younger held lands at Monktonhall, near Dalkeith (*Reg. Priv. Coun.*); he probably belonged to a family of the name still flourishing, which traces its descent from Thomas Younger of West Linton, in the Sheriffdom of Peebles, who died 1597. This adds to the probability that the family was originally Flemish, for many Flemish names are to be met with in Peeblesshire, which was a resort of foreign weavers.

Before considering the history of the family which will engage our attention, a few remarks may be made about the Youngers of Ferritoun. As there is no evidence that they were connected with the other family of the same name also living in Clackmannan, it is not necessary to give a detailed account of them, though there is no lack of information in the Parish Registers and Kirk Session Records. They remained for several generations tenants of the lands of Ferryton, under the house of Erskine. A John Younger went out with the Earl of Mar in 1715; on his return he had to submit to church discipline as a rebel before he could obtain the right of baptism for his child, who was named Francis. A brother of this John wisely left Clackmannan for Holland early in 1715 before the storm burst; he was intrusted by the Kirk Session with sundry Dutch doits which had found their way into the church collection plate and were useless in this country; with them he purchased in Holland some pepper, and duly sent it to the minister of Clackmannan. 'Clackmannan, 31 May 1715.—The which day Session mett, and after prayer the Min. reported that he had got some pepper for the dutch doits mentioned & that he had sold the same at half-crown price, which the Treasurer is charged with' (*Clack. Kirk. Sess. Rec.*). The Ferryton family became extinct, or left the parish about the end of last century. On Nov. 6th 1771 John Younger of Ferryton sold his burial-place in Clackmannan churchyard, 'comprehending five rooms and Threugh Ston,' to John M'Vey, tenant in Ferryton, reserving however, 'a Privilege of one Room in 3d Burial-place for myself' (*Clack. K. S. R.*). The Youngers of Ferryton seem to have been agriculturalists.

There was a family of Youngers in Clackmannan, connected by friendship and business with the Bruces. By trade the members of it were for several generations saltmakers. This fact makes it probable that their origin was Flemish, for in Queen Mary's reign Flemish saltmakers were invited to settle on the shores of the Forth in order that they might teach their method of working in a more skilful manner than that known to the natives. This is shown by the following act of Parliament :—

'*Anentis the making of salt within this realme.*

'ITEM, Because the Queenis Majistie hes be her prudencie and moyen, brocht certain strangers of excellent injine [skill] within this Realme, quha hes accorded to labour, discover, and manifest ane new maner of making of salt, different from the fashion used of before within the samin.' Secures them a monopoly for fifty years. (9th Parliament of Queen Mary, 4th of June 1563.) As the family whose history we are about to consider was connected with Culross and with Kincardine on Forth, in the parish of Tulliallan, as well as with Clackmannan, it will be requisite to give the result of researches made in the Register House, Edinburgh, and in the Records of these three parishes.

Henry Younger, a baxter, was a burgess of Culross; his name

occurs in the Burgh Records from their commencement in 1588 to August 1597, after which it is not found. A stent roll (list of ratepayers) was made in February 159⅞, and contains the names of 106 householders, but no Younger is amongst them. Henry Younger, 'portioner' of Blair-hill, in the adjoining parish of Muchart, died 8th August 1600. His will was administered by his executrix, his sister Agnes, wife of James Davison of Harvieston, in the parish of Easter Tillicoultry. It does not appear that he left any children. He may be identical with Henry of Culross, and have been a brother to Thomas Younger in Kincardine, in the parish of Tulliallan, who is styled in 1607 'portioner' of Kincardine and Muchart (*Reg. Priv. Coun.*), and was proprietor or feuar of the salt-pans at Culross. It is possible that Henry and Thomas were sons or nephews of Henry Younger, tenant in Ferryton in 1524. Be that as it may, it is clear that Thomas Younger in Kincardine in 1599, portioner of Kincardine and Muchart in 1607, and styled 'of Leit Green' in Kincardine 1607 (*Reg. Priv. Coun.*), was the same man who in 1606 and 1607 was engaged in a suit with Daniel Bruce in Airth about salt. In the entry for 1607 which concerns the Culross pans he is designated 'Thomas Younger in Culrois,' and is joined in the action with 'Thomas Younger in Airth,' probably his son, the Laird of Craigton. There is no statement that Culross or Airth was then the *residence* of the one or the other—but that they feued the salt-pan in these places. We know as a fact that a few years later, viz. in 1626, the pans at Culross were under the charge of Duncan Ezatt, 'Salt grieve' (*Min. of Corp. of Wrights*).

Thomas Younger 'of Leit Green,' was in 1601 (*Clack. Bap. Reg.*), witness with Sir Arthur Bruce of Clackmannan and Robert Bruce 'appeirand' of Wester Kennet to the baptism of Jonet, daughter of Sir James Schaw of Sauchie; he had been engaged in a lawsuit with Sir John Schaw of Sauchie for '2000 merks as principal, and £1000 as expenses,' 6th June 1598 (*Reg. Priv. Coun.*). What family he had we have failed to discover. There is, however, we think, no doubt that he was the father of Thomas Younger who resided at Craigton in the Parish of Clackmannan. The earliest entries of baptisms in the Clackmannan Registers are very imperfect, only two leaves being extant between 1599 and 1609; these are dated respectively 1601 and 1603. Fortunately, however, there exist entries which show that Thomas of Craigton could not have belonged to the Ferryton branch, for in 1595 is recorded the baptism of Thomas, son of Thomas Younger of Ferryton, who therefore could scarcely have been the father of Thomas of Craigton, who was married in 1598; for though instances occur of two brothers bearing the same Christian name, they are rare, and require full proof. The presumption that Thomas of Craigton was the son of Thomas of Leit Green is strengthened by the evidence we have of his intimacy with the families of Bruce of Clackmannan and Schaw of Sauchie, and by the fact that he must have been a saltmaker, for mention is made in the Kirk Session Records of the salt-pans at Craigton. It is possible that further investigation will produce absolute proof of the descent of Thomas Younger, and remove all doubts on the subject. Till these are forthcoming it will be prudent to commence the pedigree with

I. Thomas Younger (probably the son of Thomas Younger of Leit Green). His marriage is entered in the Clackmannan Registers—

'June 21, 1598. Thomas Youngar in craigtoune & Marjorie Schaw daur to the laird of Knokhall [Knockhill].'

Andrew Schaw of Knockhill, the father of Margaret Schaw or Younger, was grandson of John Schaw of Alva and Knockhill, second son of Sir James Schaw of Sauchie (alive 1483), who was grandson of Sir James Schaw of Greenock, who married Mary, second daughter and co-heiress of Islay de Annand of Sauchie, who was the lineal descendant of Islay de Annand (alive 1296). See 'General Notes anent some Ancient Scottish Families,' by David Marshall, F.S.A.Scot., privately printed.

It is impossible to state how many children Thomas Younger had by this marriage owing to the imperfect condition of the Register. Only two entries exist, viz. :—

I. James, baptized September 4, 1599.
II. Thomas, of whom below as Thomas II.
The following were also probably his children :—
[III. Andrew Younger.]
[IV. Robert Younger, described in a Bruce Charter of 1644 as servitor to Mr. Bruce of Kennet. He was in 1653 a heritor of the parish, and was on several occasions cautioner for Mr. Bruce or his son before the Kirk Session. In 1664 he left the parish. He is probably the Robert Younger who was married at Culross in 1640, and who died at Kincardine in September 1685, being father of Andrew Younger, who married Bessie Taylor at Culross, and of Thomas Younger, saltmaker, who married at Kincardine in 1688 Janet Gershom.]
[V. John, and
VI. Henry Younger, whose banns were published at Torryburn in 1640 and 1643 respectively.]

The witnesses to James Younger's baptism were James Stewart of Rossyth and Alexander Gaw of Maw. The witnesses to Thomas Younger's baptism were Edward Broun of Keir and Archibald Bruce of [illegible]. The Gaws of Maw were of good position in Fifeshire in the sixteenth century, and the Brouns were Lairds of Keir, an Estate in the Parish of Tulliallan.

Thomas Younger of Craigton was a man of good estate. In 1621 (April 7), he purchased more land, and in 1623 he was Bailie of Clackmannan. He must, moreover, have been extensively engaged in the manufacture of salt, for the name occurs in 1607 (*Pri. Coun. Rec.*) in connection with the salt-pans at Culross and Airth. It was a custom common in those days for a man possessed of capital and skill to carry on his business (especially such a one as salt-making, a foreign speciality) at several places, and thus to make provision for his sons. This arrangement is shown in the interesting account of the Lorraine glass-making families of Tyzack, Tyttory, and Henzell, written by H. Sydney Grazebrooke; it also existed in the pan-making family of Van Halen. In the case of salt-making it was perhaps necessary to have the pans at various parts of the coast. The existence of this custom proves exceedingly inconvenient to the genealogist; without a knowledge of it he is quite at sea; and even when he under-stands it, it is not easy to follow the different children in after-life, as their residences were frequently changed, till at last the various branches became more localised and thus more easy to trace.

We have not discovered when Thomas Younger of Craigton died: as Robert Bruce of Kennet purchased Craigton in 1630 that is very probably the date of his death. He was not in a position to found a family by entailing a landed estate on an elder son. He certainly had two sons, and, as we have shown, probably other children, for whom provision had to be made ; what became of James, the eldest, we know not.   A James Younger was witness to the baptism of James Younger, grandson of Thomas, in 1673. Robert Younger, probably a son, was a salt-maker at Culross ; and at the same place we find Thomas, born 1609.   The towns were so near together that communication was easily kept up, and we constantly find the same persons mentioned in the records of the two parishes.

II. THOMAS YOUNGER, son of Thomas (I.) Younger of Craigton and Margaret Schaw, was baptized at Clackmannan 18th January 1609.   In 1631 his banns of marriage were published at Torryburn, but the in- tended wife's name is not given ; ten days later he forfeited his pledge, so that the marriage did not then take place ; but before 1641 he had married Elizabeth Miller of Clackmannan, who was the mother of his children.   She is stated in the Kirk-session Records of Clackmannan to have given (August 4, 1680) to her youngest son, John Younger, salt- maker, Powside, Clackmannan, her family seat in the Parish Church. The children of Thomas (II.) Younger and Elizabeth Miller were—
    I. Thomas, of whom below as Thomas III.
    II. Bessie, baptized at Culross 22d March 1643.
    III. James, baptized at Culross 30th November 1644 ; he married at Clackmannan, 28th February 1672, Agnes, the daughter of George Tilloch or Tulloch—the sister of his brother Thomas's wife.   By this marriage he had issue—
        1. James, baptized at Clackmannan 4th January 1673, the witnesses being James Younger (probably his great-uncle) and Andrew Younger (probably another great-uncle).   James died young.
        2. George (so named after his mother's father), baptized at Clack- mannan, 7th February 1674, witnesses John Younger and Andrew Tilloch, his uncle.   He married at Clackmannan, 17th December 1709, Christian Robertson, by whom he had three sons : (*a*) James, (*b*) Andrew, (*c*) William.   The last of whom alone married, and left one daughter, Christian, the wife of James Alison.
        3. Janet, baptized at Clackmannan 22d April 1676, the witnesses being James Younger and George Tilloch.
        4. Elspet, baptized at Clackmannan 26th October 1678, witnesses John Younger and William Tilloch.
        5. John, baptized at Clackmannan 12th March 1681, witnesses James Milne and Andrew Tilloch.
        6. Andrew, baptized at Clackmannan 8th September 1683, witnesses George Tilloch and Andrew Tilloch.   Married at Alloa, 13th June 1712, Jean Chalmers.   Was a salter, and left issue.
    James Younger and his descendants were salt-makers at Powside, in the Parish of Clackmannan.
    IV. Margaret, baptized at Culross 18th June 1651.
    V. John, baptized at Culross 3d January 1658.   He was husband of Margaret Hutcheson, but the record of his marriage has not been discovered.   He had issue, and was a salter at Powside.

(*To be continued.*)

124. WITCHCRAFT.—' Clackmannan 11 June, 1706. The which day the Ministers & Elders mett in Session & after prayer William Paton Elder reported from Archibald Duncan & Robert Stupart Elders that John Scobie younger in Toun told them that he went with his Uncle the deceas'd James Scobie to a well in Grasmes Toun land two nights to wash him with the water of that well, and to cast some pouders in some papers upon him, and that there came a black man from the Kerse hill towards them, & a branded cat came out of the corn at which Robert Stuparts cattle squeel'd, & that the black man followed them doun nigh to the Walk Miln at Dovan as they were returning home to Clackmannan & that they heard a terrible noise like the noise of coaches, & that the said James Scobie fell in the water ; and that his going to be washed with the water of that well, and these pouders cast upon him were by the direction of Margaret M'Carter, and his falling into Dovan water was the reason why he was not cured, and that she forbad them to speak coming or going.' The case was heard again on 16th July 1706, and the following particulars are added : ' And that when they came to call the deponant to goe the second night he refused till the deceased Robert Reid in Toun came & took him & they both went with him the second night and saw the black man and cat, & heard the cattle squeel as aforesaid and that when they were coming back again there came a great wind upon the trees on the side of Dovan and when he was crossing Cartochy burn his uncles foot slipt & fell in the burn and Robert Reid said the cure is lost, there is no helping of you now ; and so they spoke from thenceforth till they came home, for Margaret Bruce the said James Scobies wife told them that if he fell in the water he could not be cured, and further added that when they told Margaret her Husband had fallen in the water she wept. Sic subscribitur John Scobie. This day the Session being informed that Margaret M'Carter has gone out of the parish thought fit to delay till they see if she return,' and thus the matter ended.—*Kirk Session Records.*

125. SCOT'S TRANSCRIPT OF PERTH REGISTERS [*continued from page* 170].

October 2, 1569.
William Scroggs & Isabell Leverand.

October 9, 1569.
William Dyne & Janet Dyke.

³¹/ October 16, 1569.
Nicoll Galloway & Christian Lawson.
John Fothringham & Bessie Keir.

November 13, 1569.
Paul Cousland & Elspith Scott.
William Edward & Agnis Tawis.

November 27, 1569.
Alexander Lowrie & Margaret Dyke.

December 4, 1569.
Robert Matthew & Isabell Anderson.
John Millar & Bessie Adamson.

December 11, 1569.
James Mar & Agnes Basket.

December 18, 1569.
Thomas Hardie & Janet Robertson.

January 1, 1569.
Alexander Chalmer & Isabell Maill.

January 22, 1569.
Arthur Leverand & Agnes Throskell.

January 29, 1569.
Robert Brown & Agnes Meik.

February 5, 1569.
John Anderson & Janet Watson.
William Duncan & Bessie Glass.

February 6, 1569.
James Stewart & Marion Andarson.
Fastranes Even the 7 Day of February, Anno 69 years.

February 21, 1569.
James Scott Tirsappie & Christian Adam.
George Loureinston & Marion Cuming.

March 12, 1569.
George Watson & Janet Henderson.

April 9, 1570.
Robert Cock & Janet Horne.

32/   April 16, 1570.
David Westwater & Christian Mason.

May 7, 1570.
Thomas Gibson & Margaret Mackie.

May 21, 1750.
~~Thomas Hardie & Jean Bane.~~
James Robertson & Helen Smith.

June 4, 1570.
Thomas Hardie & Jean Bane.

June 11, 1570.
John Eldar & Margaret Meik.
Alexander Anderson & Janet Gowrie.

July 2, 1570.
Patrick Wilson & Margaret Neal.

September 10, 1570.
James Cowan & Isabell Ruthven.
Alexander Maxton & Cathrine Rattray.
John Henderson & Isabell Finlayson.
William Faire & —— Gall (the wife's first name is
supplied in the memorandum of Contract viz Margaret Gall).

December 10, 1570.
John Smith & Eupheme Black.
Robert Pearson & Christie White.

December 17, 1570.
Patrick Chrystie & Margaret Dalrymple.

December 24, 1570.
Henry Williman & Christian Mathew.

Dec. 31, 1570.
Thomas Barclay & Violet Robertson.

January 7, 1570.
Patrick Tullie & Elspith Stobb.
David Johnston & Isabell Muir.

January 14, 1570.
John Peblis & Janet Whittock.

February 4, 1570.
John Young & Helen Landell.

83/ February 11, 1570.
Blaize Powrie & Janet Eldar.
Cristoll Chappell & Catherine Murray.

February 18, 1570.
Mr. Bas M'Ghie & Katherine Paterson.

(*N.B.*—I apprehend that minister or Literary Gentlemans name was Note. Basil M'Ghie. But it is written in the Register so carelessly as not to be certainly read ; it may perhaps be Mr. Thomas M'Ghie.)

February 18, 1570.
Thomas Ferguson & Helen Neving.

February 25, 1570.
John Tendall & Janet Ruthven.
John Richardson & Violet Andrew.

(*N.B.*—In the margin of the Register is written at the names of John Note. Richardson & Violet Andrew the word 'Inernathie' signifying that one of Richardson. them came from, or was Proprietor of the Lands so called.)

February 25, 1570.
John Steward & Margaret Spens.

April 22, 1571.
John Eldar & Bessie Lowrie.
Archibald Young & Bessie Law.

May 13, 1571.
Laurence Lamb & Bibbe Adamson.
James Stewart & Janet Meik.

May 20, 1571.
Andrew Donaldson & Margaret Foster

May 27, 1571.
George Hutton & Agnes Duncan.

June 3, 1571.
Michael Anderson & Margaret Murray.

July 9, 1571.
Andrew Anderson & Janet Gall.
John Rannaldson & Margaret Broun.
34/   David Wilson & Barbara Thomson.

July 16, 1571.
Stephen Black & Margaret Young.

July 20, 1571.
James Kempie & Isabell Henderson.
Robert Lovell & Janet Meik, Craigie.

July 30, 1571.
George Tait & Janet Bryden.

August 13, 1571.
David Henderson & Elspith Howie.

August 20, 1571.
John Anderson & Marjory Pitscotty.

August 30, 1571.
Walter Richardson & Janet Murray.

September 3, 1571.
Thomas Stewart & Marion Stirling.
Robert Hay & Giles Griegor.
James Ross & Christian Jamieson.

September 10, 1571.
James Colyng & Isabell Ruthven.
Alexander Maxton & Catherine Rattray.
John Henderson & Isabell Paynter alias Finlayson.

September 17, 1571.
John Young & Agnes Bowar.
John Barclay & Eupheme Murray.

November 12, 1571.
Mr. Thomas Robertson & Barbara Justice.

Note.
Robertson.

(*N.B.*—At the end of the Register Book I find a memorandum as
follows :—' The 6th day of November anno 70 years. The whilk day
Master Thomas Robertson minister has acted himself to pay to the Poor
the sum of 40 shillings money betwixt this & Andermas next, for the
slander that is raised upon [*sic*] & Barbara Justice his future spouse.'
The memorandum is subscribed with his own hand ' Mr. Thomas
35/ Robertson.' If he was minister of a Parish, I do not know at present
what Parish it was. But it would seem that either the money was paid,
& that the scandall, whether well or ill founded was done away, before
the time of his marriage.)

November 12, 1571
Andrew Thomson & Agnes Mason.
William Hepburn & Alison Raidy (perhaps Reid).

December 3, 1571.
David Hoyd (perhaps Hood) & Isabell Stewart.

December 10, 1571.
Robert Finlayson & Helen Copin.

(*N.B.*—At this place the Compiler of the Register goes back several Note.
months in the year 1571, having probably come to the knowledge, of his
having omitted to mark several marriages which had happened during
that time.)

June 10 1571,
Thomas Dundie & Violet Robertson.
John Hendry & Janet Henderson.
Robert Gaw (or Gull) & Eupheme Adamson.

June 17, 1571.
Duncan Robertson & Christian Chrystison.

July 22, 1571.
Peter Grant & Agnes Anderson.

July 26, 1571.
William Inglis & Marion Bruce.

July 31, 1571.
Adam Anderson & Elspith Snell.

August 12, 1571.
William Laird & Violet Anderson.

August 29, 1571.
Archibald Sicker & Janet Jack.

September 2, 1571.
George Ramsay & Elspith Scott.
Walter Buchanan & Bessie Mackie.
John Colt & Isabell Grieve—Muirtoun.

3d/ November 4, 1571.
James Riddy & Margaret Colt.

November 16, 1571.
James Anderson & Margaret Anderson.

(*N.B.*—James Adamson afterwards Provost of Perth & father of Note.
Mr. John Adamson Principal of the College of Edinburgh & of Adamson.
Mr. Henry Adamson Author of the celebrated Historical Poem which
according to the Humour of the Time in which it was published has the
fanciful and uncouth name of Galls Gabions.

James Adamson was a merchant in Perth, Brother of Mr. Patrick
Adamson Archbishop of St. Andrews or else nephew of that Archbishop;
and he was married to the sister of Mr. Henry Anderson the celebrated
Poet several of whose Latin Poems have been published in the Collection
called 'Delitiae Poetarum Scotorum.'

James Adamson lived to a great age. He & his Brother in law,
Mr. Henry Anderson died much about the same time in the year 1623.)

November 18, 1571.
John Cochran & Giles Kaddy.
John Brown in the parish of Methven with Margaret May.

November 25, 1571.
William Anderson & Margaret Scrimgeour.
George Hunter & Margaret Fyffe.
John Mackie & Agnes Watson.

George Stobb & Isabell Robertson.
William Robertson & —— Gaw (her first name omitted).

December 3, 1571.
John M'Griegor & Christian Ferguson.

December 16, 1571.
George Mathew & Marion Robertson.

December 22, 1571.
Troilus (perhaps Carolus) Eldar & Violet Stannis.
Alexander Brown & Catherine Cramby.
Robert M'Koyll & Bessie Forbes.
David Cuthbert & Catherine Finlayson.

37/ December 29, 1571.
David Bow & Catherine Ross.

January 1, 1571.
James Lawson & Isabell Inglis.

January 13, 1571.
Alexander Chalmer & Isabell Monipenny.
David Nicoll & Catherine Black.
James Wilson, Muirtown & Helen Wilson.

January 27, 1571.
Alexander Ferguson & Violet Balneaves.
James Eldar & Isabell Wenton.

February 10, 1571.
Robert Brown & Agnes Walker.

February 17, 1571.
George Henderson & Isabell Woddell
Walter Barnett & Janet Boy.
John Allyson & —— Nicoll.

Note.   (*N.B.*—The first name of the Bride is omitted.)
Fastrens Even the 19th day of February.

April 1, 1572.
Robert Shiell & Isabell Ruthven.

April 22, 1572.
John Rutherford & Janet Anderson.

May 18, 1572.
Thomas Barrall & Janet Dickson.
William Blair & Janet Smith.
James Sym & Eupheme Tullie.

May 25, 1572.
Thomas Fowlis & Janet Wilson.

July 13, 1572.
William Lawson & Violet Wilson.

July 20, 1572.
Robert Mason & Agnes Reddy.
William Young & Janet Malice.

[38]/ July 29, 1572.
John Pearson & Eupheme Campbell.

August 9, 1572.
John Mason & Janet Blinshall.

August 17, 1572.
Thomas Henderson & Isabell Sibbald.
David Lyall & Helen Lowdeane.
David Jackson & Marion Jakis.

September 7, 1572.
John Anderson & Isabell Brydie.
John Dow & Helen Duncan.

September 14, 1572.
Gilbert Billie & Margaret Tyrie.

September 18, 1572.
Dionysius Blacket & Janet Monipenny.

November 2, 1572.
James Henderson & Helen Cavers.
William Bower & Helen Rynd.

November 17, 1572.
George Archibald & Helen Cuthbert.
John Hewat & Janet Hoge.

126. KIRK SESSION RECORDS AND CHURCH ACCOUNTS.—The following items are selected from the Kirk Session Records of Alloa as likely to prove of interest. It would be useless to print the accounts in full, for most of the items consist of payment of money to regular pensioners or to casual poor. It may be well, however, to state that in the latter class are to be found a large number of those who suffered from the unsettled state of the kingdom. Many Irish found a refuge in Scotland about this time, and had apparently to depend for their subsistence on alms ; maimed ' souldiers ' also figure frequently ; in some cases a note is made that the recipients were gentlemen or ladies, and in one or two instances the possession of a title did not secure the possessor from beggary. If in our present number more than usual prominence seems to be given to Kirk Session Records, it may be explained that circumstances have lately enabled us to study some good specimens of these most valuable documents. Though perhaps few would be worth printing *in extenso*, none should be overlooked, and the Scottish History Society is acting wisely in printing the Kirk Session Records of St. Andrews, for the perusal of the work may lead antiquaries to extract and publish what they may find of interest in the books that exist in their own neighbourhoods. The genealogist should consult them, as they often incidentally throw light on doubtful points of family history, and amplify the otherwise bare facts entered in Parochial Registers. We shall be glad to receive extracts of general interest, and shall do our best to find room for them in our pages— if they are given *literatim et verbatim*, and are not of unnecessary length. We should specially value any that may illustrate the popular belief in witchcraft.

Extracts from 'Discharge of the Collections and Churche Money
depursed be Andrew Erskine box master beginnand July 13, 1645 ':—

for a 1000 tickets		5 lib.
for work in the kirk seats and foormes		19 sh. 4d.
to St. Andrewes busser (scholar)		6 lib. 13 sh. 9d.
for ane glassen window to the kirk		vi lib.
for yron bands nails and timber work		3 lib. 4 sh.
To the old Nowrish called bread Nourish		48 sh.
for ane windinsheit to a stranger		30 sh.
To ane old expectant suppliant		10 lib.
1646 To the old bread nourish		24 sh.
for ane Cloath to the Comunione table		xi lib. 4 sh.
for making ye blackstool timber and work		9 lib. 5 sh.
for towes to the bell and mending the bell		21 sh.
for the letron service at Comunione		48 sh.
To St. Andrewes steudent for 1646		6 lib. 13 sh. 4d.
1647 for ane lock and key to ye kirk doore		30 sh.
for tuo cowps for the comunione table		26 sh. 8d.
for meall and other furnishing to poore folk in tyme of ye pestilence		20 lib. 14 sh. 10d.
for service at letron and to the beddall the tuo comunion dayes 1647		3 lib. 1 sh. 4d.
for new foormes in the loft		49 sh. 4d.
for ane harne gowne to faulters		3 lib. 12 sh.
for leading sand and serving the sklaitters		24 sh.
for mending ye blackstoole		18 sh.
To ane stranger a scholler		58 sh
for ane bindin sheit to ane stranger		24 sh.
1648 for the table boord allowed more yn was allowed		4 sh.
for mending fallen foormes in the loft and naills and sound timber		18 sh.
The glazen wrights compt is		13 lib. 16 sh. 4d.
1649 to ane Northland stranger		8 sh.
to ane woman in Craigward taylor		12 sh.
for ane new towel for the elements		20 sh.
to the criple mans qhose goodsou was killed		30 sh.
to Andrew balk for fourmes to ye table		48 sh.
to Johne Huntar for ane kist (coffin) to ye headed man in July		3 lib. 6 sh. 8d.
to Johne Chrystie Tinkelar		1 lib. 4 sh.
1650 to ane misterfull woman		6 lib. 13 sh. 4d.
to ane honest misterfull man in the town		20 merks.
to highland men yt was seiking corne		12 sh.
to a minister cam from Irland		2 lib. 15 sh.
for a psalme buke to the kirk		16 sh.
to a ministers wyffe com from Irland called Semple		1 lib. 10 sh.
for putting bands on the seat door betwixt the kirk and the aveiw [? avenue]		10 sh.
to andrew dickie for a lock to the elders seat		7 sh. 4d.
to a German		10 sh.
to And balk for dressing the bell		15 sh.
to James Melvin for a chest		3 lib. 6 sh. 8d.

to Andr Dickies for the grave making	. . .	13 sh. 4d.
to the school maister of Newbatle	. . .	1 lib. 10 sh.
1651 mending of the bell .	. . . .	3 lib.
to on Mr Rot Wallace	. . . .	2 lib.
to on Mr George Dewar .	. . .	3 lib. 6 sh.
to Allexr Gordone a poore minister	. . .	1 lib.
to the ladie Ebitshall . .	. . .	6 sh. 8d.
to buy a winding sheit for a Souldiour	. . .	1 lib.
to Rot Young for putting up the bell	. . .	10 lib.
to Pat Meather for yron to it .	. . .	8 lib.
to Jo Short for leather to the toung of the bell .	. .	20 sh.
to Andrew Erskine to give James Steil sclatter		
for mending the church .	. . .	5 lib. 8 sh.
to Jas Melvin comed fre Ingland	. . .	18 sh.
to Pat Chalmers for a belstring .	. . .	12 sh.
1652 to the school mr of Saline	. . .	4 sh.
to one Cornet Campbell	. . .	18 sh.
to a German Js. Romaw .	. . .	12 sh.
To Wm. bean going to holland	. . .	12 sh.
to the smith for nails to the bell	. . .	15 sh.
to the merchand for a harn gown	. . .	2 lib. 2 sh.
to the tayllyour for making it .	. . .	13 sh. 4d.
to a stranger called hans Martine to help to pay		
his fraught to carie him hom .	. . .	2 lib. 8 sh.
to the glass wright for making new windows		
& mending old . .	. . .	9 lib. 7 sh. 4d.
to one Capta: Kers fre Ingl:	. . .	18 sh.
to a Sergent come from Ingl: .	. . .	12 sh.
of yt which was collected to the prisoners at		
tinmouth Castle yre was resting eight pounds		
and four shill Scotts qlk was delyverd . .		8 lib. 4 sh.
to a poor English man yt was on of the King		
domestick servants	. . .	1 lib. 10 sh.
to my lord Athols son	. . .	12 sh.

127. THE BRANKS.—1618, Oct. 4.—'Anent the Bill geven in be M'
James and his wyfe the session in ane voice ordaines hir, Janet Tailzor
[name written in above the line], to be putt in the brankes and the chain-
zie on ane Sonday fra the first bell to the third whill ye minister cums in
and the psalmes be sung, and after the preaching when the psalmes begin
to be sung whil ye people be demissed.' This is all on the case which
appears in the Records. In connection with the not unusual penance of
standing in sackcloth on the 'black stool' are two items in the Session
accounts for August 1647 :—

'for ane harne [sackcloth] gown to faulters, . 3 lib. 12sh. od.'
'for making ye blackstool timber and work, . 9 lib. 5sh. od.'

1705, Feb. 2.—'John Archibald in Bauchry stood at the kirk door
in Sackcloth between the second and third bell and also before the congregation *pro primo* the last Lords Day, and was rebuked for his hainous
guilt of adultery and exhorted to repentance for the same.'—*Alloa Kirk
Session Records.*

128. IRON COFFIN CASES.—When body-snatching was prevalent, many parishes were provided with large iron cases, which were lowered into a grave when it was dug. The coffin was deposited in it, an iron cover was placed upon it and securely locked, after which the grave was filled up. A sufficient time having elapsed, the grave was re-opened, the case taken out for future use, and the coffin was left to decay. An extra charge was made when these precautions were employed. Two of these cases existed in the neighbourhood of Alloa. One lay for many years in the churchyard at Tullibody. On missing it lately, I made inquiries and found it had been broken up for old iron. The other one was in the yard of the ruined church at Airth, and may be there yet. Without going the length of advising the Society of Antiquaries to procure such an unwieldy and repulsive article for their museum, I think it would be advisable to have a photograph taken of one, and a written description of it, for interest attaches to such relics of days when there was reason to fear that graves, even in out-of-the-way places, might be violated. Probably in a few years these cases will all be destroyed, and any chance reference to them will perplex the antiquary. Is it known what was the usual name for them ?

ED.

129. FONT OR CROSS SOCKET.—The last Report of the Scottish Society of Antiquaries contains an interesting paper on Scottish Baptismal Fonts, by J. Russell Walker, Esq., F.S.A.Scot. An engraving is given of, and allusion is made to, a stone at Inchyre House, Fifeshire. Mr. Walker states that it looks very like a gable cross or pinnacle. The engraving shows this, save that had it been used for a socket for a gable cross the hole would have been square, and not round. A stone of precisely similar character is now lying in the Churchyard of the ruined Parish Church at Culross : in this case the hole is square, and I think that it must once have held the cross. The similarity between the stones makes it questionable whether the Inchyre one had originally a round hole or basin, and whether it may not have been carved for, and perhaps used as, the finial of the gable of the Church. ED.

130. CLOCKS AND CLOCKMAKERS (see pp. 127-128, 170).—The *Burgh Records of Edinburgh* furnish evidence of an older Knockmaker than those mentioned in page 170 of *N. N. & Q.* The following extracts, the first three of which are from these Records, may prove interesting in this inquiry. The first extract, and probably the second, refers to a sundial :—

'28th Novr. 1566. The prouest baillies and counsall ordanis maister Jhone Prestoun dene of gild, to caus mend the prik of the sone orlege on the south syde of the kirk in the kirk yard and draw the letteris thairof of new.'

'24 april 1567. The dean of gild ordained "to caus paint the letteris of the orlage." Three persons appointed "to talk with the man that hes the orlage to sell desyrit to be set vp at the Nether Bow, drif it to ane price and report to the Counsall."'

'19 april 1570. It is appoyntit and aggreit betuix the baillies dene of gild and counsale on that ane pairt and Robert Creych, knok makar on the vther pairt, viz the said Robert bindis and oblissis him to mend and vphald the toun knok they furnessing irne allanerlie for the quhilk caus they ordane the thesauraris present and to cum to pay him yeirlie during his lyfetime xl s.' Is anything else known about Robert Creych?

1st August, 1589. The 'Halie bluid silver' (custom dues, so-called) were 'rowped ye space of half an hour be ye glass.'—*Acts and Statutes of the Guildry Incorporation of Dundee.* A. HUTCHESON.

131. SHAKESPEARE IN GLOUCESTERSHIRE.—The attack which has been recently made against Shakespeare has caused men to study his works with increased attention to the evidences of his knowledge of localities. No excuse is required for the presence of the following note in a Scottish magazine, for Scotsmen have shown they love the man who wrote for all time and for all races. In this note I only seek to deal with one point in his writing, but I have not seen it noticed in any of the recent literature which the Donnelly controversy has produced, and I think that at least it tends to prove that the writer of Shakespeare's plays was well acquainted with the district not far distant from Stratford. The few passages I shall produce have struck me, a Gloucestershire man, as containing indications that Shakespeare possessed a personal knowledge of that district, and I shall explain how it is probable that he had an opportunity of acquiring it. These passages have not been noted in Mr. Russell French's valuable and rare work, *Shakespeareana Genealogica*, which contains proof that Shakespeare's knowledge of Warwickshire names is shown in his plays.

In the West of England the Cotswold hills have ever been celebrated, and any one who has seen them rising in beauty, and not without dignity, from the Vale of Berkeley, will understand the influence they have exercised on the imagination of natives of a lowland district.

We find Shakespeare, as was natural in a Warwickshire man, referring to them :—

'*Slender.* How does your fallow greyhound, sir? I heard say he was outrun on Cotsall.'—*M. W. of W.*, i. 1.

The annual games on the Cotswold hills were celebrated in Shakespeare's days, and hare-coursing formed an important part of them.

In the play of *Henry IV.*, Pt. ii. iii. 2, Justice Shallow, 'at his seat in Gloucestershire,' boasts of his youthful escapades, and speaks of his former comrades, 'little John Doit of Staffordshire, and black George Bare, and Francis Pickbone, and Will Squele, a Cotswold man.' 'A Cotswold man' is the very term still applied by the dalemen to one who lives in the hill country — it would be unintelligible to a native of any other part of England.

There are other passages which indicate that Shakespeare had himself visited the most prominent of the Cotswold range, viz. Stinchcombe Hill (*i.e.* the stint or end of the combe or ridge). The subject has not been overlooked in a little work, *Dursley and its Neighbourhood*, by the late Rev. J. J. Blunt; I, as a native of Dursley, and well acquainted with every inch of Stinchcombe Hill, can speak of the correctness of his remarks.

In the play of *Richard II.*, ii. 3, we find mention of 'a wild prospect in Gloucestershire.' That this was the prospect from the hill I have mentioned seems the more probable from the following passage :—

North. How far is it to Berkeley? And what stir
Keeps good old York there, with his men of war?
Percy. There stands the castle by yon tuft of trees.

There it stands in the vale below, and is still almost concealed by the 'tuft of trees.' No such view of it can be obtained from any other spot as from Drakestone, the extreme point of the hill. From this point also the wide estuary of the Severn appears as a lake, the lower bend being concealed by rising ground. When seen at low water, Shakespeare's 'sandy-bottom'd Severn,' *Henry IV.*, Pt. I. iii. I, describes it most accurately. The river Wye is not visible from this point, and no epithet is applied to it, though it is mentioned in the same sentence. There is good cause to believe that Shakespeare himself stood on the spot, for a family of his name existed in the locality in the 16th and 17th centuries. James Shakspeare was buried at Bisley in 1570; Edward, son of John and Margery Shakspeare, was baptized at Beverstone in 1619, and Thomas Shakspeare, a weaver, was married at Dursley in 1677. Tradition has pointed out a part of the wood that lies between Dursley and the summit of the hill as connected with the poet, or at least with this family, for it has from time immemorial been known as 'Shakespeare's Walk.' Yet another coincidence remains: in *Henry IV.*, Pt. II. v. I, Davy says to Justice Shallow, 'I beseech you, sir, to countenance William Visor of Woncot * against Charles Perkes of the Hill.' Stinchcombe Hill is still known in the immediate district as 'the hill,' and on it are the traces of a house which belonged to a family named Perkis; in the year 1612 Arthur Vizar was High Bailiff of Dursley, and his descendants in the direct male line are gentlemen of coat armour still owning property at 'Woncot.' Woodmancote, an important hamlet or suburb, lies close under the hill, and 'Woncot' is a fair rendering of the way in which it is still pronounced by the rustics in the neighbourhood. The name Vizar, now Vizard, was likely to strike a sojourner in the district from its rarity and peculiarity. As Dickens noted names for future use, so probably did Shakespeare. It is quite possible that it may yet be discovered that some suit at law did exist between Visor of Woodmancote and Perkis of 'the hill.' It would be a subject for conversation when Shakespeare was staying at Dursley, as it is not unlikely he was, for, as I have stated, men of his name, possibly his relatives, were living in the immediate neighbourhood, if not in the town itself, in the 16th century. Blunt, without giving his authority, states that at Newington-Bagpath some of the family 'still exist as small freeholders, and claim kindred with the poet.'

A. W. CORNELIUS HALLEN.

132. PAYMENT OF SCOTTISH M.P.'S.—Scottish members of Parliament were formerly paid, as it was found difficult to induce country gentlemen to incur great expense as well as labour by acting as representatives of country districts. The following paper shows how the rates were levied :—

'Followes a stent roll For payment of the Somme / of Two thousand Thrie hundreth and Fyftie / pundis scottis Dew for the charges of John / Campbell of Ardchattane Commissioner of parliat / for the Schyre of Argyll maid and set doun be / Sir Dougall Campbell Sir James Lamount and / Duncane M'Corquodill of Phantellans As / haveing power and commissione fra the Lordis / of Counsell and Sessione beiring daitt at Edgr

---

* Some editions read 'Wincot' for 'Woncot,' and French (p. 325) adopts this reading, in ignorance of the family of Vizor of Woodmancote or Woncot. He supposes the poet to have invented the name, wishing not to expose a resident at Wilmcote, near Stratford, which may have been called Wincot, as Woodmancote was certainly called Woncot. The edition of 1623 reads 'Woncot.'

the nynt day of July I. MC. three scor thrie yeres / And payeable be the kinges barrones and frie holders / within the said Schyre According to the Severall / proportions of Rentis In maner efter speit

	lb	sh	d
Imprimis Sir Johne Campbell of Glenorchy .	40	oo	o
Sir Nell Campbell of Calder . . .	520	oo	o
Sir Dougall Campbell of Auchinbreck .	60	oo	o
Sir James Lamount of Innerryne . .	180	oo	o
Archibald M'Lauchlane of that ilk .	120	oo	o
Collin Campbell of Stragt . . .	60	oo	o
Angus M'Donald of Lergie . . .	120	oo	o
Duncane M'Corquedill of Phantellans .	30	oo	o
Duncane Campbell of Ellangray . .	52	oo	o
Archibald Campbell of Glencaradill .	60	oo	o
Sir Allane M'cleane of Dowart . .	720	oo	o
Lauchlane M'cleane of Lochbowie .	180	oo	o
Johne M'Cleane of Coill . . .	48	oo	o
Hecter M'clean of Torlosk . . .	60	oo	o
Johne M'cleane of Kendlochalem .	24	oo	o
M'Kinnon of Strathgrdill . .	40	oo	o
M'Kay Ugodill . . .	o8	oo	o
Suma at four pund the 100 merk rent extends to	2322	oo	o

Suma totalis extending to the said soume of / Two thousand three hundred and Fyftie punds / dew to the said John Campbell of Ardchattane / For attending the last thrie sessiones of parliament / 1661, 1662, and 1663 as his commissioner fie / according to my Lord Clerk register his attestatioune / with four days cuming and four dayes goeing at ilk / sessioune of the farsaid thrie sessiones of parliament, as / at mor Lenth is conteind in the decreitt and Lres raset tharupone.

'And we the commissioners appoyntit be the Lords of counsell and sessioune For / making of this said stent roll or any on of us according to the commissioune / grantit for that use, Have subscrybitt this pñts with our handis the sixt day of October I.MC. three scor thrie yearis.

J. LAMOND.
D. M. PHANTELLANIS.'

Endorsed.—'The scroll of / Ardchattanes fie / as commissioner / upon every frie holder / in gñall [general].'—*Ardchattan MSS.*

133. OLD SCOTTISH LAMPS, ETC.—We would draw our readers' attention to the extract we have made (with permission) from the Address of D. Bruce Peebles, Esq. (see page 28).

QUERIES.

LXXVI. FASKEN OR FASKIN.—Can any of your readers give an explanation of this surname, which has existed in Banffshire over 300 years, and has been spelt in some half-dozen different ways? M.

LXXVII. JOHN HAMILTON, music-seller in Edinburgh, also composer and versifier, *ob.* 1814. Can any one kindly inform me who owns the copyright of his poems? Is it the descendant or a publisher, and what is the present address of such owner?

O. M. M. B.

LXXVIII. GORDON OF AUCHDENDOLLY.—In the *Sherborne Journal* (Dorset) of July 21st, 1809, occurs the following announcement:—
'Tuesday se'nnight was married, Robert Gordon esq. of Auchdendolly, in the stewartry of Kircudbright, North Britain, and of Leweston, Dorset, to Elizabeth Anne, only daughter of Charles Westley Cox esq. of Kemblehouse, Wilts.'
I shall be glad to know to what family Robert Gordon belonged. His father, William Gordon, who died 1802, aged 44, married Anna, sister and heiress of Sir Stephen Naish, Knt., of Bristol, and of Leweston, through whom he became possessed of the Leweston estate. C. H. MAYO.

LXXIX. FAMILY OF WHITSON.—Information wanted about the family of Whitson in Perth, 1296 to 1500 ; especially William Quhitsoun 1379-84, Keeper of the Wardrobe to Robert II. C. H. W.

LXXX. ROSS OF PITCALNIE.—Can any reader of *N. N. & Q.* kindly give information about Anne, Christian, Isabel, Catherine, James, Charles, Angus, younger children of Malcolm Ross, fifth of Pitcalnie, by his 1st wife, Jean, eldest daughter of Mr. James M'Culloch of Piltoun? Charles and Angus, called 3d and 4th sons, are witnesses of a Sasine 22d Sept. 1730 ; in Sasines I find no further trace of them. In *N. & Q.*, O. S. XII. 149, a lady inquiring about the above children states that they were alive in 1733. F. N. R.

LXXXI. MENSHEAVIN.—At pages 202 and 203 of the fifth vol. of the *Register of the Privy Council of Scotland* is a complaint by James Lord Lindsay of the Byris, David Dundas of Priestisinche and Johnne Yallowleis, messenger, narrating the deforcement of the said Johnne Yallowleis on 12th January 1594-95 by Agnes Cokburne, wife of James Hammiltoun of Levingstoun and their family and servants, who failing to appear are denounced rebels.
Mr. Alexander Burnett then appears for himself, and as procurator for various persons in Duntarvie, Preistisinche, Westlaw, Eistlaw, Scottistoun, and Mensheavin, and gives in a copy of letters raised by the said James Hammiltoun of Levingstoun and others charging the parties residing at the above places to appear before the King and Council?
I am anxious to identify the place called Mensheavin. I find no mention of such a name in the retours; and while in the Ordnance Survey Map, plate 32 (scale 1 inch), I find Duntarvie and Priestinch in Abercorn Parish, and Scotstoun Park in the adjoining parish of Dalmeny, I can find no name resembling Mensheavin. Livingstoun appears to be Livingston in Linlithgowshire—the Byres lying in the County of Haddington. I would also be obliged if any reader of *N. N. & Q.* could

inform me of the cause or origin of the quarrel between Lord Lindsay and the Hamiltons of Livingston which gave rise to the deforcement mentioned above.   J. M'G.

LXXXII. HENRIETTA C———.—At pages 276 and 313 of vol. II. of *Lives of the Lindsays* reference is made to a Miss Henrietta C———, as governess to the daughters of James, 5th Earl of Balcarres. It requires little acumen to detect the name indicated by this initial. At page 276 it is said that she married, and at page 313 that the whole C——— family has passed away. I shall be glad to know the name of her husband and date of her marriage?   Σ.

LXXXIII. BRABONER.—This word is found in *Gleanings from the Records of Dysart,* by the Rev. Wm. Muir, 1862.

Wm. Kilgour, braboner, made a freeman 1601 (p. 48).

Thomas Dowy, braboner, 1603 (p. 49).

The editor (p. 489) states, ' This word occurs frequently both in our civil and ecclesiastical records.'

It is also found in *The Burgh Laws of Dundee,* by Alex. J. Warden, 1872.

' The braboner, or webster craft, or weaver trade, holds the eighth place amongst the nine trades ' (p. 503). But the earliest mention of the word given is 1636, the ' Deykin of the Braboner Craft ' (p. 517). There are fifteen documents connected with the weaver given, dated from 1475 to 1594, in none of which the word occurs.

What is its derivation? Elsewhere the term Brabanter is found as equivalent to a Fleming or Dutchman. It seems probable that a weaver was called a Braboner from the fact that many Flemish weavers settled in Scotland. It would be well to obtain more instances of the use of the word than those above mentioned.   EDITOR.

LXXXIV. ' O ' SUFFIX.—Many surnames and names of places in Scotland end in *o.* Does this point to an Icelandic or Danish origin?   CHIPPENHAM.

REPLIES TO QUERIES.

XXI. ARMS OF INVERNESS.—A. G. Y. will find a discussion regarding the Inverness Arms in the *Inverness Courier* of the 6th, 8th, 11th, 15th, 20th March, 8th, 20th, 25th, November, 1884 ; 7th May, 1886 ; and 18th January, 1887.   P. J. ANDERSON.

XLVI. GALLOWAY.—Permit me to disclaim the use of a disagreeable pseudo-word which your printer has introduced into my note. In three instances he has altered ' qualitative ' into ' qualitation.'   HERBERT MAXWELL.

XLVIII. Horn.—There are plenty of real difficulties in the attempt to solve the meanings of place names without raising those that are artificial. If W. M. C. chooses to reject the obvious meaning of Whithorn, *hwit ærn, candida casa*, the white house, I cannot help it ; but let the question, if it must be raised, be treated rationally. The two first steps towards getting at the etymology of a place name (and each is so indispensable that it matters not which is taken first), are to learn the local pronunciation and to ascertain the earliest written form. Had W. M. C. taken either of these steps before he had penned his last note he would not have thought it worth while to ask 'how came the "h" to be inserted?' He would have found the local pronunciation to have transposed the 'r' and the original 'œ' or 'e,' and that the name is now pronounced by the inhabitants 'hwuttren,' showing that the second 'h' is not sounded, as it would be if the accent were on the last syllable. He would also have found that in the *Anglo-Saxon Chronicle* the name is written *Hwiterne*, in Geoffery Gaimar's *Estorie des Engles* (about A.D. 1250) *Witernen*, and usually in the three succeeding centuries *Quhiterne* (*quh* representing in Scottish writings not, as W. M. C. supposes, a guttural, but the modern *wh* or the Anglo-Saxon *hw*, the latter being the more accurate symbol). Moreover the name is rendered *Futerna* in Irish-Latin MSS.

I have never stated without limitation that 'the names about Sorby are Anglian.' I have expressed an opinion that the bulk of them are Teutonic, and there can be little doubt that Sorby itself is Scandinavian.

W. M. C. quotes two names in Wigtownshire, one Pikehorn, which is Scandinavian (a peaked sea rock), and the other Knockhornan, which is Celtic, in order to disprove that Whithorn, which is Anglian, has not the plain meaning which it bears on the face of it. The longer study which he devotes to words and names, the more will he be led to disregard similarity in written forms as evidence of common origin.

Herbert Maxwell.

LXII. Kindlie Tenant.—Sir Herbert Maxwell's lucid note on the meaning of this ancient mode of tenure sums up, perhaps, all that can safely be predicated as to the conditions implied under its cognate terms.

As to the origin of the term, it has been suggested that it was applied to those who were the *natural* inhabitants of the country or of the soil; but if so it will be necessary to discriminate between such a class and that lowest or servile class, or serfs, reckoned native to the soil, designated in old charters 'nativi,' and transferred along with the land. If, in its primary significance, 'kindlie tenant' meant 'natural to the soil,' it must have implied on the part of the tenants so designed some special claims to advantage over ordinary tenants.

While conceding that the term did not necessarily originally imply the meaning of 'generous or kind,' as applied to the tenant, I must be pardoned if I dissent from the conclusion that

'the generosity lay in the landlord, who let his land on
'peculiarly easy conditions either to those who had earned his
'favour by valuable service or to his kinsfolk in humble
'circumstances.'

There is no evidence that either of these conditions
subsisted in the original constitution of a kindlie tenant. In
point of fact, we know nothing at all as to the initial relations of
the landlord and the kindlie tenant, but we know in many cases
such tenants paid what may have been a fair, if not a full rent, at
those early times, when we first read of this mode of tenure.
The difficulty is not so much that the rent was small as that it
was incapable of increase by the proprietor. Since therefore
such tenure involved fixity of rent, it is surely unwarranted to
assume generosity on the part of the landlord in not increasing
the burdens on his tenants while they possessed rights which
prohibited such increase. It has been well remarked by a
recent writer that 'the tenant was not one through favour of the
'landlord, but that he had an independent and natural right to
'his occupancy.'

On the whole, where so much must be left to conjecture, it
seems probable that the kindlie tenant was one whose original
connection with the soil was such as to give him in the eyes of
the landlord at once a hold on the land he occupied and an
importance and influence not rashly to be disturbed, and which
initiated a relationship of mutual service and good-will, which,
strengthened by time, came at length to be recognised in use
and wont, and ultimately in law, as a valid tenure, possessed of
well-recognised rights and privileges not appertaining to those
subsequent tenancies springing in later times from changed
circumstances. Since this question was raised in *N. N. &
Q.* an interesting and able paper on the subject has been
read before the Hawick Archæological Society by Mr. Oliver of
Thornwood, and noticed in a lengthy extract in the *Scotsman*
of April last.

As to Mr. Hay's explanation that a kindlie tenant was a
tenant who paid his rent in kind, and not in money, it is a pity
he does not state his authority for such a statement. Payment
in kind was often, and indeed commonly used ; but according to
Cosmo Innes (*Scotch Legal Antiquities*) 'some money was
paid,' and he further states that so early as 1290 'all services
were in process of being commuted for money rent.'

A. HUTCHESON.

LXV. COLONEL JOHN ERSKINE, DEPUTY-GOVERNOR OF STIRLING
CASTLE.—I cannot solve all the doubts of Σ, but the following
'notes' may help to clear the ground :—

As the Editor pointed out in a footnote, '*Captain* John
Erskine of Alva' was married to Lady Mary Maule, Countess
of Mar, on 29th April 1697. This was undoubtedly the same
person who was known afterwards as Colonel John Erskine, the
Deputy-Governor. He may have been designed 'of Alva' to
distinguish him from his namesake of the Cardross family, and

as he was the uncle of the then baronet of Alva—Sir John Erskine.

In 1745 I find mention made of 'the deceased Colonel John Erskine, brother to the deceased Sir Charles Erskine of Alva,' and in same year of Dame Helen Erskine, Margaret Erskine, Mary Erskine, Eupham Erskine, 'all daughters of the said deceased Colonel John Erskine'; and again, in 1748, of Dame Helen Erskine, relict of Sir Wm. Douglas of Kilhead; Margaret Erskine, relict of Mr. Wm. Erskine, merchant in Edinburgh; Mary Erskine, spouse to Mr. Alex. Webster, one of the ministers of Edinburgh; Eupham Erskine, spouse of Mr. Alex. Boswell, Advocate, children of the deceased Colonel John Erskine.'

Colonel John Erskine's testament was confirmed before the Commissary of Dunblane, 9th July 1741. This I have examined, but it contains no mention of his wives.

Will Σ pardon my pointing out that the title of the heir-male of the Alva family is Earl of Rosslyn?   MAG.

LXVII. INSCRIPTION IN MONZIEVAIRD OLD CHURCHYARD.—The Arms, three pelicans, are those of the old Perthshire family of Reid-haugh. The Rev. Henry Anderson, M.A., married Marion Ridhaugh (Scott's *Fasti Eccles. Scot.*). An account of the family of Reidhaugh of Cultibragan, County Perth, who bore for Arms *Azure*, three pelicans vulning themselves *Or*, is given in Stodart's *Scottish Arms*, vol. ii. p. 366.

The name is spelt Reidheuch, Reidhaugh, Ridhaugh, and Riddoch. Alexander Riddoch, for many years Provost of Dundee, who was born at Crieff in 1744, was probably descended from this family.   ROBERT C. WALKER.

LXVIII. William Duff was son of Hugh Duff, Minister of Fearn, 1698-1739. He graduated at University and King's College, Aberdeen, in 1721.   P. J. ANDERSON.

NOTICES OF BOOKS.

Address, chiefly on Artificial Lighting, by D. Bruce Peebles, F.R.S.E., President of the Royal Society of Arts (Edinburgh, Neill and Company), is an admirable description of more things than lighting. We wish we could give his account of travelling in old days, but can only find space for a most instructive history of the gradual improvement of lamps and candles. We have to acknowledge our thanks for permission to use the engraving, which will add to the interest of the extracts:—

'In the low country, especially in and around Lanarkshire, cannel coal was used to give light long before gas made its appearance, and it was on account of its being so used instead of candles that it got the name of cannel coal. It was first broken into splinters and then laid on an iron bracket attached to the front of the grate, so that it might be sufficiently near the ordinary coal to be kept blazing. The bracket was called the "coal airn," and the coal burned on it was called the "licht coal."

'In the Highlands long ago the bog fir was used as a common method of getting artificial light. The tree had to be sought for in the bog or moss, and an instrument was required to probe or feel for it. When it was found, the first thing necessary was to hole it, *i.e.* to dig a hole all round it, so as to free the trunk or root and allow it to be taken out. It was then cut into pieces of about 2 or 3 feet long, and the fat bits were selected and split into strips about an inch broad by a knife called a fir gullie. These splinters were called fir candles, and the bog fir came to be known as candle or cannel fir, just as the coal got the name of candle or cannel coal. These fir candles were at first held in the hand as torches are, but as time wore on some clever genius invented articles, first made of wood and then of iron, to hold the fir candles, and thus the living candle-holders were relieved of what must have been a rather tedious occupation.

'The bog or moss fir was cut into three or four feet lengths, and split into pieces three-fourths of an inch broad, and put into the holders, which are made with an angular slit to hold the fir candle. Some of these candle-holders are made to drive into the wall, and some of them have one or more joints, somewhat similar to our modern gas brackets, so that they might be adjusted and placed in a position to suit the purpose they were wanted for.

'In Aberdeenshire these candle-holders were called "puir" men, and the origin of that name is as follows : Before they came into use in the country districts it was the duty of the herd-boys to hold the fir candle at supper-time, so that the farmer and the farm-servants might see the road from the food to their mouths. After they had all got their supper it was then the duty of the farmer—so the tale goes—to hold the fir candle and let the boy get his supper ; then, if light was wanted through the evening, of course the boy had to resume the duty of candle-holder.

'At the merry meetings, when a dance was going on, the fir candles were held in the hand by some of the company, and if a disagreeable or unsociable individual, who would not join in the merriment going on, was asked, seeing that he was doing nothing, to hold the fir candle, and refused, it was said that "he would neither dance nor haud the cannel"—a saying which has become a proverb.

'Later on, in the time of James the Sixth, there was a set of beggars distinguished by the name of the king's bedesmen or bluegowns. The king granted them badges, which entitled them to hold a position far above that of the ordinary beggar. But there were also badges granted by the minister and kirk session, which were given to the deserving poor only, so that such a badge was a testimonial as to the good character of the beggar, who was thus entitled to beg on condition that he confined his operations within the boundaries of his own parish. These beggars were generally "clever with the tongue," and always welcomed at the farm-houses for the news they brought and the stories they told ; and the custom was that when a beggar arrived at a farm town about sundown the farmer was expected to give him his supper and a night's lodging in the barn, besides his breakfast in the morning to speed him on in his wanderings. Now, as a *quid pro quo*, the beggar or puir man had to give his service and hold the fir candle, paying proper attention to keeping it in good condition by taking off the ash, or, to use the Aberdeenshire phrase, "snitting the candle." This custom being established, the beggar or puir man got associated in the minds of the people he called on with the duty he had to perform, viz. the holding of the fir candle, and he, the candle-holder, came at last to be spoken of as the puir man, the name being associated with the work he did ; so thus it was that, when the iron fir-candle holder was invented, it was called a puir man or "peer man" in Aberdeenshire.

'Peer men were made to stand on the floor, and originally made entirely of wood, the stalk having a cleft, called a "clevie," at the top to hold the fir candle. A young fir tree was sometimes used for a candle-holder, being cut across at a sufficient distance from the root to allow of the branches to form "claws" or feet ; the tree was then inverted and rested on these, and the clevie was formed in what was originally the lower part of the tree. Some had stone bases to hold a round wooden stave, into which an iron clevie was

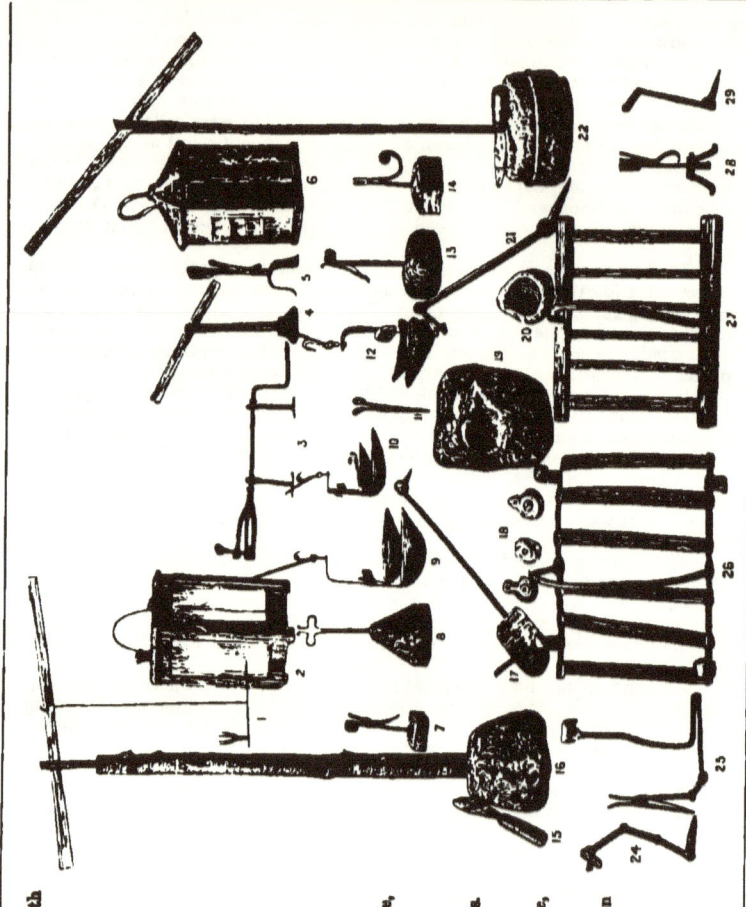

1. Puir Man, for suspension, with candleholder.
2. Bouet, for oil lamp.
3. Wall Puir Man.
4. Wooden Puir Man.
5. Puir Man and Candleholder.
6. Bouet, for candle.
7. Puir Man and Candleholder.
8. Puir Man, on wooden stand.
9. Copper Crusie.
10. Iron Crusie, with cover.
11. Puir Man, for wall.
12. Iron Crusie.
13. Puir Man and Candleholder.
14. Puir Man.
15. Fir Gailie.
16. Puir Man, wooden stem, iron clevie, and stone base.
17. Puir Man, with iron plate.
18. Three Roman Oil Lamps, of clay.
19. Stone Matrix for making iron crusies.
20. Stone Crusie Lamp.
21. Puir Man, for wall.
22. Puir Man, iron stem and stone base, hooped with iron.
24. Puir Man, jointed.
25. Puir Man, jointed for hanging on horizontal iron rod.
26. Coillichan Iron.
27. Ditto, wood.
28. Puir Man and Candleholder.
29. Puir Man, for wall.

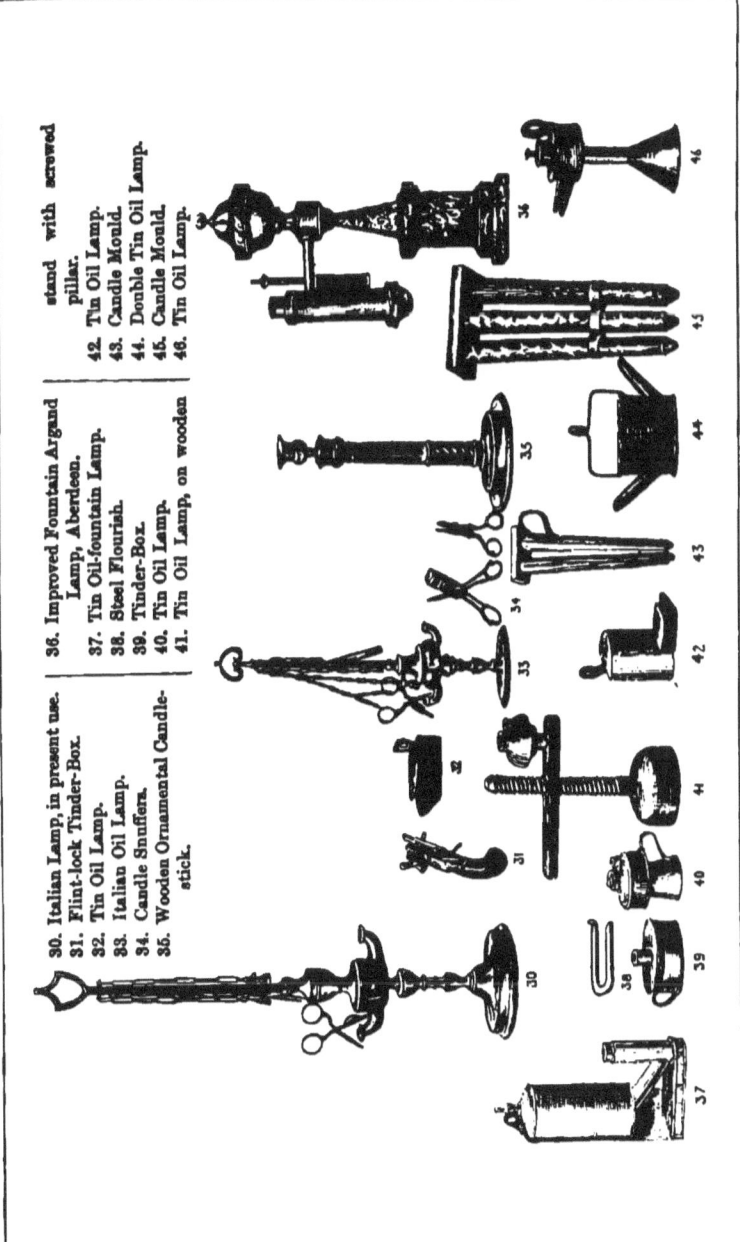

30. Italian Lamp, in present use.
31. Flint-lock Tinder-Box.
32. Tin Oil Lamp.
33. Italian Oil Lamp.
34. Candle Snuffers.
35. Wooden Ornamental Candle-stick.
36. Improved Fountain Argand Lamp, Aberdeen.
37. Tin Oil-fountain Lamp.
38. Steel Flourish.
39. Tinder-Box.
40. Tin Oil Lamp.
41. Tin Oil Lamp, on wooden stand with screwed pillar.
42. Tin Oil Lamp.
43. Candle Mould.
44. Double Tin Oil Lamp.
45. Candle Mould.
46. Tin Oil Lamp.

inserted ; others had an arrangement for holding either a fir or a tallow candle. There were also those with two clevies, by which a double light could be obtained. Another variety, as already stated, could be driven into the wall, and had joints, and were also made to slide on an iron rod, so that they might be raised or lowered.

' We have then excellent specimens of the knives, or gullies as they were called, which were used for splitting up the fir into candles. The splinters were laid to dry on the fir reist, the Gaelic name for which is "coillchan." Two of these are before us, one of wood, the other of iron, with sparred bottoms and bow handles, and they were filled with the fir candles, and· hung in a warm place in the kitchen, so that the store of candles might be thoroughly dried and ready for use.   Oil crusies made of copper or iron, such as those we have here, were well known in Scotland in the first half of the present century.   The oil used in them was fish oil, mostly whale oil, and it was carried forward to the burning point by a very beautiful natural wick formed of the pith of the common rush.   These wicks were sold in bundles, as also were spunks, a supply of which was kept to get light from the tinder-box when required.   Spunks were thin pieces of split wood about half an inch broad, five or six inches long, and tipped with brimstone.   The oil crusie, known in Banffshire by the name of " Reekie Peter," did good service in its day, and many are yet alive who were once under obligation to it.

' Another light called the " Ruffy " was sometimes used in the country, being a roughly extemporised light got by twisting or plaiting cotton rags and dipping them in tallow.   Sometimes butter was used when tallow was not to be had, in which case it was called a butter ruffy.   The flint and steel, the tinder-box, and its tinder made of half-burnt linen, and the spunks, were most important articles in every household, and indispensable for getting light before the days of lucifer matches.

' We have two bouets or lanterns, one of which was used by the bellman of St. Nicholas' Church, Aberdeen, and sent to me by Dr. Moir. One of the bouets is for an oil lamp, the other for holding a candle. At that time there was a duty on candles, and to escape from paying it the country folks got candle moulds made, and did a little contraband work by making their own candles. We have two excellent specimens of candle moulds.

History of Lochleven Castle, by Robert Burns Begg, F.S.A.Scot. Kinross, George Barnet.—Not only has Nature made Lochleven and its Isle a charming spot, but its association with Queen Mary has made it a shrine to which her admirers repair. Mr. Burns Begg fully enters into their feelings, and has produced a volume which will rank far above a mere guide-book, though as such it will be most valuable as containing a clear account of the now ruined castle, with careful drawings of it. Its chief value consists in the way in which the author, who has long resided on the shores of the lake, illustrates the period of Mary's life spent in the castle by his account of the building and its surroundings. It is not generally known that the Queen visited the castle in the year 1561 (the year of her return from France) ; then her reception was befitting her rank, and we have an account of the preparations that were made for her. Six years later she was brought back to it a prisoner. The story of her sorrows, well-known as it is, will be better understood when Mr. Burns Begg's volume has been carefully studied—and those who take it up will not quickly lay it down. The printing is exceedingly good, and the illustrations are artistic. Unfortunately, however, there is no index. The compiling of one would have given but little additional labour to the author, and would have added considerably to the value of his work.

Northern Notes and Queries

OR

The Scottish Antiquary

CONTENTS.

NOTE.—*The Editor does not hold himself responsible for the opinions or statements of Contributors.*

134. SCOTTISH TRADE WITH FLANDERS.—It is satisfactory to find that Dr. George Burnett, Lyon King, like the late Professor Cosmo Innes, recognises the great influence that Flanders had during the Middle Ages on Scottish trade and manufacture, and therefore on the nation itself. Not only is Dr. Burnett's acquaintance with this subject shown in an article in the *Scottish Review* (April 1888), but he dwells on it in his Introduction to the fourth volume of the *Exchequer Rolls of Scotland*, a work deserving the most careful consideration. In it he mentions Yair's *Account of the Scotch Trade in the Netherlands*. As this book is little known, and is now exceedingly rare, it may be well to give a few of the facts recorded by one who, as minister of the Scottish Church at Campvere in the early

half of last century, had opportunities of obtaining information from official documents.

'Florence the iii. Earl of Holland Zealand and West Friezland, married Ada, Sister of William commonly called William the Lyon; this Earl died 1190: which marriage gave occasion to his lineal heir Florence the v about a hundred years thereafter to go to England as a competitor for the crown of Scotland; and even the nephew of William king of Scotland called William, succeeding his brother Theodore went to Scotland in 1205 to claim the right of succession to the Crown in case his uncle should die without male issue' (pp. 5, 6). Yair does not affirm that this alliance gave the first encouragement to Scotch merchants to trade with the Low Countries; it however seems likely. 'The paper of the oldest date I have found, giving the Scots permission to trade in any part of their dominions, is the following

'Commeatus quibusdam Scotis a comite datus, 6 December 1321.

'Universis presentes literas inspecturis vel audituris, Gullilmus iv. comes Hanoniæ, etc.

'Nos ad instantiam gloriosi el excellentis principis nostri consanguinei karissimi domini Roberti Brussii; dei gratia Scossie, Stephano dicto Fourbour, bourgeois de Berwyc & Thomæ dicto Well, bourgeois ville Sainct Andree, cum quatuor hominibus subditis dom. reg. predicti quos secum duserunt eligendos, veniendi, redeundi, standi ac mercandi ubique per terras nostras et districtas infra hinc et unum annum, omni mala occasione remota, salvum et securum concedimus, per presentes dantes, et universis singulisque justiciariis nostris tenore presenti in mandatis quatenus iisdem, per unum annum predictum, de salvo et securi conductu provideant, ab omni injuriâ et molestia defendentes.

'Datum Zirickzee in festo beati Nicolai' (p. 6).

About two years after permission was given by King Robert to the Hollanders to trade in his dominions.

'Robertus D. Gr. Rex Scotorum, omnibus probis hominibus suis, at quos presentes litere pervenerint, salutem. Sciatis quod concessimus et concedimus, per presentes, omnibus mercatoribus de dominio terrarum Dom. Wilhelmi comitis Hanoniæ, Hollandie, Zelandie, ac Dom. Frisie. qui ad regnum nostrum, seu infra potentiam nostram, cum mercandisiis suis venire voluerint, quod libere ingressum et egressum habeant, infra omnes partes, et recepta nostri ubicunque ipsis contigerit applicare, volentes quod ipsi cum navibus et omnibus bonis suis, honorifice receptantior et de mercandiciis suis secundum leges & consuetudines Regni nostri, libere disponere permittantur. Volumus etiam quod ipsi mercatores, pro nullis debitis alienis, neque pro suis debitis propriis, in personis aut rebus aliquatenus arrestantur, quare firmiter prohibitmus, nequis contra hanc concessionem, ipsos vexare, gravare, see inquietare presumat, super nostram plenariam foris facturam. Incujus dei testimonium has literas nostras pro voluntate nostra, duraturas fieri fecimus. Datum apud Apder Alberbrochoter, decimo die Augusti, anno regni nostri octavo decimo' (p. 9).

The friendship between the two countries was interrupted in 1327, when a Scotch merchant incapable of paying his debts was put in prison at Middleburgh. The debtor escaped, but his countrymen within the Earl's reach were obliged to pay the creditors, though they had no connection with the fugitive. This event, and the disturbances both in Scotland and Holland, following on the deaths of the two princes, put a stop to commerce between the two countries for some time. In 1371 Earl Albert issued a permission to Scotch merchants to trade, but obliging them to pay the legal customs and duties. In 1382 Earl Albert settled the English staple of wool at Middleburgh and Zirichzee ; but this does not seem to have been extended to Scotland. Earl William VI., son of Albert, succeeded his father : he married a daughter of Philip the Bold, Duke of Burgundy ; by her he had a daughter, Jacobea.

John, Duke of Burgundy, son of Philip the Bold, encouraged the Scottish trade in his dominion. There is a grant in French was registered in the court books of Middleburgh. A full translation of it is given by Yair (pp. 27-33).

It is too long to give *in extenso*, but the nature of it will be seen from the brief abstract which is here given. It is addressed 'To all merchants of the kingdom of Scotland who shall come to and frequent our said country of Flanders.'

1. Received under 'guardianship' on payment of tolls.
2. To land goods at 'the stairs and the ordinary places.'
3. For the purpose of unloading, vessels may be placed side by side.
4. Vessels driven back by stormy weather may move cargo, but not sell it.
5. Provides for the appointment of commissaries to be licensed by the King of Scotland to act. These to act on behalf of merchants.
6. The commissary to be respected.
7. Scottish merchants protected by Flemish law.
8. 120 days' notice to be given before above privileges are recalled.

'Given in our town of Ipres, the last day of April 1400.

Preserved in the *Black Book* at Bruges.' Yair next gives a translation of a long paper preserved in the register of Campvere, dated at Bruges 11th May 1407. It contains 10 articles, prescribing the position and duties of the conservator and the regulations of the trade with Flanders. The city of Bruges seems to have been very anxious to lose no time in arranging matters with the Scots, as about this time the Scottish trade with Holland was interrupted by many acts of hostility committed by both parties.

In 1411 William, Earl of Holland, permitted Arnot Jokebson, Dirk Piterson, Cop Lunsea, Heyn Keniven, and others, to make reprisals by sea and land 'against our enemies the Scots.'

But on 10th December 1412 these letters of reprisal were recalled, and Scottish merchants were again protected ; this truce, however, was only to continue till 18th January (St. Peter's Day).

After the 18th of January hostilities committed by the Earl still went on. The Scots retaliated, and the Earl soon became convinced it would be wise to put the trade between the nations on a peaceful and firm footing. He therefore issued a decree, consisting of ten clauses, dated at The Hague, 1st August 1416, which was to remain in force for two years. It was, to a great extent, a repetition of the former grants and decrees, and will be found at length in Yair's book. William, the sixth Earl of Holland, died in 1417, leaving his daughter Jacobœa his heir.

(To be continued.)

135. An Account of the Family of Younger, Alloa (*continued from page* 10).—Thomas Younger spent his life in Culross ; he was dead

before 1666, but the exact date of his decease is not known. The following extract from the Culross Kirk Session Records, in which his name appears, is interesting, as showing the efforts used to put down all observances distasteful to the rigid Calvinism of the party then in power :—

1644, Jan. 7.—'. . . and Thomas Younger were accused for keeping the Yule Daie in feasting and drinking and abstaining from their ordinarie work. Confessed their fault, fined 20 sh.'

III. THOMAS YOUNGER, eldest son of Thomas Younger (II.) and Elizabeth Miller, was baptized at Culross, January 22, 1642. He married at Culross, August 21, 1680, Jane, daughter of George Tilloch or Tulloch, and sister of Agnes, the wife of his brother, James Younger. The Tillochs were saltmakers. In the middle of the 16th century they were residing at the Preston saltpans, as is shown by their wills.[1] The name is met with early in the 17th century at Torryburn, where George Tilloch married Margaret Wright, December 1, 1655, he being the son of John Tilloch, married there in 1633. He moved to Clackmannan, and died at Kennet Pans, being a Church elder and a prosperous man.

Thomas Younger had issue by his wife, Jane Tilloch—

    I. Jean, baptized at Culross, Feb. 20, 1689.

    II. George, of whom below as George IV.

    III. Margaret, baptized at Culross, October 4, 1691 ; married at Alloa, 1713, James Morrison of Alloa, Shipmaster.

    IV. Janet, baptized at Culross, Jan. 5, 1700.

Thomas Younger appears to have carried on the manufacture of salt till his death. The date of this event is not known, nor are any events in his life recorded.

IV. GEORGE YOUNGER was baptized at Culross, February 14, 1694. Nothing is known of his early life. At his marriage he is described as a sailor. As his sister Margaret was married to an Alloa shipmaster, he may have received encouragement to adopt this profession in preference to that in which his family had been so long occupied, and perhaps all the more readily that the salt-works at Culross, Tullyallan, Clackmannan, and Airth may have provided sufficient occupation for his cousins : the local records show that they carried on these works for some time. George Younger's first introduction to us after his baptism is in the position of a bridegroom. And as his grandfather had been punished for observing Christmas Day, so George was censured for an irregular marriage, the irregularity consisting in his having preferred the ministrations of an Episcopalian clergyman to those of the minister of the parish. The account of his marriage is instructive, as showing the condition of ecclesiastical affairs at the time, and it may prove interesting to give a full extract from the Alloa Kirk Session Records :—

'Alloa, the 11 of Aug. 1721, Friday.—This day the Sess being inform'd that George Younger Sailer in Alloa & Jean Thomson daught' to

---

[1] The following application for a ' Protection ' is interesting :—

In 1606, 27th November, Thomas Tilloch in Inveresk came before the Privy Council and represented that he had been ' Imployit the maist part of his youth in uncuth nationis in searching and learning the knawledge for making & practizeing of ingynis and workis for the commodious and aisie transporting of coillis betwix the colpotis, sey and salt panes of this realme, and haveing now attaint a suir knawledge thairof, in exerceing the foirsaidis practizes,' he asks for a protection of his invention. He was granted sole power to use his ' ingyne ' during his lifetime, provided it was unknown before. (*Reg. Priv. Coun.*).

Thomas Thomson Tennent in the Grange of Alloa were irregularly married and cohabited as Husband and Wife, orders them to be cited to their next diet.'

'Alloa, the 25 of Aug'. 1721, Friday.—This day compeared Geo Younger & Jean Thomson foresd and they being ask'd if they were married one to another answered that they were married and also being ask'd if they had an extract of their marriage said z' they had none but that they woud prove it by Geo Anderson, Indweller in Alloa & Hellen Mitchel his Spouse, who being called in and sworn, depon'd as follows—

'This day compear'd George Anderson Malt-man in Alloa aged about fourty nine years who being solemnly sworn depon'd that He saw George Younger, Mariner in Alloa and Jean Thomson daughter to Thomas Thomson in Grange married together by Mr. Duncan Comry an episcopal Min' for present living at Dumblane on the twenty seventh day of February last betwixt the hours of Twelve and one of the day in his own house which he pays rent for at Alloa. And this is the truth as He shall answer (Signed) Georg Anderson

'Compear'd also Helen Mitchell Spouse to the s^d George Anderson aged about fourty six years who being sworn depon'd *in omnibus usque* and this is the truth &c. And because she [cannot] write gives allowance publiquely to the Moderator and Clerk to sub^c her Deposition.

(Signed) Jo Logan Mod'

'The Session considering deposition of the Witnesses and that the s^d marriage was proven by the s^d witnesses and also that such marriages are contrary to the laws of the nation and the Acts of the Gen' Assembly did refer the s^d named persons and witnesses to the Justices of Peace to be punished according to Law.'

It should here be stated that in 1721 there was no Episcopalian congregation in Alloa, and members of the Scottish Episcopal Church had to seek the services of such clergymen of their communion as continued to exercise their functions in spite of the penal statutes against them then in force. In 1723 Mr. John Alexander, afterwards consecrated Bishop of Dunkeld, opened a church in Alloa, and resided in the town till his death in 1776. He doubtless kept a register of baptisms and marriages, but the volume has been lost, this may account for the fact that only the baptism of George's eldest child is recorded in the parish books. Thomas Thompson, father of his wife, Jane, was tenant of the Grange, a farm in the west of the town. The Alloa Kirk Session Records show that the family was highly respectable, and some of the members of it were elders. From the Records we find that George Younger had other children besides George, his eldest son, for Thomas Younger, who must have been a younger, and, probably, second son, was tenant of the Grange in 1771, and was censured by the Kirk Session for a breach of the Sabbath. The whole case is illustrative of the *modus operandi* of the local ecclesiastical court at the time, and therefore is inserted. Some features in his case are striking—the delay before the charge was brought ; the absence of all proof as to how, or by whom, if not by Andrew M'Lachlan, the injury which exasperated George Younger was committed ; and the very shaky evidence produced for the prosecution, leaves an uncomfortable feeling that Thomas Younger, the father, was, for some reason, no favourite with the reverend court before which he was summoned :—

'Alloa, 11th Jan. 1771.—The Session met and constitute. Compeared

Geo Younger son to Tho Younger in Grange and being examined concerning a Fray that happened upon a Sabbath about two years ago in the Fields between the Grange and the high road leading to Stirling, Declares, That he happened by Accident to be that day at his father's house, and hearing a report of Ducks being killed, and having a Suspicion of a Lad whom he saw in the Neighbouring field, went toward him.   Upon the Lads going off he followed him and saw some white feathers in his way, and insisted on the Lad's returning to see them.   That the Lad took up a Stone, and refused to go further, upon which Ensued a scuffle, in which the neck of George's shirt was torn.   Upon this Thomas Cullens Shoemaker came up and Struck the Declarent, which encouraged the other Lad his servant, to strike also, which the Declarant says obliged him to Strike in his own defence.

'Compeared Thomas Younger in Grange, and Declares that he saw the above Lad Andrew Mᶜlachlan wandering about the Doors on the Sabbath formerly mentioned but took little notice of him till he heard a report of Ducks being killed.   That his son George went to the adjoining field, and in a little he heard one of the Children cry that two men were killing George.   That he sent his wife and made what haste he could himself, but the Fray was over before he came.   That they brought down Thomas Cullens and his man Andrew Mᶜlachlan and showed them the Ducks, one with its back broke and another with its leg, and that Thomas Cullens promised to make up the Damage on Munday & so have no more of it.   Thomas further declares that when he went up to the field he saw Mʳ Mᶜdonald's wife the Musician.

'Compeard Andrew Mᶜlachlan and being interrogate Declared, That upon the Sabbath formerly mentioned he was in the field adjoining to the Grange herding his masters Potatoes, That George Younger came up to him and struck him several times and dragged him through the field the declarant being at that time very Lame with running sores in his Leg, That his master Tho Cullens came up and rescued him but received several blows from George Younger.   That he afterwards went down with his master to the Grange and saw the Ducks complained of, but declares he knew nothing about them, nor had any hand in hurting them.

'Compeared Tho Cullens, who being interrogate declares, That upon the before mentioned Sabbath, he went out between Sermons to see his Potatoe Ground which lay in the field above described between the Grange and the high road leading to Stirling.   That he saw two men Struggling together among the Potatoes, that leaving Mⁿ MᶜDonald whom he had met on the road, he made towards the two men by the nearest way when he saw it was George Younger and his own Servant Andrew Mᶜclachlan, who is a silly lad weak both in body and mind.   That he saw George Younger Strick him several times and upon coming up and quarrelling him for that abusive behaviour upon the Lords day the said George damned him and then Struck him to the Ground, and abused him very much. That the declarant told him he would not lift his hand to him upon the Lords day.   That Thoˢ Younger and his wife soon came up, who by the interposition of Mⁿ Mᶜdonald put an end to the Violence.   After which Tho Cullen & his Servant went down to the Grange & saw the Ducks they said were Lame.   Thomas Cullens fearing further outrage from Thomas Younger & his familie promised to talk over the matter and make it up next day.   Further Declares that through the whole Thomas Younger and his Son cursed and swore prodigiously.

'Compeared Mⁿ M'donald above designed who declared in every Article with Thomas Cullens only did not go down to the Grange but went immediately home. That before she left them she heard Thomas Younger his Wife and Son utter the most dreadful oaths she had ever heard.

' The Session after having considered the above declarations find them so very contradictory as not to know how to judge of it, only it appears from the testimony of Mⁿ M'cdonald that the Youngers have been guilty of great violence and a scandalous profanation of the Lords name and Day and are therefore of opinion That all of them ought to be seriously dealt with to bring them to a sense of this their Sin before they are admitted to Church Privileges.'

The Session do not appear to have considered what brought Andrew M'Lachlane ' herding potatoes ' on the Lord's Day ; the sin of Thomas Cullen in walking to look at his potatoes ; the sin of Mrs. M'Donald in walking for no purpose whatever ; or the fact that when, by their own declarations, they had only her evidence to rely on, they held it as sufficient to convict the persons whose property had been injured.

George Younger (IV.) and Jane Thompson had several children, but, as has been stated, only the record of the baptism of the eldest has been found in the parish register ; the order in which the others were born is therefore uncertain.

I. George Younger, of whom below as George V.

II. Thomas Younger, tenant of the Grange farm in 1771, where in 1772 he employed two women-servants (Alloa Kirk Session Records). The name of his wife is not known, nor the date of the baptism of his eldest son.

    1. Thomas, who is described (Alloa Kirk Session Records) as 20 years old in 1772, which proves that he was born 1752 ; he was unmarried in 1772, and no mention is made in the Register Records of his having a wife or family.

    2. George, who has been already mentioned in connection with the trial before the Session in 1771. He married, in 1789, Jean Belloch. For his descendants, see App. I.

    3. Alexander, baptized at Alloa, January 30, 1762 ; married Christian Martin, and had issue a daughter, Elizabeth, baptized 1791.

    4. John Francis, baptized at Alloa, March 31, 1765. He was probably the John Younger who, in 1793, married Ann Paton.

    5. Charles, probably a son, and born before Alexander ; he married at Alloa, in 1783, Jean Drummond.

(To be continued.)

136. THE SPANISH ARMADA (Note 117).—The information conveyed regarding the tradition of the supposed wreck of the 'St. Michael' is interesting, and it would have been still more so if the writer had stated whether the timber and the representation carved upon it bore the appearance of Spanish or foreign origin.

The question is, however, Do any records exist, which can be accepted as trustworthy, that give sufficient support to the truth of the traditions— of which there are several—concerning the wrecks of vessels belonging to the Armada said to have occurred upon the East Coast of Scotland ?

From the authentic records which are extant regarding the course that was taken by the fleet towards the north, from the English Channel, in August 1588, and the state of the weather at the time it passed the English coast, it appears most unlikely that any of the ships could have approached the East Coast of Scotland.

Mr. Pratt (Buchan, 1857, p. 52), refers to the representation of Abraham and Isaac, but does not mention that it was carved upon wood ; and he adds that over the figures was the inscription, 'Have faith in the Lord.' The impression conveyed by him is that the whole was cut of stone, like the other inscriptions he mentions in his work.

As regards the brass cannon said to have belonged to the 'St. Michael,' Mr. Arbuthnot (*History of Peterhead*, 1815, p. 24), says, that ' where a battery was afterwards erected, there once stood a small fort mounted with seven brass cannon which were taken out of the " St. Michael," one of the Spanish Armada which was wrecked upon this coast; and some guns of a smaller size, which belonged to this vessel, were mounted upon the Toll-booth-green in 1715 for the defence of the interior of the Town.'

In *The Annals of Peterhead*, by Peter Buchan, 1819, pp. 16 and 94, this account is repeated, and he gives a copy of a ' Deposition of Witnesses annent the Cannons of Peterhead,' made in 1740 by three inhabitants of the town, all of whom were about eighty years of age. In it they state that, ' In 1666, a Danish ship of war having been stranded on this coast, she was seized by order of the Court Marischall ; and among other things taken out of her, were two Brass, and six Iron Cannon, which were delivered to the inhabitants of the town, and mounted upon a battery erected upon the Bay, at the place called Keith Inch.'

There is no allusion made in the Deposition to any seven brass cannon having been taken out of the 'St. Michael,' nor of that number having been mounted on the battery, nor as to there being seven brass cannon belonging to the town, when, as they state in their deposition, they were carried off by order of his late Majesty in 1717.

It might be with some reason inferred from this that the tradition of the wreck originated at a later date than 1740, and that it had been founded on the story told of the wreck of the Danish ship.   J. A.

Several vessels of the Armada were wrecked on the coast of Ayrshire—in particular one sunk off Portincross Castle, in West Kilbride parish. (See Paterson's *History of Ayrshire*, vol. i. p. 89, and Sinclair's *Statistical Account* (1794), vol. xii. p. 417). Defoe, in his *Tour thro' the Whole Island of Great Britain* (1742), vol. iv. p. 234, relates the recovery of several cannon from the wreck at Portincross Castle. I shall be glad if any reader of *N. N. & Q.* can give me the names of any of the above ships, or particulars of them. This information will probably be found in the official List of the Ships of the Armada, a copy of which is preserved in the British Museum, I understand.   J. M'G.

The Howes o' Buchan (Peterhead *Sentinel* office, 1865) contains, page 95, the following : 'In one of the small bays of Collieston, the " St. Catherine," one of the largest ships of the Spanish Armada, was wrecked in 1588. This tradition was doubted for some time ; but in 1855, the minister of the parish (the Rev. James Rust) succeeded in raising one of the cannon which had belonged to this famous ship. The gun, which the writer has often seen, is in capital preservation as it now stands on a carriage in Mr. Rust's garden. Its dimensions are these—length 7 feet

9 inches; diameter of bore 3¼ inches. The gun had been loaded and shotted at the time the "St. Catherine" was wrecked, as the ball and wadding (both in good order) were taken out of the piece. The fishermen affirm that there are more guns in St. Catherine's Bay.'

The fishermen were right. A diver employed on the Peterhead harbour five or six years ago went to St. Catherine's *dub*, as it is called, and brought to his house another cannon, which was about the size and description of the one now described; it was so fixed to the rock that in tearing it from its bed part of the breach stuck to the rock and exposed the shot. Last year, when in Peterhead, I found that the diver, with his *gun*, had left for England. I think another ship, the 'St. Michael' was wrecked on Scotstown head, a few miles to north of Peterhead, and that the bell in the old churchyard was supposed to be taken from it.   THOS. HUTCHISON.

137. SCOT'S TRANSCRIPT OF PERTH REGISTERS (*continued from page* 17).

November 23, 1572.
John Constable & Margaret Brysson.
John Craig & —— Muire (the woman's first name not
    legible).
William Broun & Helen Burroch.

November 27, 1572.
John Rothray & Katherine Henderson.
James Anderson & Margaret Ogilvy.

December 6, 1572.
Patrick Black & Janet Cosland.
William Hepburn & Marion Stewart.
Nicol Lyal & Janet Richardson.
Alexander Mirglow & Christian Law.

December 28, 1572.
Andrew Henderson & Isabell Anderson.

(*N.B.*—Perhaps this was the Andrew Henderson who, about 28 years Note. after, was said to have been clad in armour and placed in John, Earl of Andrew Gowrie's study to frighten the king.) Henderson.

December 28, 1572.
George Wilson & Janet Carnie.

³⁹/ January 28, 1572-3.
John Murray & Margaret Stewart.
John Scharar & Alison Auchinleck.
Gilbert Paytt & Isabell Kinloch.
William Rollock & Janet Hill.
John Richardson & Agnes Fyffe.
John Jack & Janet Smith.
Thomas Stobbie & Isabell Anderson.

February 1, 1572-3.
David Fere (Fair) & Bessie Morieson.
Fastrans Even was the third Day of February.

February 12, 1572-3.
David Lindsay Master of Crawford & Lilias Drummond sister to my Lord Drummond.

Note.
Master of Craw- ford.

(*N.B.*—Douglas in his Booke of the Peerage says that David who succeeded to the ninth Earl of Crawford married 1st Anne, Daughter of Patrick Lord Drummond, by whom he had no issue.

By this Register it appears that the Lady's name was Lilias.

Drummond.

In his account of the Family of Drummond Earl of Perth, he rectifies the mistake of the Lady's name. He says that Lilias, third Daughter of David second Lord Drummond, was married to David Lord Lindsay son and apparent heir of David Earl of Crawford.

The Lady's father died in the year 1571, so that at the time of her marriage, which must have been a very short time after her father's death, she was sister to Patrick third Lord Drummond.

Mr. John Row.

It is somewhat extraordinary that these two young persons were married at Perth without Proclamation of Banns. Mr. John Row, minister of Perth at the time, was a man of most respectable character, and much employed in all the public transactions relating to the church. Spotswood says of him that he was of singular Piety and moderation, and gained the favour of all to whom he was known.

He seems in the Instance of the above-mentioned marriage to have shewed an Easiness of temper, and an Inclination to oblige 40/ others though he might thereby bring disagreeable consequences upon himself.

The Kirk Session and Lord Ruthven, Provost of the town, who was present with the Session, urged and commanded him to solemnise the marriage. The parties were not of his own parish, and they had no testimonial from their own ministers of the Proclamation of Banns. He could not therefore be ignorant that by the Act of General Assembly 1565 his marrieing the Parties would make him liable to 'the Pain of Deprivation from his ministry, and such other punishment as the Church should enjoin.'

In the manuscript Ecclesiastical History, written by his son, Mr. John Row, minister of Carnock, I find as follows, '27th assembly, holden at Edinburgh, March 6 1572-3, David Ferguson, Moderator—Mr. John Row censured for marrieng the Master of Crawford and my Lord Drummond's daughter without Proclamation of Banns; and what was done in it was not in due time, viz., on Thursday at the Evening Prayers: notwithstanding of this excuse, that it was at the command of the Session, whereof my Lord Ruthven was one.'

Patric, in his Church History, relating the proceedings of the Assembly, says, 'It was ordained that the act made against ministers solemnizing marriage of other Parishioners without Proclamation of Banns, shall have strength against Mr. John Row, and him to underly censure during the Churches will.'

The Assembly by censuring Mr. John Row, shewed their impartiality. But whether particular purpose was to be served by the Act 1565 at the time when it was made, it was too severe an Act to be at any time fully executed.

Mr. Row, so far from being deprived of his office, was desired by the same Assembly which censured him to do some things for them as continuing in his important office of Commissioner or Superintendant of Galloway.

William Lord Ruthven, afterwards Earl of Gowrie, was deservedly much in favour with the Presbyterian Church of Scotland.)

41/   April 14, 1573.
Patrick Eviot & Isabell Dishington.

(*N.B.*—I intend to take an opportunity of giving a particular account Note. of the ancient family of the Eviots of Balhousy.) Eviot.

April 19, 1573.
Nicol Provess & Margaret Morieson.

May 3, 1573.
Patrick Law & Janet Duckatour.

July 5, 1573.
George Hall & Violet Malcolm.
George Main & Isabell Provess.
Andrew Williamson & Christian Schars (perhaps Chalmers).
—— Gaw & Grizzel Gardener
(his first name is not legible, but has something of the appearance of Note. Walter. Almost perpetual contractions, and careless writing, render it difficulty. difficult to decypher the names, and sometimes impossible).

July 26, 1573.
James Broun & Bessie Eldar.
Andrew Douglas & Elspeth Craror.

August 2, 1573.
Thomas Lamb (His wife's name is not marked).

August 9, 1573.
John Cuthbert & Margaret Anderson.

September 13, 1573.
John Basille & Elspeth Aitkin.

September 20, 1573.
John Blair & Isabell Burnet.

October 18, 1573.
Patrick Garvie & Matie (Martha) Randie Garvie. Garvie.

November 8, 1573.
John Whittoch & Janet Maleis.
John Franklay & Margaret Holyng.
David Broun & Christian Gibson.
Henry Adamson & Helen Orme.

42/ November 15, 1573.
John Spens & Bessie Billie.

The following notes on the Perth Registers have been sent to us. We hope they will be continued.—ED.

In the Index, under Perth Registers, page 99 should be page 69.

Pp. 12 and 14.—The three entries on *Sept.* 10, 1570, seem to be repeated to a certain extent on p. 14, *Sept.* 10, 1571. The dates are one year apart, and of the first six names five are the same. The last two names on the first date are not repeated.

P. 12.—21st *Feb.* 1569. There should be a comma after James Scott ; Tirsappie was a village near Perth.

Vol. III. *N. N. & Q.*, p. 14.—*November* 12, 1571. 'Thomas Robertson *alias* Makgibbon removed from Parish of Auchtergavin, and presented to Parsonage of Parish of Moneydie' by James VI., 2d Jan. 1574. He was

afterwards minister of Kilmaveonag ; but returned to Moneydie, and afterwards was minister of Moulin ; but again returned to Moneydie, and died
in July 1596. He married, as set forth in the above page, Barbara Justice
who survived him, and had a son William and a daughter Violet.

Note, Ruthven, p. 71.—R. S. Fittis, in *Illustrations of the History and
Antiquities of Perthshire*, p. 52, and *Recreations of an Antiquary in Perthshire, History and Genealogy*, p. 290, says that Lord Ruthven had five sons
and two daughters, *all* by the first marriage.   His second wife was
daughter of the Earl of Athole, and widow of the Earl of Sutherland and
of Henry Lord Methven. William Ruthven and Dorothe Stewart are
said to have had at least three sons and eight daughters. (1) James, second
Earl, died when about fourteen years of age in 1588, (2) William, third
Earl, killed at Perth, 5th August 1600 (3) Alexander, killed at Perth,
5th August 1600.   The daughters were, (1) Marie, afterwards Countess
of Atanhole, with issue, (2) Jean, Lady Ogilvie, (3) Lilias, Duchess
of Lennox, without issue, (4) Dorothea, Lady Pittencrieff, without
issue, (5) Margaret, Countess of Montrose, (6) Beatrix, Lady Couden-
knows, (7) Elizabeth, Lady Lochinvar, and (8) Barbara, died unmarried.

P. 100.—Oct. 19, 1561. Alexander Buncle was Dean of Guild in Perth
1467.   John Buncle appears in 1471 and 1474 as Baillie, Provost in
1476.   Andrew, possibly Alexander's son, married Elizabeth, sister of
Robert Mercer of Ballief, a member of the Aldie family, and was in the
magistracy occasionally between 1492 and 1519. Their son Alexander
had a son of the same name. Possibly the latter was the Alexander
Buncle, burgess of Perth, granter of the Bond to the Carthusians for 20
merks on 28th August 1552, and the Alexander B., who is mentioned as
marrying Janet Smith there, is also known as Buncle's Vennel in Perth.
R. S. F.'s *Ecclesiastical Annals of P.*, p. 243, and Duff's *Memorabilia of
the City of Perth.*

P. 104.—Mr. William Rynd is called son to unquhil Patrick Rynd in
Kirk Session Register, 15th Sept. 1589. He was Tutor to Earl of Gowrie
and his brother Alexander.   In 1594 he went to Padua with them, and
returned in 1597. Duff's *Memorabilia*, p. 337.

P. 169.—August 13, 1568. In 1582-3 we find Nicol Ronaldson acted
as bellman, probably the same as above mentioned.

P. 133.—Decr. 26, 1563. John Boutter and Marian Duncan. Should
this not be John Soutter ?

P. 15.—10th June 1571. Reference to Thomas Dundie and Violet
Robertson will be found in *Extracts from Kirk Session Records, Spottiswoode Miscellany*, vol. ii. p. 236.

27th January 1571, James Eldar, and Isabell Wenton, at Do., vol. ii.
p. 249.

18th May 1572, James Syme and Euphame Tully at Do., p. 250.

P. 133.—2d Jan. 1563, Andrew Rogie and *James* Ruthven evidently is
a printer's error.

P. 135 and 136.—Out of a list of 355 Inhabitants of Perth in 1600, there
were only two of the name of Ross—William Ross at the Charter-house-
yett, and James, who is undesigned ; probably they are the William,
married 2d Sept. 1565, and James, married 14th Oct. 1565.

P. 100.—Euphame Conquerer married Sir Patrick Threipland on the
13th March 1665. She was a daughter of John Conqueror of the Friar-
ton. Of this marriage there were one son and six daughters.

P. 133.—19th Dec. 1563. Wm. Tyrie, probably the same William Tyrie as is mentioned at p. 106 of *Memorabilia of Perth*, as Treasurer in 1554 (by mistake 1544), who is, in a note, suggested to be of the family of Drumkilbo, afterwards proprietors of Busbie in the parish of Methven.

P. 12.—Sept. 10, 1570. William Faire, possibly the same William Fary who committed suicide by drowning himself in the Tay about the 3d December 1582. *Extracts from the Kirk Session Records*, *Spottiswoode Miscellany*, vol. ii. p. 243.

Vol. III. Nov. 16, 1571, p. 15. James Anderson & Margaret Anderson. Should it not be James *Adamson* & Margaret Anderson?

Pp. 103 and 168, Jany. 3, 1562, and Feby. 15, 1567. Possibly Gillespie M'Gregor is the same individual in both the above entries.

J. M'G.

138. CHURCHWARDEN'S ACCOUNTS, HARTSHORNE, DERBYSHIRE.—We have given our readers occasionally extracts from the Records and Accounts of Scottish Parishes. A few remarks on the accounts kept by the church-wardens of an English parish may prove of interest to our Northern readers. By the kindness of the Rev. Nigel W. Gresley, Rector of Dursley, Gloucester-shire, I have access to several volumes which were rescued from destruction by his father, the Rev. John M. Gresley. The most interesting is the Churchwardens' Account Book, which commences A.D. 1612. It commences thus :—

1. Imp' paid att london ye v^h of Maie for a bible . . . 47s. 6d.
2. Item paid att london for exchange of the Comunion Cupp . 23s.
3. Item for bringing them Dowen 2 2
October 28 gevin to aliene man . . . . . . 4d.
Item p^d Jhon Swane for candle lights for Curfew . . . 5d.
March 23. For enlarging ye kings armes with helmett crest and
mantle & paintinge lords praier and ye beleife . . . 5 4

On the third page is 'an Inventory of ye Church goods of the parish of Hartishorne.'

1. Imp. a coñin Cupp of Silver with a plate of Silver having Jhon Bapt head uppon itt.

2. Itm a large bible.

3. Itt Jewell & Hardinge.

4. Itt Erasmus paraphrase uppon ye 4 Evangelysts & ye Actes.

5. Itt A new booke of Coñon praier.

6. Itt two books of Homylyes.

7. Itt the late Queens iniunctions together wth ye Iniunctions of ye byshopp of Coventri & Lichfeild bound w^t hitt.

8. Itt certain advertisements gevin by ye L byshopp of C & L w^t other treatise bound w^t itt.

9. Itt certayne prayers sett forth by Authority to be used et.

10. Itt two register bookes y⁵ one in parchment y⁵ other in paper.

11. Itt a great chest w¹ ij lockes & kees.

12. Itt a poore mans box w¹ locke & key.

13. Itt an ould surplice.

14. Itt an new table cloth for y⁵ Comūn table & an ould.

15. Itt a Carpett for the Comūn table.

16. Itt three bells.

17. Itt Constitutions & Canons Ecclesiasticall et.

18. Itt viij boords & plancks lying in Church Sawen.

19. Itt a beare wᵗʰ a Coffin.

20. Itt a peuter bottell of ij quarts & a pint.
    pᵣ me James Royll, 1612.

It will be impossible to do more than give a sketch of how the parish money was expended. Payment was made for the destruction of hedgehogs, or, as they were more usually called, urchins. It was a popular delusion that these harmless animals sucked the cows as they lay out in the fields, so under date 1629 we find :—

'It to Tho Swan for kiling two hedghogs . . . . 4d.'
1630 'It. pᵈ unto Robte Barnes for killinge an urchin . . . 2d.'

The payments were so frequent that we are surprised that the whole genus did not become extinct. More justifiable objects of hatred were foxes and badgers :—

1631 'It pᵈ unto Robte Greene for killing a badger . . . 1s. 0d.'
1680 'to Tho. Spenser for 1 fox head . . . . 1s. 0d.'

In 1632 we find provision made for herbs for the Church :—

'It payde for Lavender to James Swan to lay the cushion & pulpit cloth 3d.'

In 1650 there is a curious entry concerning sacramental wine :—

'It pᵈ 22 of March 1650 & y⁵ 28 of March 1651 to Francis Sikes
    for 8 quarts of Clarit wine & 2 quarts of Muskadine for
    Pallme Sunday & Easter day as will appear by quittance . 11s. 8d.'

And just below is a memorial of the civil war :—

'It to y⁵ Clarke for washing out y⁵ kings arms . .   3d.'

With one item, dated 1634, we must finish :—

'It geeven to a Skottish gentleman that had house and wife and all
    his people burned by Rebels in Ierland . . . . iiijd.

                                                    A. W. C. H.

139. THE CORPORATION OF WRIGHTS, CULROSS.—The Minutes of the Corporation of the Wrights of the Royal Burgh of Culross, Perthshire, are contained in two volumes, the older of which is a small quarto of 420 pages, dating from 8th April 1612 to 12th February 1792. A curious feature is that the earliest entries seem to have been made in any part of the volume the secretary preferred, *e.g.* 1567 follows 1743, and is followed by 1632.

Though there is nothing of striking interest in the volume, it is impossible to peruse it without gaining an insight into trade customs and phrases. Of course the spirit of exclusiveness is to be met with in this, as in every trade guild of the period.

'17 March 1716.—The Corporation of the Wrights being informed that Richard Mastertoun wright was working to Rob⁴ Spitel within the toun, his teuals (tools) was taken and he was oblidged to give a bond of fortie punds scots that he should work no more after that maner upon which he had back his teuals—the bond is writen by John halkerson toun Clerk upon stamped peaper dated 17th day March 1716.   JAMES TAYLOUR.'

On the 3d of August in the same year, another interloper was dealt with more severely ; 'he was caryed to prison until he gave his Bond of fortie pund Scots.' The same day an unfreeman and his son were caught 'building a kill' on the estate of Mr. William Broun. They were brought to Culross and had to give their bond.

Before this time, viz. in 1699, a bond was granted by James M'Laren in Castelhill, 'oblidging him not to work within the toun or priviledges y'of under the penaltie of tree hundred punds Scots.'

The guild had a loft or seat of their own in the parish church, and difficulties arose between the heritors and the guild as to the maintenance of it.

A man who married a freeman's daughter could claim 'to be admitted and received a freeman and member of the Corporation by virtue of his privilege aforesaid.' This claim was allowed to Alexander Birnie, who had married Nicolas, the daughter of John Mutray, wright in Culross. The Mutrays or Moultries were an old and numerous race in and about the Royal Burgh, and three generations of them were members of the Corporation of Wrights. Other families connected with it and the town were the Primroses from whom the present Earl of Rosebery descends, and the Angels whose name is in the earlier minutes written Enzell. The Enzalls were connected both with the Wrights and with the Saltmakers.

Occasionally we meet with the admission of some neighbouring gentleman into the Corporation ; this was done with the object of securing an influential adviser and supporter in the squabbles which took place between the Wrights and the Burgh Authorities. Apprentices having served their time were admitted members on completing a say (assay) piece, the nature of which was settled by the Corporation, and two of their members were appointed to act as say masters to judge the work when done ; tables, bedsteads, and other articles of furniture were chosen as tests of skill.

The admittance of the new member was accompanied by the 'speaking pint,' which seems to mean a supply of drink at the expense of the new member. Various wholesome rules were made not only for the orderly carrying on of the business at the meetings, but for the maintenance of general good feeling. The following extract which concludes our paper bears on this subject.

'Yt guras (at Culross) the eleven day of Aug . the zeir of god 1657, the hail wrights of the broch being convenit it is concluded and agreid upone be the consent and advys of the craft yt whosoever of theme shal presoume to abus another aither in their face or behind their back or to tak speich upon them befor the craft without libertie asket and given shal pay prēstly to the bookes the soume of threi pounds Scots, in witness thirof sūcrbut be their hand.

' JAMES NASMYTH my hand.
PEITER PRỸOES (Primrose.)
JAMES MUTRAY.
JAMES SINCLAR.'
A. W. C. H.

140. CLOCKMAKERS.—Watchmakers, Gold and Silversmiths, and Jewellers who have carried on business in the city of Elgin from the years 1697 until and after the years 1820-1838.

1697 Thomas Gilgour was admitted as a Watchmaker member of the Hammermen Incorporation.

1701 William Scott Sen' and William Scot, yo' Goldsmiths in Elgin, being found qualified in their trade and occupation of Silver and Goldsmiths out of consideraion, and for ye favour and respect they bear them are admitted freemen.

1712 James Guthrie, Gold and Silversmith from Edinburgh now in Elgin having made application to the Deacons and Masters of the Hammermen Craft of the Burgh, and they being convinced of his ability and skill of working as a Gold and Silversmith and having satisfied the Craft he was admitted etc.

1715 Alexander Innes having given in his essay of Craft as a Gold and Silversmith was admitted.

1726 James Brown admitted as a qualified Watch and Clockmaker.

1729 William Livingston late apprentice to James Tait gave in his essay as ane Gold and Silversmith, and the samyn being found good and sufficient work he was admitted.

1743 John Lundie admitted having served his apprenticeship with John Brown Watchmaker.

1754 Alexander Grey, Watchmaker and Wright, created and admitted freeman for the love and favour we bear to him.

1754 James Humphrey Goldsmith and freeman of Craft had entered at that date as apprentices John M'Beath and John Cruickshank.

1772 James Grey Watchmaker admitted.
[There appears to have neither been Gold and Silversmiths or Watchmakers entered between the dates 1772-1803.]

1790 to 1820 The initials of Charles Fowler are frequently found on Elgin plate between these dates. The Rev⁴. Jas Cowper Aberdeen says he was a man of standing and ane important Silversmith, who would probably be a Burgess of Guild, as he is evidently not ane of Craft.
 |CF| |ELGIN| figure of St. Giles with Staff and Book and front view of Cathedral.

1803 George Sutherland Watchmaker admitted freeman.

1805 George Grigor Watchmaker admitted represented as having served his apprenticeship with Alexander Duncan, freeman of this Burgh.
[I can find no entry of Duncan's admission to freedom of Craft ;

probably he was a burgess of Guild, as he was an important merchant.]

1807 Alexander Archibald, freeman's apprenticeship with Alexander Duncan.

1808 John Keith, Silver and Goldsmith and Jeweller in Banff admitted freeman of the Hammermen Incorporation on condition of his paying the customary fees and producing an essay piece, the said John Keith instantly produced a Watch Chain by way of essay. This is the first notice of an essay having been submitted by a Jeweller or Watchmaker.

1820 George Sutherland, son of the preceding George Sutherland carried on the business of a Watchmaker untill within the memory of several now living.

There were also from the date 1820 carrying on business as Watchmakers and Jewellers in Elgin, George Cruickshank, Clock and Watchmaker, George Grigor (above mentioned) Clock and Watchmaker, and after these were

1838 Messrs. Grey, Spark, Duncan, Pozzie and Stewart, James Alexander, Brown, Urquhart, John Sellar.

1838 Joseph Pozzie (of Pozzie & Stewart.) Mark ⌐JP⌐ ⌐ELN.⌐ ⌐JP⌐

 (4 marks.)

J. Hardie Mark ⌐IH⌐ ⌐ELN⌐ Figure of St. Giles recumbent ⌐A⌐

(4 marks).

William Fergusson ⌐WF⌐ ⌐ELGIN⌐ (2 marks).

141. BUCHAN OF LETHAM.—In *Lands and their Owners in Galloway*, (M'Kerlie) vol. i, p. 209, it is said that John Ross of Balkail, married Jean Buchan 'of whom nothing has been traced.' She was the second daughter of John Buchan of Letham, by his second wife Ann Brown, daughter of George Brown of Coalston. Mrs. Ross's signature may be seen along with those of her brothers' and sisters' appended to a family document in an old Bible now in the possession of General Cadell of Cockenzie. The document, which is on one of the blank leaves, runs as follows :—'Ann Brown, our mother, died at Letham, the twenty sixth day of February One thousand seven hundred and ninety.

'AGED 67.

'A most pious and benevolent christian, a most virtuous, affectionate, and attentive wife, a most tender, anxious, kind, and indulgent mother, loved, esteemed respected and revered by her family, who with according hearts in unbounded filial affection, gratitude and regard, in the deepest affliction, mourn the loss of the best of parents and the firmest of friends.

'Our flowing tears have spoke what words cannot express, and our tender and grateful remembrance of her shall only cease when memory is no more.

'May she be our guardian angel, and may God enable us in brotherly love and amity to follow her pious instructions and bright example, with the heavenly assurance of again meeting her in everlasting happiness.

'Signed by her sons and daughters as follows :—

SONS.	DAUGHTERS.
Charles Buchan	Ann Buchan
Francis Buchan	Jane Ross
William Buchan	Mary Cadell
Alexander Buchan	Helen Glassel
	Janet Buchan.'

Of these signatories, Charles was Buchan of Whitsome, co. Berwick, who afterwards married the heiress of Killentringan, co. Ayr, but *d.s.p.* Francis married the heiress of Sydserff of that ilk and Ronchlaw, co. Haddington, and from him descends the present Sydserff of Ronchlaw. William was an officer of marines and served under Lord Rodney. Alexander, a Lieutenant of Fireworks in the Bengal Army, was killed at Seringapatam in 1792. (Another brother, Colonel Hew, died of fatigue at a subsequent siege of the same place.)   Ann married Thomas Lithgow, Island of Grenada.   Mary married John Cadell of Tranent, etc., and from her are descended the Cadells of Tranent, Ratho, and Cockenzie, many of whom have been distinguished soldiers.   One Cadell of Ratho was Scott's friend and publisher; another, Francis Cadell, the explorer of the Murray River, Australia.   Helen married Glassel of Longniddrie. Her only daughter and heiress married Lord John Campbell, afterwards Duke of Argyll.   Their son is the present Duke.   While Jane, Mrs. Ross herself, was mother of Field-Marshal Sir Hew Dalrymple Ross, whose son Sir John is at present military Governor of Canada.

J. H. STEVENSON.

142. FONT OR CROSS SOCKET (see 129).—With regard to the pierced stone at Inchyre House, Fife.   Should it not be Inchrye?   I think it is very likely to be a portion of what is called a Stathel, a short stone column with a large base and cap, which were used for supporting stacks.

Inchyre Abbey never was a religious house, but is quite a modern building, built, I believe, by a Mr. Ramsay, editor or proprietor of the *Scotsman* newspaper, about the year 1820.

The nearest religious house is the well-known Lindores Abbey, about one mile distant.

In some of the ancient ruined churches, notably Iona and Arbroath, there is a stone with a small square socket in the Chancel in such a position as to appear to have been in front of the centre of the High Altar.   Could this have been used for a socket or support to a processional cross or crucifix ?   J. H.

143. LEVEN.—It is stated in Colonel Robertson's *Gaelic Topography of Scotland* that the river in Fife is originally ' Levern ' (not ' Leven'). This seems supported by ' Levern ' (Renfrew) and ' Levernhope ' (Selkirk-shire), and gives rise to the question whether other ' Levens ' may not repre-sent the same contraction.   A ' Liver' flows into Loch Etive, and one into Loch Awe, and in Cornish the word ' Llyfer' seems to mean a flood—a natural name for common application to water.   The point is interesting, because theories of King Arthur's wars have been based on Llywennydd, ash-trees, etc.   W. M. C.

144. IRON COFFIN CASES (see 128, vol. iii. p. 20).—·I saw two of these

cases in Aberfoyle Churchyard about two years ago. Probably they are still there.   J. M'G.

The iron coffin cases referred to in your last are, in Fife at least, generally called Mortsafes. They are used thus, two thick planks are put in the bottom of the grave, underneath and at right angles to where the coffin will be, four strong iron rods, hinged near the upper ends are screwed into the planks, two on each side. The coffin is then lowered, the cage-like mortsafe put over it, and the hinged rods, the tops of which interlace, bent over and padlocked, the keys being given to the nearest relation. The grave is then filled up.

When the mortsafe is removed, the rods are unlocked and unscrewed, the planks being left *in situ.*

They were, I believe, first used about the time of the resurrectionists Burke and Hare, and others, and are now, I think, quite gone out of use.

       J. H.

145. THE FAMILY OF NICOLSON.—I offer the following attempt to extricate the pedigrees of the different Baronetical families of this name. Milne's List of Nova Scotia Baronets (prefixed to Foster's *Baronetage*, 1880) has six Nicolson entries, but these resolve themselves into four Baronetcies.

A. The earliest patent was sealed on 17th Dec. 1625 to 'Mr. James Nicolson of Cockburnspaith.' On the 7th Oct. of that year he had been returned as 'Magister Jacobus Nicolsone de Cokbrandispeth haeres Magistri Thomae Nicolsone, Advocati, commissarii Aberdonensis, Patris.' In a retour of the 30th April 1690 (*Inquisitiones Generales*, 7018) the following relationships are set out—

John Nicolson of Lasswade, brother of Thomas Nicolson
| of Cockburnspath
| |
John Nicolson of Poltoun   Dominus Jacobus Nicolson de
| Cockburnspath
John Nicolson of Poltoun
|
William Nicolson of that Ilk
|
Thomas Nicolson of that Ilk then served heir of the above James of Cockburnspath as his 'filii fratris abavi.'
He was succeeded by his son.

II. Thomas, a lawyer of considerable repute, consulted in 1638 as to the legality of the Covenant; named Sir Thomas Nicolson in a letter from the Marquis of Hamilton of that year. (*See* Omond's *Lives of the Lord Advocates.*) He probably succeeded his father as second Baronet, and had issue—

1. James, his successor.
2. Thomas (Sir), Procurator to the estates in 1644, King's Advocate 1649, knighted at Falkland 10th July 1650, *d.* 15th December 1656. He *m.* Rachel, daughter of Robert Burnett, Lord Crimond, and widow of John Napier, Advocate, and by her (who *rem.* as third wife of Sir Thomas Hamilton of Preston and Fingalton) left issue—
    1. Thomas, served heir to his father, the King's Advocate, on 29th September 1658, and again on 8th April 1671. Sir James

Nicolson of Cockburnspath was served heir-male of his nephew, this Thomas, on 5th September 1676.

2. Rachel, 'daughter of Sir Thomas Nicolson of Cockburnspath,' *m.* 1670 Sir William Hamilton, first Baronet of Preston, and had three daughters whose issue is extinct.

3. Marion, 'daughter of Sir Thomas Nicolson, King's Advocate,' designated (erroneously) as 'of Carnock,' *m.* George Hay of Balhousie, and had a son, Thomas Hay, who was created Viscount Dupplin in 1697, and succeeded in 1709 as sixth Earl of Kinnoull. From her descends the present Earl of Kinnoull.

4. Margaret, wife of John Cheislie of Dalry, was on 12th October 1676 served heir-portioner of her brother-german, Thomas Nicolson of Cockburnspath.

3. Agnes Nicolson, third wife of the first Lord Elibank, was (perhaps) a daughter of this Sir Thomas. Her son Thomas Murray (pupillus) was on 7th December 1637 served heir-male to her.

4. 'A sister of Sir Thomas Nicolson, King's Advocate,' *m.* David Dunsmuir, Advocate, by whom she had a daughter, Rachel Dunsmuir, who *m.* 1667 John Wedderburn of Blackness (Douglas's *Baronage*, 281). From her descends the present Sir William Wedderburn, Baronet.

5. Isabella, 'daughter of Sir Thomas Nicolson of Cockburnspath,' *m.* Sir Henry Nisbet of Craigentinny, knighted in 1641. Her son was created a Baronet on the 2d December 1669, and having exchanged properties with his cousin, became 'of Dean.' The title is extinct. John Riddell, the celebrated peerage lawyer, was descended from her.

6. Anne, 'daughter of Sir Thomas Nicolson of Cockburnspath, *m.* John Scot of Milenie (who *d.* 1709), second son of Sir William Scot of Clerkington (Douglas's *Baronage*, 2181). From her descended Major Francis Cunningham Scott of Mallenie, C.B., and William Fordyce Blair of Blair.

III. Sir James Nicolson, third Baronet, was served heir to his nephew Thomas on 5th September 1676. He seems to have been the Dominus Jacobus Nicolson de Cockburnspath, to whom on 30th April 1690 Thomas Nicolson *de eodem* was served as heir-male ; he left a daughter—

1. Joanna, wife of Gavin Elliot (brother of the Laird of Stobs), who on the same day was served heir-portioner to her father.

It may be mentioned that there were several eminent lawyers of this name. Mr. John Nicolson is mentioned in Pitcairn's *Criminal Trials* from 29th May 1596 to 29th June 1603. On the last occasion he is referred to as 'of Lasswade.' Mr. Thomas Nicolson is mentioned from 17th July 1611 to 20th June 1620, being distinguished as 'elder' for part of that time ; while Mr. Thomas Nicolson, younger, comes on the scene on the 20th July 1621. He was probably the father of the Lord Advocate.

B. The next Nicolson Baronetcy in order of date was, according to Milne, conferred on John Nicolson of Lasswade. It is dated 2d July 1629, and was sealed on 31st December of that year. The early descents are rather confused, but may be stated as follows :—

I. John Nicolson, a lawyer of eminence in Edinburgh, acquired property there and at Lasswade. He *m.* Janet, daughter of John Swinton of that

Ilk (Douglas's *Baronage*, 130), and is described as 'progenitor of the Nicolsons of Lasswade, Carnock, etc.' His 'eldest son'—

II. John Nicolson of Lasswade, served heir to his father on the 5th March 1614, *m.* Elizabeth, daughter of Dr. Edward Henderson, Advocate, and had several sons—

    1. John, his successor.

    2. Thomas 'second son,' ancestor of the Nicolsons of Carnock (see *C.*).

    3. Thomas Nicolson, founder of the family of Cockburnspath (*A.*), would, according to the pedigree set forth in the retour of 1690, have this place, but I suspect he was a younger son of John No. 1. This is the weakest point in the descents.

III. John Nicolson 'of that Ilk and of Lasswade' was created a Baronet on the 2d July 1629. He *m.* Magdalen, eldest daughter of David Preston of Craigmillar (Douglas's *Peerage*, i. 416, where he is named James). She and her sister Elizabeth were on 8th April 1640 served heirs-portioners of their brother Robert Preston, and in the retour she is designated as wife of Sir John Nicolson, Baronet, of Lasswade. He is said to have been succeeded by his grandson, and had (apparently) four sons—

    1. The father of the second Baronet, apparently identical with the first John Nicolson of Poltoun in the pedigree of 1690.

    2. James Nicolson, Bishop of Dunkeld, 'second son of the first Baronet,' *m.* Jean, only daughter of Gilbert Ramsay of Banff (Douglas's *Baronage*, 552), ancestor of the present Baronet.

    3. Robert Nicolson, to whom his brother Thomas was served heir on 24th July 1661.

    4. Thomas, to whom his nephew, Sir John, was served heir on the 6th May 1688.

IV. John Nicolson 'of Poltoun' predeceased his father, leaving a son.

V. Sir John Nicolson succeeded his grandfather as second Baronet, and was served heir to him, 5th April 1676. He seems to be identical with the second John of Poltoun in the pedigree of 1690. He was also served heir to his uncle Thomas in 1688. He *m.* Elizabeth, second daughter of Sir William Dick, Baronet of Braid (Douglas's *Baronage*, 270), and had two sons.

VI. Sir John Nicolson, third Baronet, mentioned by Milne as having 'taken out his arms as Baronet.' He was succeeded by his brother—

VII. Sir William Nicolson, fourth Baronet, was, on 21st September 1681, served as heir-male of his brother 'Dominus Joannes Nicolson miles Baronettus' in the lands of Nicolson (prius Clerkington nuncupatis), Fowlerstoun, Lasswade, etc., in Edinburgh, Cockburnspath in Berwick, and Staniepath in Haddington. He *m.* Elizabeth, eighth and youngest daughter of John Trotter of Morton Hall. (His arms are blazoned in vol. ii. of Nisbet's *System of Heraldry*, plate vi.) He is mentioned as William Nicolson *de eodem* in the pedigree of 1690, and had two sons.

VIII. Sir Thomas Nicolson, fifth Baronet, who, as Thomas Nicolson *de eodem*, was served heir-male of Sir James Nicolson of Cockburnspath, on the 30th April 1690. He is said to have *d. s. p.* (Query, was he the Sir Thomas Nicolson of Ladykirk, whose daughter *m.* Thomas Brisbane in 1715?) He was probably the Sir Thomas Nicolson in whose house carpets were used for the first time in Edinburgh, as mentioned in Ramsay's *Scotland and Scotsmen*, page 98. He was succeeded by his brother.

IX. Sir James Nicolson, sixth Baronet, who also *d. s. p.*, when the title devolved on the representative of James Nicolson, the Bishop of Dunkeld, as stated in Burke's *Peerage.*

C. The third Nicolson Baronetcy mentioned by Milne is that of Carnock. For the first two descents see *B.*

III. Thomas Nicolson of Carnock was created a Baronet on the 16th January 1637. He *m.* Isobel, daughter of Walter Henderson of Granton, and *d.* 8th January 1646; leaving issue—

    1. Thomas, his successor.
    2. John of Tillicoultrie, served heir to his sister Jane on the 28th May 1653; *m.* Sabina Colyear, and *d.* 1683, leaving two sons—

        1. Thomas, who succeeded as fifth Baronet.
        2. Colonel William, *d.* at Ypres in 1720. Ancestor of the present Baronet.

    3. Elizabeth, *m.* Thomas Drummond of Riccartoun.
    4. Anne, *m.* Sir George Stirling of Keir as his third wife.
    5. Jane.

IV. Sir Thomas Nicolson, second Baronet of Carnock, *m.* Lady Margaret (? Eleanor) Livingstone, daughter of Alexander, second Earl of Linlithgow (Douglas's *Peerage*, ii. 127), and by her (who *rem.* as fourth wife of Sir George Stirling of Keir, and again as first wife of Sir John Stirling of Garden, who succeeded to Keir); he left at his death on the 24th July 1664—

    1. Thomas, his successor.
    2. Eleanor, *m.* Sir John Shaw, second Baronet of Greenock, now represented by the Earl Cathcart and Sir M. R. Shaw Stewart, Bart. She and her sisters became co-heiresses of their nephew.
    3. Isobel, *m.* as first wife of James Dunbar of Mochrum (created a Baronet in 1694), now represented by the Right Hon. Sir William Dunbar, Bart.
    4. Margaret, *m.* (first) to Alexander Hamilton of Barcrieff (? Balnacrieff), and (secondly) to Sir Thomas Nicolson of Kemnay (see *D.*) The Marquis of Lothian is descended from her.

V. Sir Thomas Nicolson, third Baronet of Carnock, Plain, and Dunipace, served heir to his father on the 26th August and 27th, 28th September 1664; *m.* 1668 Hon. Jean Napier, eldest daughter of Archibald, second Lord Napier, and *d.* 20th January 1670, leaving one son.

VI. Sir Thomas Nicolson, fourth Baronet, born 14th January 1669, served heir to his father on 1st February 1671, succeeded his maternal uncle as fourth Lord Napier in August 1683, and *d.* unmarried in France on the 9th June 1686, when the Barony of Napier passed under its special destination, and his three aunts were served heirs-portioners to him as regards the estate of Carnock, etc., while the Baronetcy devolved on—

V. Sir Thomas Nicolson as fifth Baronet (son of John of Tillicoultrie, mentioned above), who was served as heir-male of the fourth Baronet, and as heir of his father, on the 10th August and 23d September 1686. Besides his son and successor, Sir George, he seems to have had a daughter,
    Eleanor, 'daughter of Sir Thomas Nicolson of Carnock,' *m.* (first) Hon. Thomas Boyd, second son of William, second Earl of

Kilmarnock (born 13th September 1689), and (secondly), to John Craufurd of Craufurdland. She had two daughters by her first husband—

1. Margaret Boyd, died at Edinburgh on the 7th May 1781.
2. A daughter who *m.* as first wife of Charles Hope, merchant in Edinburgh, third son of Sir Archibald Hope, Lord Rankeillour, and had by him a son, Robert, and a daughter (Douglas's *Baronage*, 60).

From this point the succession of the Carnock Baronetcy is clearly stated in Burke's *Peerage*.

D. The latest Nicolson Baronetcy was conferred on a member of an Aberdeenshire family, probably connected with the Nicolsons of Cockburnspath, the first founder of which was a 'Commissarius Aberdonensis,' as mentioned above. For some of the details that follow I am indebted to Dr. Davidson's *Inverurie and the Garioch.*

George Nicolson (probably the person who was served heir to his father, Thomas Nicolson of Pitmedden, Bailie Burgess of Aberdeen, on the 21st July 1658), was called to the bar in 1661, being then designated as 'of Cluny.' He purchased Kemnay in 1682 from Alexander Strahan, younger of Glenkindy. He was made a Lord of Session in 1682, taking the title of Lord Kemnay. He sold Kemnay in 1688 to Thomas Burnet, and bought Balcaskie in Fife. He was alive at the Union. He was twice married (first), to Elizabeth, daughter of Alexander Abercromby of Birkenbog, and (secondly), to Margaret Halyburton, who *d.* August 1722. A son by his first wife is said to have been 'Bishop Nicolson, the first Vicar Apostolic appointed by the Pope in Scotland.' Besides the Bishop he had issue—

1. Thomas.
2. William.

I. Thomas Nicolson, 'younger of Kemnay,' was created a Baronet of Nova Scotia, 15th April 1700. He *m.*, 1688, Margaret, third daughter and co-heiress of Sir Thomas Nicolson, Bart., of Carnock, and widow of James Hamilton of Barcrieff, and had several daughters but no son. One of his daughters, Margaret, *m.* as first wife of William, third Marquis of Lothian, and from her descends the present Marquis.

II. William Nicolson 'of Mergie' succeeded his brother as second Baronet. He was married four times, and had twenty-two children. He purchased Glenbervie in 1721 from Catherine, daughter and heir of Thomas Burnet of Glenbervie, whose widow (Agnes, daughter of Robert Burnet of Cowtown, etc.) he had *m.* as one of his wives. He died without surviving male issue, when the Baronetcy (granted to heirs-male general) devolved on his heir-male, stated to have been the ancestor of 'Sir James Nicolson, Bart., of Glenbervie, Co. Kincardine,' mentioned in Burke's *Peerage* of 1829 and 1837 as then alive, but regarding whom no information is recorded. Sir William's estates passed to his daughters, two of whom are known—

1. 'John,' the fifth daughter, inherited Glenbervie, and *m.* Rev. John Wilson. Her daughter, Ann Wilson Nicolson of Glenbervie, *m.* Robert Badenach of Arthurhouse. Her son, James Badenach Nicolson of Glenbervie, *m.* Eliza, daughter of James (Williamson) Burnet of Monboddo, and was recently secretary to the Lord Advocate.

2. Helen, *m.* at Montrose, 11th February 1781, Henry Ivie of Mount Alto, in Ireland.

The above notes seem to correct the double error in Foster's *Baron-etage*, where at pages 550 and 650 Sir Thomas Nicolson of Carnock is represented as Lord Advocate. They also correct the error in the pedigree of the Earl of Kinnoull in Douglas's and in Burke's *Peerages*, where Sir Thomas Nicolson, the Lord Advocate, is designated as 'of Carnock.'

Three of the four Nicolson Baronetcies seem to have been granted to 'Heirs-male general,' Carnock being the only one limited to heirs-male of the body. It would therefore appear as if Sir Arthur J. B. Nicolson of that Ilk and Lasswade, who is entered under the Lasswade Baronetcy of 1629, might be able to prove his claim to the older Cockburnspath Baron-etcy of 1625. Such an attempt would bring out any weak points in the above pedigrees.	Σ.

146. NOTES ON THE ACTA DOM. CONC. ET SESS., 1478-1495.—1. The name of the wife of Sir Patrick Hepburn, first Lord Hailes, is not mentioned in Wood's *Douglas*. From the *Acta* (page 98*) we learn that on the 24th January 1484, 'Elene Wallace the spouse of some time Patric Lord Halis,' sued Patric 'now' (*i.e.* third) Lord Hailes for her teirce. This also helps to fix the date of the death of Adam second Lord Hailes.

2. Douglas's *Baronage* says Sir John Colquhon of Luss (fl. 1440-1480) married a daughter of Thomas Lord Boyd. There is no Thomas Lord Boyd whose daughter could have married Sir John, and the marriage is not recorded in the Boyd pedigree. The *Acta*, however, show that on 25th October 1484 (page 89*), a suit was brought by Humphrey Colquhon of Luss against 'Elizabeth of Dunbar, the spous of Umquhile Sir John Colquhon of that ilk,' regarding the repair of certain family property in her hands (see also entry of 19th January of the same year, page 95* and *Acta Dom. Audm.*, 19 Oct. 1484).

3. At page 378 of the *Acta* a curious entry occurs of a petition, pre-sented on the 25th October 1494, by one Malcolm Culquhone, regarding certain land pertaining to him 'by the decease of umquhile Elizabeth Countess of M'ray (Murray or Moray), and Lady of Dûbeth, my grandame.' I can trace no such Countess of Moray. If she was Lady of Dunbeath in her own right, her name probably was Elizabeth Suther-land, but the last 'Lady of Dunbeath' I know of was Marjory Sutherland, Countess of Caithness (see *D. P.* II. 339 and 574). If for Dûbeth we read Dunbar, we may presume either that some lady of the family of Dunbar Earl of Moray, who claimed to have succeeded to that title, married (as stated above) Sir John Colquhon, the Lord Chamberlain (probably as his second wife), or that the so-called Countess of Moray was the unrecorded wife of Malcolm Colquhon, Sir John's father, who *d.v.p.*, having been mentioned in a charter of 1433. I am not aware if this difficulty has been already mooted. The entry at page 378 is composed of an unusually crabbed and contracted mixture of Scotch and Latin, and I shall be glad if any competent scholar will furnish a correct translation after collation, if possible, with the original record.

4. Douglas's *Baronage* (page 238) says that Sir David Bruce, fifth Baron of Clackmannan, married Marion, daughter of Sir Robert Herries of Tereagles. There was no such Sir Robert. She was probably daughter

of Robert Herries who had a charter of Terrachty on the 18th July 1477. And the *Acta* (page 184), under date 18th March 1490, tells us that she had previously married Sir David Stewart of Rossyth, Knight. It is to be noted, however, that on the 10th March 1490 (page 176), the *Acta* mentions an action brought by 'David Brois of Clekmanane and Mary Stewart his spouse.' Probably this is an erratum for Marioun.

5. The two printed volumes of *Acta* contain authentic references to about four hundred marriages, many of which are not elsewhere recorded, and an alphabetical catalogue of these marriages will be very useful to genealogists. Σ.

147. PARISH REGISTERS IN SCOTLAND (*continued from vols.* i. *and* ii., *p.* 172)—

Kinnoull, Perth, ...	*b.* 1618,	*m.* 1618,	*d.* 1766.
Kirkcaldy, Fife, ...	*b.* 1614,	*m.* 1615,	*d.* 1743.
Kirkden, Forfar, ...	*b.* 1650,	*m.* 1650,	*d.* 1749.
Kirkmichael, Ayr, . . .	*b.* 1638,	*m.* 1638,	*d.* 1783.
Kirkmichael, Perth, . . .	*b.* 1650,	*m.* 1650,	*d.* 1784
Kirknewton and East Calder, Edinburgh, ...	*b.* 1642,	*m.* 1642,	*d.* 1642.
Lanark, ...	*b.* 1647,	*m.* 1647,	*d. None.*
Largo, Fife, ...	*b.* 1636,	*m.* 1636,	*d.* 1767.
Lasswade, Edinburgh, . .	*b.* 1617,	*m.* 1617,	*d.* 1634.
Liberton, Edinburgh, . . .	*b.* 1624,	*m.* 1631,	*d.* 1647.
Liff, Benvie, and Invergowrie, Forfar, ...	*b.* 1651,	*m.* 1633,	*d.* 1750.
Livingston, Linlithgow, . .	*b.* 1639,	*m.* 1639,	*d.* 1718.
Longforgan, Perth, . .	*b.* 1634,	*m.* 1633,	*d. None.*
Longside, Aberdeen, . .	*b.* 1621,	*m.* 1692,	*d.* 1692.
Lyne and Megget, Peebles, .	*b.* 1649,	*m.* 1649,	*d. None.*
Markinch, Fife, . . .	*b.* 1635,	*m.* 1670,	*d.* 1634.
Melrose, Roxburgh, . .	*b.* 1642,	*m.* 1642,	*d.* 1781.
Monikie, Forfar, . . .	*b.* 1613,	*m.* 1613,	*d.* 1612.
Montrose, Forfar, . . .	*b.* 1615,	*m.* 1633,	*d.* 1670.
Newbattle, Edinburgh, . .	*b.* 1618,	*m.* 1642,	*d.* 1696.
Newburn, Fife, . . .	*b.* 1628,	*m.* 1628,	*d.* 1630.
Newton, Edinburgh, . .	*b.* 1629,	*m.* 1639,	*d.* 1730.
Ochiltree, Ayr, . . .	*b.* 1642,	*m.* 1641,	*d.* 1783.
Old Machar, Aberdeen, .	*b.* 1641,	*m.* 1621,	*d.* 1642.
Ormiston, Haddington, .	*b.* 1637,	*m.* 1637,	*d.* 1642.
Peebles, ...	*b.* 1622,	*m.* 1628,	*d.* 1660.
Peterculter, Aberdeen, .	*b.* 1643,	*m.* 1785,	*d.* 1647.
Petty, Inverness, . .	*b.* 1633,	*m.* 1657,	*d.* 1800.
Pittenweem, Fife, . .	*b.* 1611,	*m.* 1692,	*d.* 1685.
Queensferry, Linlithgow, .	*b.* 1635,	*m.* 1635,	*d.* 1782.
Roxburgh, ...	*b.* 1624,	*m.* 1654,	*d.* 1783.
St. Andrew's and St. Leonard's, Fife, ...	*b.* 1627,	*m.* 1638,	*d.* 1732.
St. Monance or Abercrombie, Fife,	*b.* 1628,	*m.* 1628,	*d.* 1674.
St. Ninian's, Stirling, . .	*b.* 1643,	*m.* 1688,	*d. None.*
Salton, Haddington, . .	*b.* 1636,	*m.* 1635,	*d.* 1644.

Scone, Perth, ... *b.* 1620,	*m.* 1620,	*d.* 1630.
Smailholm, Roxburgh, . . *b.* 1648,	*m.* 1701,	*d.* 1784.
Sprouston, Roxburgh, . . . *b.* 1635,	*m.* 1633,	*d.* 1633.
Stitchel (and Hume), Roxburgh, . *b.* 1640,	*m.* 1648,	*d. None.*
Stow, Edinburgh, . . . *b.* 1626,	*m.* 1641,	*d.* 1722.
Straiton, Ayr, ... *b.* 1644,	*m.* 1644,	*d.* 1783.
Symington, Ayr, ... *b.* 1642,	*m.* 1650,	*d.* 1783.
Tillicoultry, Clackmannan, . . *b.* 1640,	*m.* 1640,	*d.* 1639.
Torryburn, Fife, ... *h.* 1663,	*m.* 1629,	*d.* 1768.
Tranent, Haddington, . . . *h.* 1611,	*m.* 1611,	*d.* 1618.
Trinity Gark, Perth, . . . *b.* 1641,	*m.* 1641,	*d.* 1746.
Tweedsmuir, Peebles, . . . *b.* 1644,	*m.* 1644,	*d.* 1645.
Urquhart, Elgin, . . . *b.* 1647,	*m.* 1647,	*d.* 1746.
West Calder, Edinburgh, . . *h.* 1645,	*m.* 1677,	*d.* 1677.
Whittinghame, Haddington, . *b.* 1627,	*m.* 1627,	*d. None.*

EDITOR.

QUERIES.

LXXXV. 'WISH WELL.'—In conversing with an elderly lady, residing in Banchory-Devenick, Aberdeenshire, she remarked having been at a ' Wish Well,' which was described as a hollow containing a little water in a stone or piece of rock, formed by water dropping on it from the ground or rock overhead. On putting a pin in and expressing a wish, it should, on returning to the place some time afterwards, be found white.. If it is found discoloured it is not a wish well. Evidently the properties of the water characterise the well. What are they ? J. A., Abd.

LXXXVI. TIGGERS.—Dr. Robert Cowie, describing some of the duties of Ranselmen in his vol. on *Shetland and the Shetlanders*, page 26, Note 5, has ' that beggars and *tiggers* from a distance return to their own parishes.' Tig means to tantalise or annoy ; possibly *tiggers* are disturbing persons of no fixed abode. What is the explanation ? J. A., Abd.

LXXXVII. SCOTTISH UNIVERSITY MACES.—According to tradition, about the year 1683 there was discovered within Bishop Kennedy's tomb in St. Salvator's Chapel, St. Andrews, six maces which had been concealed there in troublous times. Three are kept in the University there, and one was presented to each of the other three Scottish Universities, Aberdeen, Glasgow, and Edinburgh. One, the original, is of beautiful Gothic workmanship of which the others are only copies.

There are two maces in Aberdeen, but neither of them Gothic, or in any way corresponding with those said to have been discovered in Bishop Kennedy's tomb ; the one in King's was made in 1650 by Walter Melvil, Aberdeen, the one in Marischal is after a similar make to King's, but without name of maker, townmark, or date.

On the Glasgow mace, Dr. J. F. S. Gordon writes : ' The deposit and subsequent presentation do not coincide with the inscription upon the Glasgow University mace, whereon is the word 'empta, purchased in 1465, manifesting that it was in possession 218 years before the said gift came from St. Andrews.'

The old mace of Edinburgh University was said to have been stolen by Deacon Brodie about the end of last century.

A gentleman in St. Andrews writes: ' The story of the maces is well known in this quarter, but I have never been able to find any documentary evidence to authenticate it, nor have I been able to trace the story to its origin in printed books. Billings also discredits it, and I dare say there is something legendary about it. Still it is not likely to be a pure invention, and I hope some day to hit upon something in our archives that will throw light upon it.'

What do the records of Aberdeen, Glasgow, and Edinburgh Universities say about the gifts, the maces they have, and have had ?   J. A., Abd.

LXXXVIII. MIDDLETON FAMILY.—Can G. A. W. inform me who painted the miniature of Principal George Middleton, now at Barham Court, and can he give any information connecting Robert Middleton of Caldhame, Marykirk, the Principal's grandfather, with Baillie George Middleton of Aberdeen (1574).
                                                        ALEX. M. MUNRO.

LXXXIX. JAMES CURRIE.—I will be much obliged if any reader of *N. N. & Q.* can inform me who the father and mother of James Currie, Provost of Edinburgh in 1673, were. He is said to have come from Strathaven or that district. His daughter Rachel is mentioned at page 144 of *The Guildry of Edinburgh: Is it an Incorporation?* by James Colston. Had James Currie any other children ?   J. M'G.

XC. ISABELLA ROSS.—Isabella Ross, sister of Hugh, fourth Earl of Ross, married Edward Bruce, King of Ireland, brother of King Robert Bruce. Was there any issue of this marriage ?

The aforenamed Hugh, Earl of Ross, married first, Lady Matilda Bruce, sister of King Robert Bruce, in 1308; he afterwards married Margaret, daughter of Sir David Graham, in 1329. Had he any children by Lady Matilda Bruce ?   R. P. H.

XCI. BENNET FAMILY.—Before the year 1600, there lived in *Grubet* in Scotland, *William Bennet.*

His son *William* lived in the beginning of 1600 in *Edinburgh*, and was minister during the reign of King Jacob the First. Married to Jeanna Bonnar.

His son *James* or *Jacob Bennet* was born in Scotland and went from there to *Sweden* 1640. Became a Captain in the garrison at Malmoe, and Major in the cavalry at Abo in Finland, Naturalised Swedish nobleman 1675, retaining his former name. Died 1690 at Fändern in the parish of Pernan in Liffland. Married to Christina Kinnemond. He had nineteen children, thirteen of these being sons, the greater part of whom were killed in the wars of Charles XII.

His son *Wilhelm*, Baron of Bälteberga, etc., was born 1680. He became a General in the Swedish army 1717. Raised to the rank of a Baron 1719. Appointed Governor of Holland 1728, and of Malmoehus 1737. Commanding the forces in Malmoe the same year. Died 1740 at the battle of Malmoe. Married 1712 to Magdalena Eleonora Barnekow, daughter of the Colonel Kjeld Christoffer Barnekow of Ralsvik, etc., and the Countess Margaretha von Ascheberg. From him descend those of the same name and titles still living in Sweden.

Mr. Amep in his *Pedigree of the Swedish Nobility*, says, regarding the origin of this family :—

'This family descends from Scotland and was there divided in two branches. One branch, *Bennet of Grubet*, whose motto is : " Benedictus qui tollit crucem," went to Sweden.

'The other, carrying quite another crest or three standing half lions in silver-field, remained in Scotland and England, where it has been raised to the dignity of Earl.'

Information is requested about William Bennet of Edinburgh, *circa* 1600, and his descent. C. B.

XCII. HAY.—Can any of your readers give any information regarding a family of the name of Hay who resided, and had some property (Nether Inch, it is believed), near Kilsyth, about the years 1700 or 1720? A. H.

XCIII. ST. PRUYON.—The following bequest occurs in the will of Robert Andern of Manchester, 1540 : 'I will that one be hired to go for me to S‘ Pruyons, in Scotland, and offer for me a bead flack, which is in my purse.' Where was this shrine? ED.

REPLIES TO QUERIES.

I. and XXXII. GRAHAM OF MOTE.—With reference to the articles as to the Grahams of the Borders (*N. N. & Q.* i. p. 119 and 152); in Mawson's Obits (*Genealogist*, vol. iii. New Series, p. 143) occurs 'July...1721, dyed Capt. Graham, eldest son of John Graham, late of Drogheda in Ireland'; possibly a descendant of some of the Grahams who were banished to Ireland. J. M‘G.

XIX. CRUISIE.—Allow me to add one or two particulars to your very clear descriptive note on Cruisies, page 154. These were in use in Forfarshire, and doubtless also in other parts of Scotland within the remembrance of persons now living. The saucers were called 'shells.' The wick used in country districts was usually the pith of the *Juncus communis*, called in Scotland 'rashies,' which for this purpose was divested of its outer green sheath or cuticle. The pith thus treated was then termed 'rashie-wicks,' and was tied up in bunches, and kept for use, or 'brought into towns on market-days by country dames along 'with their rural produce.'—(See Gardiner's *Flora of Forfarshire*.)

The term cruisie, while sometimes used alone, was often combined with the Scotch term for oil, *ulie* or *ulzie,* pronounced *oolie,* as 'ulie-cruisie.' There were various modes of hanging the cruisie when in use, the most common arrangement for this purpose being a short rod of iron having a swivel attachment to the cruisie at the lower end and a hook at the upper end. This rod in several examples in my possession has been twisted into a spiral form, apparently for ornament, and in one of these specimens the spiral rod is prolonged into a point beyond the hook, as if for the purpose of being inserted into a clay wall, or other permeable material. One rare specimen in this locality has an ingenious contrivance of two stout wires interlacing with each other, but free to slide to admit of the cruisie being lowered or raised at pleasure in the manner of a modern parlour gasalier. I have seen one or two cruisies made of brass, but the common material is thin iron. A specimen in the possession of the Rev. John M'Lean, Grandtully, Perthshire, has a hinged lid, made, like the cruisie, of thin iron ; and he informs me that such cruisies were common in the inland districts of the Scottish Highlands, where, when oil could not be got, tallow was used, and the lid served to support a piece of glowing peat, which melted the tallow, and kept it in the liquid condition necessary to render it a substitute for oil.

An inseparable adjunct to the cruisie was the tinder-box, made also of thin iron, usually in a circular form, four or five inches in diameter, and from an inch to an inch and a half in depth, and having a lid which fitted inside, and sank flat down on the tinder, so as to extinguish it when no longer required. The tinder was produced by burning cotton rags, and was ignited by means of a flint and a piece of steel formed somewhat like the letter U, inverted for use, called a 'flourish.' The flint required for this operation was sometimes difficult to procure, and in country districts at any rate was deliberately sought for in the fields. Many flint implements which had come down from the Stone Ages must have perished as strike-lights. Farm servants and country people knew where flints were to be found, certain fields yielding them more numerously than others. Old men have indicated such fields to me, where long ago they used to search for strike-lights, and diligent search in such fields has generally rewarded me with distinctly recognisable examples of flint implements, usually the form known as 'thumb-flints' or 'scrapers,' and flakes showing evidences of having been worked.

A. HUTCHESON.

XLV. GAELIC IN GALLOWAY.—The head-master of a Burgh School informs me that his grandmother told him that in her day Gaelic was commonly spoken in the Kells district. Sir John M'Kerlie writes that he heard from his father, that in *his* father's time it was spoken, especially in the Rhinns. The Rev. Thomas Innes wrote :—

' I have heard that some of the commonalty of that country in the remote creeks of it continue as yet to speak a particular

language different from the vulgar tongue of the Scots, but I
could get no certain information of it ' (*Critical Essay*, vol. i. p. 39).

Under these circumstances the instance quoted by G. H.
seems very probable ; but greater detail would be interesting.
Jurby (Man) about which Manx is still spoken, is not far from
Galloway.   W. M. C.

THE suggestion that one race was uppermost in Galloway
comes from Dr. Skene.

' During the latter years of Kenneth's reign, a people appear
in close association with the Norwegian pirates, and joining in
their plundering expeditions, who are termed Gallgaidhel.   The
name is formed by the combination of the two words "Gall,"
a stranger, a foreigner, and "Gaidhel," the national name of the
Gaelic race.   It was certainly first applied to the people of
Galloway, and the proper name of this province, Galweithia, is
formed from Galwyddel, the Welsh equivalent of Gallgaidhel.
It seems to have been applied to them as a Gaelic race *under
the rule of* Galle or foreigners ; Galloway being for centuries a
province of the Anglic kingdom of Northumbria, and the term
"Gall" having been applied to the Saxons before it was almost
exclusively appropriated to the Norwegian and Danish pirates.
Towards the end of the 8th century the power of the Angles seems
to have become weakened, and the native races began to assert
their independent action.'

This passage contains many assertions, and as they are un-
supported by references, one merely quotes it, reserving judgment
as to its accuracy.

Some think that the prefix Gall has nothing to do with Scan-
dinavians, but merely indicated that those who used the term were
speaking of another Gaelic people, who came from some
distance.

To the east of Loch Laggan, Inverness-shire, lies a village
called Gallovie, whose name may bear investigation.

The name Kennoway in Fife has been attributed to a Saint
Kenochi ; but in Tiree is another Kenovay.   It appears to stand
on the watershed of the island, and may be 'the head of the plain '
as has been suggested.

Quillaway (Menheniot) is noted in Bannister's Glossary of
Cornish names as requiring explanation.

                                                            W. M. C.

XLVIII. WHITHORN.—It was Sir H. Maxwell's book that revived my
    interest in Galloway Place-names, and one is grateful to any one
    who adds to our information on such points ; but they will bear
    any quantity of patient threshing out.

      Here is Ailred's account of what Ninian did :—

      ' Elegit autem sibi sedem in loco qui nunc Witerna dicitur ;
    qui locus super litus oceani situs, dum se ipsum mare longius
    porrigit ab oriente, occidente, atque meridie, ipso pelago clauditur
    a parte tantum aquilonali, via ingredi volentibus aperitur.'

Now a man's life written centuries afterwards may contain many errors; but can any one doubt that Ailred believed the *Isle* of Whithorn to have been Ninian's *locale*? We know how often saints did choose islands but had to vacate them. The only arguments I can find in favour of the *town* of Whithorn are that the chapel on the isle is not a fit commemoration of the saint, and that there is no trace of the translation of his relics. It appears, however, that the Irish life of Ninian does not make him die at Whithorn; and even if he did and was buried there, the sea-rovers may have caused a stampede, or may have disposed summarily of anything they found. The Angles may at first have held the isle, as we hold Gibraltar, without possessing the adjoining mainland.

Here is an extract from Bishop Forbes General Introduction :—

'Fergus founded several monasteries, chiefly of the " Candidus ordo," that of Premontré near Laon. Saulseat was the mother convent. From it came Holywood, Tungland and Whithorn.'

Is this the first monastery at Whithorn *town*? Rosnat certainly seems to suggest the seaboard.

When we have settled which place it is that we are trying to analyse we may proceed to details. Meanwhile, I am convinced that a word formerly written 'fut' and now sometimes pronounced 'hwutt' must *necessarily* be 'white,' nor do I see why a second *h* should be used in *writing* 'Whithorn.' The Lowlander does not often vary that letter, and the speaker of Celtic varies it according to rule. Time rather subtracts than adds consonants. The possible equivalence of *wh* and *f* I quite admit.

Speaking generally of Galloway Place-names, I submit that as the Picts are known to have held the country, we are bound to hear what Welsh, Breton, and Cornish can tell us, and cannot afford to confine ourselves to Gaelic and Gothic, the former probably, and the latter certainly, an immigrant tongue.

W. M. C.

LXI. Houston of that Ilk (p. 150).—A short article on this family is printed in the *Genealogist*, vol. v. (1881) p. 23.

'Thomas de Houston is pleased to accept from Louis XI. the seigneury of Torcy in Brie, in place of the châtellenie of Gournay, which he resigns' (*The Scot Abroad* (Burton), vol. i. p. 91).

Crawfurd, in his *History of Renfrewshire*, p. 100, gives the following inscription from the parish church of Houstoun, 'Here lyes Jhon of Houstoun, Lord of that Ilk, and Annes Campbell, his spouse, who died *anno* 1456.'

J. M'G.

LXIV. Rev. P. Murray.—Seek the Synod, Presbytery, and Session Clerk's Record of or embracing the Parish of Penpont. They may mention his native place. Also Hugh Scott's *Fasti Ecclesiæ Scoticanæ* and the references it gives. Failing these, the register of Edinburgh University, if positively known he was educated there, will state where he came from. The register of Sasines for Dumfriesshire, as he bought land in that county, and the register of marriages for Kirkcudbright might be of use.

Lex-a.

LXXII. RUSSELL.—There is no reason to attribute a Scotch origin to the Duke of Bedford. The Russells are essentially Anglo-Norman, but founded houses in Scotland and Ireland. The name frequently occurs in the *Calendar of Documents Relating to Scotland* (1108 to 1307), but only in one case can it be supposed to apply to a Scotchman. [Robert Russell of Berwickshire did homage in 1296, and he may have been an English settler.] A careful study of the arms of the different families of the name will throw light on the order of descent.

Your correspondent might also consult J. H. Wiffen's *Historical Memoirs of the House of Russell;* the article on 'Russell of Killough' in the second edition of Burke's *Landed Gentry*, vol. ii. p. 1161 ; and the *Scottish Nation*, s.v.   Σ.

LXXXI. MENSHEAVEN.—The cause of suit by Lord Lindsay of the Byres against the Hamiltons of the 'Peill of Levingston' will be found at page 345 of Pitcairn's *Criminal Trials*, vol. i. Three of the sons of James H. of L. destroyed the mill of Philpstoun, belonging to Lord Lindsay, on the 25th November 1594, and on the last day of that month set fire to the barn-yard of Duddingstone.

Σ.

NOTICES OF BOOKS.

The Scottish Jacobites and their Poetry, by Norval Clyne, for private circulation.—This little book, which has kindly been sent us, deserves more publicity than the author has seen fit to give it. Mr. Clyne shows himself a staunch Jacobite and a faithful Episcopalian ; but a Hanoverian and Presbyterian reader will none the less find the book full of interest. The selections from Jacobite poetry are judiciously made, and his remarks will cause this class of literature to be studied with a clearer perception, not only of the influence it once exercised, but of the interest which it will always possess.

An Account of the Church and Parish of St. Giles, Cripplegate, London, by John James Baddeley, Churchwarden. London, J. J. Baddeley.— This volume is written by a Churchwarden who takes more than a passing interest in the parish which has elected him to an office of dignity and responsibility. He, while attending to his present duties, finds a pleasure in studying the past, and not only so, but has given to the public the result of his labours ; and not thinking only of himself, his book is 'sold for the benefit of the Funds of the Metropolitan Dispensary.' We would ask Elders in Scotland to note all this. The Kirk Session Records are in their custody, their neighbours ready to learn the history of their parish, and charitable institutions would gladly profit by their labours. If a model is needed, Mr. Baddeley's book will supply one—*mutatis mutandis*—it is just what the history of a Scottish parish in town or country should be. Commencing with the earliest records available, an account is given of the name, the area, the local history, the founding of the Church, a list of the

Incumbents and Churchwardens. Extracts are supplied from the Registers of Baptisms, Marriages and Burials, and from the Churchwarders' accounts, nor is its present condition overlooked. The parishioners of St. Giles, Cripplegate, possess a good history of the place in which their interest centres. Many others, however, besides them, have to thank Mr. Baddeley for an admirable work.

England in the Fifteenth Century, by the Rev. W. Denton. London, George Bell & Sons.—This was the last work of a writer whose death is a sad loss. From the preface we learn that he was preparing a companion volume on the ecclesiastical state of England in the fifteenth century, which, most unfortunately, was only commenced when he was taken away. The volume he has left us is wholly taken up with the secular life of Englishmen at a period of great interest. The subject is admirably introduced in an Introduction of 65 pages, and nearly 200 pages are devoted to the manners and customs of the people of every rank ; full references are given to such authorities as are quoted, and these alone will assist the reader in enlarging his knowledge of the subject. The effect of the Scottish wars is not overlooked, and Mr. Denton's remarks on their influence on England are most valuable. The book is not a dry summary of facts, but a most fascinating description of life in the past. We can heartily recommend it.

Yorkshire Legends and Traditions, by the Rev. Thomas Parkinson, F.R. Hist. S. London, Elliot Stock.—Yorkshire, as a Northern County, is not without interest to Scotsmen, and Mr. Parkinson in collecting its legends, assists us in the study of our own. These traditions are classified, and the work forms a good model for a collection of Scottish Mediæval Legends. A chapter is devoted to Mother Shipton, who managed to gain wide notoriety. From it we learn that the earliest collection of her 'prophecies' extant was printed in 1641, or about 80 years after her death. In later editions many apocryphal sayings were added, and we are told that the most celebrated of those attributed to her was concocted as late as 1862. As it concludes with the couplet—

> ' The world to an end shall come
> In eighteen hundred and eighty one,'

we must attribute to the writer more facility of mystification than of vaticination.
Mr. Parkinson's book is one of much interest.

Records and Record Searching, by Walter Rye. London, Elliot Stock (204 pp.).—Most heartily do we welcome this exceedingly useful book, which commences with some plain directions to the Genealogist and Topographer, and then, in twelve chapters, describes the various sources from which information can be obtained. There are also seven appendices, and, we need hardly add, an excellent index.
A short Antiquarian Directory contains the names of 117 English periodicals devoted to Genealogy and Topography. Scotland follows with 7 ; but as Mr. Rye has by an oversight included *N. N. & Q., or The Scottish Antiquary* in his English list, the correct number is 8. We

trust that Scottish Archæologists will try and put the figures in a more satisfactory relative proportion to the national character for high culture and the growing taste for the study of all branches of Archæology. Mr. Rye says but little about Scottish Records; his English readers, if they visit Scotland, will find that our Parochial Registers are exceedingly interesting, and are full of valuable information, and, being all collected at the Register House, Edinburgh, they can be consulted with little trouble or expense.

Books received too late for review in present Number :—

William Shakespeare—a literary biography by Karl Elze, Ph.D., LL.D. London, George Bell.

History of Prose Fiction, by John Colin Dunlop. 2 vols. London, George Bell.

NOW COMPLETED—WITH INDEX

Vols. I. and II. (Combined)

of

𝕹𝖔𝖗𝖙𝖍𝖊𝖗𝖓 𝕹𝖔𝖙𝖊𝖘 and 𝕼𝖚𝖊𝖗𝖎𝖊𝖘

OR

The Scottish Antiquary

A Magazine of Archæology, Etymology, Folklore,
Genealogy, Heraldry, Popular Superstitions,
Customs, Proverbs, etc.

ESTABLISHED 1886 AS AN ORGAN FOR ALL SCOTTISH ANTIQUARIES.

*Published Quarterly ; now increased to 32 pages ; will again be
increased in size as soon as convenient.*

Price One Shilling, or 4s. per Annum.

DAVID DOUGLAS, EDINBURGH.

All communications to be sent to the Editor—

The Rev. A. W. Cornelius Hallen, M.A.,

F.S.A.Scot.,

Alloa,

who will also receive Subscribers' names.

Specimen Copy (back number) sent Post Free on receipt
of Six Stamps.

Part 11 (Vol. III.) will be issued December 1, 1888.

Northern Notes and Queries

OR

The Scottish Antiquary

CONTENTS.

NOTE.—*The Editor does not hold himself responsible for the opinions or statements of Contributors.*

148. THE 'RUNAWAY REGISTERS' AT HADDINGTON.—Gretna Green was not the only place where runaway couples from England were married during the last century. There was an Episcopal church at Haddington, which was convenient for such as came north *via* Newcastle and Berwick-on-Tweed, and it cannot be doubted that the services of a duly ordained clergymen of the Church were preferred by many to the rough-and-ready, though efficacious, offices of the blacksmith on the western end of the Borders. By the kindness of the Rev. T. N. Wannop, Incumbent of Holy Trinity Church, Haddington, I am able to give a transcript of the registers of these marriages, which are contained in three thin quarto volumes, which have been called, not unfitly, 'The Runaway Registers.'

VOL. I.

1762. Register of Marriages for the English Episcopal Chapel in
Hadington, N. Britain.

,,   Sep. 11.   George Birch, Esq., of Manchester, and Ann Dickenson, of Lancaster.

1763. March 21.   Thos. Septimius Dalby, Esq., and Hellen Compton, both of Hurst, Berks : [margin] married at Edinburgh.

,,   April 11.   Robt. Ellison of Staley, Dry-salter, & Ann Simondson of Stockport, Cheshire [margin] married at Edinburgh.

,,   ,, 24.   John Parker and Mary Cocke, both of Steeple-Bumstead, Essex.

,,   ,, 29.   John Wright & Mary Morrow, Chester-le-Street, Durham.

,,   Augt. 31.   Wm. How of Haughton & Jane Garthwaite of Bp. Auckland, Durham.

,,   Sep. 22.   Thos. Wragg, Esq., of St. James Par., Westminster, and Sarah Stainton, of the Burgh of Southwark* [*sic*]. An unhappy match for the poor man. [Margin] recd. a letter, signed Sarah Wragg, desiring certificate, dated London, Nov. 30 1765, which Mr. Buchanan refused.

,,   October 27.   Wm. Wynne, Esq., Par. of St. James, and Cassandra Rosina Frederic of St. Anne's, London.

,,   Novr. 7.   Richd. Lovell Edgeworth,[1] of the Middle Temple, Esq., & Anna Maria Eller of the Parish of Black Bourton, Oxford.

,,   ,, 15.   John Le Grand of the Par. of St. George, and Mary Anne Buckland of the Par. of St. Alphege, Canterbury.

,,   ,, 30.   George Farmer of Hougham & Eliz. Wade of Berkstone, Lincolnshire.

1764. March 28.   Viet Caleb Mitchell of the Par. of St. Christopher, Jeweller, and Frances Parry of the Par. of St. Peter, London.

,,   October 4.   Joseph Dowson, Par. of Morterham, Cheshire, and Mary Hanbey, Parish of Houghton Roberts, Yorkshire.

,,   ,, 8.   Thos. Pool & Mary Bradshaw, P. of Stillingfleet, Yorkshire.

[Foot of 1st page, signed] J. Buchanan, Minr.

1765. Feby. 3.   Thomas Basnet, Weaver, and Mary Shipton, widow, both of Darlington, Durham.

,,   April 13.   Dugald M'Duffie, Mercht. in Jamaica, & Janet Campbell, Argyleshire : [margin] married at Old Cambus, Berwickshire.

,,   ,, 18.   Wm. Tompson, Esq., Par. of Belgrave, & Hannah Sophia Arnold, Par. of St. Mary, Burgh of Leicester, both in the County of Leicester : [margin] married at Old Cambus . . .

,,   May 12.   Chas. Wright, A.B., St. John's, Cambridge, & Susan Holden, Greenwiche.

,,   ,, 14.   Mark Whitehead, Sailor, & Kath. Nesbitt, both of South Shields, Durham.

[1] The father of Miss Edgeworth the novelist.

1764 May 21. Ralphe Walker of Durham, & Eliz. Robson of Haughton-le-Spring.

,,   ,, 27. John Harris, Attorney at Law, of St. Andrew, Holborn, & Hannah Auberry Hill, of St. Giles in the Fields, both of London.

,,   ,, 29. Thos. Mullcaster, Par. of St. James, & Mary Woollaston, Par. of Marlebone, London.

,,   June 9. Chr. Gowland of Carleton, Surgeon, & Hellen Lang of York, both of Yorkshire.

,,   ,, 10. Jas. Mewburn, Par. of Ormsby, & Christina Ann Harrison, Par. of Upleatham, Yorkshire.

,,   July 2. Daniel Young, Surgeon, & Eleanor Lockhart, both of Berwick.

,,   ,, 12. Jerom Rudd,[1] Surgeon, & Hannah Allen, both of Darlington, Durham.

,,   ,, 14. Thos. Greenwood, Farmer, Par. of Bream, & Mary Salton of Bleadon, Somersetshire.

,,   ,, 19. Dan. Dyson, Mercht. in Hallifax, & Sarah Edwards of Northowram, Yorkshire.

,,   ,, 27. John Baptiste Darwen of St. Mildred's, London, and Sarah Petty of Rotherithe.

,,   Augt. 1. Thos. Killworth, Draper in Lutterworth, & Mary Bradley of N. Killworth.

,,   Sep. 4. John Manners, Esq., & The Rt. Honble. Lady Louisa Tollemache,[2] both of St. James Par., Westminster : [margin] married at Old Cambus.

,,   ,, 8. The Honble. Ld. Charles Greville Montague,[3] of the Parish of Kimbolton, and Eliz. Ballmere, Par. of All Saints, Huntingdon.

,,   ,, 14. John Warner Phipps, Esq., & Mary Frances Gray, St. Mary, Whitechapel, London.

,,   ,, 15. Thos. Dalby of Castle Donnington, & Ann Kirkland of Ashby de la Zouche, Leicester.

[Bottom of second page] That the Parties mentioned above, and on the former Leaf, were married according to the Rites & Ceremonies of the Church of England, is attested by   J. BUCHANAN, Minr.

[The entries are now made at the other end of the volume, and are of greater length ; the first is given *literatim et verbatim*, after which I shall only give an abstract of each entry, which however, will contain all names and designations. They are also numbered from 1 onwards.—ED.]

[On inside of Cover] Charles Horde, Esq., at Swell, near Stow on the Wold, Gloucestershire. [See marriage No. 33.]

1. Joseph Aremathea Cooper of the Parish of Tetbury in the County of Glocester, Gent., and Mary Harvey of the Parish of Cooling & County of Kent, Spinster, were married at Hadingtoun, East Lothian, N. Britaine, according to the Form of Matrimony

---

[1] In the privately printed pedigree of the Allans of Blackwell Grange the date of this marriage is given July 20, 1765.

[2] In 1821 she succeeded as Countess of Dysart.

[3] The date of this marriage in Burke's *Peerage* (D. Manchester) is September 20, 1765.

prescribed & used by the Church of England, on this seventeenth Day of September, in the year one Thousand seven hundred & sixty five by

J. BUCHANAN, Minr.

In the Presence of

Sam. Clay Harvey, ⎰ This Marriage was ⎱ Jos. Acœrin [*sic*] Cooper.
Barthw. Bower, ⎱ solemnized be- ⎰ Mary Harvey.
                tween us

2. 1765. Sep. 20. Sir Walter Abington Compton, Bart., of Hartbury, Co. Gloucester, and Anne Sarah Bennet Mosley of Chipping Campden, Co. Gloucester. *W.* W. Mosley, Wm. J. Mosley.

3. ,,   ,,   21. Stephen Bagshaw of St. Nicholas, Deptford, Co. Kent, Merchant, and Sarah Hales of St. Ann, Limehouse, Co. of Middlesex, Spinster. *W.* Ann Neill, James Fairbairn.

4. ,,   ,,   27. William Hake of Honiton, Co. Devon, and Mary Hendry of Lynn Regis, Co. Norfolk. *W.* Barbara Cooper, Barthw. Bower.

5. ,,   ,,   30. William Tateham of Stockton, Merchant, and Jane Chrisop of the same Parish, Spinster. *W.* Alice Tatham, Barthw. Bower.

6. ,,   Oct.   4. The Rt. Honble. The Earl of Effingham, of Rother-am, Co. York, and Katharine Proctor of Bothwell, Co. York, Spinister. *W.* Rose Bottiglion, Barthw. Bower.

7. ,,   ,,   5. Thos. Smart of Whickham, Co. Durham, Gent., and Margaret Carr of St. Oswald, city of Durham. *W.* Margaret Mason, Barthw. Bower.

8. ,,   ,,   25. James Petty of St. Luke's, Chelsea, Co. Middlesex, and Diana Amelia Sabine of Tewin, Co. Hertford. *W.* C. Sheffield, Barthw. Bower.

9. ,,   Nov.   6. Thomas Croft, Farmer, and Elizabeth White, Spinster, both of Sedgefield, Co. Durham. *W.* Barthw. Bower, John Foster.

10. ,,   Dec.   14. Evan Price of St. James, Bristol, Sugar Refiner, and Joanna Nicholas of the same Parish, Spinster. *W.* John Herbert, Jr., Hester Rice.

11. ,,   ,,   16. Thomas Richardson, Livery Stable Keeper, of St. Mary le Bow, and Hannah Johnson, Spinster, of St. Andrews, Holborn, both of the city of London, married at Edinburgh. *W.* John Nelson, Barthw. Bower.

12. ,,   ,,   24. William Lumley of East Wilton, Co. York, Farmer, and Ann Purchas of Middleham, Co. York, Spinster. *W.* Robert Keith, Ann Henderson.

13. 1766. Jan.   3. John Kentish of St. Michael's, Cornhill, London, Jeweller, and Mary Hiscox of the same Parish, Spinster. *W.* Wm. Bower, Barthw. Bower.

14. ,,   ,,   19. Patrick Ogilvie of Dundee, last from Newcastle, Ship-master, and Ann Burn of St. George's in the East, London, Spinster. *W.* Ka. Raitt, Barthw. Bower.

15. 1766 Feb. 8. John Green of St. Bartholomew the Great, London, Mercht., and Elizabeth Smith of St. James, Westminster, Spinster. *W.* James Fairbairn, Barthw. Bower.

16. „ „ 16. Hugh Alexander Kennedy of St. Anne's, Westminster, Doctor of Physic, and Devereux Chamberlain of the same Parish, Spinster. *W.* Wm. Garner, Barthw. Bower.

17. „ March 31. James Moore of St. Nicholas, Newcastle upon Tyne, Mercht., and Mary Adamson of the same Parish, Spinster. *W.* Helen Anderson, Barthw. Bower.

18. „ May 16. John Perier of St. Andrew, Holbourn, Gent., and Hannah Harrison of St. Ann, Soho, both of London, Spinster. *W.* James Wheeley, Barthw. Bower.

19. „ „ 27. William Menzies of Ancraft, Co. Durham, and Ann Crowther of Lowich, Co. Durham. *W.* Selby Crowther, Barthw. Bower.

20. „ June 28. Francis Chalie of St. Dunstan's in the East, Co. Middlesex, Wine Merchant, and Priscilla Bridges of Newchurch Parish, in the Strand, Co. Middlesex, Spinster. *W.* Wm. Garner, Barthw. Bower.

21. „ July 7. John Dewar, Esq., Ensign in the First Regimt. of Foot Guards, and Caroline Vernon of St. Clement Danes, Spinster, both of Co. Middlesex. *W.* John Hurst, Barthw. Bower.

22. „ „ 23. John Hall of Branspeth, Co. Durham, Mercht., and Alice Bedford of the city of Durham and Parish of Elvet, Spinster. *W.* Wm. Gurner, Barthw. Bower.

23. „ Aug. 17. John Redhead of St. Nicholas, city of Durham, Grocer, and Isabella Aisley of same Parish, Spinster. *W.* Wm. Garner, John Dunlop.

24. „ „ 25. John Cole, Gent., and Sarah Salkeld, Spinster, both of Chester le Street, Co. Durham. *W.* James Fairbairn, Barthw. Bower.

25. „ Oct. 2. William Humphrey of Titchfield, Co. Southampton, Gent., and Mary Drake of Hound, Co. Southampton, Spinster. *W.* Wm. Garner, Barthw. Bower.

26. „ „ 6. Charles Western, Esq., and Frances Shirley Bottan, both of Rivenhall, Co. Essex. *W.* Barthw. Bower, David Mayne.

(*To be continued.*)

149. GENEALOGY A SCIENCE.—The following extract from the *Athenæum* is worth a place in *N. N. & Q.*—ED. :—

Family history is a subject of surpassing interest. Now that men have come to know that Genealogy is a branch of Science, which, if rationally pursued, will be productive of important knowledge, it is ceasing to be degraded by being a mere slave to those who possess rank and title.

The American Antiquaries have taught us that the story of a peasant race may be as fraught with human interest as the chronicles of the Nevilles or the De Courcis. *Athenæum, Sept.* 29, 1888.

150. Sculptured Stones at Dundee.—Recent alterations and improvements on the Street Architecture of Dundee have caused the removal of many of the older buildings which have been associated with the civic life of the burgh for centuries. Upon several of the buildings, which have been thus removed, there were sculptured coats of arms, merchants' marks, initials, and dates, most of which belonged to the sixteenth century. A few of these were preserved during the later demolitions, and they have been placed, most appropriately, in a chamber in the old steeple of Dundee, where they will be preserved for the inspection of future generations. The room where they are now kept also contains several pieces of antique sepulchral sculpture of a much earlier date, regarding which little has been written. The illustrations which we give afford some idea of the class of antiquities thus preserved, and may serve to direct the attention of antiquaries towards them.

1. The oldest of the five stones figured in the plate is delineated in Dr. Stewart's *Sculptured Stones of Scotland*, though not so accurately as one might have wished. It forms the cover of a stone coffin, also preserved, which was found when excavations were being made for the foundation of the new churches that were erected in Dundee after the disastrous fire in 1841. The carving is in high relief, and in a fair state of preservation. The appearance of the floriated and inscribed cross proves that it belongs to the Early Christian Period. The lower portion is filled with sculpture representing a ship with an animal—apparently a bear—climbing up the rigging. At the stern of the boat a hand in the attitude of benediction is shown, and above the panel another hand is shown drawing a sword. No satisfactory explanation of the symbolism of this momunent has been given.

2. The next stone in point of age shown in our illustration also forms the cover of a stone coffin, the carving of which has been very elaborate. The incised cross-hilted sword with which it is decorated makes it probable that the coffin had been occupied by a Knight-Templar, though his name and date cannot now be traced. The Templars had extensive possessions both in the burgh of Dundee and the surrounding country, and there are still preserved amongst the Town's charters records of sasines given by the Preceptor of St. John of Jerusalem towards the close of the sixteenth century.

3. The very beautiful sculpture of the arms of Charles II. with the date 1660 are notable as showing the Tudor badge as well as the emblems and arms of Scotland, England, Ireland, and France. This panel formerly decorated the street front of a building in the Nethergate of Dundee where was the entrance to a passage called Whitehall Close. As the building was erected *circa* 1750, the panel must have been removed from some previous structure, although it is difficult to tell where its original position was. Many doubtful stories regarding Whitehall Close are still in existence. It is asserted that the dwelling of the royal family of Scotland in Dundee stood within this Close, and that it obtained its name of Whitehall Close immediately after the Restoration. We have found no evidence whatever upon which to found such a statement. In early times the Kings who visited Dundee resided at the Monastery of the Franciscans, or with some wealthy citizen, and we can find no trace of any royal residence in Dundee after the destruction of the castle. It is true that there were some ancient vaulted chambers under one of the houses in Whitehall Close, and also that several of the houses in the close had sculptured

(150. SCULPTURED STONES—)

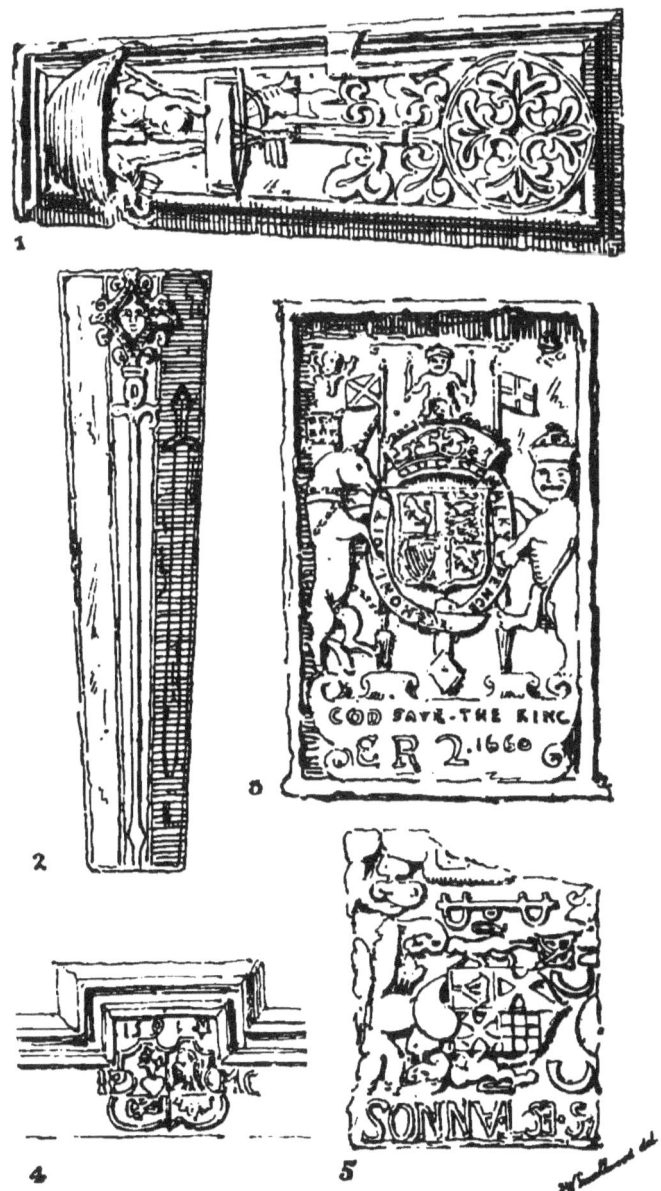

fragments built into them bearing the royal arms accompanied by sententious injunctions to loyalty, but the existence of these does not necessarily imply that there ever was a royal palace there. The name of Whitehall Close is quite a modern invention. In 1560 the passage was called 'Spenss' Close,' and in 1727 it was described as 'David Jobsons' Close,' from the name of a wealthy brewer who occupied a large portion of it. It does not appear to have obtained the name of Whitehall Close before the end of last century. The original site of this carved panel is merely a matter of conjecture, and the following theory is put forth simply as a suggestion :—

One of the most extensive dwelling-houses in Whitehall Close was the property of James Lyon, baker, a scion of the Strathmore family. His son, Sir Patrick Lyon of Carse, an eminent judge previous to the Revolution of 1688, was a most pronounced Royalist, and was deprived of his office in consequence. He is known to antiquaries as the author of a collection of genealogical manuscripts now in the Advocates' Library, Edinburgh, and is often quoted as an authority upon heraldry. Who then would be more likely than Sir Patrick to testify his loyalty and to commemorate the Restoration by erecting such a panel as this? It is not improbable that the panel was removed from Sir Patrick's house, which had become ruinous, and was inserted over the entrance of the Close where it had stood.

4. Another of the stones in our illustration is interesting as giving both the family arms and the merchant's mark of a Dundee burgess. It appears to have been the lintel of a mantel-piece, and bears the initals J. P. = James Pierson, and M. C. = Margaret Carnegy, with the arms of the two families marshalled, with the date 1591. James Pierson was a merchant, and was entered on the Roll of Burgesses of Dundee on 7th February 1570, claiming his privilege through his father Walter Pierson, *institor*, who was enrolled in 1541.

5. The last of the stones shown in our picture is a fragment of the tombstone that was erected in the Church of Dundee as a memorial of Magister Colin Campbell who was minister there from 1617 till his death in 1638. He was born in 1577 and took his degree at St. Andrews University when in his twentieth year. In 1604 he was ordained as minister of Kettins in the Presbytery of Meigle and was translated to the third charge in Dundee in 1617. Though at first one of the Protestors against Episcopacy, he latterly became an ardent supporter of the king in his attempts to impose that form of Church government upon Scotland. His services were highly appreciated in Dundee, and are repeatedly recognised in the Council Minutes of the Burgh. He died on 13th June 1638, and was buried in the South Church. The tombstone which marked his resting-place was excavated from the ruins after the fire of 1841. He was married to Margaret Hay and three of his sons were engaged in the ministry, James Campbell being minister of St. Madoes, David, of Menmuir, and John, of Tealing.

To some of the other interesting sculptured fragments preserved in the Museum room of the old steeple of Dundee we may refer at some future time.   A. H. MILLAR.

151. ULSTER KING OF ARMS AND THE LAIRDS OF WESTQUARTER.[1]—
I. *The Ogleface Baronetcy* [?].—During my researches into the history of
the ancient and once powerful Scottish house of Livingston, I have had
occasion to refer to the pedigree of the late Sir Thomas Livingstone[2] of
Westquarter and Bedlormie, by whose death in 1853 the male line of
the Lords Livingston of Callendar, Earls of Linlithgow, etc. etc., has
apparently become extinct in Scotland ; and for some time past I have
been much puzzled over the 'Lineage' of the late baronet as given by
Ulster in his popular *Landed Gentry* and other genealogical works.[3] For,
not only does he give a generation too many in Sir Thomas's undoubted
line of descent from Sir George Livingstone of Ogilface or Ogleface, the
fourth son of William, sixth Lord Livingston, but he also distinctly asserts
that this same Sir George 'was created a baronet of Nova Scotia, 30th
May 1625,' when, as a matter of fact, I contend that not only had Sir
George died before the above date, but, moreover, that no such baronetcy
has ever existed.[4] Hence the long line of baronets—ten in all—that
figures in Sir Bernard Burke's pages is purely mythical ! The strangest
circumstance, however, in connection with his account of this family is,
that though there was never any Ogleface creation, yet some years later,
in 1699, a baronetcy was conferred by William the Third on a Sir James
Livingstone *of Westquarter*, from whom the late Sir Thomas was *not*
directly descended, and, moreover, owing to the unusual wording of this
patent it is open to doubt whether collateral heirs could inherit. This
latter and authentic baronetcy is not referred to by Sir Bernard Burke !
It is therefore my intention to endeavour to prove here, in the first place,
the non-existence of the Ogleface baronetcy and the true lineage of the
Livingstones of Ogleface, Bedlormie, and Westquarter ; and, secondly, to
give what I consider to be the real history of the Westquarter estates and
title, as Ulster only vaguely alludes to the fact of these estates having
passed from their former possessors—the Livingstones of Westquarter—into
the ownership of the Ogleface or Bedlormie branch of the same family.

That Sir George Livingstone of Ogleface was never created a baronet
of Nova Scotia can be demonstrated from the following facts :—

I. No such patent is to be found in H. M. General Register House,
Edinburgh, or elsewhere, that I know of, nor is his name entered in any
authentic list of Nova Scotia baronets that I have come across in the
course of my researches into my family history now extending over a period
of ten years and more.

---

[1] Vide *Vicissitudes of Families* (remodelled edition), by Sir Bernard Burke, C.B.,
LL.D., Ulster King of Arms, vol. ii. pp. 219-239.

[2] The later generations of Bedlormie and Westquarter usually spelt their patronymic
with the final *e*, hence I have followed their example in the above article as far as
regards the members of their particular branch of the Livingston family.

[3] For the purpose of this article I am quoting from the edition of *The Landed Gentry*
published in 1868, the only copy by me, but on an examination of the last edition issued
in 1886 I find the portion of the 'Lineage' treated of above is identical in both issues.

[4] On the *above-mentioned date* a baronetcy of Nova Scotia was conferred on a David
Livingston of Dunipace, but he was quite a different person altogether from his kinsman
Sir George Livingstone of Ogleface, and from this David the late Sir Thomas was in no
way descended. David Livingston's grant is entered in the Great Seal Register on that
date—30th May 1625. *Registrum Magni Sigilli*, Liber li, No. 54. See also *Regist.
Precep. Cart. pro Baronettis Nov. Scotiæ* MS., fol. 19. The *only other* Livingston
Baronetcy granted about this period was the one conferred on John Livingston of
Kinnaird, 25th June 1627. This gentleman was ancestor of the Earls of Newburgh, now
represented in the female line by Prince Giustiniani Bandini.

II. That a baronetcy of Nova Scotia was granted *on the date given by Burke* to David Livingston of Dunipace. (See *ante.*)

III. That in no *original documents* in which his name occurs, either during his lifetime or after his decease, is he thus designated. For example, in documents prior to August 1594, in which month he was *knighted,* as will be shown later on, he appears simply as 'George Levingstoun of Ogilface,' while after that date he is designated 'Sir George Levingstoun of Ogilface, *knight';* and a curious circumstance in connection with this apocryphal baronetcy is that Ulster himself gives a copy of a formal deed or attestation drawn up in 1676 to prove, to quote his own words, 'the exact degree of relationship betwixt the ennobled families of Linlithgow and Callendar and the Ogleface or Westquarter branch [which] appears to have formed the subject of some legal inquiry, and immediately formal declarations and attestations under the hands and seals of both earls are prepared, and are afterwards recorded in the Register of Probate Writs. That by the Earl of Callendar is as follows :—"Wee Alexander Earl of Callendar Lord Livingstone and Almond &c. Doth hereby testify and declare that Sir Alexander Livingstone, *Knight,*[1] now of Craigengall, is lawful son and air to umquhile William Livingstone of Craigengall, who was lawful son and air to umquhile Sir George Livingstone of Ogleface, *Knight,*[1] the which Sir George Livingstone was next brother german to umquhile Alexander Earl of Linlithgow, our grandfather. Written by William Duncane, our servant; given under our hand at Callendar, this twenty-ane day of October, 1676 zeiris, Before thir witnesses Normand Livingston of Milnhill, and William Duncane above written." The attestation by the Earl of Linlithgow is precisely in the same terms, and is dated from the Castle of Midhope, this 20th September 1676.'[2] And yet, in the face of this document, which is perfectly correct in all its particulars, he must introduce *another* Alexander between the above Alexander of Craigengall (afterwards of Bedlormie) and his father William Livingstone of Craigengall, and, moreover, style them all baronets !

IV. That Sir George Livingstone of Ogleface died prior to the creation of the order of Nova Scotia Baronets is proved from a document in the possession of Mr. Fenton-Livingstone, the great-nephew of the late Sir Thomas Livingstone, and the present owner of the Westquarter estates. This document, which bears date 6th December 1616, is a 'Bond by John Bellenden, brother-german to the late Sir James Bellenden of Broughton, to William Livingstone, lawful son of *umquhile* George Livingstone of Ogilface,' etc., etc.[3] As, owing to the wide circulation of Sir Bernard

---

[1] The italics are my own.

[2] Vide *The Vicissitudes of Families,* vol. ii. p. 225.

[3] Westquarter MSS. reported on by Sir William Fraser in the *Seventh Report, Historical Manuscripts Commission,* Appendix, pp. 732 *et seq.,* Deed No. 13.

[*N.B.*—I may as well remark here that just as I had completed the above article, my contention as to the non-existence of an Ogleface baronetcy of 1625 received satisfactory confirmation from quite an unexpected quarter. For on my attention being called by a Scottish antiquarian friend to a volume catalogued in a second-hand bookseller's list as relating to the 'Calander Peerage Case,' I bought this book, and found it to be a very scarce privately printed copy of the 'Abstract of the Written Evidence to be laid before the Inquest for proving Sir Thomas Livingstone, of Ogilface and Bedlormie, Baronet, nearest and lawful Heir-Male in General of James, First Earl of Calander [Callendar], Lord Livingstone of Almond, who lived and died in the seventeenth century,' in which volume—printed in 1821—*no mention is made of Burke's creation of* 1625, the only reference in its pages to any baronetcy being to that of *Westquarter,* granted in 1699, of which more anon.]

Burke's justly popular publications, the lineage of this branch of the Livingston family has been largely copied from by the authors of other kindred works, I consider it may be advisable to preserve in the pages of *Northern Notes and Queries* what appears to me to be the correct pedigree of the late Sir Thomas Livingstone of Westquarter and Bedlormie, whose undoubted descent from a once illustrious, though unfortunate, house needs no embellishment by the insertion of a fictitious baronetcy. For the sake of comparison a copy of that portion of the *Landed Gentry* lineage containing the descent of Sir Thomas from Sir George Livingstone of Ogleface is printed in parallel columns.

Landed Gentry
LINEAGE.

LINEAGE
as
reconstructed,
with proofs.

WILLIAM,
SIXTH LORD LIVINGSTON.

I. The Hon. George Livingstone of Ogleface, co. Linlithgow, was created a baronet of Nova Scotia, 30th May 1625, and was succeeded by his eldest son,

NOTE.

It is highly probable that Sir Bernard Burke may have got his idea of an Ogleface baronetcy from Playfair's *British Family Antiquity,* for in the account of Sir Thomas's ancestors contained in volume viii.—*The Baronetage of Scotland*—of this ponderous work, the creations are given as follows:—
' *Creations,*—of Ogleface in 1625, and Westquarter in 1699.' To the *latter creation* is appended a note to the effect that ' Sir Thomas is heir and representative of this branch of the family.' The above volume of Playfair's work was published in 1811. It is a curious fact, however, that this writer does not make any other reference to this creation in his account of this family. What makes me think Burke followed Playfair is that the former *also* gives an Alexander too many, but it was apparently left to the latter to fill in the full date of the Ogleface creation, and hence, finding the Dunipace baronetcy the only Livingston patent registered under that year, it appears to have been made to do for Ogleface !

II. Sir William, who was succeeded by his son,

I. George Livingstone of Ogilface or Ogleface was the fourth son (the second that left issue) of the above William, sixth Lord Livingston. On the 19th April 1588 a charter under the Great Seal was granted to ' Willielmo Domino Levingstoun &c &c ac Georgio Levingstoun suo filio legitimo &c &c de totis et integris terris de Ogilface &c &c.'[1]
This George was knighted by King James VI. at the baptism of his eldest son, Prince Henry, in August 1594.[2] He married Margaret Crichtoun previous to 20th June 1597, on which date he assigned to her as a liferent provision after his decease the lands of Woodquarter of Ogilface, etc.[3] He became one of the adventurers for the plantation of forfeited estates in Ulster, and was enrolled on the 25th July 1609 for 2000 acres.[4] He died prior to December 1616,[5] and was succeeded by his son and heir,

II. William Livingstone, of Craigengall, Linlithgowshire, and Shancrekan in Ireland.[6] He married Margaret

[1] *Registrum Magni Sigilli,* Liber xxxvi. No. 507.
[2] *Tracts Illustrative of Scotch History,* p. 486.
[3] *Westquarter MSS.* (*Seventh Report, Hist. MSS. Commission*), No. 8. Playfair says this lady was a ' daughter of the Hon. William Crighton, son of Lord Viscount Frendraught.'
[4] *Register of the Privy Council of Scotland,* vol. viii. p. 330.
[5] See *ante* for proof of this statement. Burke says in his *Vicissitudes of Families,* vol. ii. p. 223, that he died ' prior to June 1628.'
[6] ' Willielmus Levingstoun, hæres Domini Georgii Levingstoun de Ogilface militis, patris,' according to a retour dated 21st January 1636 (*Inquis. Generales,* 2197). He is designated ' of Craigengall ' in the ' Attestation of 1676 ' (see *ante*), also in sasine quoted from below, etc. etc. ; and of ' Shancrekan,' in a pass or safe-conduct, dated 3d August 1616 (vide *Westquarter MSS.* No. 12).

III. Sir Alexander, who was succeeded by his only son,

NOTE.
This is the Alexander too many mentioned above.

IV. Sir Alexander, designated of Bedlormie, who married Susannah Walker, heiress of Bedlornie, and was succeeded by his only son,

V. Sir Alexander. This gentleman married Henrietta, daughter of Alexander Scott, Esq., by whom he had seven sons and three daughters, and was succeeded by his eldest son,

VI. Sir George, at whose decease without issue in 1729 the baronetcy devolved upon his brother,

Stewart,[1] and was succeeded by his eldest son,

III. Sir Alexander Livingstone of Craigengall, who acquired the lands of Bedlormie in the same county through his marriage to Susanna Walker, sole heiress of Patrick Walker of Bedlormie.[2] Sir Alexander died in May 1690,[3] and was succeeded by his eldest son,

IV. Alexander Livingstone of Craigengall and Bedlormie. He married Henrietta Scott, 'daughter of the late Alexander Scott, goldsmith, burgess of Edinburgh,' in 1683,[4] and died on the 13th of November 1720,[5] when he was succeeded by his eldest son,[6]

V. George Livingstone of Craigengall and Bedlormie, who was retoured heir to his father on the 27th February 1722.[7] He married in same year 'Francisca Kerr, lawful daughter of the deceased John Kerr, brother-german of the late Robert, Marquess of Lothian;'[8] and died, without leaving issue, prior to the 13th of November 1729,[9] when he was succeeded by his next younger brother under the entail of 1702, namely,

[1] A sasine proceeding on a charter of sale by James, Lord Livingston of Almond and Callendar, was granted in favour of ' William Livingston of Craigengall and Margaret Stewart his spouse, and Alexander Livingston, their son, and his heirs-male in fee, of an annual rent of 160 merks furth of the lands of Scheirhill, in the barony of Callendar,' and registered on the 24th November 1637 (*General Register of Sasines*, vol. 45, fol. 508).

[2] *Vide* sasine on charter of alienation granted by Patrick Walker of Bedlormie, heritable proprietor thereof, to 'Alexander Livingston, eldest son of William Livingston of Craigengall, and Susanna Walker, his affianced spouse,' in conjunct fee, and to their heirs, of the lands of Bedlormie, reserving to said Patrick Walker his liferent thereof. Charter is dated at Pinkie, 26th March 1645, and sasine given on 2d April, registered 19th April 1645 (*General Register of Sasines*, vol. 54, fol. 540). The contract of marriage, dated 14th March 1645, is still preserved at Westquarter (*Westquarter MSS.*, No. 17).

[3] *Commissariot of Edinburgh, Testaments*, 20th February 1696.

[4] *Vide* charter by Charles II. to Alexander Livingstone, eldest son and apparent heir of Sir Alexander Livingstone of Craigengall, etc., dated at Windsor Castle, 11th May 1683 (*Registrum Magni Sigilli*, Liber lxix. No. 76).

[5] *Commissariot of Edinburgh, Testaments*, 14th June 1721.

[6] On the 17th December 1702, the above Alexander Livingstone executed a deed of entail of his estates in favour of his eldest son, George, and the heirs-male of his body, whom failing, they were to go to the other sons in the order of birth, viz. Alexander; James (of whom more anon, as he was the first of the Ogleface or Bedlormie Livingstones to possess the Westquarter estates); William (the second of his family to own Westquarter); Thomas, and their respective heirs-male; whom failing, to the other heirs-male of the body of the said Alexander Livingstone, etc. etc. (*Registrum Magni Sigilli*, Liber xc. No. 64). Besides the sons mentioned by name in the above entail he had two others, Robert and Michael, probably born after the execution of this deed. Robert's eldest son ultimately succeeded all the persons mentioned above. There were also *four* daughters, not three as mentioned by Burke.

[7] Retour of service registered under date 26th April 1722.

[8] *Vide* marriage contract, dated 21st April 1722 (*Registrum Magni Sigilli*, Liber xc. No. 64).

[9] *Services of Heirs*, H. M. General Register House, Edinburgh. Recorded 25th November 1729.

VII. Sir Alexander, who died unmarried in 1766, and was succeeded by his brother,

VIII. Sir William, designated of Westquarter and Bedlormie. This gentleman, dying without issue in 1769, was succeeded by his nephew,

IX. Sir Alexander, of Westquarter and Bedlormie, who married Anne, daughter of John Atkinson, Esq., of London, by whom he had seven sons and one daughter, viz. :—

    I. Alexander Small, *d.* unmarried.
    II. William, *d.* unmarried.
    III. Thomas, his heir.
    IV. John Robert, *d.* unmarried.
    V. Thurstanus, *d.* without legitimate issue in 1839.
    VI. James, *d.* an infant.
    VII. George Augustus, killed in battle.

    I. Anne, who married the Rev. John Thomas Fenton, Rector of Ousby and Torpenhow, Cumberland, and had issue—

      1. John Thomas Fenton.
      2. Alexander Fenton.
      3. Robert Fenton.

VI. Alexander Livingstone, designated 'surgeon in Dalkeith' in his retour of service of above date.[1] The date of his death is probably as stated by Burke,[2] and, being unmarried, he was succeeded by his next surviving brother,[3]

VII. Captain William Livingstone (of whom more anon), the successful claimant to the Westquarter estates in the action 'Livingstone *v.* Lord Napier,' finally decided in the plaintiff's favour by the House of Lords in 1765.[4] He married Helen ——,[5] and died at Bedlormie on the 22d February 1769.[6] By the above lady he had no issue, and was thus succeeded by his nephew,

VIII. Alexander Livingstone,[7] who was, on the 18th August 1769, retoured heir to the estate of Bedlormie as the nearest male representative of his uncle George, under the entail of 1702 ;[8] and on the 1st January following was also served heir to the Westquarter estates as 'Heir-Male of Tailzie and Provision-General' to his uncle, Captain William Livingstone of Westquarter,[9] to which he was granted seisin six weeks later.[10] Between the years 1775 and 1778—as will be referred to again under the second portion of this article—he assumed the baronetcy of Westquarter, which had apparently been unclaimed since the death of Sir James Livingstone, of the original male line of Culter and Westquarter, the first baronet, in 1701. Thus this Alexander was the *first* of the Bedlormie branch of whom any authentic proof can be found in con-

[1] *Services of Heirs*, H. M. General Register House, Edinburgh. Recorded 25th November 1729.

[2] I cannot find any original evidence to prove the correctness of this date, but Burke has evidently copied it from Playfair's *Baronetage of Scotland*, p. 16.

[3] James Livingstone of Westquarter, the *next younger* brother, had died previous to 1745 ; Playfair says in 1743. I cannot, however, find any record among the *Services of Heirs* of this William's succession to the Bedlormie estates, though the fact of his possessing these as well as Westquarter previous to his death in 1769 is undoubted.

[4] *House of Lords Journals*, 11th March 1765, Appeals 88.

[5] I have been unable to ascertain this lady's maiden name.

[6] *Commissariot of Edinburgh*, *Testaments*, 28th March 1769.

[7] He was the eldest son of Robert Livingstone, sixth son of Alexander Livingston of Bedlormie (*see* No. IV. in my list). Robert's wife was a Miss Baillie of Polkemmet.

[8] *Services of Heirs*. Registered on 29th November 1769.

[9] *Services of Heirs*. Registered on 24th of same month. In this retour he is described as ' being the son of Robert Livingstone.'

[10] Dated in Register of Stirlingshire Sasines, 14th February 1700.

4. George Livingstone Fenton, in holy orders, Chaplain of Poona, Bombay.

　1. Anne, married William Henry Clarke, Esq., of Hexham House, Northumberland, and has two sons, Clement Henry and Livingstone.

　2. Caroline, married to her cousin Robert Fenton, Esq.

　3. Mary.

The eldest son, John Thomas Fenton, Esq., married Selina Heathcote, and has an only son, the present Thomas Livingstone Fenton Livingstone, Esq. of Westquarter.

Sir Alexander, married, secondly, Jane, daughter of the Hon. Captain Cranston, son of Lord Cranston, by whom he had two sons and a daughter—

　Francis, an officer in the army, *d.s.p.*

　David, killed in battle, *s.p.*

　Eliza, married to J. Kirksopp, Esq. of Spital.

Sir Alexander died in 1795, and was succeeded by the third but eldest surviving son of his first marriage.[3]

nection with the title of baronet.[1] He married twice, as stated correctly by Burke,[2] and died in 1795,[3] when he was succeeded by the third son of his first marriage,

X. Sir Thomas, Admiral of the White, married, in 1809, Janet, only surviving daughter of the late Sir James Stirling, Bart., of Mansfield, by whom (who died in 1831) he had no issue. Sir Thomas died 1st April 1853, and was succeeded at West-quarter, under a deed which he executed, by his great-nephew, the present Thomas Livingstone Fenton Living-stone, Esq. of Westquarter.

IX. Sir Thomas Livingstone of Westquarter and Bedlormie, by whose death, on the 1st of April 1853, the male line of the Ogleface Livingstones became extinct.

II. *The Westquarter Estate and Baronetcy.*—The original male line of Westquarter is said to have been descended from Robert, a younger son of the Sir John Livingston of Callendar who fell at the battle of Homildon Hill in 1402. I have, however, not been able to ascertain the correctness of this statement, but this is not of much importance, as, for the purpose of this article, we need not go further back

---

[1] For example, in the Registers of Sasines, quoted from above, his designation from 14th February 1770 to 21st August 1775 is that of 'Alexander Livingstone, Esquire of Westquarter,' simply; while in the next sasine in order of date in which his name occurs, and which was registered on the 26th May 1778, he is designated 'Sir Alex. Livingstone, of Westquarter, Baronet.'

[2] According to the *Annual Register* for 1795 Sir Alexander died on the 8th April in the above year, while the *Scots Magazine,* vol. lvii. p. 276, says he died on the 9th.

[3] With the exception of a few additional particulars as to dates of marriages, etc., the account of Sir Alexander's family in the edition of 1886 is the same as above.

than the owner of Westquarter, *temp.* Mary Queen of Scots and her son James VI., and the contemporary of Sir George Livingstone of Ogleface.[1] This individual also bore the name of Robert, curiously enough, and died in January 1615,[2] when he was succeeded by his eldest son, Alexander, who died in August 1626,[3] leaving an only daughter, Helenor, to inherit his estate of Westquarter. This lady at the time of her father's death was betrothed to her kinsman William Livingston of Culter, the son and heir of Sir George Livingstone of Ogleface's younger brother Sir William Livingston of Culter, who had died in 1607, and whose tomb is still to be seen in Dundrennan Abbey.[4] This gentleman she subsequently married, and thus the estate of Westquarter came to be possessed by a nephew of that Sir George whose own direct descendants were ultimately to be its owners. William Livingston, the younger, of Culter, afterwards better known as 'Westquarter' from his wife's estate, served under his cousin the Earl of Callendar when the Scottish Army unsuccessfully attempted the rescue of Charles I. in 1648. On the capture of Carlisle he was left in charge as deputy-governor, and on the defeat of this expedition by Cromwell he had to surrender the town to the English, and returned home to meet with the usual reception accorded to the unfortunate 'Engagers' by the fanatical ministers of the Kirk Session of his parish. 'Westquarter' and his wife appear to have both died in 1679[5] when their eldest surviving son James succeeded to the family estate of Westquarter. This James married the widow of his kinsman Alexander Livingston, second Earl of Callendar, and 'on account of his known fidelity and integrity' was created a Knight Baronet by William III. by patent dated the 30th of May 1699.[6] Sir James died in November or December 1701,[7] and having no children his estate of Westquarter, in accordance with the terms of his marriage contract, passed into the possession of his widow, who shortly afterwards married again[8]—her third husband being James, third Earl of Findlater. Before she could legally become the owner of Westquarter, she had to obtain the consent of Sir James's nearest living relative, who happened to be his niece Helen Livingston, Lady Newton, and who had, as 'heir-general,' been retoured as such to her uncle early in 1702.[9] This latter lady thereupon, by a deed

---

[1] Unless otherwise stated, the above pedigree of the male line of Westquarter is compiled from researches made among the Particular Registers of Sasines for Stirlingshire in H. M. General Register House, Edinburgh.

[2] *Commissariot of Stirling, Testaments*, vol. ii., 19th April 1615.

[3] *Commissariot of Stirling, Testaments*, vol. iii., 15th August 1627.

[4] The inscription on his tomb reads as follows :—' Heir . Lyis . Ane . Right . Honorable . [M]an . Sir . Will[iam] . [Li]vingstoun . Of . Culter . Knight . Brother . To . The . Noble . Earle . Of . Linlithgow . Quha . Died . 2 . May . Anno . 1607 ' (Hutchison, *Memorials of Dundrennan Abbey*, pp. 27, 28). Wood's *Douglas Peerage*, vol. ii. p. 126, styles him also ' of Westquarter' from probably confusing the father with the son, as both bore the same Christian name.

[5] *Commissariot of Stirling, Testaments*, vol. ix., 20th June 1679 and 26th June 1679.

[6] *Registrum Magni Sigilli*, Liber lxxvi. No. 70.

[7] *Commissariot of Stirling, Testaments*, vol. xi., 22d June 1705, and *Com. Edinburgh, Testaments*, vol. lxxxii., 13th Sept. 1705.

[8] This lady was Lady Mary Hamilton, a daughter of William, second Duke of Hamilton.

[9] *Services of Heirs*, H. M. General Register House, Edinburgh, booked 23d Jany. 1702, also as ' heir-special in Westquarter, etc.,' 29th May 1702.

dated 29th December 1704, divested herself 'of the fourth part of the lands of Redding, called Westquarter, with mansion house, seat in Parish Church of Falkirk, and the great lodging in the said town,' which she as 'brother's daughter and heir of the deceased James Livingston of Westquarter' had been granted sasine of, in favour of 'Mary, Countess of Callendar, then Countess of Findlater,' with the consent of Sir Richard Newton of that Ilk, her husband.[1]

The Countess of Findlater having no children of her own, and probably considering that it would be a pity to let an estate which had belonged for so many generations to the Livingstons go out of the possession of that family, executed a settlement on the 8th March in the following year by which, with the consent of her husband, the above lands were entailed after providing for their joint life interest in the same, on 'James Livingstone, third son of Alexander Livingstone of Bedlormie (No. IV. in my Lineage), and the heirs-male of his body, whom failing to his other heirs-male, whom failing, to such person as the said Countess Mary should name by writing under her hand, and failing thereof to the said James Livingstone his nearest heirs or assignees whatsoever.'[2] The Countess having died two months after the signing of this deed,[3] the succession opened to the above James, then a minor, who, in 1706, took infeftment upon the precept contained in Helen Livingston's disposition to the Countess.[4] After coming of age James, who evidently did not wish to be bound by the entail, resigned the estate into the hands of the superior, from whom, in 1728, he obtained a fresh charter without the restrictions he objected to. He, thereupon, shortly afterwards still further complicated matters by selling these lands to Mr. William Drummond of Grange, who again in 1734 sold the same to Francis Lord Napier.[5] Thus the original intention of the Countess of Findlater to keep this estate in the possession of her first and second husbands' family had been so far frustrated by the very first person of that surname on whom she had disponed it by the entail of 1705. James Livingstone died within a few years after Lord Napier's purchase of Westquarter, and leaving no issue, his immediate younger brother, Captain William Livingstone, would, in the natural course of events, have been his successor.[6] For some time the latter took no steps to recover the estate, probably being ignorant of the fact that his brother's right to sell Westquarter was illegal ; but from whatever reason the delay arose from,[7] it

---

[1] Recorded in *Stirling Sasines*, vol. xx. folio 393.
[2] *Ibid.*
[3] She died on the 4th May 1705, without, however, ever having been infeft in these lands (*Com. of Edinburgh, Testaments*, vol. lxxxii. 13th Sept. 1705 ; *Dictionary of Decisions*, vol. iv. pp. 334-5).
[4] *Faculty Decisions*, 1757-1760, vol. ii. pp. 38-41. Sasine registered 8th January 1707, vide *Stirling Sasines*, H. M. General Register House.
[5] *Faculty Decisions.*
[6] Playfair says he died in 1743 (*British Family Antiquity*, vol. viii. p. 15).
[7] According to a family tradition of which Sir Bernard Burke gives an account in his *Vicissitudes of Families*, vol. ii. pp. 228-230, the recovery of Westquarter was delayed by the loss of the title-deeds, and it was not until the unexpected and romantic discovery of these important documents by Sir Alexander Livingstone of Bedlormie, the father of the late Sir Thomas Livingstone of Westquarter, at a wayside inn, that led to Sir Alexander successfully ousting the Napiers. Though this tradition is still credited by his descendants, researches among the decisions of the Court of Session and House of Lords Appeals clearly prove, as stated above in the text, that the action was fought and won, not by Sir Alexander, but by his uncle and predecessor, Captain William Livingstone.

was not until the early part of 1756 that the gallant captain commenced proceedings by obtaining a retour of service 'as heir of tailzie and provision to the deceased Mary, Countess of Findlater,' on the strength of which document he was thereupon infeft in these lands.[1] This led to his bringing an action at law against Francis, Lord Napier, for improper possession, which first came on for hearing before the Court of Session on the 9th March 1757.[2] The plaintiff's, or 'pursuer's' (according to Scottish legal phraseology) case being briefly as follows :—Firstly, that James Livingstone had made up no title to the estate, that a service was necessary, and without it the infeftment and subsequent charter were of no effect; Secondly, if James Livingstone was held to have completed his title, he was bound by the conditions of the entail, which had been inserted in his first infeftment, and in either case, the deeds in question were null, and ought to be set aside. Lord Napier's defence was that James Livingstone was joint heir with the Countess, and not a substitute, and consequently was not bound by the fetters of the entail.[3]

The preliminary action of the 9th March 1757 went in favour of Captain Livingstone, as the Lords of Session found 'that the pursuer had a sufficient title to force production of all deeds granted by the Countess of Findlater on James Livingston.'[4] It was not, however, until five years later—3d March 1762—that the plaintiff won his case in the Scottish Courts, when 'the Lords found that James Livingstone was called to the succession as heir substituted to the Countess, and as the Countess's right was personal and incomplete, a general service of James to the person last infeft was necessary, and therefore that his base infeftment did not vest the lands.'[5] This judgment being appealed against by Lord Napier, this hard-fought action was not finally decided in Captain Livingstone's favour until the 11th March 1765, on which date the House of Lords confirmed the above decision of the Court of Session, and dismissed Lord Napier's appeal.[6] The successful plaintiff did not live long enough to derive much personal benefit from his victory, for he died at his mansion-house of Bedlormie, within four years of the dismissal of Lord Napier's appeal by the House of Lords, when he was succeeded in the possession of both the Bedlormie and Westquarter estates by his nephew Alexander.[7]

So far I have traced only the succession of the Ogleface or Bedlormie Livingstones to the 'Westquarter Estate': it now remains for me to relate briefly what I consider to be the true facts of the case as regards their title to the 'Westquarter Baronetcy,' which was conferred on James Livingstone of Culter and Westquarter by William III. in 1699. The copy of the original patent granting this baronetcy, as recorded in the Great Seal Register in H.M. General Register House, Edinburgh, contains the following limitation (see below) as to the destination of the title after the first

---

[1] *Services of Heirs*, dated 23d January 1756, and registered 4th February same year.

[2] 'Captain William Livingston against Francis, Lord Napier. Whether the fee of an estate vests *ipso jure* without a service in a nominatim substitute in a tailzie.'—*Faculty Decisions*, 1757-1760, vol. ii. pp. 38-41.

[3] *Dictionary of Decisions*, vol. iv. pp. 334-5.

[4] *Faculty Decisions*, 1757-1760, vol. ii. pp. 38-41.

[5] *Dictionary of Decisions*, vol. iv. p. 335.

[6] *Journals of the House of Lords*, vol. xxxi. p. 71.

[7] He died on the 22d February 1769.

baronet's death, and as he never had a son, or any child at all, it appears very doubtful to me whether a collateral heir could inherit the dignity, simply on the strength of his possessing the lands. And it is a very curious fact that, as already mentioned in the corrected Lineage, it was not until some years after his succession to the estates that the above Alexander assumed the title of baronet, to which, moreover, neither of his uncles and predecessors had laid claim.[1]

(Limitation as to heirs referred to above.)

. . .'Damus concedimus et conferimus In Jacobum Livingstoun de Westquarter ob notam suam fidelitatem et integritatem *Et in filium natu maximum de ejus corpore* (post suum decessum) *Ejusque hæredes masculos successive* Titulum honorem ordinem gradum et dignitatem Militis Baroneti perque præsentes facimus Creamus et constituimus eundem Jacobum Livingstoun ejusque antedictos successive in perpetuum Milites Baronetos ac ipsos Eorumque uxores et liberos respective et successive dicto Titulo cum loca et præcedentia tum in privato et in publico post datum præsentium frui et gaudere Ordinamus sicut quivis alius Miles Baronetus in dicto Regno etc. etc.' . . . [2]

TRANSLATION.

. . . 'Do give, grant, and confer upon James Livingston of Westquarter, on account of his honour, fidelity and integrity, *and upon the eldest son of his body* (after his decease) *and his heirs-male in succession*, the title, honour, rank, grade, and dignity of a Knight Baronet, and by these presents do make, create, and constitute the same James Livingston and his aforesaids successively for ever Knights Baronets, and do ordain them and their wives and children respectively and successively, after the date of these presents, to possess and enjoy the said title with place and precedency as well in private as in public like as any other Knight Baronet in the said kingdom.' . . .

The intentions of the above clause appears to me to be to limit the succession to *the heirs of the body* of the above Sir James Livingston of Westquarter, and as he left no heirs of the body, then the title would have become extinct on his death in 1701. With the following tables, which will better explain the position of affairs, I must now close this article :—

[1] Even in the 'Abstract of Evidence,' referred to before, and which was printed by the orders of the last baronet, Sir Thomas, son and successor of the above Alexander, the latter is given as the first of the Bedlormie branch that 'succeeded to the Scottish Baronetage of Westquarter.' (*Vide* p. 17, also pedigree attached to this 'Abstract.')

[2] *Registrum Magni Sigilli*, Liber lxxvi. No. 70. The above patent is dated at Kensington Palace, 30th May 1699, or exactly seventy-four years later than the date assigned by Burke to his Ogleface creation !

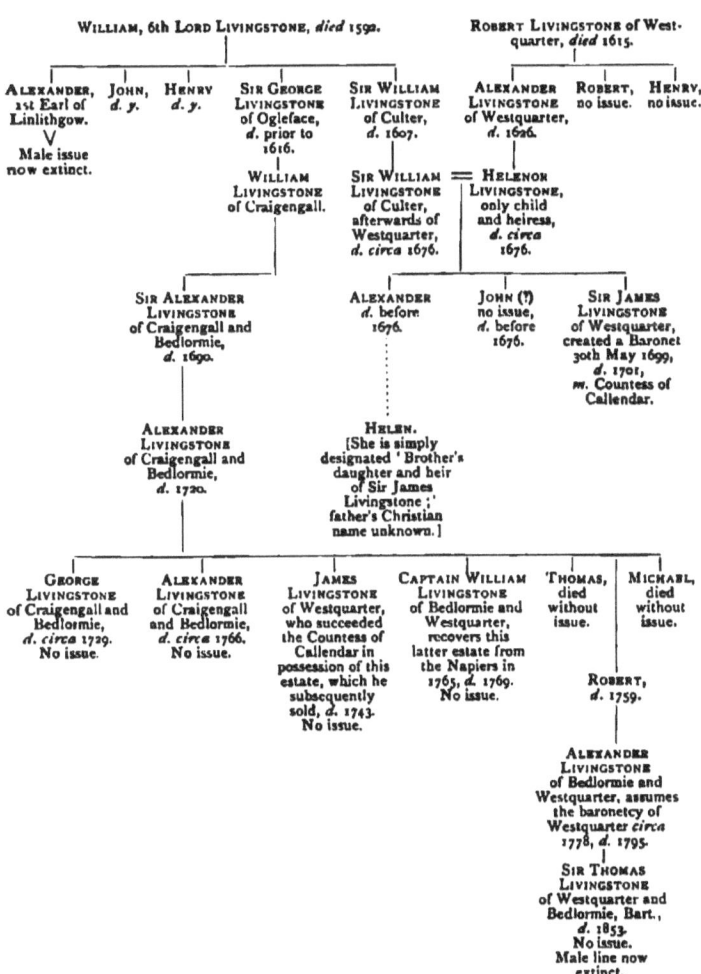

E. B. LIVINGSTON, F.S.A. Scot.,
Author of *The Livingstons of Callendar and Their Principal Cadets.*

152. DRAGON LEGENDS.—Doubtless to the prevalence of serpent worship in very early times we owe the existence of the numerous stories, all of which bear some resemblance to the classical myth of Andromeda and Perseus or the early Christian myth of St. George and the Dragon. Several instances of such legends are given in Mr. Parkinson's *Yorkshire Legends and Traditions,* and others are given below, as it is desirable that such stories should not be lost sight of. It will be seen

that whether occurring in Gloucestershire in England, or in Forfarshire in Scotland, they bear a strong resemblance to each other.

(1) The Dragon of Deerhurst, Gloucestershire.—'The story is that a serpent of prodigious bigness was a great grievance to all the country about Deerhurst, by poisoning the inhabitants and killing their cattle. The inhabitants petitioned the king, and a proclamation was issued out, that whosoever should kill the serpent should enjoy an estate on Walton-Hill in this parish, which then belonged to the crown. One John Smith, a labourer, engaged in the enterprise and succeeded: For having put a quantity of milk in a place to which the serpent resorted, he gorged the whole, agreeable to expectation, and lay down to sleep in the sun, with his scales ruffled up. Seeing him in that position, Smith advanced, and striking him between the scales with his axe, took off his head. The family of the Smiths enjoyed the estate, when Sir Robert Atkins compiled this account, and Mr. Lane, who married a widow of their family, had then the axe in his possession.'—Rudder's *History of Gloucestershire,* pp. 402, 403.

(2) The 'Worm' of Linton, Peeblesshire.—'A piece of rude sculpture still visible on one of the walls of the church, above the principal door, represents a horseman in complete armour, with a falcon on his arm, in the act of driving his lance down the throat of a nondescript fierce animal. An inscription is affirmed to have run thus—

> " The wode Laird of Lariston
> Slew the worm of Wormes glen,
> And wan all Lintoun parochine,"

in allusion to a traditionary exploit of Somerville of Linton, the founder of the Scottish branch of that family in 1174.'—See *Memories of the Somervills,* p. 45; *Origines Parochiales,* vol. i. pp. 431-432, *vide* Pennecuik's *Description of Tweeddale,* p. 158, etc.

(3) Arbuthnot, Perthshire.—'In the church is a stone effigy said to be a memorial of a certain "Sir Hugh the Blond," who killed a dragon which infested the district. There is a carved monster at the feet of the knight, such as is often met with in mediæval tombs. This may have given rise to the tradition.'

(4) The Dragon of Strike Martin, Forfarshire.—About three miles north from Dundee, in the hollow of Strath Dighty, and close to the little stream bearing the latter name, are a few houses called Strath Martine, locally denominated Strike-Martine. It appears that, long long ago, a wealthy farmer occupied an adjoining farm called Pittempan, who was blessed with a family of nine bonny daughters. Coming from the labours of the field one sultry summer evening, he desired his eldest daughter, as he was fatigued, to bring him a draught of cool water from the well. . . . As she did not return . . . the second was sent on the same errand, and so on until the whole nine sisters were sent. There being no appearance of any returning, . . . he went himself to learn the cause. . . . On coming to the spring he beheld the nine girls lying weltering in their blood within the folds of an enormous dragon. He alarmed the neighbourhood, and a large concourse of people gave chase to the monster, among them a young man named Martin, a lover of one of the maidens. Coming up with the monster as it was crossing the Dighty, making for the hills, he attacked it with a club—the crowd exclaiming 'Strike, Martin!' About two miles north from this the monster was killed; the spot is in one

of the fields of the farm of Balbeuchly, and is marked with an ancient-looking stone covered with a representation of the reptile. In the eastern gable of one of the buildings in a row of old ruinous farm-buildings on the north of Strathmartine Church, an old monument is built bearing the figure of a man with a head having some resemblance to a swain, and on his shoulder he is carrying some kind of implement or weapon. A short distance from this, at the gate of the school-master's garden, there is another monument upon which two serpents are sculptured. These two monuments, in connection with the one on the farm of Balbeuchly, are traditionally believed to have reference to the tragical event. The fountain is still known as 'the Nine Maidens' Well,' and the following doggerel has been handed down from time immemorial :—

> ' It was tempit at Pittempan,
> Draggelt at Ba-Dragon,
> Stricken at Strike-Martine,
> And killed at Martin Stane' (p. 158).

—Abridged from *Rambles in Forfarshire*, by James Myles. Dundee, James Myles, 1850.

153. GLASGOW FASTING MAN IN ITALY.—*Extracted from the State Papers (Venetian),* 1527-1533.

789. Bull of Clement VII. for John Scott, Layman of the Diocese of Glasgow.[1]

1532.
July 21,
Sanuto Diaries
v. lvi.[2]

Is induced to accede to his pious demands. His competitors and enemies who sought to obtain certain estates and possessions belonging to him by inheritance, and certain adherents of theirs having thrown him into prison, he was sustained in said prison during thirty-three days, without food and without drink or human consolation, remaining comforted solely by our Lord Jesus Christ, the blessed Virgin Mary, and by St. Ninian, bishop and confessor, whose miracles in Scotland become daily more and more resplendent. Having been released from that prison, and revived with meat and drink, and his competitors and enemies persecuting him more rabidly, he was driven to take refuge in the Monastery of Holyrood. He remained there without food and drink for 106 days, and in the meanwhile made a vow that if released from such distresses and tribulations, he would visit the Sepulchre of Christ at Jerusalem, and the places of the Holy Land, as also the body and relics of St. Ninian, deposited in the Church of Whitehern (*in ecclesia Candidæ Casæ*),[3] without eating flesh or fish. Shortly afterwards, being freed and at liberty, he visited the relics of St. Ninian, and then directed his steps towards Jerusalem, traversing the kingdom of England, where he suffered much adversity.

The Pope therefore grants to him, and to one companion to be chosen by him, license to visit Jerusalem and the Holy Land. As his own means (*vires*) do not suffice, the Pope remits to all Christians who shall have supplied him and his companion with necessaries, so many seven years, and the like number of fasts enjoined them as penance.

Rome, at St. Peters, 1532, 21st July, 9 pont. *Signed :* Friar Bernardo.
[*Latin.*]

[1] Another bull of a similar tenour, dated Bologna, 6 *id.* Feb. 1532, 10 pont., is printed in Rymer, xiv. 447. There is an allusion to John Scott in Mr. Froude's *History of England,* vol. i. pp. 294, 295, ed. London, 1856.

[2] The translation was made from the original Diaries, which are not paged.

[3] The Church of Whitehern was situated in Galloway, and the relics of St. Ninian were preserved at Whitehern until the Reformation.

1532.
Sept. 1.
Sanuto Diaries,
v. lvi.
(Originals.)

801. John Scott, the Glasgow Faster.

Attestation of his abstinence by the Bolognese Vianesio Albergati.

Vianesio Albergati to his candid readers, greeting.

The Rev. Father in Christ the Lucchese Silvestro Dario, auditor of the 'Rota' of our Holy Lord Pope Clement VII., and Nuncio to the King of Scotland, notified to me that John Scott, a man of probity, and of noble Scottish lineage, moved by piety towards God, abstained from food and drink during three consecutive months. Lest this should appear incredible, I interrogated the said Scott, by an interpreter, whether he had remained for so long a while without eating or drinking. As he maintained that it was perfectly true, I asked him whether he would abstain for some days from eating and drinking, which, with God's help, he promised to do. Having stripped him of all his apparel, lest he should secrete anything whereby to recruit his strength and deceive me, and having clad him in other raiment, I kept him for 11 consecutive days and nights in my house, in a bedchamber (*cubiculo*), most carefully closed and sealed (*clauso et obsignato*). I kept the strictest watch, lest anything should enter that could serve for food and drink, for I always kept the keys of said bed-chamber (*ipsius cubiculi*) in my own possession, in order that I might convince myself whether any one could live so long without eating and drinking. On the expiration of 11 days, the said John having most con-stantly endured so long an abstinence, and having always preserved the same complexion (*colorem*), vigour, and pulse, which seemed singularly marvellous to the learned physicians who came very frequently to visit him ; and as he had now exceeded the number of days during which a man can live without food and drink, I let him out of the bedchamber (*cubiculo*), he neither requesting nor expecting his discharge ; and I enabled him to depart (*ac ei abeundi facultatem feci*).

During the whole time that I watched him under close custody, he prayed God and the saints continually, save when he talked or slept ; of which thing I call to witness God Almighty, whose Majesty may not be deceived ; and if I lie, I do not deprecate His eternal wrath. Farewell, excellent readers, and as no advantage can accrue to me from so impudent a lie, in case I do lie, believe the thing itself to be most true and most certain, as it is.

Rome, 1st September 1532.

Vianesio Albergati, Bolognese.

So it is with my own hand.

Registered by Sanuto, 30th September 1532.

[*Latin.*]

1532.
Sept. 30.
Sanuto Diaries
v. lvii. p. 25.

810. Marco Antonio Venier, Venetian Ambassador at Rome, to the Signory.

John Scott, who came from Scotland, his country, on his way to the Holy Sepulchre, is here ; he offered the Pope to remain many days without any food, and his Holiness gave him in custody to trustworthy persons, who kept him securely locked up for 13 days without having eaten. He remained there the whole time, always in prayer, and would have staid longer had not the Pope desired him to be set at liberty, and that food should be given him. This proceeds from divine grace rather than from deceit, '*o otto alcuno.*' On his aforesaid voyage he will visit Venice. Has been requested both by him and by the chief personages here to recommend him. Beseeches the Signory to concede him favour.

Rome, 30th September.

Registered by Sanuto, 5th October.

[*Italian.*]

812. John Scott.

Reading in the Senate of the letter from Marco Antonio Venier. (*Note by Sanuto.*)

1532.
Oct. 5.
Sanuto Diaries,
v. lviii. p. 28.

A letter came from our ambassador at Rome, dated 30th September. He writes that one John Scott has arrived there on his way to Jerusalem. He professes to remain many days without eating. The Pope placed him with a guard; he remained thirteen days, praying the whole time, without taking any food; on their expiration the Pope gave him leave to restore himself. He is coming to Venice with a brief of recommendation from the Pope, for his voyage to Jerusalem. The letter was read in the Senate.

[*Italian.*]

814. John Scott at Venice. (*Note by Sanuto.*)

1532.
Oct. 6.
Sanuto Diaries,
v. lvii. p. 29.

This morning came to the Doge, Dom. John Scott, who, according to the letter from Rome, remains many days without eating. His Serenity sent him to the Chiefs of the Ten. He was accompanied by Ser Michiel Morosini, to whom he brought a letter of recommendation from Cardinal Pisani. He cannot speak (Italian?); is about 50 years old; long hair, red face, rather fat; is wrapped round the body in a very sorry cloth garment; and holds in his hand a book of offices (*uno officio*), on which his eyes are bent. He has with him a Scot, who can speak nothing but Scotch, and no one understood him. On his departure from Rome the Pope gave him twelve crowns for his journey hither. He exhibited a certificate '*di uno di Scozia*,' how that he (Scott) had passed three months without eating anything, during which interval he communicated twice. There is also a certificate from Rome, to the effect that he had been locked up in a chamber for ten days without taking any food. The Chiefs of the Ten then sent for the cellarer of S. Giorgio Maggiore, and desired him to keep the two Scots for ten days, after which they will be sent to San Spirito,[1] and to other friaries, until a safe passage to Jerusalem can be procured for them. Many persons went to see him (John Scott).

[*Italian.*]

154. SIR FRANK VAN HALEN, KNIGHT OF THE GARTER.[2]—Sir Francis van Halen, Hale, or Halle, for the name is spelt in various ways, was not

---

[1] In the year 1532 the island of S. Spirito, in the Venetian Lagoons, was inhabited by the 'Canons of S. Spirito.' (See Flamingo Corner.)

[2] As this paper deals with a subject in no way connected with Scotland, I may be permitted to explain that it was written for and accepted by *The Genealogist.* As, however, some changes are being made in the management of this valuable magazine, I have been advised to print it in the *Scottish Antiquary.* I do this chiefly because the forthcoming volume of the Harleian Society will, I believe, contain the Pedigree of Hall of Northall, and some of my readers may value the light I have been able to throw on the history of the knight so rashly claimed by that family as their ancestor.

A. W. C. H.

one of the twenty-six knights who are styled 'Founders' of the Order of the Garter. He was admitted as thirty-fourth on the roll in place of Sir Otho Holland, who died 3d September 1359. His valour, his high social position, and his personal services to King Edward III., both in arms and finance, made him a worthy comrade in a band which contained such heroes as the Black Prince, Sir Walter Manny, and the Captal de Buch. Sir Frank's warlike achievements are recorded by Froissart, but little has been hitherto known of his personal or family history. Beltz, in his history of the Order of the Garter (pp. 122-127), confesses that he has been unable to obtain a reliable account of this knight. He very naturally rejects the only one which is available when he wrote, viz. one given in the pedigree of the Halls of Northall (Vincent, No. 134, fol. 479, in Coll. Armor.). Vincent is regarded as a painstaking and accurate herald ; it is strange that he passed a pedigree full of blunders, only some of which Beltz points out. As this pedigree contains the name of Sir Frank van Halle, it will be necessary to print at least a portion of it, and then to give an account of the family to which he really belonged, drawn from authentic sources, which will utterly disprove Vincent's statements. The following is taken from the Hall pedigree amongst the Harl. MSS. 1396, fol. 143*b*; it agrees with all that Beltz says of the one in the College of Arms which I have not seen ; it will, I believe, appear *in extenso* in the forthcoming volume of *Pedigrees of Shropshire Families*, printed for the Harleian Society.

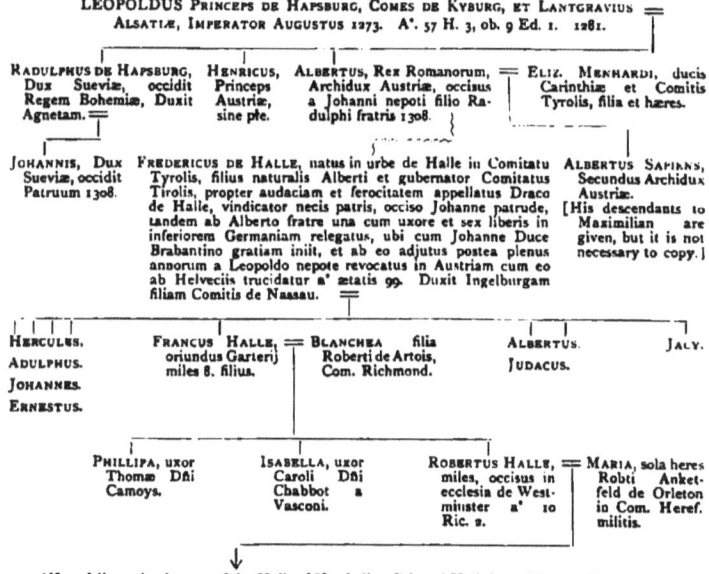

[Here follows the descent of the Halls of Northall to Edward Hall the well-known Chronicler.]

Beltz remarks, 'For these statements no voucher is offered, and several other averments in the document . . . are disproved' (p. 123). The 'other averments' I need not consider. I shall now proceed to give an account of Sir Frank's descent, marriage, and issue, founded on official records and the works of distinguished foreign genealogists, some of which Beltz probably did not consult; even had he done so, he would not have derived the assistance from them which I have found, as I have had to guide me in perusing them more than three hundred extracts from the archives of the city of Malines, made for me by the Archiviste en Chef, M. Victor Hermans—whose skill as a genealogist has enabled him to add many notes and references to standard works which have proved exceedingly useful.[1]

In the 13th and 14th centuries many wealthy and noble Italians settled in Brabant and Flanders, their skill in finance making their residence profitable to the Flemings, whose wares were sent to every market in the world. The family of Mirabelle[2] was of great antiquity and distinction in Italy, where the adage was known in early times, 'I Mirabelli sorsero presto, e presto si estinsero.' 'Teatro Araldica, du L. Teltoni. E. F. Saladini. vol Terzo. Lodi 1843 (art. Dalla Porta)' mentions 'Dai Conti di Lomello, e Mirabello, e Langosco . . . ed altre grandi ed illustri genovesi famiglie;' and again, 'I conti de Mirabello, di Langosco . . . fu uno dei maggiori capitani che sorra il ogni altro si sia segnalato nelle guerre di Lombardia.' They bore *gu.* a lion *or*, armed, langued, and crowned *az.* These, their paternal arms, have been always borne by the descendants of John de Mirabelle, although the name was gradually given up for that of Halen. The Mirabelle CREST is a demi-lion *or*, armed, langued, and crowned *azure*, between two wings *sable*. The CRI is 'Mirabello,' and the MOTTO 'Sine deo nil.' The accompanying plate is from an old drawing sent me by the late Colonel van Halen of Brussels.

A branch of the family settled in Sicily bore the arms, with the lion supporting a flag charged with France *az.*, three fleurs de lys, with a label of three points *or* for Anjou.

Though I have not yet succeeded in discovering the exact nature of it, it is almost certain that a connection existed between the noble Italian house and John de Mirabelle of Malines, who is described as a Lombard. He must have been a man not only of wealth, but also of good family, for he was permitted to contract a marriage with 'la Dame van

---

[1] Some of the information given in this paper is to be found in my *History of the Van Halen or Hallen Family*, privately printed in 1885. Since its issue I have learned many more facts concerning Sir Francis van Halen. I still hope to be enabled to trace the family of Mirabelle of Brabant to its home in Italy, and shall feel grateful to any student of Italian genealogy for such assistance as he may be able to give me. 'Mercatores de Italia in Flandria' were a wealthy and a noble race, and it is surprising that no attempt has been made to write an account of them.

[2] Mirabello is a village near Benevento in Italy.

Halen.'[1] The date of this marriage I have not discovered; she, however, was alive December 25, 1348, when her name occurs in the city accounts. At this time she must have been an old woman, for her grandsons were grown up. By this marriage John de Mirabelle had at least two sons.

    1. John de Mirabelle dit van Halen, of whom below.

    2. Francis de Mirabelle, who is mentioned in Grammayre's *History*.

Probably Leo de Mirabelle, who in 1340 lent King Edward III., when at Antwerp, ten thousand pounds (Rym. *Fœd.*, tom. ii. part iv. p. 63), was another son.

John de Mirabelle dit van Halen, elder son, was a person of considerable importance ; he became Receveur-General of Brabant, and acquired the important seigneurie de Perwez and other domains, he, however, made many enemies, and is said to have died in prison, where he certainly was in 1318, as the accounts of the city of Malines (1318-19, fol. 148. v°.) prove. His first wife was Mary, la Dame de Perwez,[2] by whom he had two sons.

    1. Simon, who married Isabelle, Dame de Somerghem Ecclo., etc., and was assassinated 9th May 1346, leaving one child, a daughter. His name occurs (Pat. 26, Edw. III., p. 1, m. 18), where I find that his widow sued for certain unliquidated pecuniary claims upon Edward, for which the king granted a patent to Sir Frank de Hale, brother of Simon, in which it is also recited that Sir Frank had engaged to attend the king's service with twenty-five men-at-arms during his life at £300 per annum.

    2. Frank or Francis, of whom below.

John de Mirabelle dit van Halen, after the death of the Dame de Perwez, married, 29th May 1312, Mary (or Sophia) de Berthout,[3] 'la Dame de Malines' (*Accounts of the City of Malines*, 1311, 12, fol. 167, r.) ; by her, who survived him, he does not appear to have had any children.

Francis de Mirabelle dit van Halen, second son of John, is known more frequently by the name Halen. The name Mirabelle was seldom used by his descendants, though it was occasionally, as is proved by an epitaph in the Abbey Church of St. Michel, Antwerp, 'Venerando Johanni de Mirabelle dicto de Halen præclaro hujus urbis multis Annis Senatori . . . decessit . . . anno 1570.'

I have not been able to find the date of Sir Frank's birth, which must have occurred about 1300-1310. The proof that he and Simon were

---

[1] The fief of Halen was near Diest. I have not, however, discovered any account of the family of which John de Mirabelle's wife appears to have been the heiress. As she survived her grandson, Sir Simon de Mirabelle, the Sire de Perwez, her title would be merged in those possessed by his only daughter and heir.

[2] Mary, Dame de Perwez, was a daughter, by Alice de Audenarde, of Godfrey, Count de Vianden, Sire de Perwez, son of Philip, Count de Vianden, by Mary, dame de Perwez, daughter, by Alice de Grimberg, of Godfrey, Sire de Perwez, son, by Alice d'Orbais, of William de Lovaine, Sire de Perwez, son by his second wife, Ymane de Los, of Godfrey, Count of Brabant, who died A.D. 1190. Through his mother, Sir Francis was descended from Charlemagne, Alfred the Great of England, and the most distinguished families of Europe. The arms of the Counts de Vianden were *gu.* an escocheon *arg.*, but Count Godfrey, the father of Mary, adopted in place of these the arms of Perwez, viz. *gu.* a fess *arg.*, which arms Sir Francis and his descendants could quarter with Mirabelle and Halen.

[3] She married after John de Mirabelle's death Reignold II. Earl of Gueldres, and had by him a son, Reignold III. After her death the Earl married Eleanor, daughter of King Edward II. and sister of King Edward III. (Reusner, *Op. Gen.*). Sophia de Malines ('cousine du duc de Brabant') was in 1291 the widow of Henry Sire de Breda (Arch., *De la ville de Malines*, vi. 263). John de Mirabelle was therefore her second husband. She was under full age in 1287.

sons of John de Mirabelle is clear, 'Simon de Mirabelle, chevallier, dit de Halle, fils de Jean, Seigneur de Perwez, par son testament fait en 1345, a donné et fondé la cloitre de Grœnenbriele. Il donne par son testament à François de Mirabelle son frère (Olivier Vrede, *Genealogiæ Comitum Flandriæ* (Preuves), p. 267).

An account of the martial achievements of Sir Frank van Halen taken from Froissart's *Chronicles*, and other sources, is given by Beltz. I may be permitted to insert here the summary of his career sent me by M. Hermans. 'He was invited to the coronation of the King of England in 1326, was engaged in the war in Scotland, 1331; distinguished himself at the Battle of Ecluse, 1340; was in London, 1342; at the Battle of Bergerac, 1344; the Battle of Auberoche, 1345; Envoy in Gascony, 1350; in Champagne, 1359; at the concluding of the Peace of Brittany, 1360; elected a Knight of the Garter, 1360; Captain of the Castle of Rochefort in Gascony, 1366.'

I have now shown that the Brabant knight had no connection with Frederick, the Dragon of Halle, who most probably was a mythical person, for Reusner does not mention him. As to his marriage, the Northall Pedigree gives the name of his wife as Blanche, daughter of Robert d'Artois. Beltz points out that d'Artois had no daughter so named, so that here, as in some later instances, the line was carried on by people who had no existence, a state of matters, to say the least of it, awkward.

Butkens (*Trophées du duché de Brabant*) gives the pedigree of the Berthout de Duffle family. From it I find that Sir Francis married Marguerite Berthout de Duffle, daughter of Henry, descended from Walter Berthout, Sire de Grimberg and 'de Pays de Malines,' who was also the ancestor of John de Mirabelle's second wife. By Marguerite, Sir Frank had one child, Marguerite, the wife of the Sire de Beaumont. After her death he contracted a morganatic marriage[1] with Marguerite van Werffelt, by whom he had four children.

1. John, who left three sons, John, Francis, and Henry.
2. Sir Francis, 'Chef homme des Archers,' 1397, who left a son Francis.
3. Sir Andrew, Sire de Helmaele and de Berendrecht, who left three sons, John, Francis, and a second Francis.
4. A daughter, Elizabeth, married Sir Gerard van Tiechelt.

---

[1] But little is known of the nature of the marriage laws in Germany, Flanders, and Brabant during the middle ages. The Church regarded marriage as a Sacrament—the State made use of it as a convenient institution for consolidating parties, reconciling quarrels, and placing the fief of a weak female child in the hands of a powerful court favourite. The Church's blessing was not deemed necessary to the validity of a State marriage, though from the commencement of the fifteenth century it was rarely dispensed with. On the other hand the Church frequently joined in holy matrimony those who did not obtain from the State a formal recognition of their union. These originated 'Morganatic' or 'left-handed marriages.' As long as such alliances did not affect any State interests they were informally acknowledged with some limitations. Children born of them were debarred from succeeding *de jure* to hereditary and feudal honours. Their fathers were, however, empowered to legitimise them, and thus free them from any taint the absence of a legal status might be supposed to leave. Society naturally regarded the Church's marriage as sufficient, and recognised both wife and offspring as being *sans reproche*. The pedigrees of Flemish and German families contain no wavy line (indicating illegitimacy) in such cases, and the armorial bearings are handed down with no mark of inferiority on them. It is almost needless to add that such a state of things was unknown in Scotland and England. A good account of marriage in Germany in the middle ages is to be found in the *Journal of Jurisprudence*, Nos. 373, 374. See also *De Jure Connubiorum apud Batavos recepto*, Henrici Brouwer, J. C. Amstelodami, 1665.

On the 10th June 1367, a grant of the fief of Lilloo was made to Sir Frank by Louis, Count of Flanders, and his wife, Margaret de Brabant, on the occasion of his marriage with Marie de Ghistelle [1]—by this marriage he had a son, John, who succeeded as Sire de Lilloo, and died after 1445, leaving no male issue.

It will be seen that the list of Sir Frank Halle's children given in the Northall Pedigree is purely imaginary. The Malines records speak of those I have given above as acting severally and conjointly in the transfer of land, etc. A pedigree of the family is in a MS. collection made by Butkens, now in the British Museum (add. 12451). Another pedigree which I have consulted is at Malines, and was drawn up by Henri van Huldenberghe dit van der Borch van Moesic, Chevalier, Commune Maître de Malines, A.D. 1633, this is not so complete as Butkens', but neither gives any sons other than those I have mentioned.

Sir Frank van Halen was buried in St. Rombaud at Malines, as the following extract from the city accounts shows, ' 1375. 25. September—Vingt

deux archers sont rangés devant l'hôtel de ville, à cause du grand nombre d'étrangers venus a Malines pour assister à la pompe funèbre de Messire

[1] Mary de Ghistelle married (after 1329), as second wife, Thomas de Diest, Sire de Zeeland, by whom she had two sons, Henry and Simon; he died 1349. She married, 1352, le Sire de Morianes. She married thirdly, in 1367, Sir Francis van Halen, by whom she had one son, John, who died without male issue.

Franco van Halen' (*fo.* 83 *vo.*). A monument was erected to his memory in the same church at the expense of the city, as is shown by the accounts. The canopy is still to be seen, but his effigy, and that of his last wife Mary de Ghistelle, were damaged during the Revolution of 1830 ; the fragments are, however, preserved at one of the royal palaces. Sanderus (*Theatr. Sacr.*) gives an engraving of it ; the inscription, in Flemish, is

' Dit is de Sepulture myns Heren H. VRANCX VAN HALEN, Here was van Lilloe, die starf in't jaer M.CCC.LXXV, ix daghe in Oegxt. Ende myns Vrouwe MARIE syn wyf was, Docht. was myns Heren van Gistele, die starf M.CCCC en v. x daghe in Meerte.'

The following portion of the Van Halen pedigree will illustrate what I have already stated :—

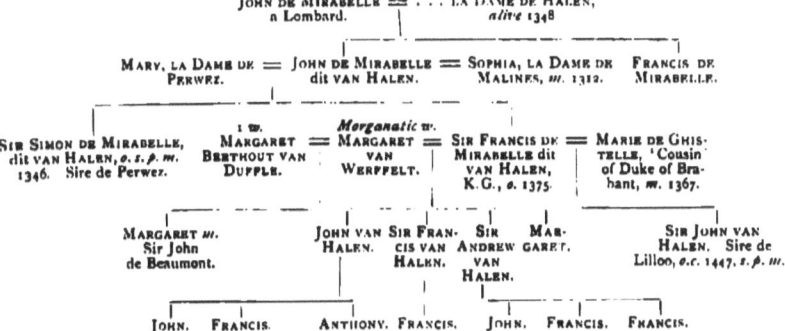

A few words as to the arms given in the Northall pedigree must conclude this paper. They have been clearly fabricated with reference to the ' Dragon of Halle ' and to Sir Frank's service to the English king. They are tricked with three quarterings for Aubermond, Mortimer, and Antingham, though the right to assume these is questionable. They are thus described by Beltz (p. 126),—ARMS : *Gules*, a wyvern, wings elevated, crowned *or* ; pendent from the neck an escocheon of the field, thereon an eagle displayed, with two heads *argent* ; all within a bordure *az.*, charged with six lioncels rampant

(? passant), and as many fleur-de-lis alternately—of the second. CREST : on the battlements of a castle *argent*, a wyvern *sable*, the wings addorsed

guttee d'or, gorged with a ducal coronet, therefrom a chain reflected over the back, of the third, in the dexter claw a sword erect, *azure.*' Beltz, in a footnote, remarks : ' These bearings rest upon the doubtful authority of a plate, affixed, at a long subsequent period, to the stall which Sir Frank van Hale occupied, and of a drawing annexed to a pedigree imposed upon Vincent, both emanating, as it would seem, from a common source. Above the crest on the plate there is an escroll bearing this inscription ' *Mons Franke van Halle, Capp de Calais,*' over the escroll is the date ' 1360.' Under the arms, which are surrounded by the garter, is the Motto, ' OIE (omne ?) SOLUM FORTI PATRIA.'

The true arms of de Mirabelle I have already described. On the monument of Conrad van Halen at Malines, the arms of van Halen are  quartered, and are thus described by Henri van Huldenberghe, 'd'azur a la bande d'or chargé de 3 roses de gueules boutonnées d'or et feuillées de sinople et accompanée de 2 étoiles à 5 rais d'or.' The same arms, with other colours, are given in Riestop, and some not unlike them are, according to Burke (*Armory*), borne by English families whose names bear a resemblance to Halen.[1] If these are descendants of Sir Frank van Halen, they must trace from some of his descendants who left Brabant in the 16th century. My own ancestors at Malines were descended from his third son, Sir Andrew van Halen, and it is known that the descendants of John de Mirabelle dit van Halen, who died at Antwerp 1570, and was also descended from Sir Andrew, came to England about that time.

A. W. CORNELIUS HALLEN.

155. JACOBITE NOTES.—It may perhaps interest some of your readers to hear that before the death of Prince Charles, and the return of those who had been in arms for him, the Almighty was always entreated in reading the Litany to show His pity upon all prisoners, EXILES, and captives. This was the practice in Pittenweem, and probably elsewhere, and seems very touching. The lady from whom this information was derived was twelve years old when Prince Charles died, and had therefore a distinct recollection of its being done.

Another curious piece of information, which I heard from an old woman in that neighbourhood, was that her father was a young Edinburgh apprentice during the 'Forty-five, and that he and a number of other Jacobite apprentices joined the Edinburgh volunteers *in order to run away*, and thus to spread a panic among them. This fact, which I believe to be perfectly true, will account for the extraordinarily ludicrous and otherwise unaccountable pusillanimity which that gallant body displayed. The old woman whose father thus risked his life in the cause, was Chapel Mary, who at one time opened the doors of the pews in Pittenweem Chapel.

A. H.

---

[1] Flemish names underwent many changes in England, and often settled down into forms under which they can scarcely be recognised.

156. URBS GIUDI.—In giving the genealogy of Vortigern, Nennius says :—'GUITAUL (was the son of) GUITOLION ; GUITOLION of GLOUI. BONUS, PAUL, MAURON, GUOTELIN, were four brothers who built GLOIUDA, a great city upon the banks of the river Severn, and in British is called CAIR GLOUI, in Saxon, GLOUCESTER.'

This makes UDA and CESTER correspond. I have been struck with the likeness of the former to the Spanish CIUDAD (of which the last consonant is often little pronounced). Troude's *Breton Dictionary* says :—' Dans les écrits du VIe siècle on trouve parfois KAER au lieu de KEAR et KER. Le mot KEUDET semble avoir été usité au sens de ville, cité.'

The idea is probably CAUED, shut, corresponding to the Gaelic DUIN. If URBS GIUDI was an enclosed site, the probability of its having been on an island seems reduced. Corroboration or refutation will be welcome in this and in all cases. W. M. C.

157. SCOT'S TRANSCRIPT OF PERTH REGISTERS *(continued from page 45).*

November 22, 1573.
David Johnston & James Wilson.

November 29, 1573.
Pate Murray & Christian Gardener.

December 8, 1573.
William Edward & Janet Marshall.
Patrick Garvie & Malie Randie (viz. Randall). Garvie.

(*N.B.*—They were before mentioned as being married October 18 ; Note. such inaccuracy is very blameable in any person who is entrusted with the keeping of a Register.)

December 15, 1575.
William Cook & Catherine Robertson.
Alexander Stewart & Catherine Ruthven.

(*N.B.*—In an ancient manuscript chronicle of memorable occurences, Note. I find as follows, 'The first Downfaling of two Bows of the Brig of Tay, Bridge of Perth. & of Louis work, by Inundation of water on the 20 Day of December Inundation. 1573 years after midnight.'

Another old manuscript calls the Inundation 'the great water bolliter,' by which I suppose was meant the breaking, dissolving, or loosening of the Ice in the River. The falling of the two arches at that time seems to have been the first remarkable Failure, then remembered, of the old Bridge of Perth.

The Bridge was more ancient than the time of King William the Lyon. Fordun & Johannes Major both speak of it as being at Perth in the year 1210, at which time it suffered much by an Inundation. Major calls it ' Pontem Sancti Johannis ingentem apud Perth,' the large Bridge of St. John at Perth : and says that King William, his brother David, & the Prince Alexander, were in Danger from the waters, & sailed in a Boat from the House in which they were.

The Fable fabricated by a later writer viz. Hector '*/ Boethius, is not to be regarded.

Louis, or as it may be called, Lollius work is of great antiquity ; without Louis or Lollius it a Town in the situation of Perth could not have subsisted any Length of work. time. It is necessary for the Distribution of the waters of the Almond, which if they were to run in one Channel, would at times prove very dangerous to the Town. No mills could be at Perth without it. And in ancient times the water which is conveyed by it circulated the walls of the Town, and rendered Perth famous as a Place of Defence against the Enemy.

There is certain Evidence from one of the Charters of the Blackfriars' Monastery at Perth that Louis Work is of more ancient Date than the year 1244.

Antiquity of Perth.

The Itinerary, Map, and Commentary of Richard of Cirencester, accidentally discovered at Copenhagen in the year 1747, have thrown great light on the Roman Antiquities in Scotland. The old Opinion, before Hector Boece time, was that Agricola the Roman General in Britain began the building of Perth about the year 81. Agricola's Conquests on the north side of the Forth were soon relinquished. But in the year 140 Antoninus sent Lollius Urbicus into Britain to be governor of the Island, who immediately passed the North, and having subdued six of the Tribes or nations formed them into the Roman Province called Vespasiana.

Sibbald of ye Roman Ports, Colonies, &c.

Sir Robert Sibbald, who carefully inspected the Roman Streets or military ways, observes that there was one which led from Aberdour to Perth: another from the Bridge of Stirling to Perth: and another from Abernethy to Perth. He supposes therefore that where the Town of Perth stands there was a Roman Colony, & that it was the Place called in the Roman Maps 'Ad Taum.'

Since the discovery of Richards Itinerary, Dr. Stukeley in his Publication "/ concerning it, in the year 1757, makes different suppositions relating to Perth; he mentions it sometimes as the 'Ad Taum,' sometimes

Victoria.

as the 'Orrea,' & sometimes as the Victoria of the Romans.

But Mr. Whitaker, in his celebrated History of Manchester, who had before him the whole of Richards Itinerary Map & Commentary, has now fixed Perth to be the Victoria of the Romans, and Victoria or Perth, he says, appears to have been what was called a Latin Town enjoying the Jus Latii or Latin Privilege. The inhabitants of a Latin Town were no longer governed by a foreign Prefect & Quæstor, but by a Prefect & Quæstor elected among themselves. A Briton was then President, a Briton their Justiciary, & a Briton their Tax-gatherer, and any inhabitant of such a Town, who has borne the offices of Prætor or Quæstor, was immediately entitled to the Privileges of a Roman Citizen.

The sixth Legion called 'Victorian' and the twentieth Legion called 'Valerian and Victorian' were resident in Britain and continued to be so in the time of Lollius Urbicus. A Part of one of these Legions having their principal station at Perth seems to be the reason assigned for giving the Town the name of Victoria.

After the Conquest of six of the Nations on the North of the Forth by Lollius Urbicus in the year 140, the Romans continued in this Country about thirty years, viz. till the year 170, when they were obliged to retire to the south side of the Forth. Most of their works therefore in this part of the Country must have been made during that period.

The same sagacity and industrious spirit which excited them to construct so many Military Roads to Perth may well be supposed to have excited them to make what might be then called Lollius work, & which afterwards by a shortening & corruption of Pronunciation of which there are many similar examples, came to be called Louis work.

None of the Roman Towns or Stations on the North side of the Forth now retain the names which the Romans [46]/ gave them. The name Victoria would be particularly obnoxious to the People of the Country. In the Pictish times the town was called Beartha, Bearth, Bert; and when in St. Patrick's time the letter P was introduced into the Galic language, & B and P came to be indiscriminately used the Town was generally called Perth or Pert, and by the Highlanders at this Day is called Pheairt which seems to be the softened manner in conversation of pronouncing the words Berth or Pert.

Beartha in the Galic language signifies clean, fine, genteel. Bertha, Berth or Bert, according to Dr. Samuel Johnson, is a German word, and signifies the same as Eudoxia in the Greek, viz. illustrious. Berth in the Pictish times was, according to Fordun L. 10 c. 16, 17 a strong fortified town, and was unsuccessfully besieged by the Norwegians.

It was called Perth or Pert in Charters extant granted about the year one thousand one hundred; about a hundred years before the time of the fancied change of the name invented by Boece.

On the north side of the Almond there might probably be a Roman Post, or what was commonly called a summer camp, which the Romans generally had about two miles from their winter quarters or chief place of residence. This was probably the case because urns evidently belonging to the Romans have been found on the north side of that river. It seems certain that several of them that were slain in Battle were interred there. That other fort might possibly come under the same name with the other fort & town to which it was reckoned an appendage, though I am rather of opinion that the ground on the North of the Almond never had the name of Bartha till after the time of Hector Boece. After the most careful examination of the ground by skilful persons & making allowance for the Ravages made by the water, it has been declared to be absolutely impossible that there could [46]/ be at any time a Town at what is now called Bartha.

If Perth in the time of the Romans was a Latin Town, by which the inhabitants had the privilege of choosing their own magistrates, it may be conjectured that in the Pictish times it would enjoy also some peculiar privileges, so as to bear some resemblance to what is now called a Royal Burrow.

Hector Boece's story was adopted by Buchanan & by many after writers both Scotch & English. The truth of it was justly questioned by the Publisher of Fordun's *Scoti-Chronicon*—and the testimony of its falsehood, which I have met with in the course of Historical reading and in the Examination of Records, are so numerous that to insert or even to quote them would take up too much room in this Book.)

December 22, 1573.
William Strachan & Janet Rollock.

February 7, 1573.
Robert Lyn & Helen Watson.
William Edgar & Christy Rogge.

February 13, 1573.
William Rynd & Janet Murray.
Thomas Malcolm & Helen Richardson.

F

February 21, 1573.
John Bathlay & Janet Howeson.
John Lamb & Christian Sym.
Gabriel Stawker & Christian Marshall.
John Chalmers & Elspeth Malcolm.
Fastrein even the 23 day of February.

April 5, 1574.
Willie Roll & Marian Edmonston *alias* Cowart.

April 18, 1574.
William Anderson & Christian Wilson.
John Henderson & Janet Black.

47/ April 25, 1574.
Laurence Strathmiglo & Janet Wright.

May 9, 1574.
David Haw (viz. Hall) & Janet Wilson.
William Fyd & Christian Whittock.

158. STRANGE NAMES.—We give our readers the result of a perusal of some old Parochial Registers, English and Scottish. The strange names we have found, are worthy consideration, for they offer some interesting problems as to their derivation. Localities, trades, and physical peculiarities gave rise to surnames when men found it convenient to adopt them. Foreign names often assumed strange and ludicrous forms which became permanent, but still we must seek for an explanation for the existence of many names which cannot thus be accounted for.

All ranks of life in Church or State are met with, from Pope and Emperor downwards. The vast tribe of Smith is subdivided into Goldsmith, Shoesmith, and others, till we get Naesmith, or No Smith at all, bearing for motto ' Non arte sed marte,' and for crest a broken hammer. We like better the spirit of a distinguished holder of the name, who has adopted ' Non marte sed arte' and the hammer in good working order—this however, is a digression. The wrights, though not so numerous as the smiths, have many branches—Wheelwright, Cartwright, Plowright. Then come stranger names, Swordslipper (*i.e.* sword sharpener), Ironmonger, Huntsman, Armourer. A class of names of Dutch origin existed, but is now almost lost, Shoemaker, Panmaker, Slaymaker.

Of quaint names, the following may serve as a sample—' Eightshillings,' ' Halfpenny,' ' Too large,' ' Go to bed,' ' All the world,' ' Helmet,' ' Conqueror,' ' Conquergood,' ' Horsenayle,' ' Bargain.' ' Ann next Truelove,' offers a hard nut to crack. ' God be near,' ' Milksop,' ' Chance,' ' Cakebread,' ' Parchment,' ' Churchyard,' ' Rottenherring;' ' Fairservice,' used by Scott, but is found as a real name; ' Mustard,' ' Coachman,' ' Thorowgood,' and ' Toogood,' ' Holdupp,' ' Scattergood,' ' Midwinter,' ' Careless,' ' Justice,' ' Crucifix,' ' Pyx,' ' Javelin,' ' Cripple,' ' Catchmaid,' ' Hell,' ' Heaven,' ' Paradise,' ' Eden,' ' Spur,' ' Stirrup,' ' Goodgame,' ' Skill,' ' Churchman,' ' Unthank,' ' Temperance,' ' Gooddeknow,' ' Reuniting,' ' Goedowne,' ' Tomorrow,' ' Thrift,' ' Rawbone,' ' Barebone,' ' Piesmith,' ' Ratt,' ' Screewe,' ' Doubtfire,' ' Posey.' ' Land ' and ' Coast ' and ' Flood ' were buried the same day; ' Nurse ' married ' Child,' so did ' Bird,' ' Nest.' ' Tongue,' ' Faith,' ' Pride,' lay near each other, and ' Joy ' was buried a few days later. ' Pine,' soon followed ' Paine ' and

'Stillgo' ended his race. 'Leasure,' 'Swift,' 'Speed,' 'Lovely,' 'Vinegar,' 'Wildgoose.' Of colours we have Scarlet, Brown, Pink, Violet, Black, White, Gray, Blue, Greene, Red, but Yellow is not met with save in 'Yellowlees.' 'Measures,' 'Self,' 'Friend,' and 'Ego,' Register 'Shame,' 'Orange,' 'Pretious,' 'Mangowne,' 'Breath,' 'Harness,' 'Thirdketle,' 'Hornbuckle,' 'Hatter,' 'Halfehead,' 'Blackstar,' 'Crosskeies,' 'Dragoone,' 'Buttress,' 'Tarpenny,' 'Farthing,' 'Holdeforth,' 'Haddock,' 'Dudgeon,' 'Hardtasker,' 'Love,' 'Hostage,' 'Porloine,' 'Pistoll,' 'Muskitt,' 'Canon,' 'Rainmortar.' What 'Joseph Sparks Last Ellis' means we do not know, as the owner of the name died in 1651, before the multiplication of Christian names, 'Sparks Last Ellis,' must stand for the surname. 'Sugar,' 'Wassaille,' 'Jackett,' 'Justice,' 'Thunderman,' 'Sign,' 'Velvit,' 'Basin,' 'Godbid,' 'Eatebread,' 'Comfort.'

We have given the names as we met with them. It is difficult to classify them. It will be apparent that in many cases the peculiarity is due to the spelling adopted by the clerk. The following are instances of rare Christian names, or of strange combinations—'Parsada,' 'Darby,' 'Island,' 'Attoway,' 'Ziphora,' 'Hosanna,' 'Repentance,' 'Avis,' 'Lyney,' 'Pound,' 'Bethulia,' 'Mirabel,' 'Flower,' 'Virtue,' 'Oringa,' 'Hamiah,' 'Devee,' 'Dedoria,' 'Isbrood,' 'Creature,' 'Renathaniell,' 'Johnbaptis' (*sic*), 'Comparini,' 'Lazarus,' 'Maximilian,' 'Gamaliel,' 'Prudence,' 'Balthazar,' 'Hamlet,' 'Damaras,' 'Fermine,' 'Zacheuss,' 'Uriall,' 'Dulcibell,' 'Charity,' 'Zechoniah,' 'Lemuel;' 'Nicholas' as a woman's name frequently in Clackmannan Registers. 'Fortune,' 'Tuball,' 'Phœnix,' 'Marruria,' (? Mercurius), 'India' 'Plesant,' 'Dorris,' 'Dilsiah,' 'Conyway,' 'Isamore,' 'Jaffa,' 'Izzard,' 'Deverill,' 'Calip,' 'Selora,' 'Hediene,' 'Jodocker,' 'Lacarria,' 'Luther,' 'Zannan,' 'Habbakkuk,' 'Temperance,' 'Tristram,' 'Venter,' 'Athaliah,' 'Mehathabell,' 'Faith,' 'Patience,' 'Mercy,' 'Eunice,' 'Lakehorn,' 'Micah,' 'Farros,' 'Crescent,' 'Lesprience,' 'Damarest,' 'Wyborow,' 'Blythe,' 'Haverline,' 'Quintine,' 'Livewell.' Of combinations, 'Only too large,' 'Collect Wood,' 'Christian Helmet,' 'Ann Angell,' 'True Blue,' 'Prudence Stage.' ED.

159. RINGS GIVEN IN PLEDGE.—The following extracts from the East Anstruther Kirk Session Records are interesting as showing an unusual way in which rings were made use of in connection with matrimony. Perhaps more light will be thrown on the custom which does not appear to have been very common.

'1665, 26 December. There was this day two ringes put with ane purse in the boxe on off which was for a rent George Wilbrie contracted with Margret Meyven the 29 of Julie having I.N. ingraven upon it. The other ring haveing E.D. ingraven wes for a rent Peter Wilsone contracted with Helen Cunninghame the 3d day off November.'

'1673, 6 Oct. Given ys day be Robert Young in hand before his marriage, a gold ring qh was put into ye box.'

'1674, 17 Aug. This day Rob. Young received back his pande towitt a gold ring.'

'1678, 16 April. Alexʳ Adamson being ctracted with Janet Phyall consigned a gold ring for his pledge.'

'1678, 12 Nov. William Farefull gave in a ring for his pledge which was put in the box.'

'1678, 26 Nov. Collected at Baillie Gourlay's son christening and William Farefulls marriage on Nov. 14., 00. 12. 02.'

'1680, 9 May. Given by William Farefull at the receiving of his ring which he pauned at his contract of marriage, oo. 18. oo.'

160. LEVEN (see Note 142).—A discussion on the etymology of 'Leven' took place in *Notes and Queries*, 7th S. iii. pp. 30, 113, 177, 295, etc., when a variety of derivations were suggested. Dr. Reeves and Dr. Joyce, both eminent Celtic authorities, incline to the derivation from *leamhán* (pronounced *lavan*), an elm or *llamhnach* (*lavnagh*), a place where elm-trees grow. *Gleann leamhna* of the Irish Annals is identified (*Vita S. Columba*, p. 378, *note*) with the Leven which flows from Loch Lomond; and the name of the district Lennox, anciently Levenax, probably is formed from the adjectival form *leamhnach*. The tree is the indigenous wych-elm (*ulmus montana*), not the so-called English elm (*ulmus campestris*), which is an imported species.

There is always a tendency to assimilate names which have a similarity; hence it is quite possible that some of the Levens in Scotland and Ireland arise from *liath abhuinn* (pronounced leeavven), the grey river. The numerous rivers named Lee have this signification.

HERBERT MAXWELL.

In my note on this river-name, I stupidly wrote ash for *elm*-trees. Crosby Ravensworth (Westmoreland) is on the Lyvennet (so spelt on maps), which may have something to do with 'the lofty LLWYVENYDD' of Taliessin.

At Innerleithen, the TH is pronounced as in the English word THE, corresponding with the Welsh LLYDO, to pour, and suggesting that the Water of LEITH was probably pronounced in like manner. We have INVERLEITH yet; but is there any trace of *Aber*leith, corresponding to Abercorn to the WEST, and Aberlady to the EAST of it?

A book I recently read, stated, I think, that there were no Abers south of the Scots' water.   W. M. C.

161. MARRIAGES RECORDED IN *Acta Dom. Conc.* AND *Acta Dom. Aud.*, 1466-1495.—The following alphabetical catalogue of the marriages recorded in the *Acta Dom. Conc.*, 1478-1495, and *Acta Dom. Auditorum*, 1466-1494, has been prepared in accordance with the suggestion made at page 57 of last number of *Northern Notes and Queries*. The letter *A* prefixed to an entry indicates that the marriage has been met with in the *Acta Auditorum* only. The figures /91, and so forth, indicate the year (1491), under which the reference to the marriage occurs. The letter (*d*) added in brackets after a name shows that the person named was dead at the date of the reference. The figures (1), (2), or (3) placed after or before a name show that the person so marked was first, second, or third husband (or wife, as the case may be).   Σ.

Abernethy, Jonet, 1488, Thomas Ogilvy.

Abernethy, Margaret, /91, Gilbert Fordis.

Abernethy, Katherine, /94, Alexander Esse or Effe.

A Abernethy, ... (1), /91, Christian Cockburn.

A Agnew, Quintin, /94, Marion Waus.

Akynhead, John, /92, Violet Elphinstone.

Aldicraw, Patrick, /91, Margaret Lindsay, Lady of Cräling.

Allardyce, George (*d*), /88, Jonet Pitcairne.

A Anderson, George, /79, Margaret Dewar.

'Angus Herald,' /90, Katherine Hamilton.

Arnot, John, /94, Marjory Balfour.

Auchinleck, James, /92, Gelis Melville.

Auchinleck, James, /95, Gelis Ross.
Auchinleck, Adam (*d*), /95, Jonet Inglis.
Auchinleck, father of Adam (*d*), /90, Christian Douglas.
Bailzie, William, of Watstoun (2), /94, Marion Crechtoun (Mrs. Tweedie).
A Balbirny, Elizabeth, /74, William Carribers (*d*).
A Balcasky, Mary, /74, John Grenschelis (*d*).
Balcolmy, James (2), /92, Isobel, Lady of Bar.
Balfour, Christian, /78, William Bonar (*d*).
Balfour, Andrew (2), /84, Mirabel Kinnear.
Balfour, Marjory, /94, John Arnot.
Balfour, James (Glendowglas), /95, Jonet Stewart (?Baldarran).
Bannatyne, Thomas (*d*), /91, Agnes M'Connell (*see* Isles).
Bar, John (*d*) (1), /92, Isobel, Lady of Bar.
Barbour, Katherine (*d*), /90, Lucas Brois (Bruce).
Barcare (Barker?), Jonet, /90, David Blindsele.
Baroun, Sir Patrick (*d*), of Spittalfield (1), /90, Marion Liddale.
A Belton, (? Boulton), Mary, Lady of, /91, George Hume, of Aiton.
Berclay, Christian, /95, Peter Monypenny (*d*).
Berclay, David (*d*), of Collairny, /95, Margery Dowglas.
Berclay, David (*d*), of Collairny, /95, Margaret Dury.
A Berclay, Marjory, /91, David Rollock.
Bissait, father of George, /94, Annabel Kinnear.
Blackadder, Baldred (2), /92, Margaret Melville.
Blair, ... (*d*), of that Ilk, /76, M. Makmorane.
Blair, David (*d*), of Adamton, /91, Agnes Brois (Bruce). (He was alive in 1483.)
Blair, David (*d*), of Bendachy, /93, Jonet Rattray.
Blindsele, David, /90, Jonet Barcare.
Blith, Alexander (2), /92, Agnes Todrik.
Bonar, William (*d*), /78, Christian Balfour.
Borthwick, Jonet, /91, Peter Murray.
Borthwick, Elizabeth, /93, Andrew Gray (*d*), of Balheloy.
Boswell, Effame, /90, David Meldrum, of Newhall.
A Boswell, John, /76, Marion Lothresk.
A Boyd, Margaret (1), David Cathcart (*d*) (*see* D.P.I. 340); /88, (2), John Crawford.
A Boyd, Archibald, /94, Christian Mure.
Boyis, Margaret, /93, John Wemyss (*d*).
Boyis, Margaret, /95, Archibald Ramsay.

A Bris (? Brison), Jonet, /88, John M'Cailzie.
A Broun, Jonet, /71, ... Scougale.
Bruce (Brois), Robert, /90, Margaret Preston.
Bruce, Lucas, /90, Katherine Barbour.
Bruce, Sir David, of Clackmannan (2), /90, Marion Herries.
Bruce, Agnes, /91, David Blair (*d*), of Adamton.
Bruce, Edward, /93, Christian, sister of Sir David Stewart, of Rosyth.
Buyt, Jonet, /95, Henry Mondwell, Burgess of Wygtoun.
Campbell, James, of Carsewell, /93, Margaret Waus.
Campbell, Margaret, /94, Hector M'Gilline, of Lochboyg.
A Campbell, Duncan (2), /81, Margaret Drummond.
Cant, Christian, /88, Archibald Dundas.
Cant, Walter, /91, Margaret Libbertoun.
Carkettle, Jonet, /90, Thomas Turing.
Carkettle, Jonet, /92, George Levingstone (*d*), Burgess of Edinburgh.
A Carlile, Sir William, /91, Jonet Maxwell.
A Carmichael, Beatrix, /82, James Dunbar (*d*).
A Carruthers (? Carribers), William (*d*), /74, Elizabeth Balbirny.
A Carruthers (? Carribers), William (*d*), /74, Agnes Fawlaw.
A Carruthers, William, /78, Christian Kinglassie.
A Carruthers, Marion, /78, John Menzies (*d*), of the Weme.
A Cathcart, Christian, /89, Alexander Hamilton.
A Chaip (Cheape), Margaret, /78, Robert Dowy (*d*).
Chalmer (Chawmr), Gelis, /90, Robert Maknare.
Chalmer, Sir John, of Gaitgirth, /92, Jonet Hamilton.
A Chalmer, Christian, /94, Humphrey Cunningham.
Charteris, Sir William (*d*), of Cagnor, /80, Elizabeth Stewart.
A Charteris, William, of Kinfauns, /76, 'Christian, Lady, the Graham.'
Clóstoun (Clogstone), Michell (*d*), /95, Christian Walcare (? Walker).
A Cocherane, Michell, /88, Euphame Erskine.
Cockburn, Alex., of Ormiston, /88, Margaret Schaw.
Cockburn, Christian, (1) . . . Abernethy (*d*), /91, (2) James Sinclair.
Cockburn Margaret, (1) Gavane Crichton (*d*), /91, (2) John Wardlaw.
Cockburn, Gelis, /93, Alexander Murray (*d*) of Shillinglaw.
Cockburn, Margaret, (1) John Lindsay (*d*), /94, (2) William Hay of Tallo.

Cockburn, George, /95, Jonet Giffard.

Colp, William, /92, Christian Turing.

Colquhon, Sir John, /95, Elizabeth Dunbar.

A Colquhon, Margaret, /89, David Douglas.

Colrode, . . . (1)(*d*), /94, Jonet Hervey.

Congalton, Edward (2), /90, Jonet Seton, Lady of Dirleton.

Corour, Margaret, /78, Henry Hepburne of Westfortoun.

A Corry, Herbert, /89, Esot Murray.

Cosoᵣ (? Corser), Adam (*d*) (1), /91, Katherine Fotheringham.

Cosoᵣ, Elene, (1) John Schaw (*d*) /94, (2) John Ogilvy.

Crage, John, of that Ilk, /92, Christian Hog.

A Craigmillar, Jonet, Lady of, (1) Wᵐ· Preston of Craigmillar, /91, (2) William Somerville of Grealton.

Crake, Philip, /71, Margaret Scougall.

Cramy, Arthur (*d*), /84, Isabel Murehead.

Craufurd, Isobel, /94, James Forrester.

A Craufurd, John (2), /90, Margaret Boyd.

A Craufurd, Marion, /93, Robert Cunningham (*d*) of Polquharne.

Crawmond, Thomas (*d*), /90, Margaret Gardin.

Crichton, Sir James (*d*), of Ragorton, /91, Margaret Symple.

Crichton, Gavane (*d*) (1), /91, Margaret Cockburne.

Crichton, Christian, /92, John Martin (*d*) of Medhope.

A Crichton, Marian, /78, (1) James Tuedy of Drumelzare, /94, (2) William Bailzie of Watstoun.

A Crichton, . . . /91, James Hering (*d*).

A Crichton, Margaret, /91, Lawrence Wallace.

A Crichton, Christian, /78, Alexander Erskine.

Cromy, Richard, /93, Marion Martin.

A Culane, Margaret (2), /94, James Innes (*d*) of that Ilk.

A Cumyn, Alex. (*d*), of Ernefield, /88, Mary Leslie.

Cunningham, Agnes, /93, Thomas Galbraith (*d*) of Kilcroich.

Cunningham, Robert (*d*), of Cunninghamhead, /95, Elspeth Ross.

A Cunningham, Robert (*d*), of Polquharne, /93, Marion Craufurd.

A Cunningham, Humphrey, /94, Christian Chawmer.

A Dempster, Gelis, /91, father of Robert Fotheringham.

A Dewar, Margaret, /78, George Anderson.

A Dewar, Margaret, /89, Archibald Hume.

Dickson (Diksone), /89, Marion Moubray.

A Dishington, Elizabeth, /91, John Wemyss (*d*).

A Donaldson, Patrick (*d*), /73, Elizabeth Ruthven.

Douglas, James, /80, Jonet Hume.

Douglas, Sir William (*d*), of Whittingham, /84, Margaret Fleming.

Douglas, John, /76, Jonet Rynd.

Douglas, Christian, /90, father of Adam Auchinleck.

Douglas, Jonet, /92, William Somerville (*d*).

Douglas, James, /92, Elizabeth Ugstoun.

Douglas, Marjory, /95, David Berclay (*d*) of Collairny.

A Douglas, Elspeth, /84, Alex. Ramsay (*d*) of Dawolly.

A Douglas, David, /89, Margaret Colquhon.

A Douglas, (?) Archibald, of Colschogill, /82, Euphame Maxwell, 'Lady of Pothouse.'

A Douglas, James, /93, Elizabeth Hay.

A Dowy, Robert (*d*), /78, Margaret Chaip.

A Drummond, Walter, /78, Elizabeth Scrymgeour.

A Drummond, Margaret, (1) Andrew Mercer (*d*), of Drumberny; /81, (2) Duncan Campbell.

A Drummond, John (2), /91, Marion, Countess of Menteth.

Dunbar, Elizabeth, 'Lady of Luss,' /82, Sir John Colquhon (*d*).

A Dunbar, James (*d*), /82, Beatrix Carmichael.

A Dunbar, Margaret, /84, father of Robert Livingstone, executor of late Edward Livingstone of Balcastle.

A Dunbar, Patrick (*d*), /88, Annabel Boyd.

A Dunbreck, William, /91, Conny Gordon.

Dundas, Elizabeth, /90, Robert Stirling.

A Dundas, Archibald, /88, Christian Cant.

Dury, Margaret, /95, David Berclay (*d*), of Collairny.

Edmonstone, John, of that Ilk, /82, Margaret Maitland.

Edmonstone, James, /95, Elene Murray.

Elphinstone, Violet, /92, John Akynhead.

A Elphinstone, Agnes, /91, Gilbert Johnstone of Elphinstone.

Erskine, Patrick (*d*), /91, Alison Spens.

A Erskine, Christian, /66, Alexander Erskine.

A Erskine, Euphame, /88, Michell Cocherane.

A Erskine, Alexander, /78, Christian Crichton.

Esse, Alexander, /94, Katherine Abernethy.

Fawlaw, Agnes, /74, William Carribers (*d*).

Ferne, Agne⁵, /95, John Williamson (*d*), Burgess of Elgin. [But at page 397 his name is given as Robertson.]

Fleming, Margaret, /84, Sir Wᵐ. Douglas (*d*), of Whittingham.

Fleming, Malcolm (*d*), (1) /92, Euphame (?)

Fleming, William, of the Bord (2), Euphame (?)

A Fokkart, Alexander, /94, Christian Lowis.

Fordis, Gilbert, /91, Margaret Abernethy.

Forrester, David (*d*), of Torwood, /92, Marion Somerville.

Forrester, James, /94, Isabel Craufurd.

Fotheringham, Katherine, (1) Adam Cosoʳ (Corser?) (*d*), of Stirling, /91 ; (2) Michell Levingston.

A Fotheringham, father of Robert, /91, Gelis Dempster.

Fraser (Frisale), Annas, /94, Kenzoch Mackenzie (*d*).

A Fraser, Margaret, /82, James Murray (*d*).

A Fraser, Elizabeth, /90, Thomas Gudelad (*d*).

A Frost (?), Margaret, /79, William Stevyn.

Fullarton, Alexander, /94, Katherine Lyale.

Galbraith, Thomas (*d*), of Kilcroich, /93, Agnes Cunynham.

A Galbraith, John (*d*), of Ballindrocht, /83, Elizabeth Stewart.

Gardin, Margaret, /90, Thomas Crawmond (*d*), of Melgund.

Gardin, Katherine, /94, 'Ross Herald' (*d*).

Gargunnock, Laird of (*d*), /93, Marion Seton.

Giffard, Jonet, /95, George Cokburn.

Glen, Marion, /90, Robert Schaw of Balgerry.

Glendonwyn, Mathew (*d*), of Glenrath (1), /92, Margaret Waith.

A Glendonwyn, Elizabeth, /73, William Weir.

A Glendonwyn, Margaret, 'Lady of Lag,' /88, . . . Grierson (?).

Goldsmyth, David, /78, Margaret Knichtsoun.

A Gordon, Conny, /91, William Dunbreck.

Gorty, Elizabeth, /95, Fulane Strogeith of that Ilk.

Graham, John (*d*), /91, Margaret Muschet.

A Graham, 'Christian, Lady the,' /76, Wᵐ. Charteris of Kinfauns.

Gray, Thomas, /84, Marjory Scott.

Gray, Andrew (*d*), of Balhelvy, /93, Elizabeth Borthwick.

A Gray, Marion, /84, Alexander Straiton of the Knox.

Grenschelis, John (*d*), /74, Mary Balcasky.

Grierson, ... (*d*), of Lag, /88, Margaret Glendonwyn.

Grundiston, David (*d*), (1), /84, Mirabel Kinnear.

Gudelad, Thomas (*d*), /90, Agnes Nemoch (Nimmo).

Gudelad, Thomas (*d*), /90, Elizabeth Fresale (Fraser).

Guthrie, Christian, /94, George Somyr. *or* Sumiʳ.

Guthrie, Elizabeth, /94, William Murray (*d*), of Cullon.

A Guthrie, Malcolm (*d*), /83, Marjory Straithbachᵉ.

Haldane, Patrick (2), /95, Isobel Murray.

Hallis, Lord (Hailes), /84, Elene Wallace.

Halkerston, William, /84, Margaret Lamb.

Halyburton, Jonet, /88, John Knolles.

Halyburton, Alexander (*d*), /84, Margaret Lamb.

Halyburton, Elene, (1) John Mossman (*d*), /91 ; (2) Lawrence Tailziefer.

Halyburton, Walter (*d*), /91, Christian Stewart.

Hulyburton, Jonet, /92, John Sinclare.

Halyday, John, /94, Elizabeth Moffet.

Hamilton, Adam (*d*), of Prestgill, /88, Agnes Levingston.

Hamilton, Jonet, /92, Sir John Chawmʳ of Gaitgirth.

A Hamilton, Robert, of Fengalton, /88, Marion Johnstone.

Hamilton, Katherine, /90, 'Angus' Herald.

A Hamilton, William, /88, Christian Inglis.

A Hamilton, Alexander, /89, Christian Cathcart.

A Hamilton, Elizabeth, /78, Helise Makcoulach.

A Hamilton, Alexander, /94, Isobel Hog.

Harlaw, Marion, /91, George Robison (*d*).

Hart, Alison, /95, Adam Young.

Harvy, Robert, /92, Elizabeth, daughter of Wm. Smith in Inveresk.

Hay, William, of Tallo, (2) /94, Margaret Cockburn.

A Hay, William (*d*) of Tallo, /79, Margaret Mowbray.

A Hay, Elizabeth, /93, James Douglas.

Henryson, John, /80, Christian Schank.

Henryson, George (*d*), /92, Elizabeth Peeblis.

Hepburn, Henry, of Westfortoun, /78, Margaret Curour.

Hepburn, Katherine, /92, George Robison.

[1] I think this was the Controller of the Household in 1468.

QUERIES.

XCIV. ROSEMARY DACRE.—In a pamphlet by Ellen K. Goodwin (Kendal, T. Wilson, 1886), reprinted from the Transactions of the Cumberland and Westmorland Antiquarian and Archæological Society, on 'Rosemary Dacre and the White Cockade,' a letter from Rosemary Dacre (Lady Clerk) is quoted, in which she states that she was born at Rose Castle, 6 miles from Carlisle, on Nov. 15, 1745, and baptized immediately afterwards, and records the well-known incident of a party of Highlanders arriving, waiting till the ceremony was concluded, and their leader taking off his white cockade, and leaving it as a protection against any stragglers of the Highland army.

The author then quotes an entry from the parish register of Kirklintow, Cumberland, in which the baptism of 'Mary, daughter of Joseph Dacre, Esq.,' is stated to have taken place at Rose Castle, on Nov. 3, 1745.

Further, the author refers to 'An Authentic Account of the Occupation of Carlisle in 1745,' by George Gill Mounsey, p. 41 (London, Longmans & Co.) where it is stated that none of the Highlanders crossed the Border before the 7th or 8th of November.

Could these dates be made to agree, if we assume that the first and last dates given were calculated according to New Style; and that the date in the English parish register was calculated according to Old Style? J. M. G.

[See footnote to the 'Runaway Registers,' p. 69. That confusion did sometimes exist is shown by the well-known lines of Burns,—

'There was a lad was born in Kyle,
But what'n a day o' what'n a style,
I doubt it 's hardly worth the while
To be sae nice wi' Robin.' D.]

XCV. ARCHBISHOP SHARP.—Archbishop Sharp married Helen, daughter of Moncrieff of Randerston. Is the date of their marriage known? W. T. W.

XCVI. SIR WILLIAM SHARP OF STONYHILL.—William, son of James Sharp, Minister of Crail, afterwards Archbishop of St. Andrews, was appointed Deputy Keeper of the Signet in 1660, on a Commission issued by John, Earl (Duke) of Lauderdale, Hon. Secretary. He must then have been very young, for the date of the Archbishop's birth is given as either 1613 or 1618. He became owner of Stonyhill near Musselburgh. On the 29th of October 1669, he still appears in the official minutes as 'Mr. William Sharpe.' On the 11th of March 1670 he is first described as a Knight. He remained Deputy Keeper until 1682. Is anything more known of his history? W. T. W.

XCVII. RINGING A MILLEN-BRIDLE.—In the Kirk Session Book of Alves the following entries occur :—

'March 15th, 1663. This day the minister represented to the Eldership that he had heard of a verie sinful miscarriage in some people in Easter Alves the last week, viz. the ringing of a millen-bridle (as they call it) upon ane aged and diseased poor woman called Margaret Anderson, thereby to hasten her to death as they conceived. Their names are Andrew Angouse and Agnes Rob. The Session appointed them to be cited to the next dyet.

'March 22d, 1663. Compeared Andrew Angouse confessed he rang the bridle, he being interrogated what were the words he spake at the ringing of it answered that he said crans flesh or wrans flesh come out thy way. Agnes Rob confessed she went and sought for and brought to the house the bridle at the diseased woman her own desyre. They are appointed to be reproved publickly the next day, with certification if the like carriage be practised by them on anie others of the parish *pro futuro* they shall be censured with sackcloth, and this to be intimated the next day.'

The questions requiring solution are (1.) What is a millen-bridle? (2.) How was it 'rung?' (3.) Why should the 'ringing' of the bridle hasten the death of one who was supposed to be unable to die easily? (4.) Is any other instance of this superstition known? J. A.

XCVIII. MITCHELL AND BUCHANAN.—James Mitchell [*b.* about 1705] came from Glasgow, or its neighbourhood, about 1730, to New England, and settled in Wethersfield, Connecticut.

His elder brother William Mitchell [*b.* about 1704], Agnes Buchanan his wife [*b.* about 1700], and their son William [b. about 1735], came from Glasgow in 1755 to Chester, Connecticut. Can the ancestry of these Mitchells be traced?

Family records say that Agnes Buchanan, wife of William Mitchell, was 'aunt of Rev. Claudius Buchanan,' D.D. As he was born in 1766, she was probably his great-aunt. Dr. Buchanan was a son of Alexander Buchanan, supposed to be a native of Inveraray, who was Rector of the Grammar-School of Falkirk.

Can the ancestry of these Buchanans be ascertained? Are there any living descendants of the brothers and sisters of Dr. Buchanan, or of his daughters Charlotte and Augusta? Kindly reply to this Magazine, or to Mrs. Edward Elbridge Salisbury, New Haven, Connecticut.

REPLIES TO QUERIES.

LXXXIII. BRABONER.—"The Netherlanders were masters of the Linnen Trade as well as the Woollen; and during these civil wars [in the Netherlands, in the 16th century], several of their manufacturers in both, settled themselves amongst us; as in the old Burghs, weavers go still under the designation of Brabanders, from their masters who taught them the art" (p. 77, *The Interest of Scotland Considered*). London: printed for T. Woodward, at the Half-moon, between the two Temple Gates in Fleet-street, and J. Reele, at Locke's Head, in Amen Corner, Paternoster Row, 1736.   H.

[The word is used in the marriage registers of Wandsworth, Surrey, now being printed by Mr. Squire :—

' 1672, July 30. Dennis de Prince and Katherine Culveneer, Brabanters, licence.']

LXXXVI. TIGGERS.—The specific instructions for dealing with 'Tiggers' is contained in Act 4 of the Abridgment of the ancient 'COUNTRY ACTS OF ZETLAND,' an early printed copy of which is before me. By this it is provided :—

'That all Tiggers of wool, corn, fish, and others, be apprehended wherever they come, by any that can find them, and to put them in firmance, to be punished with the stocks and joggs, and that none receipt them in their houses, nor give them hospitality, or service, under the pain of Ten pounds (Scots) *toties quoties.*'

In the INSTRUCTIONS TO RANSELMEN, the body of officials in Shetland parishes formerly appointed to make inquisition in cases of theft, petty crimes, and misdemeanours, these officials are directed not to allow 'any beggar, or thigger, from any other parish, to pass through your bounds; and if they offer so to do, you will secure them till they be punished, conform to the Country Act 4th.'

The term, as used in these instances, would at first sight seem to indicate a *thief*, but the explanatory alternative, 'or Beggar' in the last quotation, and on the margin in the original of the 'Country Acts,' seems to point at another class of offenders, who, at the same time, were perhaps not altogether common mendicants. The word 'Thiggar,' which is the form of the spelling in early copies of the Acts, is defined by Jameson as 'One who draws on others for subsistence in a genteel sort of way.'

The word is identical with the modern Danish *tigger*, 'a beggar,' and has its origin in the Old Northern *thiggja*, 'to receive,' 'accept of,' which, according to the Cleasby-Vigposson Lexicon, was sometimes used elliptically as—'to take lodging, or receive hospitality for a night,' thus coming to be applied to persons of the class who made free with other people's hospitality, and craved their property at the same time.

                     GILBT. GOUDIE.

XCI. BENNET FAMILY.—The following is an Extract from Dr. Hew Scott's *Fasti Ecclesiæ Scoticanæ*, part ii. p. 483.

ANCRUM.

1622 William Bennett, A.M., was laureated at the Univ. of Edin. 30th July 1614, presented by James VI. 25th July 1622. He was a member of the Commission for maintaining Church discipline, 21st Oct. 1634, about which time he gave xl. lib.

towards erecting the Librarie in the Univ. of Glasgow. Having purchased an estate, he exercised his privilege as a freeholder by voting for a commissioner from the county to the Convention. The General Assembly, 16th Aug. 1643, found these powers incompatible with the ministry, and recommended him to abstain from civil courts and meetings, etc. He died between 3d Feb. and 1st Sept. 1647, aged about 54, leaving a son, William, who was retoured heir to his lands of Grubet, Wydehope, etc., 29th Dec. following. [*Reg. Laur. Univ. Edin., Sec. Sigill., and Pres., Presb. Reg., Calderwood, and Stevenson's Hist., Mun. Univ. Glasg. iii., Bannatyne iii., and Maitland Miscell. ii., Baillie's Lett., Ing. Ret. Roxburgh,* 195 *de Tut.* 58.]

J. T. M.

XCIX. MARRIAGE OF HUGH ROSE AND CHRISTIAN INNES.—It is a matter of some importance to obtain the registration of the marriage of Hugh Rose (of Kilravock Roses) to Christian Innes daughter of Alexander and Catherine Innes of Cairnend, Speymouth parish, which took place about 1735-40; or of the baptism of Euphemia Rose, their daughter, about 1740. It is not known where the marriage or the baptism took place, only it is not in any of the Parish Registers, and Dean Ferguson writes me it is not in his. A brother of Euphemia's was baptized at Tain. It is not known where the married couple may have wandered, but they finished life in the parish of Tyrie.

G.L.

[G. L. may find some information in Cosmo Innes's work on the Rose family, which, however, I have not seen.—ED.]

NOTICES OF BOOKS.

Anstruther, or Illustrations of Scottish Burgh Life, by George Gourlay. Anstruther: George Gourlay.—Mr. Gourlay is not only a burgess of Anstruther, he is a man who does his duty by his native town. As such he may be held up as an example to be followed by others. We do not suppose the history of Anstruther surpasses in richness that of other Scottish towns. Its treasures, however, have been brought to light as other like treasures should be, by an inhabitant of the place. If Mr. Gourlay seems occasionally to lean to old wives' fables, we can forgive him, in consideration of the many undoubted facts he records. The volume of 177 pages is well printed, well bound, and reasonable in price, and may serve as a model of what a Burgh or Parochial History should be.

Stratford-upon-Avon Note-Books. No. I., Shakespearian Extracts from 'Edward Pudsey's Booke.' Collected by Richard Savage, Secr. and Lib., Shakespeare's Birthplace. London: Simpkin & Marshall.—We welcome the appearance of No. I. of what we trust will be a goodly collection of 'Note Books.' The Library at Stratford-on-Avon must contain many literary treasures, and Mr. Savage is well fitted for the task of extracting such as may prove of special interest. This volume consists of extracts from a common-place book kept by a country gentleman who lived near Stratford when Shakespeare was residing there. Passages from the plays then fresh from his pen are given; a good proof that they were regarded as genuine by one who had every opportunity of knowing. Mr. Savage has, we believe, discovered that he was mistaken in considering that 'Irus' was a play of Shakespeare's hitherto unknown. 'Irus' being a character in a work of another author. The error has, we believe, been corrected in a later edition of the Notes. Edward Pudsey's evidence is most valuable, and Mr. Savage is to be congratulated in producing a volume, attractive outside, and singularly interesting when opened.

The Sutherland Papers. Pocock's Tour, 1760. Printed for the Sutherland Association, Edinburgh.—Last year the Scottish History Society issued *Bishop Pocock's Tour in Scotland.* The volume was only printed for members. The Editor, Mr. D. William Kemp, has wisely produced for the members of the Sutherland Association that portion of the work which treats of that county. The result is an interesting little volume, well illustrated, and furnished with valuable Notes and Appendix.

History of Prose Fiction, by John Colin Dunlop. London: George Bell & Sons.—This is a reprint of a work which was first published as long ago as 1814. The author died in 1842. The two volumes now before us are well annotated, which adds considerably to their value. The range taken by the author is a wide one. Commencing with Greek Romance, he works down to the present century, tracing the family likeness of many of the tales, and following them through their wanderings. Carefully prepared charts afford much assistance in studying a subject which is too little appreciated by those who would read with more profit if they studied the influence which romance has had on the world.

William Shakespeare, a Literary Biography, by Karl Elze, Ph.D., LL.D. London: George Bell & Sons.—This book, which was published in Germany in 1876, has now been translated by L. Dora Schmitz. Its appearance at the present time is most opportune, and those who have taken any interest in the Bacon-Shakespeare controversy should study it. It is interesting throughout, and not only is a careful literary biography of England's great poet, but an interesting description of the period in which he lived. He cannot be accused of fulsome flattery, for occasionally his opinion of the poet seems unduly harsh, but he is never guilty of the coarseness which is to be found in the writings of some of those whose attacks on Shakespeare have lately excited some attention. An Appendix contains an interesting account of the Portraits of Shakespeare.

Northern Notes and Queries

OR

The Scottish Antiquary

CONTENTS.

NOTE.—*The Editor does not hold himself responsible for the opinions or statements of Contributors.*

162. OLD LINEN.—*Northern Notes & Queries* for December 1886 contained some notes, sent in response to a query, upon some old table linen brought to Scotland by Major-General James Ferguson of Balmakelly, who died in 1705. There have recently been shown to me two pieces of old linen, one of which commemorates events of the same kind, though posterior in date, as those recorded on the linen then described, while the other, curiously enough, belonged to a near relative of its owner. They are the property of Mr. James Bruce, W.S., 23 St. Bernard's Crescent, Edinburgh.

The first—much finer in texture than the other—contains in the centre a representation of two Christian horsemen, each firing a pistol at a turbaned Turk.   In each case another Turk is already down beneath the heels of the rearing charger, while the one at whom the pistol is fired bends back, with uplifted scimitar, holding in his left hand a flag bearing the Crescent and Star.   Beneath is the word ' *Belgrade* ' above the representation of a city, the topmost tower of which is crowned with a crescent, while a river flows past it.   Across the river, and nearer the edge of the cloth, are guns in position, a gunner firing them, and another apparently engaged in handing a shell.   Between the batteries, which converge and balance each other in the pattern, as do the horsemen above, are two other soldiers, holding banners, and with fascines beside them.   Above the horsemen again is another town with the word ' Temesvar,' and above that the two-headed eagle, and on each side of it a shield with many quarterings.   Below each shield is a turbaned figure on its knees, with the hands manacled, while one of two chains, attached to the manacles in each case, is grasped by the eagle's talons, and the other is fastened to the quartered shield.   Round the whole runs a border containing representations of towns, alternating with the usual trophies of guns, trumpets, drums, flags, etc.   The names of these towns are ' Waradin,' ' Beuda,' ' Semlin,' and ' Palanka.'   The conjunction of names points clearly to the campaign of 1716-17.   The names on the linen described in my previous communication were ' Buda,' ' Pesth,' ' Gran,' and ' Nie.'   Gran was taken by the Imperialists in 1684, and Buda in 1686.   The linen now described is marked with the letter G, and was given to Mr. Bruce's maternal grandmother by the Rev. George Garioch of Old Meldrum, who belonged to a well-known family in, or near, the district of the same name.   The name Garioch of Kilstearis occurs frequently in Aberdeenshire records.

The other piece seems to have been cut from a larger cloth, as the border is only found on one side, and the figures are repeated, as if they had been carried on in lines.   At the top are the words ' Friedrick August Konigin Pollen,' repeated above a crowned figure on horseback.   Below come a succession of flying cherubs, then a series of shields, flanked by sprigs of laurel, surmounted by large crowns, and bearing *two crosses potent in pale*.   Still lower is a city, with ships riding on the waters before it, and the word ' Dantzig ' above its towers.   Beneath this again are a series of figures of a single soldier holding a lance, and seemingly standing guard over what look like barrels and bales of goods.   Then again come the words ' Friedrick August.'   The border has nothing remarkable, consisting simply of conventional flowers.   Mr. Bruce has inherited this piece of linen, which is marked with an F, from his father's mother, who was the great grand-daughter of William Ferguson of Badifurrow and sister of the General.   This Janet married—it is said, after a courtship of the kind immortalised in Longfellow's *Miles Standish*—her cousin John Ferguson, and went with him to Poland, where they lived for many years.   One nephew at least also went to seek his fortune there in 1703, with such success that when his son or grandson was next heard of in Scotland, he was a member of the Polish Diet, had been congratulated by the King of Prussia on becoming a Prussian landowner, had a son in the Prussian Guards, and was said to be the richest banker in the East of Europe.

J. F.

163. THE ROYAL ARMS IN SCOTLAND.—In the Pheasant House in the grounds of St. Fort, near Newport, there is a stone, of which a sketch is annexed. It has been lying there for many years, and its history is unknown, but it is supposed to have been originally built into the old mansion-house of St. Fort, probably above the entrance door. That house was demolished when the new one was built about sixty years ago. The stone, which is much weather-worn, has on it the Arms of James VI. after he succeeded to the throne of England, and is interesting as showing the manner in which the Royal Arms were borne in Scotland after the Union of the Crowns. It will be observed that the Scottish Arms get the more honourable place in every way. The Scottish lion occupies the first and fourth quarters of the shield; the Scottish supporter, the Unicorn, which is crowned, is on the dexter side, so is the Scottish Ensign, the St. Andrew's Cross, while the Scottish Crest, the lion sejant, is used with the Scottish motto, 'In defence.' Below the shield, where the Orders of the Thistle and the Garter are shown, St. Andrew's Cross is placed above St. George's Cross, thus giving pre-eminence in every detail to Scotland.

It will be remembered that at the opening of the Glasgow Exhibition a number of letters appeared in the Glasgow newspapers as to the proper manner of marshalling the Royal Arms when used in Scotland. The stone at St. Fort is valuable as showing how they were borne in this country after the accession of James VI. to the throne of England. Below the Royal Arms is a curious inscription :—

> Ther is no fisching to the Sie,
> Nor serves lyk a King's thats fr[ee];
> God gives them means weil to reward,
> Such as to [virtue have] regard.

Alexander Nairn, of Sandfurd, was Private Chamberlain to the Queen of James VI., hence probably the use of the Royal Arms on his house. Mr. and Mrs. Corbet, of St. Fort, have had their attention directed to this interesting stone, and have taken means to protect it from further dilapidation.   R. C. W.

[A description of this stone appeared in the *Dundee Advertiser*. By the kindness of the Editor we are able to give our readers a sketch of it.]

164. RUNAWAY REGISTERS, HADDINGTON (*continued from page* 71).—

27. 1766. Oct. 25. John Norris, Esqr., of St. James, and Catherine Maria Fischer of St. George's, Hanover Square, both in the city of Westminster. *W.* John Pollard, Barthw. Bower.

28. „ Nov. 9. Evan Prichard of Lantrissant, Gent., and Susannah Thomas, Spinster, of Lamblethian, Co. Glamorgan. *W.* John Gidding, Barthw. Bower.

29. „ „ 19. Thomas Wright of Birstall, Clothier, and Lydia Birkhead of the same Parish, Spinster, both in Co. York. *W.* Timothy Crowther, Barthw. Bower.

30. „ Dec. 6. James Ballmer, Esq., and Sophia Escutt, Spinster, both of St. Antholin, London. *W.* Mary Van Wylick, Barthw. Bower.

31. „ „ 9. William Dawkin, Esq., and Charity Mansel, Spinster, both of Swansea, Co. Glamorgan. *W.* Timothy Kelly, Amy Mansel, Mary Mansel.

32. „ „ 21. William Burdon of Stranton, Shipmaster, and Mary Claxton of Hart & Chapelry of Hartlepool, both Co. Durham. *W.* James Fairbairn, Barthw. Bower.

33. 1767. Feb. 21. Charles Horde, Esq., of Lower Swell, Co. Glocester, and Mary Lydia Robins of Ittringham, Co. Norfolk. *W.* Wm. Garner, Barthw. Bower.

34. „ Mar. 12. James Ward of Bury St. Edmunds, St. Mary's Parish, Co. Suffolk, and Ann Dickens of the same Parish. *W.* Barthw. Bower, Clementina Whitlock.

35. „ Apr. 29. Thomas Melson, Husbandman, and Elizabeth Hallam, Widow, of Heyburgh in the Middle Marsh, Co. Lincoln. *W.* Wm. Philips, Barthw. Bower.

36. „ „ 29. Joseph Sealey and Marion Wood, both from Glasgow. *W.* Barthw. Bowers, John Brown.

37. „ May 8. Anselm Odling of Market Raisin, Co. Lincoln, Fell-monger, and Anne Clarke of the same Parish, Spinster. *W.* Wm. Garner, Barthw. Bower.

38. „ „ 8. Henry Henderson of Embleton, Co. Northumberland, Butcher, and Catherine Brooks of Alnwick, same County, Spinster. *W.* John Johnston, Barthw. Bower.

39. „ July 13. Richard Reeve, Surgeon and Apothecary, and Mary Knight Olive, Spinster, both of St. Nicholas, in the city of Rochester, Co. Kent. *W.* Elizb. Burgis, Wm. Garner, Barthw. Bower.

40. „ Aug. 2. Gerrard Selby, Esq., Commander of His Majesty's Cutter 'Meredith,' and Catherine Pemble, Spinster, both of the Chapelry of Belford, Co. Northumberland. *W.* James Fairbairn, Bw. Bower.

41. „ „ 12. John Dinely, Esq., Lieut. in His Royal Highness the Duke of Glocester's Regimt., and Eleanor Olive of St. Nicholas, in the City of Rochester, Co. Kent. *W.* Wm. Garner, Robert Williams.

42. „ „ 16. Nevil Goodman, Farmer, and Susannah Goodman,

Spinster, both of Elm, in the Isle of Ely, Co. Cambridge. *W.* Jonathan Phillips, Bw. Bower.

43. 1767. Sep. 7. Thos. Pigott, Esq., of Horsted Keynes, Co. Sussex, and Hannah Coupe of Maldon, Co. Essex, Spinster. *W.* Thomas Maitland, Anne Wicksteed.

44. „ „ 8. Claude Scott, Corn Factor, of St. Mary, Whitechapel, and Martha Eyres of Stepney, Spinster. *W.* Sarah Elizb. Bird, Barthw. Bower.

45. „ Oct. 28. William Dent of Darlington, Co. Durham, Mercht., and Mary Robson of the same Parish, Spinster. *W.* Edwd. Lister, Will Andrews, John Carfrai.

46. 1768. Jan. 12. Wm. Turner, Esq., and Sarah Bedford, Spinster, both of Leeds, Co. York. *W.* Samuel Kay, Mary Ross, George Hall, Wm. Garner.

47. „ „ 24. William Anderson, late of Virginia, last from St. Olave's, London, Mariner, and Mary Gist, Spinster, of the same Parish. *W.* Isobell Garner, Barthw. Bower.

48. „ Feb. 1. John Mitchison of All Saints', Newcastle, Plummer, and Elizabeth Greenhow of St. Andrews', in Newcastle, Spinster. *W.* Barthw. Bower, Wm. Garner.

49. „ Apr. 2. Samuel Turner of the Town of Sheffield and County of York, Mercer, and Margaret Burton of Mills of the same Parish, Spinster. *W.* Robt. Burton, Barthw. Bower.

50. „ „ 3. Lancelot Carwardine, Cyder Mercht., and Ann Drew, Spinster, both of Ledbury, Co. Hereford. *W.* George Garner, Barthw. Bower.

51. „ „ 5. Thomas Lindsay of Alnwick, Schoolmaster, and Elizabeth Reay of St. Andrews, Newcastle, Co. Northumberland. *W.* Susannah Mitchison and Barthw. Bower.

52. „ „ 12. Thomas Greenwell of All Saints, Newcastle, Tallowchandler, and Ann Smith of Wolsingham, Co. Durham, Spinster. *W.* John Greenwell, Barthw. Bower.

53. „ „ 16. James Wagstaff of Morterham, Co. Chester, Tobacconist and Grocer, and Esther Hill of the same Parish, Spinster. *W.* Nicholas Hill and Barthw. Bower.

54. „ May 20. William Turner of Sevenoaks, Co. Kent, Wine Merchant, and Sally Stonehouse of the same Parish, Spinster. *W.* George Wye, Barthw. Bower.

55. „ June 21. Thos. Sample of Eglingham, Co. Northumberland, Farmer, and Margaret Smith of Belford, same Co., Spinster. *W.* William Garner, Gilbert M'Gilivray.

56. „ July 21. Thomas Dail of Whitby, Co. York, Mariner, and Ann Durham of South Shields, Co. Durham, Spinster. *W.* Martha Major, Barthw. Bower.

57. „ Sept. 17. Joseph Hutchinson of Thirsk, Co. York, Merchant, and Mary Robertson of Watermillock, Graystock, Co. Cumberland, Spinster. *W.* William Sanson, Barthw. Bower.

58. 1768. Sept. 27. John Landell of St. John, Newcastle, Merchant, and Jane Greenhorn of Pryton, Spinster. *W.* John Brown, Barthw. Bower.

59. „ „ 29. Samuel Hooper of St. Clements Danes, Bookseller, and Mary Plaisted of Marybone, Spinster, both of London, Md. 'in the Chapel' of Haddington. *W.* Thomas Viguers, James Fairbairn.

60. „ Oct. 2. George Dods of Stepney, Baker, and Esther Wes of Aldersgate, in the City of London, Spinster. *W.* John Sibbald, George Sibbald, William Grieve, William Dods, Christian Cunningham.

61. „ „ 28. Joseph Sturgis of Sibbertoft, Co. Northampton, Esq., and Martha Gamble of Willoughby Waterless, Co. Leicester, Spinster. *W.* Wm. Gurner, Barthw. Bower.

62. „ Nov. 14. John Sherratt of St. Martins in the Fields, Co. Middlesex, Esq., Lieutenant in the Royal Regiment of Foot, and Jane Jefferies of Ford, Co. Northumberland, Spinster *W.* Barthw. Bower, Gilbert M'Gilivray.

63. „ Dec. 17. Richard Larkin of Offham, Co. Kent, Farmer, and Elizabeth Lee of West Packham, same Co., Spinster, married at Old Cumbus, in the Co. of Berwick. *W.* F. Christopher, Barthw. Bower.

64. 1769. Jan. 20. Thomas Harrison of Scarborough, Co. York, Mariner, and Ann Harrison of Easingwold, same Co., Spinster. *W.* James Fairbairn, Barthw. Bower.

65. „ Feb. 2. John Dickinson of Putney, Co. Surrey, Esq., and Sophia Smith of Cheswick, Co. Middlesex, Spinster. *W.* Juliet Smith, James Fairbairn, Barthw. Bower.

66. „ Mar. 17. Simon Slingsby of St. Georges, Hanover Square, Esq., and Elizabeth Jelfe of Mary-le-bonne, Spinster, both of the City of Westminster. *W.* James Fairbairn, Barthw. Bower, William Messing.

67. „ „ 22. Richard Wignall, Farmer, and Rachell Leroo, Spinster, both of Peterborough, Co. Northampton. *W.* Susannah Leroo, James Fairbairn, Barthw. Bower.

68. „ April 6. John Heptinstall of Pontefract, Co. York, Grocer, and Anna Tomlinson, same Parish, Spinster. *W.* William Garner, Barthw. Bower.

69. „ „ 29. The Rev. Daniel Halloway, Clerk, Curate of Rayleigh, Co. Essex, and Mary Woodford of Hockley, same Co., Spinster. *W.* William Garner, Barthw. Bower.

70. „ May 9. Thos. Baylis, Marble Mason, and Elizabeth Hughes, Spinster, both of Banbury, Co. Oxford. *W.* Thomas Millington, Barthw. Bower.

71. „ „ 30. James Kirk of Scarborough, Co. York, Marriner, and Ann Rennock of the same Town, Spinster. *W.* James Fairbairn, Gilbert M'Gilivray.

72. „ June 1. George Denshire, Esq., of All Saints in Stamford, Co. Lincoln, Capt. in the 9th Regimt. of Foot, and

Ann Brackinbury of Spilsby, same County, Spinster. *W.* George Digby, Barthw. Bower.

73. 1769. June 25. Thomas Carse of Berwick-upon-Tweed, Miller, and Eliz. Scot of same Town. *W.* John Hoy, Alex. Fraser.

74. „ Aug. 16. John Burn, M.D., and Elizabeth Alder, Widow, both of Berwick-upon-Tweed. *W.* Sarah Fairbairn, Barthw. Bower.

75. „ „ 18. Thomas Palmer of St. Michael, Roper and Flax-dresser, and Sarah Geness of St. Mary, Spinster, both of Stamford, Co. Lincoln, md. 'in the Chapel.' *W.* John Palmer, James Fairbairn, Barthw. Bower.

76. „ Oct. 27. Joseph Hazard of Lincoln, College, Oxford, and Susannah Maria Shippey of Highgate, Co. Middlesex, Spinster. *W.* James Fairbairn, Barthw. Bower.

77. „ Dec. 6. John Edgar of St. Thomas, Salisbury, Co. Wilts, Apothecary, and Mary Tatum, both same Parish, Spinster, md. 'in the Chapel.' *W.* James Fairbairn, Barthw. Bower.

78. „ „ 12. James Thorburn of Ford, Farmer, and Elizabeth Menzies of Brankstone, both Co. Northumberland. *W.* James Fairbairn, Francis Thorburn.

79. 1770. Mar. 5. Bartholomew Nenny of Spitalfields, Silkweaver, and Delahaize Ann Cook of St. Mathews, Bethnal Green, Spinster. *W.* Barthw. Bower, John Juck.

80. „ May 1. John Harrison of Little Ouseburne, Co. York, Common Brewer, and Ann Coopland of Easing-wold, same Co., Spinster, md. 'in the Chapel of St. Katherines, Hadington.' *W.* James Fairbairn, Ruth Ellerton, Barthw. Bower.

81. „ „ 11. The Rev. John Stephens, Rector of Blowfleming, Co. Cornwall, and Jane Stiell of Belhaven, Parish of Dunbar, N.B., Spinster, md. at Beltonford in the Parish of Dunbar. *W.* James Fairbairn, Eliz. Buchanan.

END OF VOL I.

VOL. II.

Register of Marriages for the English Episcopal Chapel in Hadingtoun, N. Britain.

1. 1770. May 31. John Dalton of St. Mary's Parish, Bury St. Edmunds, Co. Suffolk, Gent., and Sarah King of Diss, Co. Norfolk, Spinster, md. 'in this chapel.' *W.* Clementina Whitlock, James Fairbairn, Barthw. Bower.

2. „ June 11. John Ward of Torrington East, Co. Lincoln, Grasier, and Ann Wright of North Kelsey, same Co., Spinster. *W.* James Fairbairn and Barthw. Bower.

3. 1770. June 20. William Muke [or Micke] of Wighill, Co. York, Esqr.,
and Mary Stainsby of Kirby, Moorside, same Co.,
Spinster. *W.* Mary Lanes, [?] James Fairbairn.

4.   „   „   30. John Mills of Morpeth, Co. Northumberland, and
Ann Scott of the same parish. *W.* William Willey,
Barthw. Bower.

5.   „   July 15. John Stirling of Middle Temple, London, Attorney
at Law, and Elizabeth Harriott Bromwell of St.
John, Hackney, Spinster, both in Co. Middlesex.
W. James Fairbairn, Barthw. Bower.

6.   „   Aug. 10. Thomas Clarkson of Hull, Co. York, dealer in
horses, and Elizabeth Brigham of the same parish.
W. Barthw. Bower, Jane Lincoln.

7. 1771. Feb. 6. James Hamilton, Musician, of the parish of Lady
Yester in the city of Edinburgh, and Katherine
Dewar of parish of New Greyfriars in the same
city, Spinster. *W.* Robert Scott, Wm. Garner,
Georgina Dallas.

8.   „   Sep. 2. Sir Steven Anderson, Bart., of St. George, Hanover
Square, and Maria Elsegood of St. Martin's-in-
the-Fields, Spinster. *W.* T. Innocent, James Tait.

9.   „   Oct. 15. John Dodds of Warkworth, Co. Northumberland,
Mason, and Elizabeth Pattison of the same parish.
W. Barthw. Bower, John Pierie.

10.   „   Nov. 6. Archibald Megget, Esq. of Gifford, East Lothian,
and Elizabeth Wells of Darlington, Co. Durham,
Spinster. *W.* T. Innocent, Jas. Fairbairn.

11.   „   „   11. Edward Finlason, Surgeon of the Queen's Dragoons,
and Dorothea Peach of Derby, Co. Derby, Spinster.
W. Abram. Cormack, Barthw. Bower.

12.   „   Dec. 16. William Paul, the younger, of Nafferton, Co. York,
Esq., and Ann Taylor of St. Mary's, Beverley,
same Co., Spinster, md. 'in the chapel of St.
Katherine's, Hadington.' *W.* E. Hutchinson,
Stephen Croft, Barthw. Bower.

13. 1772. Feb. 19. Alexander Clapperton, Writer in Edinburgh, and
Jean Black of Whittinghame, Spinster. *W.* John
Craw, James Fairbairn.

14.   „   „   23. Nehemiah Bartley of Temple, Bristol, Distiller, and
Sarah Trout of St. Philip and Jacob, same city,
Spinster, md. 'in the chapel of St. Katherine.'
W. Mary Hawkins, James Fairbairn.

15.   „   April 11. Henry Hammond of Newport Pratt, Co. Mayo, but
late of Berwick-upon-Tweed, and Mary Nealson of
Berwick. *W.* George Goodwill, Barthw. Bower.

16.   „   „   25. John Crawford of West Kirk, and Betty Crawford of
Tron Church, both of Edinburgh. *W.* James Fair-
bairn, Barthw. Bower.

17.   „   June 3. John Billing of Wing, Co. Rutland, Farmer and
Grasier, and Catherine Turner of the same parish,
Spinster, md. at Blackshiels. *W.* Ann Baines,
James Fairbairn, Thos. Fairbairn.

18. 1772. June 19. George Young of Stepney, Co. Middlesex, Ship Carpenter, and Mary Tuthill of St. Mary Aldermary, London, Spinster, md. at Blackshiels. *W.* Harriott Kerr, James Fairbairn.

19. ,, ,, 24. John Breedon of Pangbourn, Co. Berks, Esq., and Elizabeth Pryse of Fulham, Co. Middlesex, Spinster, md. in 'Hadingtoun Chapel.' *W.* James Fairbairn, Barthw. Bower.

20. ,, July 9. Simonides Cridland, Lieutenant in the Seventeenth Regiment of Infantry, and Mary Syme of the West Kirk, Edinburgh, Spinster. *W.* Richd. Aylmer, Barthw. Bower.

21. ,, ,, 28. The Revd. James Cruikshanks, Minister of the Congregation of Protestant Dissenters in Shaw's Lane, Berwick-upon-Tweed, and Margaret Dods of the same congregation. *W.* Barth. Bower, Wm. Garner.

22. ,, Aug. 6. Francis Stuart, Esq., Captain in the Twenty-Sixth Regiment of Infantry, and Mary Nicholson of St. George's, Hanover Square, London, Spinster. *W.* Jas. Stewart, Anne Stewart, Wm. Garner.

23. ,, ,, 6. William Wanley, Esq., of the Inner Temple, London, and Jane Wetherill of Stokesley, Co. York, Spinster. *W.* Barthw. Bower, James Fairbairn.

24. ,, Oct. 10. Thos. Dodds of Cornhill, Co. Durham, Toll-bar keeper, and Mary Miller, late of North Shields, now of Cornhill, aforesd. *W.* John Nisbet, Thomas Hann.

25. ,, Nov. 2. John Farrer of St. Mary, Aldermary, London, Gent., and Rosa Adams of Walkern, Co. Hertford, Spinster. *W.* James Fairbairn, John Swanston.

26. ,, ,, 11. John Baillie of Berwick-upon-Tweed, Shopkeeper, and Margaret Jeffiry [signed Geffiry] of the same. *W.* Barthw. Bower, Gabriel Wilson.

27. ,, ,, 12. Thomas Kent of Leeds, Co. York, Wooll Stapler, and Elizabeth Illingworth of same parish, Spinster, md. 'in this chapel.' *W.* Barthw. Bower, Gabriel Wilson.

28. ,, ,, 19. Thomas Watson of Syston, Co. Lincoln, Farmer and Grasier, and Elizabeth Calcraft of Ancaster, same Co., Spinster. *W.* Tho. Reid, Barthw. Bower.

29. ,, ,, 19. John Scott[1] of the parish of All Saints in Newcastle-upon-Tyne, Fellow of University College in Oxford, and Elizabeth Surtees of St. Nicholas Parish in the same town, Spinster, were married at Blackshiels, N. Britain ~~according to the form of~~ [*sic*]. *W.* James Fairbairn, Thos. Fairbairn.

30. ,, Dec. 6. John Walker of Rudston, Co. York, Blacksmith, and Mary Wellburn of the same parish. *W.* Wm. Garner, Barth. Bower.

31. 1773. June 12. James Bolton of Wooler, Co. Northumberland,

[1] Afterwards Lord Eldon.

Mason, and Isabel Jamieson of the same parish. *W.* William Litster, Sarah Fairbairn.

32. 1773. July 26. John Harnwell of North Lopham, Co. Norfolk, Linnen Weaver, and Elizabeth Whitebread of the same parish. *W.* Robert Gardner, Eliza Buchanan.

33. „ Aug. 16. George Hall of Felton, Co. Northumberland, and Jane Carr of the same parish. *W.* Wm. Garner, George Horsbrough.

34. „ „ 19. John Wilson of Alnwick, Co. Northumberland, Surgeon, and Ann Wilson of the same parish. *W.* James Fairbairn, Barthw. Bower.

35. „ Sept. 29. Alexander Geddes, Esq. of St. Margarets, Westminster, Co. Middlesex, and Sarah Fry of the same parish, md. at Dunbar. *W.* Eliza Buchanan, John Lorimer.

36. „ Oct. 13. Samuel Widdel of Shillbottle, Co. Northumberland, Farmer, and Jane Paxton of the same parish. *W.* Barthw. Bower, Betty Smith.

37. 1774. Apr. 29. George Henderson of Newton, Co. Northumberland, Miller, and Jane Menzies of Cornhill, Co. Durham. *W.* Barthw. Bower, James Fairbairn.

38. „ June 1. Thomas Peacock of Northorp, Co. Lincoln, Grazier, and Keturah Scales of the same parish, Spinster. *W.* Thomas Fairbairn, Barthw. Bower.

39. „ „ 12. Charles Arthbuthnot, Captain in his Majesty's Sixty-sixth Regiment of Infantry, and Elizabeth Rombley of Kendal, Co. Westmoreland, Spinster. *W.* Thomas Reid, Barthw. Bower.

40. „ Aug. 3. Charles Edward Stewart, Fellow of Magdalen College, Oxford, and Ann Alethea Wallen of Long Milford, Co. Suffolk, Spinster. *W.* Hannah Prior, Barthw. Bower.

41. „ Oct. 20. Thomas Hindmarsh of Berwick-upon-Tweed, Joiner and Cabinetmaker, and Elizabeth Alder of the same parish. *W.* Wilfrid Younghusband, James Fairbairn.

42. „ Nov. 25. John Jackson of Godmanchester, Co. Huntingdon, Lieutenant of his Majesty's Marine Forces, and Sarah Paine of Stoke Damarel, Co. Devon, Spinster. *W.* E. Mallett, Barthw. Bower, James Fairbairn, M. B. (?) Home.

43. 1775. June 21. Sir Alexander Purvis of Eccles, Co. Berwick, Bart., and Mary Hume of Coldingham, same Co., spinster. *W.* Barthw. Bower, Alex. Stille, Janet Baird.

44. „ „ 28. Edward Brooksby of Newark-upon-Trent, Co. Nottingham, Mercer and Draper, and Hannah Toplis of the same parish. *W.* Barthw. Bower, Elizabeth Watson.

45. „ Aug. 24. Stephen Hoddle of Newport Pagnell, Co. of Buckingham, Grocer, and Sarah Miles of Hanstope, same Co., spinster, married 'in this chapel.' *W.* Mary Hollingworth, Barthw. Bower.

46. 1775. Sep. 16. Simon Brown of His Majesty's Navy, Surgeon, and Ann Campbell of Haddington, Spinster. *W.* Eliz. M'Call, Janet Durham.

47. „ „ 27. Edward Steel of Berwick-upon-Tweed, Mariner and Isabella Hog of the same parish. *W.* Thomas Carss, Josiah Dods, Isable Steel.

48. „ Oct. 11. Patrick Roy of St. Martins-in-the-Fields, London, Merchant, and Lillias Moodie of Chigwell Co., Essex. *W.* John Hirkes, Mary Hirkes.

49. „ „ 15. Gavin Thompson, Surgeon in His Majesty's Navy, and Isabella Nairn of the City of Edinburgh, Spinster. *W.* Will Brodie, Isable Whithead.

50. „ Nov. 13. Richd Kerney [signed, Kearney], Lieutenant in His Majesty's Thirty-sixth Regiment of Infantry, and Elizabeth King of St. Lawrence, Winchester. *W.* Joseph Bennett, Daniel Davidson.

51. „ Dec. 3. James Black of Tweed-mouth, Co. Durham, Barber and Peruke maker, and Mary Lambert of the same parish, widow. *W.* Barthw. Bower, Henry Jacobson.

52. 1776. June 29. James Brodie of the West Church Parish, Edinburgh, Merchant, and Ann Gough of Coldingham, Co. Berwick [*sic*], widow. *W.* George Lawers, Eliza. Buchanan.

53. „ Aug. 3. Philip Gills of Holt, Co. Norfolk, Surgeon, and Henrietta Winn of the same parish, Spinster, md. 'in this Chapel.' *W.* James Fairbairn, Barthw. Bower.

54. 1777. Jan. 11. James Dodd of the Tolbooth Parish, Edinburgh, Late Ensign in His Majesty's 102nd Regiment of Infantry, and Christian Smeaton of the same parish. *W.* James Fairbairn, Barthw. Bower.

55. „ „ 24. James Forster of St. Mary, Alt Hill, Co. Middlesex, Policy-Broker and Christiana Gwyor of St Mary-le-bonne, same county, widow. *W.* James Fairbairn, Alexr. Fraser.

56. „ Feb. 28. Richard Brackenbury, Ensign in the 70th Regiment of His Majesty's Infantry, now lying in the Castle of Edinburgh, and Janetta Gunn, of the city of Edinburgh, spinster. *W.* James M'Beath, James Fairbairn.

57. „ Mar. 23. Robert Spooner Haddilsay, of St. Andrew, Holborn, London, Draper, and Mary Higgs of St. Mary, Islington, Spinster. *W.* Geo. Ridpath, James Fairbairn, Barthw. Bower.

58. „ April 23. William Johnson of London, Esq., and Jane Hume of South Leith, Spinster, md. 'in the Chapel of Hadington.' *W.* Alex. MacBean, Margt. Murray.

59. „ June 27. John Williams of Badshott, Parish of Farnham, Co. Surrey, Esq., and Frances Thomas of St. George's, Hanover Square, Co. Middlesex, Spinster, md. 'in

this Chapel.'   *W.* Audley, James Fairbairn, William Ansell.

60. 1777. Oct. 5. William Augustus Cane, Lieutenant in His Majesty's Second Regiment of Foot, and Dorothy Ogle of St. Johns, Newcastle.   *W.* Gilbert M'Gillivry, John Butler.

61. „ Nov. 13. Henry Constantine Jennings of South Weild, Co. Essex, Esq., and Elizabeth Catherine Nowell of the Chapelry of Havering Bower, same Co., Spinster. *W.* Jas. Nisbet, Eliza Buchanan.

62. 1778. Feb. 11. Wm. Graham, Esq., of the city of Aberdeen, and Isabella Abernethy of the same city.   *W.* James Fairbairn, Patrick Thomson.

63. „ „ 12. John Hart of Felton, and Sarah Potter of the same parish.   *W.* James Fairbairn, Ann Hart.

64. „ June 4. Robert Gillies of Berwick-on-Tweed, Mason, and Margaret Clark of the same Town.·   *W.* Jas. Nisbet, Geo. Foster.

65. ., „ 27. William Bacon Forster of Adderstone, Co. Northumberland, Esq., and Lady Katherine Turnour of Kirisford, Co. Sussex, md. 'in this Chapel.'   *W.* Jas. Nisbet, James Fairbairn, Ann Boxall.

66. „ July 2. Charles Elston of Lutterworth, Co. Leicester, Innkeeper, and Ann Jenkins of Husbands Bosworth, same Co., md. 'in this Chapel.'   *W.* James Nisbet, William Swanston.

67. „ „ 8. Hugh Lord of St. Mary, Pembroke, Esq., Major to Prince of Wales' Foot, and Eleanor Mathew of Lanfoist, Co. Monmouth, Spinster, md. 'in this Chapel.'   *W.* Eliz. Morgan, John Lloyde, Jas. Nisbet.

68. „ Sep. 22. Robert Richardson, Junr. of Alnwick, Co. Northumberland, Attorney at Law, and Mary Watson of Embleton, Spinster.   *W.* Edwd. Henderson, Sarah Fairbairn.

69. 1779. Jan. 19. James Potts of Norham, Co. of Durham, Overseer of the Coalworks at Greenlaw Walls, and Rose Potts of the same Parish.   *W.* Ja. Nisbet, Mark Proudfoot.

70. ., July 24. Wm. Speir of Rawston, Co. Dorset, Gent., and Mary Wardner [signed Mary Maria Wardner] of Alverdeston, Co. Wilts, md. 'in this Chapel.'   *W.* Anna Gutch, James Fairbairn.

71. „ Sep. 3. Michael Coulter of Lisbury, Co. Northumberland, Farmer, and Mary Coulter of Morpeth, Spinster. *W.* Jas. Nisbet, Thomas Fairbairn.

72. 1780. Feb. 18. Willm. Tripp of Wiveliscombe, Co. Somerset, Mercer and Linnen Draper, and Joan Good of Huish Champflower, same County, Spinster.   *W.* Joseph Hayter, John Hasswell.

73. „ Mar. 21. James Stuart, Esq., of Hadingtoun, and Mary, widow to the late Francis Stuart, Esq., Major in the

Twenty-sixth regiment of Infantry, md. at 'Edinburgh.' *W.* Mary Boyd, Alex. Wood, David Boyd.

[We acknowledge with many thanks some annotations on these registers. These, with any others that may be sent us, will be printed when the transcript is completed.—ED.]

165. SCOTSMEN NATURALISED IN ENGLAND.—The fourth volume of *Calendar of Documents relating to Scotland,* edited by Joseph Bain, F.S.A. Scot., has just been issued by the Treasury. One interesting subject is well illustrated in it, viz. the frequency with which Scotsmen were made denizens of England in the fifteenth century. Special encouragement was given to this, as is shown by a 'warrant' (July 21, 1461) to the Chancellor to grant letters patent (in a form enclosed) to all manner of 'Scottes' within England that come to him and make their oath of allegiance to the King (in a form also enclosed) [*Privy Seals (Tower)* 1, *Edw. iv. File* 9]. Several lists are given, and we think it probable that the genealogist may obtain much assistance from them. We also notice that frequent reference is made to the family of Stewart settled in the east of England. A sharp controversy has been carried on lately as to the history of this family. The information contained in this volume is likely to prove of use.[1] The same may be said of the Scot family which held land in Surrey in the fifteenth century.   ED.

166. SCOTTISH NOTES ON THE ARMADA (vol. i. 159, vol. iii. 2, 39).—In the Collection of Armada relics lately exhibited at Drury Lane Theatre was— ' 281. Piece of timber of the *Florida,* Treasure Ship of the Spanish Armada, wrecked in the Sound of Mull, near Tobermow [? Tobermory], 1588.   *Lent by Colonel Mac Lachlan.'*

We do not know from what sources the name of this vessel has been ascertained, but the State Papers of Scotland throw an interesting light on the wreck and its consequences.

' *3rd Jan.* 158⅞.

' Kings letters raised by Mr. David M'Kgill of Nesbitt, His Majesty's Advocate, state that, in October last, Lauchlane M'Clayne of Dowart, "accumpanyed with a grite nowmer of thevis, brokin men, and sornaris of Clannis, besydis the nowmer of ane hundreth Spanyeartis, come, bodin in feir of weir, to his Majesteis propir ilis of Canna, Rum, Eg, and the Ile of Elennole, and, eftir thay had soirned, wracked, and spoilled the saidis haill Illis, thay tressonablie rased fyre and in maist barbarous, shamefull and cruell maner, brynt the same Illis, with the haill men, wemen and childrene being thairintill, not spairing the pupillis and infantis, and at the same tyme past to the Castell of Ardnamurchin, assegeit the same, and lay about the said castell three dayis, using in the meantyme all kynd of hostilitie and force, baith be fyre and swerd, that micht be had for recovery thairof: fra the persute of the quhilk thay had not returned, unless be the force and power of his Majesteis gude subjectis they wer putt bak and the house relevit. The like barbarous and shamefull crueltie hes sendle bene hard of amangis Christeanis in ony kingdome or age, the said Lauchlane being movit heirunto in respect the inhabitantis of the saidis Ilis wer his Majesteis proper tennentis, destitute of the conforte and assistance of the clannit men of the Ilis to participat with

---

[1] See a foot-note to the Introduction, page xxxiii.

thame in thair awne defens."—The Advocate appearing, the Lords order
the said Lauchlane, who has made no appearance, to be denounced rebel.'
—Registers of the Privy Council of Scotland (1585-1592), vol. iv. p.
341. Further proceedings in the same case took place, as the following
extract shows:—

'The samyn day, Lauchlane M'Clane of Dowart, being accusit and
persewit be the said Mr. David M'Gill, Advocat (of the crimes following),
committit be him.

'Dittay *against Lauchlane M'Clane of Dowart.*

'That he, be himselff, and utheris in his name, of his caussing, aganis
the estait of his Maiestie and Croun, as also aganis the estait of the
countrey, in the moneth of November 1588 yeiris, tuik up bandis of Men
of weir, strangearis, Spanzertis, quha were ane pairt of the armie, callit
"The Halielvg," destinat for suppressioun of all that professit the trew and
Cristian Religioune; and swa to subuert the estait of the Kingis Maiestie,
his Croun, countrey, and Commoune-welth thairof: Quhairthrow, they wer
fund and declarit, oppin and publict inimes, and swa to be resistit, be Act
of Counsall; as in the samin, of the dait the fyrst of August 1588, att
mair lenth is contenit: neuirtheless, he retenit and kepit thame in
cumpanie with him, under his waiges, within the Ile of Mvlle, and remanent
North and West Iles, invadand and persewand, vpoun his particuler deidlie
feid borne aganis Angus M'Conill of Dinneveg; the said Angus, his kyn,
freindis, allya, assisteris and pairt-takeris, being subjectis and inhabitantis
of his Maiesties realme. In the quhilk invasioun, he, accumpaneit with
the said men of weir, strangearis, Spanzertis, publict inimeis of the estait,
as said is, maid sindrie slauchteris, heirschipis, birningis, depredatiounes,
and otheris notorious murthouris and oppressiounes; and speciallie, in the
said moneth of November, he brint with fyre the landis of Canna, Rum,
Eg, and Ellen-ne-muk, and hereit the same; he slew and crewillie murdreist
Hector M'Cane Channauiche and Donald Bayne his brothir, with ane
grit nowmer of wyffis, bairnis and puir laboreris of the ground, about aucht
or nyne scoir of sawles, quha eschapit the fyre, was noch spairit be his
blindie sword. And all the same tyme, accumpaneit with the saidis
strangearis, Spanzeartis, publict inimies as said is, he tuik with him the
cannoune, tressonablie besageit the hous of Ardenmvrche, be the space of
sax or sewin dayes, he causit schwit diuers schottis thairat, and slew diuers
gentilmenne thairin, callit[1] . . . vsurpand thair throw his hienes authoritie—'
[a long list of other crimes—but no more mention of Spaniards]. 'Incar-
cerat in Castro de Edinburghe' until his majesty's will should be declared.—
1590-1, *Criminal Trials,* Maitland Club, vol. i. p. ij. p. 230.

The Registers of Privy Council show that the prisoner got out on bail
which he forfeited.   A. W. Cornelius Hallen.

There are records of the wreck of a vessel of the Armada at Mull,
and of another at Fair Island. But beyond these none are known to exist.

The official list referred to was printed in Spain before the Armada
left, and does not contain any information regarding what became of the
vessels afterwards.

The copy of the list which is in the British Museum belonged formerly
to Lord Burghley, who made several notes upon it. In one of these he
records the wreck of the ship Gran Grifon at Fair Island, but not of any
other in Scotland.   J. A.

[1] A line left blank in the Record.

In reply to the strictures of J. A. in your September number, I perfectly well remember the slab or tablet bearing the inscription alluded to in Dr. Pratt's 'Buchan.' The wood-carving representing the offering of Isaac was affixed to the surface of this, so that the words at the top of the tablet appeared above the wood-carving.

At the lower edge of the tablet was a sort of corbel, representing a human head, cut out of the same stone as the tablet itself. On this the lower end of the wood carving rested. The corbel was painted in the same brilliant tints as the carving. From time to time, as the colours faded through exposure to the weather, they were renewed by some artistic hand.

When I last visited Peterhead some years ago the carving had disappeared, but the tablet remained with its stone corbel; the latter still retaining traces of the flesh-coloured paint which had once adorned it.

The tradition referred to by Mr. Thomas Hutchison in connection with the bell in the old church tower at Peterhead was long a popularly received one. It has however no foundation in fact. It probably arose from a hasty reading of the inscription on the bell, which runs as follows: 'Soli Dei Gloria *Michael* Burgerhuys me fecit 1647.' The name of the worthy Dutch bell-founder had apparently been identified in the popular mind with that of the luckless war-vessel. W. B.

'ARMADA STONE,' NEWHAVEN.—The *Edinburgh Evening Despatch* of December 21, 1888, contained some interesting notes on Newhaven, illustrated by well executed engravings. By the kindness of the Editor, I am permitted to make use of one of these which shows what is called the 'Armada Stone.' The account given of it is unfortunately meagre. We are not told how long the name has been attached to it, or if old writers have given any history of it, or of the house where it is placed or the former owners of it.

We should be glad to know any facts that might connect this stone with the Armada; the date appears to us the only thing suggestive of such connection. The writer speaks of 'a Romish Cross on a pennon at each Masthead,' but clearly this is a mistake. The well-known ensign of St. Andrew is shown in the sketch; besides, if a Spanish ship had been intended, it would surely have been represented in a shattered condition. The emblems underneath point rather to its indicating the residence of some opulent and successful mariner well skilled in the science of navigation. A. W. C. H.

167. VERSES ON A SUN-DIAL.—The following verses, with the date 1632, are engraved on a sun-dial in a garden at Whithorn:—

The Orcades that Hants in Mearock's Mote:
And Satyres tripping aye from Hill to Hill,

Admiring Phœbus cours, and Phœbe's lote ;
The Edub cauld quhairofe they hade no skill.
Them all agreeing with teares that did distlll
Out our thair cheeks, to mak a bullerand strand,[1]
The Earth to breack, as they were warned till
Be Arladge,[2] voice at Keyloche they me fand
Out throwe my centre a gnomon they made stand
At morning, noon and even of an lengthe
The Zodiack signs weel till wnderstand
With Equinox and solstices the strenthe
Sen Phœbus heer brings trouble, caire, and toyll,
Pray vnto God to send an better soyll.

Mearock may be the hill (2750 feet) now written Merrick, in the Stewartry of Kirkcudbright, visible from Whithorn. There is also a Mearock Hill in Portpatrick parish. But what are 'Orcades' and 'Edub'?

HERBERT MAXWELL.

168. OLD DESCRIPTION OF SCOTLAND, ETC.—The manuscript of which the following is a copy is written in a very careful hand on both sides of a folio sheet of paper. It is very much frayed and worn at the folds. It appears to be a portion only of a large work, but what nature the rest of it was of is doubtful. It appears to have been written about the year 1639, as Stirling Castle was then held by the Earl of Mar.

The contents in the column at the beginning of the paper appears to have been the order of work of the Court of Session, and the divisions of Scotland would probably be for the Circuit Courts.

The portion of the following, entitled, 'The memorial of the rare and wonderful things in Scotland,' was printed in 'The Scottish Journal of Topography, Antiquities, Traditions, &c. &c.,' vol. i. pp. 127, 128. It is not quite so full there as in the present instance, and is said to have been taken from an early Geography. I have given the continuation (note 10), as it is contained in the Journal. Can any reader give further particulars regarding this fragment. The document has a few notes in a different handwriting, but as they are mostly on the margin they have almost disappeared.

J. M'G.

THE ORDER OF THE CALLING OF THE TABLE OF THE . . .

MUNDAY.	
Redemption of Lands. Reductions of all kynds. Transferrings. Losse of Superiories. For making, sealing, and subscribing of Reuersions.	The Shyres of the first Quarter as followeth, That is to say —Forfair, Kinkardin, perhaps Aberdeene Shyres is omitted, Bamff, Elgin, Forresse, Narne, Innernese, Crom(arty), ... Cathnesse, Orknay. The Shyres of the Second Quarter— Edinburgh, Linlithgow, Selkirk, Roxburgh, Peblis, Berwicke, and Haddington. The Thrid Quarter—Striuling and Renfrew, Lanerk, Wigton, Dumf(ries), Kikcudbright and Annandaill. The fourth Quarter—Perth, Clackmannan, Argile and Bute.
TEWSDAY. Recent spoiles without the tyme of vacants. Actes of Adjournal.	The Senators of the Colledge of Iustice begin ther rysing and . . . as followes. They begin to sitt downe in Edinburgh, on the Morne after Trinitie Sunday while the first day of August, and thereafter to be vacant (while) the . . . of November nixt

(*sic.*)

---

[1] *Bullerand strand*, a gurgling stream. ' *To* BULLER, to emit such a sound as water does when rushing violently into any cavity.'—*Jamieson.* 'STRAND, a rivulet.'—*Ibid.*
[2] *Arladge,* =horloge or orloge, *i.e.* horologe.

to come, and then to begin and sit while the xi day (of) March nixt thereafter, and then to be vacant while the morning after . . . Sunday as aforesaid.

The . . . es of the Scotland.

WEDNESDAY.

The Common Table of the foure quarters of the Realme by order euery one after ane other, as is prouided in the Actes of the Institution, in the print books of Parliament.

THURSDAY.

(The same Table.)

FRYDAY.

The King's actions, Strangers, and the Poore.

SATERDAY.

The Lords of Session and Members thereof, the Prelates, Paiers of Contributiõ, and the Common Table foresaid.

And upon the Wednesday and Thursday to call all common priviledged Matters, such as Hornings, fre persons -nings Letters conforme to Rolements, Decreits Arbitrals, Tacks, Pensions, Ordinarie Letters, gifts, Registring of Contracts, actions to become Civil or Prophaine, Dowble poyndings, Billes, Supplications, and ther Last Actions to be called of Newe, by ordinance of the Lords of Session for Expedition of Causes.

The Shyres.]

SOWTH.	NORTH.
Edinburgh.	Abirdene.
Sterling.	Dundie.
Lithgow.	Sanct Ihonston
Rothsay.	alias Perth.
Dumbarten.	Banff.
Renfrew.	Dunfermeling.
Ruglen.	Carraill.
Aere.	Forfair.
Irwing.	Brechin.
Glasgow.	Mont-rosse.
Kirkcudbright.	Elgene.
Wigtain.	Innernes.
Whithorne.	Arbrothe.
Laynerick.	Saint Androis.
Iedburgh.	Cowpar.
Selkirk.	Cullane.
Peblis.	Fores.
Haddlington.	Narne.
North-Barwick.	Ih—m ?
Dumbar.	Dysert.
Drumfries.	Kirkadie.
	[I think ther lakks yet some few.

The Castl and Fortalice of Dumbar, a hous of great stre¬th, till w^{th}in these late zeares, it was demoleist by Iames Earle of Murray, Regent of Scotland, in Lothien, desert.
1. The Castel of Edinburgh, inhabit by Iohn Earle of Mar.
2. The Castel and Stɪength of Blacknes in Lothien, inhabite by Sʳ. Taes Sand . . . .
3. The Castel and Strength of Sterling, inhabite by the Earle of Mar and his Deputie.
4. The Castel of Dumbarton, inhabited by the Lord Hammilton.
5. The Castel of Lochmaben in Annandaill, occupied by the Lord Maxwell.
6. The Castel of Kirkwall in Orknay, appˉtaining to the king, inhabite by (the) Earle of Orknay.

Pallaces appertaining to the King.
1. The Pallace of Halyrudhouse, beside Edin(r), in Lothien.
2. The Pallace of Dalkeyth reserued for the (use?) of the Prince, wth the Orchard, Gardens, and wood adjacent thereunto, foure m(yles) distant from Edinburgh.
3. The Pallace of Lithgow, w^{th}in the Towne of Lithgow, in Lithgowshire.
4. The Pallace of Falkland, and the Towne of Falkland adjacent therunto, wth the Park in Fyfe.

Castels appartaining to the King.
The Castle of Roxburgh, now demolis(hed) by the law, and by the Commandem(ent of) the King and Thrie Estates in . . . daill. The Monumento yet . . . this houre, but desert.

A Memoriall of the most rare and woonderfull things in Scotland.
Among many Commodities that Scotland hath cõmon with other Nations, it is not needfull to re(her)se in this place, in respect of ther particulars declared at lenthgh before. It is beautified wth some rare gifts in its self wonderfull to consider which I haue thogtht good not to obscure (for the good Read(er)).
As for Exemple
In Orknay, besides the great store of Sheep that feed upon the Main La(nd) therof . . . Ewes ar of (such?) fecunditie, that at everie Lambing

I think this by of . . es . . aʳt, which . . trash of Hector . . se therof. [*sic*]

(Note here illegible.)

tyme they produce at lest two, and ordinarilie thrie.   (Th)er be niet(-her) venemous or ravenous beasts bred there, nor do live there, althoght they be transported thither.

3   In Scotland, the Yles called Thulæ, at the tyme when the Sunne enters in the Syne of Cancer for the space of (20 ?) dayes ther appeares no night at all.*   And among the Rocks thereof growes the delectable Lambre (?) called Succ(inŭm ?)

Note here gible.)
5   Hither is also great resort of the beast called the Merrik.   The Skinnes whereof ar costlie Furrings.

6   In Rosse ther be great Mountaignes of Marble and Alabaster.*   Fay.

7   In the Sowth of Scotland, speciallie in the Countries adjacent to England ther is a Dog of marvelous natur called The Sleuth-hund *or true*; because when he is certified by woordes of Arte spoken by his Master what G(oods ?) ar stolne, whether Horse, Sheep, or Neat: Immediatelie, he addresseth him suthly to the sent, and followeth, wth great impetuositie, through all kynd of ground and water, by as many ambages as the Theeves haue vsed, till he attain to ther place of residence.   By the benefit of the which Dog, the Goods are recovered.   But now of Late he is called by a new popular name, The Sleuth-hound: because whereas the People do liue in Sleuth and Idleness neither by themselves, or by the office of a good Hound, or by the strenth of a good House, the do preserve ther goods from the incursion of Theeues and robbers, Then have they recourse to the Dog for reparation of ther sleuth.

8   In the West and northwest of Scotland, ther is great repairing of a Fowle, called the Erne, of a marvelous nature, and the people are verie curious and solicit to catch him, whome thereafter they punze of his Wings, that he shal not be able to flie againe.   This Fowle is of budge quantitie: and althought he be of a rauenous nature, like to the kynd of Haulks, and be that same qualitie gluttonous, neuertheles the people do giue him such sorte of meat as they think conuenient, and of such a great quantitie at a tyme, that he liues contented wth that Portion, for the space of fourteen, sixteen, or tuentie days, and some of them for the space of a moneth.   The people that do so feed, do vse him for this intent, That they may be furnished wth the featheris of his wings, when he doth cast them, for the garnishing of ther arrowes, either when they are at warres, or at hunting.   For these feathers only do neuer receaue Raine or Water as others do, but remaine alwayes of a durable Estate and vncorruptible.

9   In all the Moore-Land, And Mossland of Scotland, doth resorte the Blacke-Cock, a Fowle of a marvelous vertue, and marvelous bountie, for he is more delectable to eat than a Capon, and of a greater quantitie, cled with thrie sorts of flesh, of diuerse colours, and diuers tastes, but all delectable to the vse and nouriture of m(an).

10   In the Two Riuers of Dee and Done, besides the maruelous plentie of Salmond Fishes gotten there, There is also a maruelous kynd of Schellfishe, called the Horse mussill, of a great quantitie: Wherein ar engendered innumerable fayre, bewtifull and delectable Pearles, conuenient for the pleasure of mã, and profitable for the vse of Physick, and some of thame so fayre, and pollished, that they be equal to any mirrour in the World.

11   And generallie by the prouidence of the Almightie God, whence

dearth and scarcitie of Victuals do abound in the Land ; Then the fishes are more plentifullie taken for support of the People.

12   In Galloway The Loch called Loch-Myrton ; althought it be commõ to all fresh water to freeze in Winter, zet the one half this Loch doth neuer freeze at any tyme.

13   In the Shyre of Inuernes : The Loch called Loch-nes, and the Riuer flowing frõ thence into the Sea, doeth neuer freeze. But by the contrarie, in the coldest days of Winter, the Loch and Riuer are both seen to smoke and reecke, signifiing vnto ws, that ther is a myne of Brimstone vnder it, of a hote qualitie.

14   In Carrik ar Kyne, and Oxen, delicious to eat : but ther fatnes is of wonderfull temper(ature ?) that althocht the fatness of all vther commes-table beast for the ordinary vse of Man, do congeale wth the cold ayre ; by the contrarie, the fatnes of these beasts, is perpetually liquid lyk oyle.

15   The Wood and Park of Cummernauld, is replenished wth Kyne and Oxen, and those at all tymes to this day, haue bene Wyld, and all of them of such a perfect wonderfull Whiteness, that there was neuer among all the hudge numbre so much as the smallest black (spot found to be upon one of their skins, horns or cloove ?). . . . . .

16   In the Park of Haly-rud-houss are Foxes and Hares, ...

17   In Coyle, now called Kyle, is a rock of the height of tuelue foot, and as much of (breadth) called the Deaf-Craig, for althoght a man should crie neuer so lowde to his fellow from one syde to the other, he is not hard, althought he make the noise of a gunne.

18   In the Cuntrie of Strathierne, a little aboue the old Towne of the I think Robert Pights called Abernithie There is a maruelous Rocke, called the Rockand- . . . . observed stone, of a reasonable bignes, that if a man will push it wth the least motion . . . this . . . of his finger it will mooue werie lightlie, but if he sh(ould) addresse his himself. whole force, he profits nothing, which moues many people to be wonderfull when they consider such contrarietie.

19   In Lennox is a great Loch called Loch-Lowmand, being of length 24 miles ; in Breadth 8 miles ; containing the numbre of 30 Yles : In this Loch are obserued thrie wonderfull th(ings) one is, Fishes verie delectable to eat, that haue no fynnes to mooue themselves w^{t}all (as) other fishes do.

20 The Second Tempestuous waues and surges of the water (perpetually rag-ing ?) without winds, and that in tyme of greatest calmness, in the faire

21 (pleasant time of summer ?) when the Ayre is quyet. The third is one of these Yles that is (corroborate ?) nor vnited to the ground, but hath bene ppetually loose ; and althought (it be fertil of good grass, and replenished with nolt, yet it moves by the waves of the ?) water, . . . is transported sometymes towards on point and (other whiles towards ?) another.

. . . .

In Argyle is a stone fund in diuers parts, the which laid vnder (straw or stubble ?) consume them to fyre by the great heat : that it collects there. In Buquhan at the Castel of Slaynis is a caue from the top wherof (dis-tills water ?) wthin (w^h in ?) schort tyme doth congeale to harde stones, whyte in collour : In this caue ar no Rottons seen at anie tyme althought the land be wonderfull fertill.

24   In Lothien, within two miles to Edinburgh, sowthward is a well spring, called St. Catherine('s) well, which flowes ppetuallie wth a kynd of black fatness, above the water whereof . . . ridge make mention. This fatnes is called Bitumen aquis supernatan . . . . it is thought to proceid of a (fa ?)tt

[*Sic.*] myne of Coale . . . which is frequent in all Lothien and speciallie . . . of Coale, called vulgarlie The Parret Coal, [whereof it proceeds, is sudden to conceive fire or flame, so is this oil of a sudden operation to heal all salt scabs and humours, that trouble the outward skin of man : commonly the head and hands are quickly healed by the virtue of this oil, it renders a marvellous sweet smell.   At Aberdeen is a well, of a marvellous good quality to dissolve the stone, to expel sand from the reins and bladder, and good for the cholic, being drunk in the month of *July*, and a few days of *August ;* little inferior to the renowned water of the *Spaw* in *Almain.*   In the north seas of *Scotland*, are great clogs of timber found, in the which are marvellously engendered a sort of geese, called Clayk Geese, and do hang by the beak, till they be of putrefection, oftimes found and kept in admiration of their generation. At *Dumbarton*, directly under the castle at the mouth of the river of *Clyde*, as it enters in the sea, there are a number of Clayk Geese, black of colour, which in the night-time do gather great quantity of the crops of the grass, growing upon the land, and carry the same to the sea ; then assembling in a round, and with a curious curiosity, do offer everyone his own portion to the sea flood, and there attend upon the flowing of the tide, till the grass be purified from the fresh taste, and turned to the salt ; and lest any part thereof should escape, they hold it in with their nebs, thereafter orderly every fowl eats his portion ; and this custom they observe perpetually.   They are fat and delicious to be eaten.]

169. THE YOUNGER FAMILY (*continued from vol.* iii. *page* 39).— V. GEORGE YOUNGER was baptized at Alloa 17th February 1722.   He is mentioned in the Kirk Session Records (27th March 1767) as a Brewer, being the founder of the present firm of 'George Younger and Son.'   He married, at Clackmannan, 14th April 1755, Catherine Allan, whose family appear to have been of great respectability in that parish. She died 14th April 1785.   George Younger died 28th September 1788, and was buried with his wife in Alloa churchyard, where a monument was erected to their memory.   The dates of the birth of their children are given in the Family Bible now in the possession of their great-great-grandson George Younger.   They are as follows :—

    I. Robert, born 19th May 1756, baptized at Alloa, died 15th August 1775, unmarried.

    II. George, born 15th March 1758, baptized at Alloa, died young.

    III. Charles, born 19th February 1760, died 30th September 1784.

    IV. Catherine, born 13th June 1761.

    V. James, of whom below as James VI.

    VI. George, born 31st May 1765, married, 1789, Jean Bleloch,[1] sister to Mary, the wife of his brother James.   He was a maltster by trade, and was buried with his wife in Alloa churchyard, where their monument still exists.   He had two sons, viz. :—I. George, born 1790, who died unmarried, having sold his property in Alloa ; and II. John, born 1791, married, 1814, Mary Bleloch, and had issue—i. George, born 1816, died unmarried : ii. John, born 1819, died in infancy : iii. James, born 1826, married,

[1] The statement, page 39, that another George Younger married Jean Bleloch has been found to be incorrect.—ED.

1854, Mary Andrews. He resides at Birkenhead, and has had the following children :—(1) John Bleloch, born 1855, married, 1882, Mary Swinburne, and had one daughter, Edith; (2) Robert, born 1857, married, 1884, Martha Whalley, and has issue (*a*) James, (*b*) George Christopher, (*c*) Georgina, (*d*) Flora; (3) David, born 1858, unmarried; (4) James, born 1860, married, 1882, Annie Ellis, and has issue (*a*) Ethel, (*b*) Mary Alice; (5) Margaret, married Edward Hughes, and has issue (*a*) Robert, born 1885, (*b*) Margaret, (*c*) Mary; (6) Flora Elizabeth; (7) Mary Ana, died in infancy; (8) George died 1870, unmarried: iv. William, born 1829, died 1865, in New Zealand, without issue: v. Robert, born 1833, married Margaret, daughter of James Drysdale, Wellmyre, Clackmannan, and died   having had issue—(1) John, born 1857, married Catherine, daughter of John Muil, Merchant, Alloa, has issue (*a*) Jessie, (*b*) John Robert, born 1887, (*c*) Catherine Margaret; (2) James Drysdale, born 1861, married Lilly, daughter of —— Elliott, Esq., M.D. He lives in America, and has issue two children (*a*) Madge, (*b*) Lilly; (3) Robert, born 1867, died young; (4) Jessie, married David Simpson, and died 1884; (5) Mary Jane Bleloch; (6) Margaret Drysdale.

VII. Francis, born 30th January 1767, baptized at Alloa by Mr. Heugh of the Associate Presbytery of Stirling. He died 10th October 1788, unmarried.

VIII. Frances, born 9th August 1768, died 1792, unmarried.

VI. JAMES YOUNGER, fifth child but eldest surviving son of George Younger (V.) and Catherine Allan, was born 1st July 1763 and baptized at Alloa 10th July of that year. He married at Alloa, 4th December 1789, Mary Bleloch of Clackmannan, whose sister Jean married his cousin George Younger. The family of Bleloch held farms in Clackmannan for several generations, and several of the name were elders in the Kirk. She died 15th November 1837, James Younger her husband having died 19th February 1809. Both are buried in Alloa churchyard. Mr. Younger carried on his father's business of Brewer. His children were :—

I. George, of whom below as George VII.

II. John, born 31st May 1792, baptized at Alloa.

III. Robert, born 4th September 1796, baptized at Alloa, died young.

IV. Allison, born 1st August 1800.

V. Robert, born 15th February 1802, died 10th October 1851, having married, at Dumfries, in 1833, Ann M'Dowall, who died 1884. He had issue—1. James, born 1834, died 1840; 2. Ann, married, 1st, —— Craig, 2d, J. Robinson; 3. George, born 1838, died 1843; 4. Robert, born 1840, drowned at Alloa Ferry, aged 5 years; 5. Mary, married —— Hunter, Aberdeen; 6. Hannah, married Robert Glass; 7. James, born 1846, died at Durham 1873; 8. William, born 1848, now in Aberdeen; 9. Robert, born 1850, died at Weston, Co. York, 1887.

VI. Margaret, born 12th May 1805, died 15th January 1835.

VII. James, born 10th April 1808, died at Inverness, 29th April 1834.

VII. GEORGE YOUNGER, eldest son of James Younger and Mary Bleloch, was born 19th August 1790, and baptized at Alloa. He married, 16th December 1816, Jane, daughter of James Hunter at Woodhead, Tillicoultry. She was born November 11, 1792, and is now (1889) alive and in the enjoyment of powers mental and physical rare at such a great age. Mr. Younger was a Brewer, and much increased the business which his grandfather commenced. He died 25th September 1853, and was buried in Alloa churchyard. His children were—

I. James, of whom see below as James VIII.

II. Robert, born 16th March 1820, married, 24th February 1853. ——, daughter of John Henderson, and had issue—1. George, born 3d November 1858; 2. John Henderson, born 17th August 1862; 3. Robert James, born 17th November 1868; 4. Jane Hopkirk, married, 30th October 1877, William Rutherford, Barrister-at-Law, London; 5. Mary Wilhelmina, married, 6th March 1883, Noel Smith, London.

III. George, born 20th May 1822, married, 16th August 1855, Margaret, daughter of Robert Tannahill, Merchant, Glasgow, and has issue—1. George William, born 14th May 1859; 2. Robert Tannahill, born 5th December 1860; 3. Henry James, born 14th June 1865; 4. Margaret Tannahill; 5. Jane; 6. Ann Christina; 7. Mary Francis; 8. Jessie Alice.

IV. Francis, born 1824, married, 1852, Jane M'William. He died without issue.

V. William, born 1831, died 1839.

VI. John, born 1837, died at Buenos Ayres 1865, unmarried.

VII. Jessie, married Robert Henderson, Lorns Hill, Alloa, and has issue.

VIII. Mary, died 1853, unmarried.

IX. Jeannie, married Walter Wylie, Park Head, Alloa, who died leaving issue.

VIII. James Younger, eldest son of George Younger (VII.) and Jane Hunter, was born February 1818. He died 1868, having married, November 1850, Janet, daughter of John M'Ewan, Shipowner, Alloa, and had the following children :—

I. George, born October 1851, educated at the Edinburgh Academy, married, June 1879, Lucy, daughter of Edward Smith, M.D., F.R.S. of Heanor, Derbyshire, and Harley Street, London, by whom he has issue—1. James, born 1880; 2. Edward John, born 1882; 3. Charles Frearson, born 1885.

II. John M'Ewan, born 1852, died 1867.

III. James, born 1856, married, February 1886, Annie, only daughter of Thomson Paton, Esq., Norwood, Alloa, and has issue Mary Graeme.

IV. William, born 1857.

V. Robert, born 1861.

VI. Annie, married, 1878, the Rev. D. M'Lean, and has issue one son and four daughters.

NOTE ON YOUNGER ARMS.

The plate of Arms which we give on p. 138 is composed of—

1. The Arms of the family of Jonckeer, Flanders, given by Rietstap, *or,* a fess *gu,* between three Martlets in chief *sa,* and a rose in base of the second.

2. The arms of Captain Henry Younger, Comptroller General of the train of Artillery (*tem.* Charles I.), they are *or,* a bend between two cannons *sa.* On 10th May 1645 he had a grant of honourable augmentation, viz.: 'On a Canton *or,* a rose *gu.,* surmounted of another *arg.*' 'No pedigree of this gentleman or of his descendants has ever been recorded.'—*Information from Heralds' College.*

3. John Yonger of Stratton recorded his pedigree at the visitation of Hereford 1634, and claimed for arms 'on a bend between two dolphins three Martletts,' but his right was 'queried.' The pedigree is as follows:—

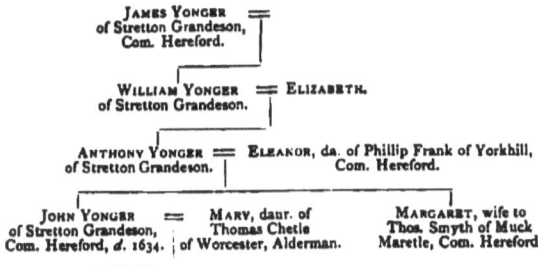

JAMES YONGER
of Stretton Grandeson,
Com. Hereford.

WILLIAM YONGER == ELIZABETH,
of Stretton Grandeson.

ANTHONY YONGER == ELEANOR, da. of Phillip Frank of Yorkhill,
of Stretton Grandeson. Com. Hereford.

JOHN YONGER == MARY, daur. of   MARGARET, wife to
of Stretton Grandeson,   Thomas Chetle   Thos. Smyth of Muck
Com. Hereford, *d.* 1634. | of Worcester, Alderman.   Maretle, Com. Hereford.

ELEANOR YONGER.

—*Information from Heralds' College.*

4. Younger of Auchencass, Co. Dumfries, granted, 1866, '*Arg.* on three piles in point *sa.,* as many annulets *or,* a chief *gu.* charged with a crescent between two mullets of the first.' These arms, however, bear a strong resemblance to the arms of the Scottish family of Young.—*Information from Lyon Office.*

N.B.—Other Coats of Arms of Jonckeer and of Younger are given by Rietstap and Burke.

YOUNGER ARMS.

1. Arms of JONCKEER, Flanders.

2. Captain HENRY YOUNGER, 1645.

3. YONGER of Stratton, Co. Hereford, 1634.

4. YOUNGER, Co. Dumfries, 1866

170. FONT OR CROSS SOCKET AT INCHRYE (pp. 20, 129, 142).— In company with Dr. Laing of Newburgh, I had an opportunity of examining this stone on October 6th, and have no doubt that originally it was the socket stone of a gable cross or finial, turned to account in later times as a 'Knockin Stane.' It is a freestone block 1 ft. 8½ in. × 1 ft. 6½ in. × 1 ft. 1 in. in depth. Its principal features are four gables, two of them having the flat tympanum marking the back and front of the stone, as is frequently the case, the side gablets being deeply recessed. On one of the flat faces is a very distinct mason's mark, which may probably indicate the front of the stone. These gablets have a three-inch moulding in each case, terminating in the broad spreading side-lobes of a *fleur-de-lis*, the central lobe having been no doubt carved on the upper stone, whether cross or finial. Sunk in the upper bed is the bowl 11 inches in diameter, and 7½ inches deep. It is very roughly tooled, and could not possibly be a font, and in its present form just as improbably a socket. If the upper stone were socketed at all, the tenon would most likely, as in the example noted at Culross,[1] be square, and as in scores of other instances there can be little doubt that, whether with a central orifice to suggest it or not, the basin has been hewn out for the comparatively humble purpose of shelling pot barley. Nothing is more common here than to find privy stones—some of them finely moulded —so turned to account. Just as its incomplete character forbids the stone at Inchrye being a font, so does its architectural character forbid its being in any way connected with a stathel. It has evidently formed a prominent feature in some large and ornate building, and although not 'one mile,' as stated by your correspondent, but nearly two and a half miles distant, there is no building in the vicinity at all answering this character except the Abbey of Lindores, from which no doubt it was originally purloined. WILLIAM GALLOWAY,
Whithorn, Wigtownshire.

Your correspondent J. H. is quite right that the name of the house near the loch of Lindores should be Inchrye, not Inchyre, but he is wrong in saying that it was built by the proprietor of the *Scotsman*.
Patrick Rigg Ramsay, who built the modern house, was proprietor of the now defunct *Edinburgh Courant.* W. J. HAIG.

171. MILK (vol. i. pp. 77, 114, 138).—The Introduction to the *Munimenta Gildhallie Londiniensis* (1859, London, Longmans) gives a description of life in London in the 14th century. The following passage concerns a subject which has been mentioned in *Northern Notes & Queries*:—' Milk is nowhere mentioned as an article of sale or otherwise. . . . Milk perhaps was little, if at all, used by the city population' (p. lix).

172. BRASS MORTAR FOUND AT KINROSS.—We give a sketch of an interesting mortar of Dutch manufacture recently purchased by a Kinross gentleman at an old-metal store in the town. The design is excellent. The handles are formed to represent Dolphins, while round it runs an inscription 'LOF GODT VAN AL'—Love God above all. The dimensions of the mortar are—height about 6 inches, diameter 3½ inches, its weight is 2½ lb., and its capacity is 10 oz. liquid measure.

---

[1] A sketch of the Culross Cross socket is given, page 151.—ED.

The inscription seems to indicate that it was used by a doctor or compounder of drugs, as prescriptions were in old days usually prefixed by a devotional invocation.

A. W. C. H.

173. GENEALOGY.—From a short story entitled 'They were married,' occurring in a book entitled *The Captain's Room*, by Walter Besant, 1887, p. 324 :—

'It makes one weep to think how our middle-class people neglect their genealogies, so that they know nothing of their own people, and have no pride, and learn no lessons from the past. Cannot something be done, my friends? Can we not write the annals of our own generation, each for his own family, so that whatever the fate of our children, and grandchildren, they, too, may feel that they have ancestors who lived, and loved, and hoped, and made a little success, perhaps, and died and were forgotten, as they, too, in their turn, shall die?'

174. THE ROSS FAMILY.—The pedigree of the branches of the Ross family, of which the Earls of Ross were Chiefs, is to be published in the following numbers of *N. N. & Q.* It has been compiled from family papers, sasines, and other sources, and the accompanying Key Chart refers to it. Besides the Branches given in the Chart, whose descent is clearly traced to the Earls of Ross, an appendix will contain the pedigrees of many families, who certainly derive from the same source, but for whom the connecting-links have yet to be found. In these tables there are probably many omissions, and possibly many errors ; it is however hoped that their publication will bring to light fresh material, and enable what is faulty to be corrected. A life passed chiefly abroad has rendered it impossible for me to consult authorities which are easily accessible to others.

I am anxious to thank all those friends who have given me during many years of research so much valuable assistance.   F. N. R.

175. SCOTTISH TRADE WITH FLANDERS (vol. iii. p. 35).—John, Duke of Lorraine and Brabant, second husband of Jacobœa, daughter and heiress of William VI. Earl of Holland, who died 1417, ratified and confirmed the privileges granted to the Scottish merchants by his late father-in-law (31st March 1418), but though the two years during which the decree of 1st August 1416 obtained were almost expired, no provision was made for prolonging the privileges; as a consequence, for some years the regular course of merchandise was interrupted, and both countries had recourse to privateering. This was the more disastrous as Scotland was dependent on Flanders for the ordinary furnishings of man, beast, and house. Pinkerton (*Hist.* vol. i. p. 163) states that about this time 'the arms and armour used in Scotland came from England or Flanders;' again, 'The simplest implements of agriculture, horse shoes, cart wheels, harness, saddlery, were imported from Flanders' (p. 408). 'Even in the best parts of Scotland the inhabitants could not manufacture the most necessary articles' (Mercer's *Hist. of Dunfermline,* p. 66). The fine old wooden chests or ambries, and other carved furniture, which are sometimes spoken of as proofs of Scottish skill, are in old inventories referred to as Flemish—in fact these documents contain the word Flemish *usque ad nauseam.* It is necessary, however, to swallow the fact if a right idea of the importance of Flemish trade is to be arrived at. In 1423 commissioners were appointed to settle disputes, those on the Scottish side being Alexander, Archdeacon of Dunkeld, and Patrick Johnston of Linlithgow, and on 7th August 1423 peace was signed, to continue for a year and a half. There were four items, 1. Liberation of prisoners; 2. Letters of protection on both sides; 3. The rights bestowed by the treaty of 1416 to be recognised; 4. Ambassadors empowered to inquire into past outrages.

On the 22d May 1424, this treaty was prolonged for two years, and as irregularities took place, the Duke of Burgundy pacified King James, and made satisfaction for any damage done. It was on this occasion that Middleburgh in Zetland was opened out especially to Scottish trade—and the 'Scottish House' still remaining in the town dates, we believe, from this period. The document conferring the right for Scottish merchants to trade there is given by Yair, both in Latin and English; it is a long document, containing seven clauses, the sixth of which permits Scottish merchants to import in bales their white cloths to any part of Flanders, and there have them dyed, and carry them back to their own country. This treaty was signed 6th December 1427, and therefore after the expiry of that signed 1424.

Mary, daughter of James I. and sister of James II. of Scotland, was married, 1444, or seven years after her father's death, to Wolphaert van Borselen, son to Henry van Borselen, Lord of Campvere, 'who had the compliment made him of the title of Earl of Buchan' (Yair, p. 80). This peerage is not to be found in any lists of the Earls of Buchan we have met with. It seems that the title was most probably 'Dominus de Buchan.' Sir Robert Stewart, *de jure* Earl of Buchan, appears never to have been recognised as such. He was living 1431. In 1469, Sir James Stewart, 2d son of Sir James Stewart of Lorn, was created Earl of Buchan (*Complete Peerage,* vol. ii. p. 55). Mary Stewart died in 1467. Her husband married again, and died in 1487, so that he could not well have been

Earl of Buchan. Though the only child of the first marriage, a boy, died at the age of 12, it is quite likely that the alliance had something to do with making Campvere, or 'The Pheir,' as we find it called in old records, available to Scottish merchants. Yair, however, does not favour this view, and states there is no evidence that would support it.

The next special reference to Scottish trade with Flanders is to be found in the Scot. Acts of Parliament, 1466 (28th Oct.), which can easily be consulted. In the opinion of Yair, Middleburgh and Campvere vied with each other 'which of them should make the most engaging offers to draw' the Scottish merchants 'to themselves, the former of these having at this time, 1495, a large trade and ready market for Scotch and English goods lying in the Scald and near Antwerp, and not yielding for a flourishing trade to any other town in the neighbourhood. Campvere had much the same advantages with regard to the conveniency for the Scotch market, only Middleburgh was better furnished with goods which the Scotch wanted to buy and carry home to their own country' (p. 92). For some time the trade with Flanders had been under the management of a duly recognised official, known as the Conservator, but in 1503 an Act of Parliament (Jan. 4, Parl. 19, Act 81) made his office fixed, legal, and established. As this officer had to come yearly to Scotland to report on his official acts, the greater proximity of Campvere was an inducement to make it the headquarters of this trade. The later history of the Scottish traffic with Campvere will be found not only in Yair, but in the *Records of the Convention of Royal Burghs*, a work to be found in any good Public Library.   A. W. C. H.

176. GRAHAM OF GARTMORE.—It is stated in Burke's *Landed Gentry* (7th ed. p. 770), that Sir William Graham, first Baronet of Gartmore, was eldest son of William Graham of Gartmore, whose daughter married Hon. John Alexander, fourth son of the first Earl of Stirling. George Crawfurd, in his *Peerage* (p. 331), says that Sir William was the son of John Graham originally of Duchray, afterwards of Galingad, and that he acquired Gartmore from John Alexander, Lord Stirling's son, who had married, not Sir William's sister, as stated by Burke, but the daughter and heiress of Robert Graham of Gartmore, descended from Gilbert Graham of Gartmore, third son of William, third Earl of Menteth (*Ibid.* 332 ; also *Douglas*, ii. 228).

In the pedigree of the Alexanders, Earls of Stirling, given in Wood's *Douglas* (ii. 537), John's wife is said to have been a daughter of Sir John Graham of Gartmore. In this matter Crawfurd shows greater research and information than Douglas, and I am inclined to prefer his account. However this may be as between Crawfurd and Douglas, both are opposed to Sir Bernard Burke's version, which should be corrected.   Σ.

177. PARISH REGISTERS IN SCOTLAND (vols. i. ii. combined, pp. 89, 130, 172, vol. iii. p. 57).—We have already given the names of 32 parishes possessing registers commenced before 1610, and of 127 possessing registers commenced between 1610 and 1650. We are glad to know that these lists have been found useful, and we propose to give two more, viz., (*a*) for the period between 1651 and 1675, and (*b*) between 1676 and 1700. It appears scarcely necessary to classify the later registers, but it is evident that the genealogist receives assistance from lists which show at once what are his chances of gaining information by a visit to the Register House Edinburgh. Third List, A.D. 1651-1675.

In the following list the date of the earliest entries are given (*b.* for baptism, *m.* for marriage, *d.* for burial) :—

Aberdour, .	*b.* 1663,	*m.* 1669,	*d.* 1658.
Abernyte, .	*b.* 1667,	*m.* 1667,	*d.* 1666.
Airth, . .	*b.* 1660,	*m.* 1660,	*d.* 1670.
Alva, . .	*b.* 1655,	*m.* 1664,	*d.* 1726.
Arbroath, .	*b.* 1653,	*m.* 1653,	*d. None.*
Athelstaneford,	*b.* 1664,	*m.* 1664,	*d. None.*
Auchterarder,	*b.* 1661,	*m.* 1668,	*d. None.*
Auchterderran, .	*b.* 1664,	*m.* 1681,	*d. None.*
Ayr, . . .	*b.* 1664,	*m.* 1687,	*d.* 1766.
Ballingry, .	*b.* 1670,	*m.* 1670,	*d.* 1670.
Banchory Ternan,	*b.* 1670,	*m.* 1670,	*d. None.*
Barony, . .	*b.* 1672,	*m.* 1672,	*d.* 1805.
Bathgate, . .	*b.* 1672,	*m.* 1672,	*d.* 1698.
Beith, . . .	*b.* 1661,	*m.* 1659,	*d.* 1783.
Borrowstouness, .	*b.* 1656,	*m.* 1648,	*d.* 1736.
Bothwell, .	*b.* 1671,	*m.* 1692,	*d.* 1754.
Burntisland,	*b.* 1672,	*m.* 1672,	*d.* 1734.
Cadder, . .	*b.* 1662,	*m.* 1663,	*d. None.*
Cambuslang, .	*b.* 1657,	*m.* 1657,	*d.* 1731.
Caputh, . .	*b.* 1670,	*m.* 1671,	*d.* 1784.
Cargill, . .	*b.* 1652,	*m.* 1653,	*d.* 1709.
Carmunnock, .	*b.* 1654,	*m.* 1653,	*d.* 1783.
Carnock, . .	*b.* 1652,	*m.* 1652,	*d.* 1653.
Carrington or Primrose,	*b.* 1653,	*m.* 1653,	*d.* 1698.
Carstairs, . .	*b.* 1672,	*m.* 1672,	*d.* 1674.
Channelkirk, .	*b.* 1651,	*m.* 1653,	*d.* 1730.
Chirnside, . .	*b.* 1660,	*m.* 1660,	*d.* 1784.
Colinton or Hailes, .	*b.* 1654,	*m.* 1654,	*d.* 1716.
Cortachy and Clova, .	*b.* 1662,	*m.* 1662,	*d. None.*
Craig, formerly Inchbrayock,	*b.* 1657,	*m.* 1666,	*d.* 1726.
Cramond, . .	*b.* 1651,	*m.* 1651,	*d.* 1816.
Cromarty, . .	*b.* 1675,	*m.* 1679,	*d. None.*
Cupar, . .	*b.* 1654,	*m.* 1654,	*d.* 1654.
Deskford, . .	*b.* 1660,	*m.* 1659,	*d. None.*
Dingwall, . .	*b.* 1662,	*m.* 1753,	*d.* 1786.
Dirleton, . .	*b.* 1664,	*m.* 1664,	*d.* 1664.
Drymen, . .	*b.* 1672,	*m.* 1721,	*d.* 1729.
Dumbarton, .	*b.* 1666,	*m.* 1682,	*d.* 1642.
Dunbar, . .	*b.* 1672,	*m.* 1651,	*d.* 1737.
Dunblane, . .	*b.* 1658,	*m.* 1653,	*d. None.*
Dundonald, .	*b.* 1673,	*m.* 1676,	*d.* 1763.
Dunkeld, . .	*b.* 1672,	*m.* 1707,	*d. None*
Dunnottar, .	*b.* 1672,	*m.* 1755,	*d.* 1755.
Eaglesham, .	*b.* 1659,	*m.* 1723,	*d. None*
Eastwood, . .	*b.* 1674,	*m.* 1693,	*d. None.*
Ednam, . .	*b.* 1666,	*m.* 1666,	*d.* 1694.
Fala and Soutra, .	*b.* 1673,	*m.* 1675,	*d. None.*
Falkland, . .	*b.* 1669,	*m.* 1661,	*d.* 1670.
Fettercairn, . .	*b.* 1720,	*m.* 1669,	*d.* 1721.
Fintry, . .	*b.* 1659,	*m.* 1667,	*d. None.*

Fogo, .	*b.* 1660,	*m.* 1660,	*d. None.*
Fordyce,	*b.* 1665,	*m.* 1723,	*d.* 1718.
Forres,	*b.* 1675,	*m.* 1682,	*d. None.*
Foveran,	*b.* 1658,	*m.* 1677,	*d. None.*
Fowlis Wester,	*b.* 1674.	*m.* 1674,	*d.* 1719.
Galston,	*b.* 1670,	*m.* 1693,	*d.* 1762.
Glencross, formerly Woodhouse-lee,	*b.* 1672,	*m.* 1673,	*d.* 1673.
Gordon,	*b.* 1652,	*m.* 1652,	*d.* 1748.
Guthrie,	*b.* 1664,	*m.* 1663,	*d.* 1716.
Home and Paplay,	*b.* 1654,	*m.* 1654,	*d.* 1765.
Inverary and Glenaray,	*b.* 1653,	*m.* 1651,	*d. None.*
Kemnay,	*b.* 1660,	*m.* 1660,	*d.* 1660.
Kilbarchan,	*b.* 1651,	*m.* 1650,	*d.* 1743.
Kilspindie, .	*b.* 1656,	*m.* 1656,	*d.* 1783.
Kinnell,	*b.* 1657,	*m.* 1657,	*d.* 1657.
Kirkintilloch, formerly Lenzie,	*b.* 1656,	*m.* 1656,	*d. None.*
Kirkliston, .	*b.* 1675,	*m.* 1675,	*d.* 1817.
Kirkwall and St. Ola,	*b.* 1657,	*m.* 1657,	*d.* 1666.
Langholm, formerly Staplegor-toun,	*b.* 1668,	*m.* 1668,	*d.* 1668.
Larbert,	*b.* 1662,	*m.* 1760,	*d.* 1758.
Leochel Cushnie,	*b.* 1669,	*m.* 1658,	*d.* 1657.
Leslie,	*b.* 1673,	*m.* 1729,	*d.* 1761.
Leuchars,	*b.* 1665,	*m.* 1665,	*d. None.*
Logie,	*b.* 1660,	*m.* 1660,	*d.* 1780.
Logierait,	*b.* 1673,	*m.* 1681,	*d.* 1779.
Loudoun, .	*b.* 1673,	*m.* 1673,	*d. None.*
Longformacus,	*b.* 1654,	*m.* 1654,	*d.* 1716.
Lunan,	*b.* 1654,	*m.* 1654,	*d.* 1783.
Lundie and Fowlis,	*b.* 1667,	*m.* 1677,	*d.* 1723.
Manor,	*b.* 1663.	*m.* 1664,	*d.* 1663.
Marnock,	*b.* 1676,	*m.* 1672,	*d.* 1713.
Mauchline, .	*b.* 1670,	*m.* 1670,	*d.* 1753.
Methlic,	*b.* 1670,	*m.* 1696,	*d.* 1663.
Methven,	*b.* 1662,	*m.* 1662,	*d.* 1783.
Moneydie,	*b.* 1655,	*m.* 1655,	*d.* 1783.
Monimail,	*b.* 1656,	*m.* 1656,	*d.* 1697.
Monquhitter.	*b.* 1670,	*m.* 1693,	*d. None.*
Newburgh, .	*b.* 1654,	*m.* 1654,	*d. None.*
Nigg, .	*b.* 1675,	*m.* 1720,	*d.* 1803.
North Berwick,	*b.* 1653,	*m.* 1653,	*d.* 1662.
Oldhamstocks,	*b.* 1664,	*m.* 1664.	*d. None.*
Penicuik,	*b.* 1654,	*m.* 1654,	*d.* 1658.
Peterhead,	*b.* 1668,	*m.* 1664,	*d.* 1673.
Polwarth, .	*b.* 1652,	*m.* 1652,	*d.* 1652.
Prestonkirk, formerly Preston-haugh,	*b.* 1658,	*m.* 1658,	*d. None.*
Rattray,	*b.* 1665,	*m.* 1665,	*d.* 1699.
Renfrew,	*b.* 1673,	*m.* 1673,	*d.* 1732.
Rothiemay, .	*b.* 1658,	*m.* 1677,	*d. None.*
St. Andrews,	*b.* 1657,	*m.* 1657,	*d.* 1792.

Scoonie, ...	*b.* 1675,	*m.* 1667,	*d.* 1765.
Speymouth, formerly Essil and			
Dipple, ...	*b.* 1654,	*m.* 1729,	*d.* 1731.
Strathblane,. . . .	*b.* 1672,	*m.* 1678,	*d.* 1673.
Strathdon, formerly Invernochlie			
including Corgarff, . .	*b.* 1667,	*m.* 1672,	*d. None.*
Strichen, ...	*b.* 1672,	*m.* 1679,	*d.* 1721.
Tulliallan, . . .	*b.* 1673,	*m.* 1673,	*d.* 1680.
Wandell and Lamington.	*b.* 1656,	*m.* 1645,	*d.* 1702.
Wemyss, . . .	*b.* 1660,	*m.* 1779,	*d.* 1707.
West Linton, . .	*b.* 1656,	*m.* 1657,	*d.* 1667.
Westruther, . .	*b.* 1657,	*m.* 1658,	*d. None.*
Yester, . .	*b.* 1654,	*m.* 1654,	*d. None.*

178. GENEALOGY OF EARLS OF FIFE (vol. i. p. 114).—The early ancestry of the Duffs, Earls of Fife, is purely mythical. If Gordon (quite from memory), who writes a history of Keith, Banffshire, is to be believed, he states that a tombstone erected in the fifteenth century in either Mortlach or Cullen church to a Duff of Muldavit was really erected to one Lunes de Maldavit, and that their surname had been erased and Duff substituted.   M.

179. SCOT'S TRANSCRIPT OF PERTH REGISTERS.—At p. 44, vol. iii. 1563, I should say that John *Soutter* should be *Boutter*, probably a progenitor of Butter of Faskelly, county Perth.   S. K.
[*N.B.* These transcripts will be continued in our next number.—ED.]

180. THE FAMILY OF NICOLSON (*continued from vol. iii. p.* 51).—Since my note on the Nicolsons has appeared in print, I have been struck by its numerous imperfections, due partly to conflicting information and partly to want of research. I have now consulted the Acts of the Scottish Parliament, and annex the following notes to be read as part of my paper. I fear they only complicate the matter to a greater degree. I shall gratefully accept any criticisms or suggestions, and with their help I will if possible construct a chart pedigree of the family for future insertion in these pages if the Editor consents.

I may mention that although there is good reason to suppose that the Nicolsons of Cockburnspath, Lasswade, and Carnock, were connected with the Aberdeenshire Nicolsons, yet there is evidence to show that the name was not uncommon in the Lothians, so far back as 1449.

(*a.*) Page 51.—'Mr. James Nicolson of Cockburnspath.' From an Act of 1633 (v. 135), confirming to him the Barony of 'Coldbrandspeth,' it appears that his father, the Aberdeen Commissary, obtained them by a charter of alienation, executed by John Arnot in August 1621. It is to be remarked that the Act of 1633 does not recognise the title of Baronet, said to have been conferred in 1625.

(*b.*) Page 51.—It appears from the records of Parliament that Sir Thomas Nicolson (afterwards King's Advocate), was Procurator to the Estates in 1641. The appointment of the 8th January 1644 (to which Mr. Omond refers) being evidently a reappointment, with a special direction that in case of difficulty he was to consult 'the Lord Advocate Sir Thomas Nicolson,' and other counsel named (vi. 69). It is probable that the mode of printing this sentence (and of another at vol. v. page 383), has led to the erroneous idea that there were two Lord Advocates of the name of Nicolson. There should have been a comma between 'Advocate' and 'Sir.' The Lord Advocate in 1644 was Sir Thomas Hope; and the Sir Thomas Nicolson whom the Procurator was to consult was Sir Thomas Nicolson, first Baronet of Carnock, who was also an Advocate. This is clear from an entry at vol. vi. page 183.

Vol. vi. also tells us that Thomas Nicolson was appointed King's Advocate, 10th March 1649, sworn in as such on the 12th, and as a Privy Councillor on the 16th of that month, and his appointment ratified on the 7th August. In 1651 he is referred to as 'our trusty and familiar Councillor Sir Thomas Nicolson, our Advocate.'

(*c.*) Page 52.—Sir James Nicolson, third Baronet of Cockburnspath, was a member of the War Committee for Berwickshire, from 1643 to 1648 [at page 212, vol. vi., the name of his estate is spelt Cobethspeath].

(*d.*) Page 52.—In connection with the numerous Advocates of this name, the Acts of Parliament mention that Mr. Robert Nicolson, appears for the Provost of Lincluden in 1592. In the same year a very remarkable Act was passed (iii. 608), for rescinding the forfeiture of the children of Euphame M'Kalzeane, who had been executed for witchcraft (I think the case occurs in Pitcairn). The Act grudgingly deprives the unfortunate children of certain rights, acquired by Sir James Sandilands, and John Nicolson, Advocate, and mentions that the house of the latter was on the 'north side of the Kingis Streit.'

(*e.*) Page 52.—Regarding the Lasswade Baronetcy, it should be noted that two ratifications were passed in 1669 (vol. vii. 623), in favour of the second Baronet of this line. The first Act names him Sir John Nicolson, Baronet of Lasswade, and confirms a charter of 1607, granted by the Archbishop of St. Andrews, to 'umquhile Sir John Nicolson of Lasswade, Knight Baronet, goodfather of His Majesty's Lovite Sir John Nicolson, now of Lasswade, Knight Baronet.' Of course there were no Baronets in 1607, so that this recital merely means that the grantee was at a later date created a Baronet. The Act likewise confirms the charters, etc., made in favour of 'Mr. *James* Nicolsone of Lasswade, father of said umquhile Sir John.' Elsewhere this person's name is given as John. The second Act ratifies the Barony of Clerkington, now to be called Nicolson, to the same person, now designated as Sir John Nicolson of that Ilk. These Acts show that the name of the first Baronet's eldest son was John, and that he died in his father's lifetime.

(*f.*) Page 53.—Sir John Nicolson, first Baronet of Lasswade, was a Commissioner of Supply for Edinburgh in 1667. He is probably the same person designed as John Nicolson of Poltoun in 1644, 1646, and 1647, and as Sir John Nicolson of Poltoun in 1661 and 1663 (see vols. vi. and vii.).

(*g.*) Page 53.—There is some difficulty about James Nicolson, the Bishop of Dunkeld, from whom the present Baronet derives. Burke says he was 'son of the first Baronet.' But the James Nicolson who died as Bishop of Dunkeld was a prominent minister, selected by the General Assembly to sit on the 'conference' regarding stipends in 1592, 1596, 1606 and 1607. He died soon after 1607, for in 1609, Gavin, Bishop of Galloway, was appointed to the stipend conference, 'in place of the said umquhile Maister James Nicolson, Bishop of Dunkeld.' A man raised to the rank of Baronet in 1629, and alive in 1640, cannot have had a son, who flourished from 1592 to 1607, and was dead, as Bishop, before 1609.

(*h.*) Page 53.—The second Baronet of Lasswade was a Commissioner of Supply for Edinburgh in 1678, and is probably identical with the 'Sir John Nicolson of Cockburnspath' who held the same office for Berwickshire in that year (viii. 223, 224). This is however the only passage where I have met with a Sir John Nicolson of Cockburnspath, and might well be a misprint for Sir James, the third and last Baronet of Cockburnspath, who seems to have survived till 1690, were it not for another entry, referred to in the next note (*i*).

Sir John Nicolson of Nicolson, was representative for the County of Edinburgh in the third session of the second Parliament of Charles II. (1672). From an Act passed in 1673 (viii. 212), it appears that the King had, of his own authority, imposed a special tax on tobacco, and had by letter under the great seal of 2d December 1671, given the collection thereof to Sir John. This Act revokes the imposition and the gift. From an entry in the Acts of 1696 (x. 69), it appears that he was one of a company of twelve who took a tack of the customs in 1674, and who were 'great losers' thereby.

(*i.*) Page 53.—Sir William Nicolson, the fourth Baronet, was Commissioner of Supply for the county of Edinburgh in 1685, and was probably the 'Sir William Nicolson of Cockburnspath' who filled that office for Berwickshire in the same year (viii. 464). This seems to show that Cockburnspath had passed away from the branch of the Nicolsons that took their designation from it, before the date I have assigned for the death of the Sir James, the third Baronet of Cockburnspath. At Sir William's death, or soon after, the family became bankrupt, and Cockburnspath and Stanipeth were judicially sold on the 7th July 1694 to the Right Hon. Sir John Hall of Dunglass, to whom was confirmed in 1695 (Acts, ix. 505) all rights therein 'competent to umquhile Sir John and Sir William Nicolsones of that Ilk.'

(*j.*) Page 54.—The first Baronet of Carnock was an Advocate, as stated above in note *b*. It is mentioned (v. 273) that a ratification in his favour, passed in 1639, probably the same as is set forth at page 533 of that volume, and from which it appears that he got Carnock under a charter of 15th February 1634, on the resignation of John Drummond, and Playne or Plain under a charter of the 28th June 1634, on the resignation of James Somerville. As Sir Thomas Nicolson of Carnock, he was elected and appointed a member of the Committee of Estates, by the Parliament sitting at Edinburgh, on the 2d June 1640 (vol. v. 309 and 479). He was a Commissioner of Supply for Stirlingshire, 1643-1645. In a case heard in 1661 (vol. vii. page 167), it is mentioned that he lent a large sum to James, Earl of Southesk, and others in 1645, for maintaining the efficiency of the Fife Militia.

(*k.*) Page 54.—John Nicolson of Tilliecoultrie (=Dilliecoultrie), was a Commissioner of Supply for Clackmannanshire, 1661-1663.

(*l.*) Page 54.—Sir Thomas Nicolson, the second Baronet of Carnock, was a Commissioner of Supply for Stirlingshire in 1648. He was one of those exempted from the Act of indemnity of 1662, unless he paid a fine of £6000. In 1695 (ix. 395-406) is a lengthy entry of the suit between his three daughters and their cousin, the heir-male, who succeeded as fifth Baronet ; and from this it appears that Sir Thomas, the second Baronet, was still a minor when, on 22d August 1648, he executed the contract for his marriage with Lady Margaret Levingstone; that on the 22d April 1646, curators had been appointed, none of whom was a consenting party to his marriage contract, although some of them acted as curators at a later date; and that he had four daughters, Helenor, Isobel, Anna, and Margaret, all of whom were alive on the 21st July 1664, when, being on his deathbed, he executed a bond of provision in their favour. Of those, Anna probably died unmarried, as she is not a party to the suit. It was held that the marriage contract did not, and that (owing to the non-consent of curators) it could not, alter the entail of Carnock and Plain, which therefore passed to the three daughters as heirs-portioners of their nephew.

(*m.*) Page 55.—Kemnay. George Nicolson was one of the Commissioners for Aberdeenshire in the Parliament of 1617. Mr. George Nicolson was in 1669 allowed to hold annual fairs at the Kirktoun of Cluny, and was a Commissioner of Supply for Aberdeenshire in 1678. In 1685 there was a double return, and that in favour of 'Sir John Nicolson of Kemnay' was rejected (viii. 455, 458). As Sir George Nicolson of Balcaskie, he was a Commissioner of Supply for Fife in 1690.

(*n.*) The following Advocates of the name are mentioned in Lord Hailes' Catalogue—

Thomas Nicolson, admitted			1594.
Sir Thomas	,,	,,	1612.
Robert	,,	,,	1614.
Thomas	,,	,,	1661.
Sir George	,,	,,	1661.
Thomas	,,	,,	1687.

Σ.

28th October 1888.

181. Dragon Legends (vol. iii. p. 85).—The church of Arbuthnott is not in Perthshire, as you give it in your interesting notes, but in Kincardineshire. Sir Hugh the Blond, according to Jervise, was the reputed founder of the family of the Arbuthnotts. 'Fable says that he received large additions to his estates in consequence of having killed some wild animal that frequented the Den of Pitcarles, greatly to the danger of the neighbourhood; and a *cannon ball*, preserved in a niche of the wall of the aisle of the church, is shewn as the *stone* with which Sir Hugh killed the animal!'—*Memorials of Angus and Mearns*, p. 28*; see also the ballad of 'Sir Hugh le Blond,' in *Legendary Ballads*, p. 206.

The legend of the Dragon of Strike-Martin is well-known in the district, and few traditions are so well supported by place-names and sculptured stones as this one. The 'Nine Maiden Well' is a fine spring, locally supposed to exhibit nine springs, one for each of the maidens of the legend; but the writer was present some years ago when the well was uncovered, and instead of nine there were thirteen springs boiling up among the sand in the bottom of the well, which is not more than 2 feet deep below the covering planks. When a boy, the writer had pointed out to him in the old burying-ground of Strike-Martin nine mounds side by side, which were said to mark the graves of the nine maidens, but probably in this instance tradition was being supplemented by imagination. A. Hutcheson.

182. BRIDGES AND HARBOURS.—In the 16th and 17th centuries the kirk-sessions not only made collections for purposes purely ecclesiastical, but they did much to improve the condition of the country. Records contain frequent entries of collections made for the building of bridges, generally in the district, but not necessarily in the parish. More rarely also, the smaller harbours were put in repair with the proceeds of collections made in inland parishes. Briefs such as existed in England were unknown in Scotland, and it is not clear what machinery was put in motion to induce the Church to take into consideration any pressing case. Perhaps some of our readers will explain how this was done.—ED.

183. MARRIAGES PERFORMED IN THE CHURCH.—The Easter Anstruther Kirk Session Records may be quoted on this point, as having marriages in houses was formerly the exception and not the rule: '1701, 25 Feb. It is enacted by the Session that if any person shall desyre to be privately married, and not in the church, they shall pay to ye poor of ye paroch before their marriage, oo6. 13. 04.'

184. ARMS OF SCOTTISH FAMILIES ON FLEMISH MONUMENTS.—The following are given in Sanderus, *Theatre Sacr. de Brabant:*—

1. 'Douglas dit de Schott 1682. Ermine, three estoiles sable' (vol. i. pp. 59, 70).

N.B.—In the Inventaire des Archives de la ville de Malines, vol. vi. is entered—
1582. Arrestation de l'espion Douglas-Schot—Lettre signée Melander, jésuite — Interrogatoire — Aveuse — Procès — Deposition du capitaine Simpel (p. 174).

1676. Pretention de Douglas-Schot, ancien bourgmestre de Malines, pour affairs independantes de ses fonctions, terminée par transaction, le 18 août 1676, moyennant la somme de 1000 florins (p. 47).

2. 'Le Cabinet d'armes de noble et bien née Dame Elizabeth Murray, Epouse de Noble Seigneur Pierre Grahame, morte en 1724, avec 8 quartier suivant Murray of Newton, Murray of Blackborn, Sterling, Marr, St. Amant, De Claer, De Boyart, Couper.' Monument in the Parish Church of Tilbourg (vol. iv. p. 123).

185. A PLEA FOR PLACE-NAMES.—May I reproduce in *N. N. & Q.* what I wrote in a contemporary about four years ago :—
'Many interest themselves in the derivation of place-names, believing them to contain evidence (racial and historical) which is sometimes more trustworthy than that of documents. The difficulty is not so much to get derivations as to reject the swarms of conjectures which infest every district. There are throughout the country numbers of men of leisure and education who might do much towards systematising the facts, state-ments, and even surmises on such points; and comparisons of evidence (documentary and verbal), would gradually conduce to accuracy. One of the first points seems to be to record the names themselves, both as cur-rently written and as pronounced. The pronunciation would have to be indicated on a uniform system, and it would be for experts to consider

whether that adopted by the new English dictionary is the best. We have on the 6-inch Ordnance Survey a great many place-names recorded, but the numbers that have escaped entry must far exceed those that are in print. Names of fields, gates, stiles, lanes, etc., are almost of more value than those of larger places which have been worn down by attrition. If those interested in such things would get survey-sheets of their districts, and carefully note thereon (say in red) any unrecorded names as usually spelt, and underneath (say in blue) the current pronunciation, so as to make speech visible, a mass of evidence would gradually be formed from which cumulative inferences might be drawn. Notes as to sources of information, etc., might be appended to each survey-sheet. Much that is of value passes away from us daily, and many are deterred from making a beginning by a sense of the immensity of the question. If the above sketchy idea finds favour with any of your readers, it is to be hoped that they will discuss it.'

The remarks on the above generally expressed concurrence, but had a decidedly Saxon tinge, as was to be expected in the South-east. No opinion specially favourable to Dr. Murray's system of indicating sound was expressed. My own impression is, that the first point would be to get rid of that remarkable mixture called English with its eccentric vowels and confusing spelling, and to take as a basis some well-known tongue, with an established literature and phonetic system—say modern Welsh, German, or Spanish. This might be safer than relying on the inventions of individuals. Welsh has the advantage of indicating the important difference between the two sounds which are expressed in English by TH; but whatever language were used, modification would be necessary to suit special sounds. The Greek character would do for the guttural C or CH; but the guttural G would want a symbol. It would also be necessary to provide for the Welsh LL; the Gaelic L; the York-shire äa and D; and those pauses in Gaelic which often mean so much. To indicate those vowel sounds which are not A, E, I, O, or U (Italian), reversed letters or new symbols seem better than diphthongs or overhead accents—indeed tildes or any small marks seem objectionable. All place-names should be printed (not written) and the syllable on which the chief stress is laid might be in capitals.

When the time came for drawing inferences, the partisans of Scandinavian, Erse, Brythonic, or Saxon, could each have their say; but more important than any of them would be the eventual judicial element.

W. M. C.

186. SCULPTURED STONES AT CULROSS.—*N. N. & Q.* (vol. i. pp. 7, 26) contains an account of some of the epitaphs in the burying-ground of the ruined parish church of Culross, which is situated about a mile to the west of the town, and which was in a dilapidated condition in 1633. when an Act was passed making the Abbey the Parish Church. See *Proceedings of Society of Antiquaries of Scotland* for 1877, pp. 251, 252.

Some of the monumental stones are interesting, especially some early slabs of which Nos. 3 and 5 are examples; they are, however, built in as lintels to doorways, which must have been opened into the church in the 16th century. No. 7 is a fragment of a massive slab, the arms are some-what similar to those of Erskine, the fork (?) on the pale may be for difference. The arms of Erskine of Balgownie (in the Parish) are found

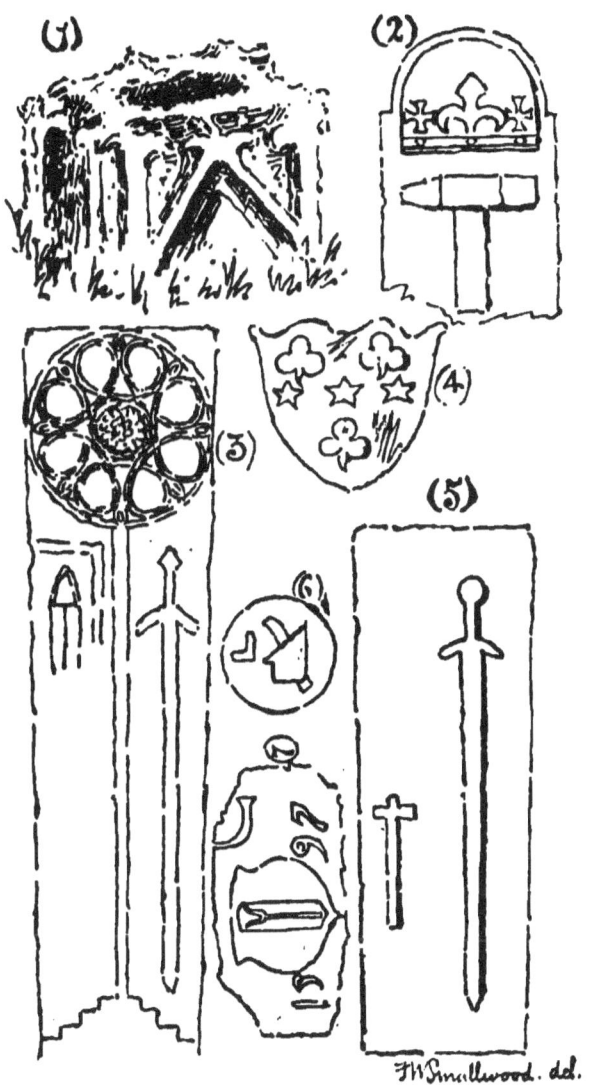

F. W. Smallwood. del.

on 16th century slabs, and James Erskine, the first of Balgownie, had a younger son, Adam, whose arms those on the broken slab may be. The only initial now left is much injured, but it may form the lower portion of an E. The Coat of Arms, No. 4, has no name or initial to indicate to whom it belonged; perhaps some reader may be able to throw light on it. No. 2 is a headstone with a well-cut Badge of the Guild of the Hammer-men. No. 6 displays the share and coulter, together with another instrument, the nature of which is uncertain. No. 1 is a sketch of the Cross Socket referred to at page 139.   A. W. C. H.

187. THE PRESENT BRITONS A MIXED RACE.—The following forms part of an article which appeared in the *Standard* of August 27th. It is satisfactory to find that the daily press has commenced to point out the evident, but to some unpalatable fact, that very few Britons of the 19th century, whether on the north or south of the Tweed, can assert that their lineage is wholly or even chiefly insular, or that many family names now common are indigenous :—

'Our standing policy has been to admit the foreigner—good, bad, and indifferent—without let or hindrance. From the Flemings in Pembroke in the reign of Henry 1., to the Russian Jews in Whitechapel at the present day, persecuted and distressed foreigners of all races and creeds have found their way into different portions of this country, and no one has said them nay. As a rule, it must be admitted that this policy of free settlement has paid very well indeed. The foreigners who have come here have added on the whole a useful element to the population. The Laureate's famous line, "Saxon and Norman and Dane are we," is considerably within the mark. We are also Fleming and Walloon, and Dutchman, and Low German, and Huguenot Frenchman. Numerically small as most of these immigrations have been, they consisted, as a rule, of the pick of the various countries of origin. The process is still going on. There is a German colony in the City, and an American at the West End, and an Indian colony, which at present seems to be chiefly settled in Bloomsbury. Like their predecessors in the Middle Ages and the 17th century, our modern colonists, with few exceptions, soon become absorbed, and after a generation of two, men whose names are foreign, and whose forefathers were born under alien skies, are the most patriotic and sometimes the most insular of Britons. Yet this process of constantly adding fresh blood to the old stock is a healthy one, and it is possible that not a little of that physical toughness on which we pride ourselves is due to its influence.

QUERIES.

XCIX. SCOTS IN POLAND.—'His (Sir John Denham) ode or song upon the Embassy to Poland by which he and Lord Crofts procured a contribution of ten thousand pounds from the Scotch that wandered over that kingdom. Poland was at that time very much frequented by itinerant traders, who, in a country of very little commerce and of great extent, where every man resided on his own estate, contributed very much to the accommodation of life by bringing to every man's house those little necessaries which it was very inconvenient to want and very troublesome to fetch. I have formerly read without much reflection of the multitude of Scotchmen that travelled with their wares in Poland ; and that their numbers were not small, the success of this negotiation gives sufficient evidence.'— Johnson, *Lives of the Poets,* i. p. 105, ed. 1783.

On this I note as follows :—

That there were a great number of Scotch pedlars is certain, for the 'Scotch Pedlar in Poland' was a proverbial expression (see *Epistolæ Ho-Elianæ* in letters dated 1633, page 316 of 7th ed., London 1705), but there must surely have been some more considerable trade or commerce. See *Lithgow's Travels* (1609-1619), p. 334, in 12th ed., 1814, who speaks of *thirty thousand Scotch families that live incorporate* in Poland, *beside* the yearly emigration from Scotland, which grew to such an evil that Patrick Gordon, the King's agent at Dantzic, wrote to entreat King James to put a stop to it (*Analecta Scotica,* ii. 286). What was the attraction to so distant a country as Poland ? The £10,000 was not contributed by a few wealthy persons, but was raised by a tax *or decimation.* Sir John Denham says in his poem :—

> ' For when
> It was moved, there and then
> They should pay one in ten,
> The dyet said, Amen.'

Any information or suggestion would be most thankfully received. **N.**

March 24th, London.—Vol. cxx. 38, Chamberlain to [Carleton] : The Polish Ambassador has had an audience, and requests men to resist the Turk. The king promises well ; it is thought he will have leave to raise Scotch or Irish troops, there being thirty thousand Scotch families in Poland.—*Dom. Ser.* 1621, page 237.

December 9th.—Certificate of Sec. Conway that Alexander Chambers, in obedience to the king's proclamation, had quitted service in the wars of Poland, and had offered to serve the king. [*Minute,* Lord Conway's *Foreign Letter Book,* France, vol. clxxviii. p. 248].—*Dom. Ser.* 1625, page 174.

We earnestly request that any of our readers who are able to afford ' N.' information will send it *at once* addressed to me. It is required for literary purposes and *for immediate use.* It will of course be also inserted in the next number of *N. N. & Q.,* as the subject is one of much interest. **Ed.**

C. GILL FAMILY.—(*a*) Information wanted about the family of Gill, in the south of Scotland, and particularly of the old family of the Gills of Perthshire. John Gill, Burgess, Bailie, and afterwards Provost of Perth, sat in three of the Parliaments held by David II., the first at Perth, 1364 ; second at Edinbro', 1367 ; third at Perth, 1369 ; and also in the Parliament held by Robert II. at Perth,

1373. He was, conjointly with John Mercer (progenitor of 'Mercer of Aldie'), collector of the customs at Perth, besides holding many other offices connected with the business of the town and county. John Gill was also Laird of Halton or Haldoun (what parish is it in?) co., Perth. Another John Gill is about 1380 designed Lord of Tarsopie or Tarsappie—near Perth. What parish is this in? Is there any evidence to show who these persons married, and what family they had? In the Index of special services of Perth we find :—

'1648, April 28.—Thomas Gill in Ludgerlaw. Naeses, Robert Gill, Calcearii, burgensis, de Perth, filii fratris avi, in tenementis in Perth.'

'1648, Nov. 1.—Catherina Gill, filia legitima Patricia Gill, vestiarii in Stuir. Naeres pestionaria, Robert Gill, burgensis de Pearthe, filii fraternis avi.'

'1649, Sep. 4.—Helena Andersone, filia legitima. Toeunces Andersone, burgensis de Perth, inter illum, et Agnetum Gill. Naeses, Robert Gill, calceadii burgensis de Perth, avunculi in tenementis in Perth.'

In vol i. No. 8, *Notes & Queries.*—'Perth Reg. :—Thomas Robertson and Isabell Anderson were *m.* 24th Feby. 1565.'

'1648, Nov. 1.—Margareta Elizabetha et Barbara Gillis, filiae legitima quandam Patricii Gill vestiarii in Stuir. Naeredes posticia asiae Roberti Gill, burgensis de Pearthe filii frateris avi.'

The above four entries, not including your Robertson-Gill marriage, all doubtless refer to descendants of the old Perth family.

Another John Gill was one of the three first Lecturers in Philosophy and Logic, anno 1410, under Bishop Henry Wardlaw. Can any one give me more information about him? I have heard there is a tombstone to his memory at St. Andrews.

1633-5 Feb.—'Mr. Gill is one of the advocattis (Edinburgh) employed in the proceedings respecting the reduction and con-cilation of the retours and patents concerning the Earldom of Stratherne (see *Hist. of the Earldom of Stratherne*, Appendix 43).'

Patrick del Gyll, who was among the gentlemen of Peebles-shire who submitted to Edward I. 1296 (see Chambers's *Peebles-shire*). Is anything more known of him?

(*b*) Cattanach family.— ——Cattanach, otherwise Macin-tosh, said to be *of,* or *in* Ballochbuie, in the Braemar district of Aberdeenshire, *m.* about 1724 . . . daughter of . . . Lumsden, Laird of Corrachree in Logie, Coldstone, co. Aberdeen, and had an only daughter: Margaret Cattanach *b.* 1725. (Miss Lumsden was Cattanach's first wife). Can any one give more information?

(*c*) Pennycuick of that Ilk, afterwards of Newhall, co. Edinbro'. —Does any reliable information about this family exist in a pedi-gree form? The descendants, and it is believed representatives, of the family, settled, in the last century, in the Kirkmichael and Cluny districts of Perthshire, and acquired the small estates of Soilsasie and Logie. These were sold by the late General J. T. Pennycuick, who *d.* this year, not very long ago.

(*d*) Who was Middleton of Stenhouse, and where is it? Janet

Middleton, *b. circa* 1637 (stated in an old pedigree to be daughter of Middleton of Stenhouse), *m.* at Aberdeen, 16th July 1667, James Byres, merchant of Aberdeen and Rotterdam, progenitor of the Moir-Byres family of Tonley, Aberdeenshire. A George Middleton appears as one of the witnesses at the baptism of their daughter Jean, 13th October 1668.

(*e*) Can your Banffshire correspondent give any information, from the Sheriff Court Records or otherwise, of a Patrick Gill in Alihouseburne, near Banff, in the early part of the seventeenth century; and of a George Gill, in Warielip, parish of Boyndlie, where, as a curious old raised letter tombstone in that churchyard shows us, he departed this 'lyf' 3d April 1689, *m.* (her initials on tombstone are M. C—)? Or about the parentage of Alexander Clerk or Clark, of Banff, Shipmaster, *b.* about 1680, *m.* Christian Gordon (parents wanted), *ob.* 1732. Captain Clerk (so the name is there spelt, Burgess Diploma) was admitted Burgess of Guild of Fortrose, co. Ross, in August 1732.   S. K.

CI. GOLF.—In what book are the following lines on golf to be found?—

> In winter too, when heavy frosts o'erspread
> The verdant turf, and naked lay the mead,
> The vig'rous youth commence the sportive war,
> And arm'd with lead their jointed clubs prepare.
> The timber curve to leathern orbs apply,
> Compact, elastic to pervade the sky.
> These to the distant hole direct they drive,
> They claim the stakes who thither first arrive.
> Intent his ball the eager gamester eyes,
> His muscles strains and various postures tries
> Th' impelling blow to strike with greater force,
> And shape the motive orb's projectile course.

C. D. DONALD, Glasgow.

CII. COLONEL ARCHIBALD CAMPBELL.—In the beginning of the present century, a Colonel Archibald Campbell acquired the liferent of Finlaystone, Renfrewshire, from the then Cuningham Graham, and resided there for some years. Any information about him will be a favour.   C. D. DONALD,

172 St. Vincent Street, Glasgow.

CIII. THE M'DOWALLS OF FREUGH.—For the sake of quoting an authority, I will say—according to M'Kerlie in *Lands and Their Owners in Galloway,* edition of 1870, vol. i. p. 66, Uchtred M'Dowall of Freugh who married Agnes Agnew had issue—

'Probably Umphray, who married Jean Drummond, and is supposed to have predeceased his father.

'Patrick, was Uchtred's heir.

'William.

'Patrick succeeded his father, and had sasine of the lands of Freuch, etc., 12 May 1670. He married on the 12 Nov. 1662, Barbara, daughter of James Fullertoun of Fullertoun, parish of Dundonald, Ayrshire. . . . He appears to have taken an active part as a covenanter, and suffered severely in consequence. He had to become a fugitive. . . . On 18 Feb. 1680, he was summoned before the Justiciary, and sentenced to be executed when taken, and his property confiscated to his Majesty's use.'

Page 67—' Uchred M'Dowall de Freugh had a charter of the lands of Knokencrosh, 24 July 1691. Uchtred must have been the son of Patrick, although the family historians are altogether silent in reference to him. He appears to have died early, and nothing seems to be known as to whom he married; but that he had at least two sons seems certain from the Public Records. . . .'

' Patrick M'Dowall was served heir of his grandfather, Uchtred M'Dowall of Freugh, 26 August 1692; his own father, Patrick, having been passed over in consequence of the forfeiture. . . . William, his brother-german, had sasine of certain lands in the parish of Stonykirk, 28th Oct. 1702. Patrick M'Dowall married Margaret, daughter of William Hattridge of Dromore, county Down, Ireland.'

Page 68.—' Patrick, it would appear, died in 1733 . . . and was succeeded by his son, John M'Dougall of Freugh, who married Lady Elizabeth, daughter of Lord Crichtoune of Sanquhar, in 1725. . . . He had also in the year a reversion by William M'Dowall, his uncle. . . .'

I shall be much obliged by any further information as to this part of the family, particularly :—

a. Whether it is known where Patrick, Uchtred's son, and the fugitive, settled when he fled.

b. Whether he had any other sons than (1) Uchred, the name of whose wife is unknown ; (2) Patrick, who succeeded his grandfather ; and (3) William.

c. Whether Uchred's sons married and had issue, what were their names, and in what public records are they mentioned, also what became of them.

d. Whether Patrick, Patrick's son who succeeded Uchtred in 1692, had any other sons than John who succeeded him, and if so, what became of them.

e. Whether any of the family settled in Ireland, and if so, what is known about them and their issue.

S. S. M'DOWALL, 54 St. James's Street, Piccadilly, London.

CIV. TOWERS FAMILY.—Can any reader of *Northern Notes & Queries* give any information concerning the early members of the Towers or Touris family who settled near Dunblane about 1630, and rented the farm of Quoigs near that town? A John Towers or Touris married a daughter of M'Lauchlane who held the farm of Quoigs in 1630. Were they an offshoot from the Towers family of Inverleith near Edinburgh? WALTER F. LYON.

CV. TERMS ATTACHING TO DOMESTIC ANIMALS.—In controlling the movements of domestic animals by the voice, besides words of ordinary import, man uses a variety of peculiar terms, calls, and inarticulate sounds—not to include whistling—which vary in different localities.

The undersigned is desirous of collecting words and expressions (oaths excepted) used in addressing domesticated animals in all parts of Great Britain and abroad.

In particular he seeks information as to—

(1) The terms used to start, hasten, haw, gee, back and stop horses, oxen, camels, and other animals in harness.

(2) Terms used for calling in the field cattle, horses, mules, asses, sheep, goats, swine, poultry, and other animals.

(3) Exclamations used in driving, from the person, domestic animals.

(4) Any expressions and inarticulate sounds used in addressing domestic animals for any purpose whatever (dogs and cats).

(5) References to information in works of travel and general literature will be very welcome.

Persons willing to collect and forward the above-mentioned data will confer great obligations on the writer; he is already indebted to many correspondents for kind replies to his appeal for the *Counting-out Rhymes of Children*, the results of which have been published in a volume with that title. (Elliot Stock, London.)

To indicate the value of vowels in English, please use the vowel-signs of Webster's Unabridged, and in cases of difficulty spell phonetically.

All correspondence will be gratefully received, and materials used will be credited to the contributors.

Address,

PROFESSOR H. CARRINGTON BOLTON,
UNIVERSITY CLUB,
NEW YORK CITY, U.S.A.

CVI. STEWART FAMILY.—Information—or a likely place to obtain such —concerning the family of Stewart of Stenton, Perthshire. I know all about them from present date back to John S. of S. who died in 1791. I have traced another John S. of S. who apparently died about 1730, another Thomas S. of S., a Commissioner of Supply for Perthshire, 1685 to 1691, and another John S. of S. living 1660, who had a brother Gilbert, a merchant in Edinburgh, stated in Douglas's *Baronage* to have married a daughter of Wedderburn of Kingussie. Can any one say if this family is linked on to the royal tree? W. L.

REPLIES TO QUERIES.

VIII. In vol. i. p. 29, should be Patrick Leslie of *Eden*, not *Aden*.

X. Was not Dr. John Arbuthnot one of the Arbuthnots (who always spelt the surname with one *t*) who were an early branch of the Arbuthnott family, and owned Cairgall in the parish of Langside, Aberdeenshire, in end of the sixteenth century?

They were long almost the leading family in Peterhead—the Arbuthnot Barts. are descendants from them. Mrs. James Arbuthnot of Innernettie, Peterhead, has in her possession a very good genealogy of the family. *Ibid.* p. 48.—Lumsden of Clova.—For as numerous as this Aberdeenshire family have been, and still are, there is only one registered coat of arms, that of Lumsden of Cushnie, which all the cadets, in ignorance no doubt, bear indifferenced.

I. Robert Lumsden, the first designed of Cushnie, *m.* Isobel, daughter of John Forbes of Lespersie, and *d.* 1546, leaving, it is said, nineteen children, of whom—

   1. Thomas.

   2. Matthew of Tillycairn, author of *A Genealogical History of the House of Forbes, m.* but *d. s. p.*

   3. Robert of Clova, the first we find designed *of Clova, m.* Elizabeth Keith, and left two daughters and co-heiresses, of whom one, Christian Lumsden, spouse of Alexander Duff of Torrestoun, is in 1605 second co-heir to her father, 'umqll Mr. Robert Lumsden of Clova and umqll . . . Keith, his spose' (*Sheriff Court Records of Aberdeen*).

   1. Marjory, *m.* Patrick Forbes of Carse, and had issue.

   2. Euphan, *m.* Alexander Forbes of Newe, and had issue.

   3. Jane, *m.* Alexander Chalmers of Balnacraig, and had issue.

II. Thomas Lumsden, yr., of Cushnie, *m.*, and *d.* before his father; issue at least two sons.

   1. James, *d.* in 1550, who left an only son Patrick, who *d. s. p.* 1563.

   2. John, who carries on the line.

III. John Lumsden of Cushnie and Clova, *m.* first and secondly Elizabeth Menzies, probably a daughter of the old Aberdeenshire family of 'Menzies of Pitfodles;' issue—

   1. John, succeeded to Cushnie, and *m.* Janet, daughter of John Mortimer of Craigievar, and had a son Robert, who *d. s. p.*

   2. Alexander of Clova, *m.* Christian Irvine, whose descendants carry on the Cushnie family.

   3. Arthur.

   1. Elizabeth, *m.* John Burnett of Leys.

Pedigree in Burke's *L. G.* of Lumsden of Pitcaple, not nearly correct.

XIX. 'Cruisie' (vol. i. 19, vol. iii. pp. 32, 60).—Scotch etymologists should note the 'rude flickering lamps' which lit the kitchen of the country-house at Milly in the days of 'The Terror.' From the painful light they gave they were 'called, not inappropriately, *creuse-yeux*'—eye-scoopers. Have we here the derivation of our own familiar 'crusie'?   *Scotsman.*

XXV.   P. 50. Rev. Alexander Rose or Ross, Laird of Tusch, in the

Garioch, and of Rosehill (now Turner Hall) in Ellan parish, and was Minister of Monymusk, all in Aberdeenshire, issue—

1. John, Rev., of Feveran (D.D. 1684), *d.* 1690, succeeded to Tusch, *m.* a daughter of the family of ' Udny of that ilk,' their daughter Margaret *m.* 1693 Robert Turner, who had previously bought Rosehill, and called it Turnerhall.

2. Alexander was consecrated 1686 Bishop of Moray, and 1688 Bishop of Edinburgh, *d.* 1720. See *Scot's Fasti*, and *Homes of Moir and Byres*, pp. 8, 9. They were a branch of the family of Kilravock.

Arthur Rose or Ross (brother of the Rev. Alexander Rose, Laird of Tusch) was Bishop of Argyll 1675, of Glasgow 1679, and who, in 1684, became Archbishop of St. Andrews and Primate of Scotland. Σ.

XLIII. P. 122. Read *Laithers* not *Southers*, in Aberdeenshire (near Turriff), not Banffshire. Σ.

LVIII. P. 149. Mr. Thomas Fraser had doubtless been a descendant of the ancient family of the ' Frasers of Durris,' represented by ' Fraser of Findrack ' (see Burke's *L. G.*). Σ.

LXI. P. 150. An old branch of the Houston family were long burgesses and leading residents at Fortrose, in Ross-shire, and their arms are still to be seen on an old tombstone there. Σ.

XCI. BENNET FAMILY.—I do not think the William Bennet of Edinburgh, *circa* 1600, regarding whom C. B. inquires, was a son of the family of Bennet of Grubet. William Bennet, one of the ministers of Edinburgh, was in 1644 appointed one of the visitors for the University of St. Andrews. He may possibly have been father of the Jacob Bennet who went to Sweden in 1640.

The person in question may have been connected with Sir George Bennet of the shire of Fife, who was created a baronet on the 28th July 1671, and regarding whom Mylne writes : ' His father was minister of the College Kirk of Edinburgh. He was in the service of Carsimor, King of Poland, and was one of his noblemen, and came to great riches.'

The Grubet family was founded (as stated by J. T. M. in last number, pp. 112-113) by Rev. William Bennet, laureated 1614, rector of Ancrum, returned in an inquisition *de tutela* as next of kin to Robert, son of Raguel Bennet of Chester, on the 7th November 1637 ; purchased Grubet, and *d.* 1647.

William Bennet was served heir of Grubet 29th December 1647. He (or his son) was created a baronet of Nova Scotia 18th November 1670 ; and was a Commissioner of Supply for Roxburghe 1684-1707. He had a son and two daughters.

1. William Bennet, younger of Grubet, M.P. for Roxburgh 1693 to 1707, and in the first Parliament for Great Britain, *m.* (1) Margaret Scougall, dead before 2d July 1694, when James Scougall, Advocate, was served heir to her, and (2) Elizabeth Hay, probably daughter of ' Sir David Hay,

Doctor of Medicine' (see *Acts P. S.* ix. 199), alive in 1707, when he had a ratification of the Grubet charter (*Idem*, xi. Appendix, p. 130). There is no mention of his succeeding to the baronetcy or leaving issue.

2. Christian, *m.* 1697 as first wife of Charles Stuart of Dunearn, and had a son, Alexander Stuart of Dunearn, Keeper of Ludlow Castle, who *d.* 13th February 1787 without leaving issue.

3. Elizabeth, *m.* as second wife of Sir John Scott, first baronet of Ancrum, and had two daughters, from whom are descended Sir Hector Maclean Hay, Bart. of Alderston, and Sir William Henry Walsingham Calder, Bart.

Raguel Bennet of Chester, mentioned above, was probably a brother of the rector of Ancrum. His name is spelt Baguel in *Douglas's Baronage* (page 219). His daughter Marian *m.* Robert Scott of Burnhead, and his son and successor Robert was served heir to Raguel, his father, on the 17th January 1670, and was a Commissioner of Supply for Roxburgh 1662 and 1696. He was dead in 1704, when his son Archibald Bennet of Chester was appointed a Commissioner of Supply for Roxburgh. Archibald's grand-daughters Helen and Isabel *m. circa* 1780 Archibald Douglas of Semperdean and Archibald Hope (see *Douglas's Baronage*, p. 60).

I have notes of families of Bennet of Easter Liveland in Stirlingshire, of Wester Both or Wester Beath in Perthshire, and of Bussis or Wester Quylts in Fifeshire; but none of these throw any light on the question asked by C. B. There seems also to have been families of the name in Pittenweem, Burntisland, Anstruther, and other parts of Fifeshire.   Σ.

XCVI. Sir William Sharp of Stonyhill.—I offer the following contribution towards a history of this family :—

1. In the index to the Acts of the Parliament of Scotland there are three entries of the name Sir William Sharp, viz. of Scotscraig, of Stonyhill, and of Stratyrum. The last entry (vol. xi. p. 148) is probably a misprint due to transposing the names of Stratyrum and Scotscraig, which both occur in the same line.

2. There can be no doubt that 'Scotscraig' and 'Stoniehill' refer to one and the same family, that descended from the Archbishop. The King's cash-keeper in 1681 is Sir William Sharp of Stainehill (*Acts*, vol. ix. 155, where he gives an assignation to Robert Adair, on the 6th December of that year); and in the proceedings of 1693 (ix. 275), and 1696 (x. 69), the same cash-keeper is referred to as Sir William Sharp of Scotscraig.

3. Sir William Sharp of Scotscraig was a Commissioner of Supply for Fifeshire in 1678, 1685, and (if my surmise about Stratyrum be correct) in 1704. Sir William Sharp of Stonyhill was a Commissioner of Supply for Midlothian in 1678, 1685, 1686, 1690, and 1706. It is clear from what follows that there

were two Sir Williams, father and son, and that the early entries refer to the father, and the later ones to the son. '

4. Sir William Sharp and Dame Agnes Clelland, his spouse, had a charter of Naeton, Staniehill, and other lands near Musselburgh, dated 20th October 1680, ratified in 1681 (*Acts P. S.* viii. 270).

5. Sir William Sharp of Stonyhill represented Clackmannanshire in the Parliament of 1681, and was elected a Lord of the Articles. This Parliament had only one session, and in the convention of 1678 that preceded it, and in the first Parliament of James II. that followed it, Clackmannanshire was represented by Bruce of Clackmannan.

6. Sir William Sharp of Scotscraig was created a Baronet of Nova Scotia on 21st April 1683, with remainder to the heirs-male of his body. I think this was Agnes Clelland's husband.

7. Sir William Sharp, 'Knight and Baronet,' had a charter of Staniehill, dated 31st July 1706, ratified in 1707 (*Acts*, xi. 463). The ratification refers to the 'deceast Sir William Sharp and his spouse.' This must have been the second Baronet. There is no mention of Naeton in this ratification.

8. Archbishop Sharp is said to have had a son Sir William, and three daughters, one *m.* Erskine of Cambo (see Wood's *East Neuk of Fife*, p. 259—I cannot trace this marriage), the second *m.* John Cunningham of Barns, and the third to William, eleventh Lord Salton.

9. Dominus William Sharp de Staniehill was on 1st November 1678 served heir of Robert Sharp of Castlehill, his brother-german.

10. Dominus William Sharp de Scotscraig, miles, was on 6th May 1680 served heir of the Archbishop, his father.

11. Sir James Sharp of Scotscraig, *m.* Sophia, one of the four daughters of the Hon. Sir Charles Erskine, first Baronet of Cambo. Douglas makes her third daughter, but in Wood's *East Neuk*, p. 296, she is represented as the eldest daughter. Her brother, Sir Alexander Erskine, was *b.* 1665, and *m.* 1680, so that the date of her marriage may be set down as 1680-90.

12. Lady Mary Lundin or Drummond, youngest daughter of the first Earl of Melfort (by his first marriage), *m.* first, Gideon Scot of Highchester (ancestor of Harden), who *d.* 1707, and secondly, 'Sir James Sharp, Baronet, and had issue to both' (Douglas's *Peerage*, ii. 21, and *Baronage*, 216). I suspect this was the same Sir James Sharp as is mentioned in preceding paragraph, and that he was second son of Sir William, the first Baronet, and that he succeeded his brother.

13. Sophia Erskine, niece of the Sophia Erskine mentioned above, and daughter of Sir Alexander Erskine, second Baronet of Cambo, is said to have *m.* 'Sir Alexander Sharp of Scotscraig' (Douglas's *Peerage*, ii. 21). He was probably a son of Sir James mentioned above.

14. From these notices, and from the information recorded by W. T. W., we may construct the following tentative pedigree :—

DAVID SHARP, Merchant in Aberdeen.
|
WILLIAM SHARP, Sheriff-Clerk of Banff, *m.* Isabella, eldest daughter of John Leslie, fourth of Kinninvie
[In Burke's *Landed Gentry* he is named James Sharp, Laird of Banff Castle.]

JAMES SHARP, the Archbishop, *b. circa* 1613, consecrated 1661, murdered 1679, *m.* Helen Moncrieff.

SIR WILLIAM SHARP, Deputy Keeper of the Signet and Cash Keeper, knighted before 1671, *m.* Agnes Clelland, created a Baronet 1683.	ROBERT SHARP of Castlehill, dead in 1678.	Daughter, said to have *m.* 'Erskine of Cambo.' ?	Daughter, *m.* John Cunningham of Barns, and had issue.	MARGARET, *m.* William Frazer, Lord Salton, and had issue.

SIR WILLIAM SHARP, 2d Baronet, alive in 1707. No wife or child mentioned.	SIR JAMES, seems to have succeeded as 3d Baronet ; *m.* (firstly) *circa* 1680-90 Sophia Erskine, and (secondly) after 1707 Lady Mary Drummond.

SIR ALEXANDER, probably 4th Baronet, *m. circa* 1710 Sophia Erskine.

NOTICES OF BOOKS.

The Scottish Paraphrases, an Account of their History, Authors, and Sources, by Douglas J. Maclagan. Edinburgh, Andrew Elliot, 1889.— This is a volume well got up, both inside and outside; it will prove a valuable contribution to the Hymnology of the Church. Englishmen have well-nigh forgotten both the new and old versions of the Psalms to be found at the end of former editions of the Prayer Book. Scottish Presbyterians are more slowly giving up their Metrical Psalms. To the Paraphrases more recently introduced into the Church worship they will cling when the Psalms are wellnigh forgotten, save some few and deserving favourites. Mr. Maclagan, in the first sixty pages of his work, gives not only a history of the introduction of Paraphrases, but an account of the writers of them. Though most of them were Scotsmen, the works of Englishmen were by no means overlooked. Addison, Darracott, Doddridge, Mason, Tate, and Watts, are all represented.

The book contains all the Paraphrases, with such different versions as exist printed in parallel columns. Not the least interesting portion of the work consists of the manipulation—may we not say mutilation—the words endured at the hands of the committee of divines appointed to sit upon the works of poets. Some suggestions were fortunately not carried out. We give an instance—

Cameron wrote thus :—
                    ' The planets from their orbits shoot,
                        For evermore disjoined ;
                    As when a fig-tree drops its fruit,
                        Shook by some boisterous wind.'
The alteration suggested runs thus :—
                    ' The stars now from their orbs disjoined,
                        Shower through ethereal space ;
                    As figs shook by the boisterous wind
                        Pour from their boughs apace,'
where the vigour of the last two lines of the stanza seems to us to be utterly destroyed.

The work Mr. Maclagan has undertaken has been well done.

INDEXES TO VOL. III.

I.—GENERAL INDEX.

II.—INDEX TO PERSONS.

NOTE.—*As the marriages extracted from Acta Dom. Conc. et Sess. (p. 56) are given in alphabetical order, the names are not given in the following Index.*—ED.

III.—INDEX TO PLACES.

Note.—*As the lists of Parish Registers (pp. 57, 142) are printed alphabetically, the names are not given in the following Index.*—Ed.

Edinburgh: T. and A. Constable, Printers to Her Majesty.